MYTHS

of

ORIGIN

OTHER BOOKS BY
CATHERYNNE M. VALENTE

Deathless

A Dirge for Prester John, Volume One: The Habitation of the Blessed

A Dirge for Prester John, Volume Two: The Folded World

A Dirge for Prester John, Volume Three: The Spindle of Necessity

The Girl Who Circumnavigated Fairyland In A Ship Of Her Own Making

The Grass-Cutting Sword

The Ice Puzzle

The Labyrinth

The Orphan's Tales, Volume One: In the Night Garden

The Orphan's Tales, Volume Two: In the Cities of Coin and Spice

Palimpsest

Under In the Mere

Yume no Hon: The Book of Dreams

MYTHS
of
ORIGIN

CATHERYNNE M. VALENTE

MYTHS OF ORIGIN

Wyrm Publishing
www.wyrmpublishing.com

ISBN: 978-1-890464-14-1

Printed in Canada

For all those I loved then and now,
who had a part in the life that surrounded these books:
Dmitri, Sam, Melissa, Kaite, Matt, Ryan, and Seth

TABLE OF CONTENTS

INTRODUCTION

BY JEFF VANDERMEER

"We are finished. Our smile is beatific and mouthless. We have no more body to puzzle us, and our voices multiply in infinite combinations, through the trees and stones and snow . . . "

Catherynne M. Valente is a force unto herself, one of those quadruple threats who can burn her way into your brain with novels, short stories, poetry, or blog entries. She's unapologetic about using a poetic style, although she's underrated in terms of the muscularity, the toughness, the sheer bloody-mindedness of her prose. At heart, Valente is a unique member of the writers' bestiary: a creature made of words who swims like a dolphin through pages of prose. Pure writers hardly ever come as pure as this . . .

It's no surprise, then, that in just a few short years Valente has risen from obscurity to become one of the most important and unique fantasists of the early twenty-first century. Whether it's the fascinating and convoluted stories-within-stories that typified the Orphan's Tales duology, the mythic, pseudo-historical storytelling of her Prester John series, the sensuous, Decadent human landscapes of her one-off novel *Palimpsest,* or her most recent, based on Russian folktales, *Deathless*, Valente is always pushing herself and her readers toward the visionary allied with the all-too-human. Her intense education in the classics is often finely balanced against the uncompromising nature of her prose. In an era when many preach the virtues of invisible prose, Valente's having none of it—exploding the myth that you can't have both lush, intricate prose and accessibility for the reader.

But what might not be as clear to Valente's fans is that she started out writing fiction just as compelling and rich as the works for which she has received wider acclaim. This omnibus edition bristles and sparks with evidence of that auspicious beginning, containing four works that provide valuable corroboration of her talent: *The Labyrinth, Yume no Hon: The Book of Dreams, The Grass-Cutting Sword*, and *Under In the Mere*.

My own first encounter with Valente's work was that first novel, for which I wrote the introduction. As I wrote then, "Have we been here before? Yes and no—we've seen these mountains, those valleys, before (at least from afar), but that makes no difference. Every time language dislocates and damages us with the intensity of its unexpected beauty, and the truth of that beauty, we undergo a similar transformation—and we return so we can be dislocated and beautifully damaged once again, albeit in a slightly different way . . . That the author is drunk with words belies the control with which she uses them."

In contrast to the continuous phantasmagorical dream that is *The Labyrinth*, Valente demonstrates other strengths in, for example, *Yume no Hon: The Book of Dreams*, which combines revisionist folktale approaches with an often generous sense of humor. Her attention to detail is exemplified by a chuckle-inducing section with a Snail "moving within his ponderous shell towards the thickest and most delicious of my vines" whose "oilskin rippled slightly and eye-stalks swiveled vaguely in my direction" when the narrator raps "imperiously on that iridescent shell." A rich style, yes, but grounded in close observation of the world.

By contrast yet again, *The Grass-Cutting Sword* consists of a series of short, sharp shocks: a condensed storytelling that demonstrates Valente's effectiveness within a somewhat smaller-scale narrative. The compression in these connected, open-ended moments is impressive: "Yet I have always wondered—what marvelous, secret things could have been woven from that wet, black thread, the thread that smelled so sweet burning?"

Pivoting yet again, away from Eastern influence and toward a re-imagining of Arthurian legends, Valente in the novella *Under In the Mere* that ends this book engages in a different kind of elevated language that manages to also modernize the source material: "Around me, before I could draw breath, was a town of oak-shacks and dark seal-heads floating grim in the morning, a town full of trickling wells and streets that blew dust at themselves . . . I rode into the Underworld on the singing angle of my golden sextant, eyes open, charts asplay, and yet, and yet. I suppose I ought to have known." Journeys of both a physical nature and of the characters' inner life permeate *Under In the Mere*, both stranger and more familiar than the quest in *The Labyrinth* and yet allied with it.

Have I given the impression that Valente is an intensely visual writer? I hope so. Painters and writers are somewhat similar with regard to style, although they often have different goals with regard to the idea of narrative. Like writers, painters have a palette of colors to work with, which they then deploy to create a painting using brushstrokes. These brushstrokes are dictated by the types of brushes they use, and their personal approach to creating the brushstrokes. How they mix and layer the paint. The resulting image of a person will seem to exist independent of the brushstrokes, but it has no such autonomy: it is dependent on the use of charcoal rather than watercolor, oils rather than acrylics. In this regard, Valente demonstrated from the beginning of her career an ability to create very different effects within her lush style.

And if you are a writer like Valente, style doesn't exist just in the syllable because style doesn't encrust a story, form on top of it. Instead, style permeates. It inhabits. Here, in *Myths of Origin*, it exists in every meaning and derivation of the words, and in the hearts of her characters. This is a special kind of obsession, beautiful and true.

"And the book lay between us, bulging and dark, promising. The Fox retained her beatific face; I opened the cover with a careful hand and read these things."

THE LABYRINTH

THIS IS FOR YOU—THE BLAME IS YOURS.
WRITTEN ON YOUR SKIN
SPOKEN IN YOUR VOICE:
A GLAMOUR AND A LIE.

All that I know is contained in this book,
written without witness,
an edifice without dimension,
a city hanging in the sky.
—**Anaïs Nin**, ***House of Incest***

A human being who has not only come to terms and learned to get along with whatever was and is, but who wants to have what was and is repeated into all eternity, shouting insatiably *da capo*—not only to himself but to the whole play and spectacle, and not only to a spectacle but at bottom to him who needs precisely this spectacle—and who makes it necessary because again and again he needs himself—and makes himself necessary—What? And this wouldn't be—*circulus vitiosus deus?*

—Friedrich Nietzsche

CANTO
THE FIRST

1

Look closely. This is not the Way.

Up or down, I could not say, I could not say. I ate the severed halves of a Compass Rose seven-hundred-and-negative-eight miles back, covering the yellow red meat with lime skins and choking it down. Now it is Within. So I could not say northwest or south, only the veil-fire *that way* and the moon-forest *this way*, this turn or that turn, round the oleander Wall rippling underwater or over the mandrake Wall salivating on my hand as I execute a three-quarters pike half-caffeinated flip over its thick shoulders. My body is bound with guitar strings, nipples like fawn's hooves strumming E minor chords and finger-picking a Path through resonant briars, redolent of the desert bellies of blue lizards. By now my feet are worn through, holes like mouths gaping and smacking in cathedral soles, pounding, thrusting on the Path like a drum-skin stretched into incandescence, finding that old comfortable rhythm that by now I know so well, that I invented out of dust and the sweat beading prettily on my own calves.

It is all familiar now, after the passage of constellations and the ingestion of the Compass Rose, holding now that flaming cross inside me, *in this sign thou shalt conquer,* north-brow south-hips east-wrist west-thigh, in this sign thou shalt walk until the end of days, in this sign thou shalt blaze and burn, in this sign thou shalt stride tall through this Place, this happy Garden of Lies, in this sign thou shalt eat berries and lie under the moon, and let it tan your skin silver.

I carry Direction inside me like a child, a watery infant daughter of a circuit of dawns, connected by the fibrous strength of my spinal fluid and thread sun from the enamel of my teeth. She, in all her diamond gills and sunfish fins is anchored in my rich belly, wrapping her precious little Compass-form in my umbilicus like a mummy, and so I am her sarcophagus, too. Her mother and her coffin.

And the directions never change, magnetic north is always at the crown of my mercurial head, south always at the arch of my holy foot, for I carry the Rose within, growing like a Vedic moon. O serpentine I, having a tail fat with scales linked like opaline chain mail, and thus no way to give birth to this precise little cat-child, kept inside an adamant muscle wall. It pushes against my ribcage, stretching the skin of my lifting belly. Amphibious and infertile, webbed into frozen fecundity, Great-With-Child, never Birthed, never Mother. Trapped in the swallowing, breasts heavy and pendulous with milk, unable ever to feel the tug of that small mouth against them. Ever huge with the weight of oceans, of a thousandthousand mountains, halted in freeze frame like an urn. Ambrosial blood swimming between us, the eater and the eaten and the eater again, sucking at the soil of the womb like a clear-petalled lilac. And in this habit of motion-forward, I have learned:

The Void of the Labyrinth does not exactly stretch, or exactly coil, or exactly twist. But it *snarls*. A bolt of belligerent lightning-silk angrily unraveled, corded, torn, circumnavigating itself in a rattling feint, coming apart and crushing in. And it changes, like the horned moon, cycling without pattern. Walls mutate like film noir rape scenes, tearing at pearl skirts with mud-brick fingers that leave stigmatic bruises.

Roads. Oh god, I cannot speak of it, but the Roads have filled me entirely, stuffed and crammed into every corner, oozing out of my body like icy caviar. They are my avenue-bracelets and my fat sapphire street chokers, my gold scarab short-cut armbands and my boulevard harem anklets, they are my cobblestone coin belts and my alleyway-agate earrings. Long Paths criss-cross my torso like ammunition belts, and the innumerable dead-ends pierce my breasts beautifully, hanging pendulously, swinging with laughter, slapping triumphantly against my bronzed belly.

And. There are here tremors of Doorways. They appear in the morning like dew-dampened butterflies, manic and clever. They travel in packs. At night the hinges change from right to left, or vanish completely. Some are no more than flaps of fur, iridescent in the light of the Walls, or sweeping veils of gauze and silk, long curtains like a woman's hair. Like my hair.

Some are hard and ornate, carved with a fantastic code of Arabic and Greek, letters drawn in a paste of crushed diamonds and the hooves of a drowned horse, written with the elegant tip of a black cigarette holder. These have heavy knockers and bulbous knobs, brassy and baronial, in intricate shapes; I have seen a knob like a griffin's fierce mouth, open in a scream with her tongue made of rose quartz, feathers fanning out magnificently in silver on the face of the Door. And a falcon-claw knocker all of amber, the reptilian talon, the three terrible nails ending in their razor points, all wrapped about with the leather of bondage, the flying trails of a hunter's bird cascading down the polished Door, ending in a large lacquered ball with which to strike and enter.

But they are not beautiful to me, any longer. They cluster whispering and break and dance in and out of vision. And they hunt. Like sleek foxes they creep along the places where the Wall meets the Road and wait. They will glide up silently and swallow you as you lie beneath a sighing willow, or stalk you through three dozen twists and turns of the Labyrinth, seizing you as you come upon one of the long boulevards. They are savage creatures, and hungry. On what do they open? I have learned only to avoid them, and I could not say.

I did not exactly *come* here, and I will not exactly *go*. I have always been Here, I have always been about to escape. I have never been *arrived*, always *in transit*, slowly digested by the Road with Doors snapping at my heels. I will never tell the tale of:

"One day I woke up and I was here."

But perhaps it was so, I could not say. Then equally perhaps I shall one day fall asleep and be not here. If this is true, what came before has dissolved from me, lost like milk teeth. But I think, rather, that it has always been as it is, and there was never a *beforethis* nor will be an *afternow*. I am accepting. This is not a thing to be solved, or conquered, or destroyed. It is. I am. We are. We conjugate together in darkness, plotting against each other, the Labyrinth to eat me and I to eat it, each to swallow the hard, black opium of the other. We hold orange petals beneath our tongues and seethe. It has always been so. It grinds against me and I bite into its skin.

I accept. It is not always unpleasant under this particular cubic yardage of sky. I once (will? never?) thought in miles and leagues, counting my measured footsteps with my abacus-lips. I once chanted the low, quiet black magic of numbers and distance, of meters and kilometers like coiled snakes in baskets. I wrote over my whole body with sap, calculating how many times my feet had abused the earth, how many times the stones had gnawed my toes. No more, I have forgotten numbers. I washed the sap in a marble fountain of a serpent-woman spewing clear water from her gaping mouth, that despairing cavern. And I walked on, my pack secure on squared shoulders. I accept.

I am not exactly alone. There are Others. Of course there are the Doors, and they are company of a brutal sort, but I glimpse now and again a flash of golden fur or tinfoil tail in a stream. And I hear rustling in the nights that is not the sibilant gliding of an impending Door. I could not say what creeps and whispers through the branches and down the threaded Road, but I hear it, and I am not afraid.

2

I HAVE STRIPPED MYSELF OF LIGHT.

The Wall-light and the moonlight and the Road-light and the willow-light. I have pulled it down like a pair of blue jeans, scuffed and spattered with paint. Fountainlight and shadowlight and cobblestonelight, roselight and ivylight and dragonflylight, hyacinthlight, applelight, fleshlight and Doorlight. I have pulled it all away, the yarrowlight and Mazelight and fingernaillight and eyelight. Slid off the pirate's planks of my thighs like a river of nascent rain. Waterlight. Underneath that mummification of light, underneath that other body which was so well-wrought, like Milanese leather over my little scaffold of bone, I have grown a new skin. The color of sun-heated coffee skimming the cream off of my shoulders, perforated with cinnamon and licorice, tinted with wind-etched Sea-pebbles. It sloughs down over my arms and elbows, creasing itself like the thick folds of a marble toga. The heat causes ripples; it is not yet accustomed to my frame. We shiver and slithe around each other, combining slowly, slowly.

It is not quite like a molting, for I am not quite like (but not quite unlike) a snake; more the regeneration of a limb by a desert creature, tongue lapping in and out. There was the setting of the sun red on red on red, and the sky scalding, and the new skin over my fingers like petroglyphic gloves. Sand caked my hair into long sheaves, curling sticks of stiff driftwood, frozen fleshy-fat river eels. I am a stone Medusa sitting by the Wall, late afternoon light nosing her face like a curious wolf, knifing the supper-meat savagely, turning a pitiful hare and wild greens to jasper and sodalite. And all around her form the crackle and hiss of new skin, growing, growing, growing, covering her serpent-hair with that fabled horse-flesh. And now I walk in a body of darkness that is light, skin seething black, seeking the next sinuous trine of this Path.

I stand as I have stood a meaningless number of times on one of the long thoroughfares, lined with wild pear trees alternating whitethorn and prairie grasses, blooming as though they were planted with some purpose, to shade the heat chattering off this Road, pushing into the air with oily hands, tracing a finger-pattern into the image I see. (Though it may not be real, the Void of the Labyrinth has no shape, and thus no constancy). I have come through a considerable snarl, and the new body I have won does not make it easier; I cannot see my legs move beneath me, they blend so into the liquid night and shadow, swallowing stars into my knee pits.

When I bend to examine the Path, nebulae are crushed to glittering dust beneath thigh on the anvil of calf. It went: left left right straight left right circle back right straight through the portcullis and under the bridges three sharp lefts two gradual rights through the roundabout over the creek and seventy perpendicular left turns spiraling inward.

But it has all changed by now, of course, so that map does little good. And it means nothing, to say that I have come through a snarl or found a thoroughfare. I catch myself thinking in the old ways of distance and arrival, of a goal, of a center, of an end. And even then thinking in the ways of time and linear movement. But there are infinite tangles and straight Roads; that I have traversed one (of a multitude my feet have enumerated into meaninglessness) and spilled out in my dark puddle of self onto another is less than nothing at all. I have found the Colossus and been enfolded.

A whale's ribcage is almost visible against the sky, long and bleached white. The comfort of its linearity glows in a spectral nova. And there is something comforting about the length and breadth, the Road like a woman's smooth brown leg extended into the infinite, her toe brushing the corona of the sun, heel pressing the rim of eradication. Yes, it alters and mutates and flicks through its shapes like a nickelodeon, but it cradles me and keeps me and I am defined more by Walls and Roads now than limbs and brain. It is a wide womb and I am born over and over.

It is a game we play. There is Vision here, to be stolen, seized, taken at knifepoint from the black-scaled baobab. Vision, yes, but no Will. Will has no meaning, or has lost it, under the dusty whitethorn leaves with their filtered light, no meaning behind or before the marauding Doors, no meaning in my palm or a greater one, crossed by arcane lines that I cannot read, cannot say. I move like the breath in a pan pipe, and walk as I may, but it ends in nothing, the Path determines. I am within the Colossus, within the Whale, and though my footfalls echo on its entrails and my voice stabs the lining of its stomach, I am in the fish and I go whither it swims. No meaning. I balance on a crown of babble, teetering and tottering on four-inch heels over a cobblestone Road, straps of biting black scoring my ankles with pricks of blood like decimals. The fan of four bones demarcate. My stride is weary with gin-streaked sighs. Grey sky wind in my face and breath of thorns. Swamps and marshes and crushed cellos, cracked air and bamboo beatings. There is no other than this Road that looks so linear and ever-going. Plod, plod, plod, one lacquered/unlacquered toe after another, red, white, red. Into the horizon, perpendicular I against the degreeless slope of hills and dales. All the paints in my boxes are ash, all the inks black. I carve my world in monochrome.

I am at the sword-point of all amplitude and fold/unfolding. I reside in voluminous wreckage. It is beautiful, the hide of the leviathan reflected in mud-brick and trellis-work, the suggestion of a thing concealed: a Queen, a Talisman, a Treasure, a Castle, a Monster. At the very least some secret knowledge to be won. The threat of an oblong head rising blackly out of the water, lake beading off its reptilian brow makes the liquid promise shine with voluptuous beckoning. I am I, can be no other, and my little mind, encapsulated in skull and void, insists that a center exists within Wall after Wall. I promise myself not to think on it, knowing as well as I do that there is nothing, that the whisper is a lie, but I slip. I slip and drown in the root system of the Labyrinth.

3

TIME FLICKERS ON AND ON.

A half-realized body stretches out coral-encrusted fingers to seize it. Useless, of course it is useless—each spindle-moment gone before my limbs could ever escape the glassine softness of their essential corporeality, could achieve escape velocity and roar away from themselves in a bloom of fire. I walk (will walk, have walked, I told you there is no coming and going here) in the Maze, a spinning silver coin in the sky, and the names of the flowers float out of my honeycombed skin, the mystic botany I once knew when I was (am, will be) wrapped in my sanguine turban. Crocus, narcissus, chrysanthemum, orchid. I name them for the air's ears, for the benefit of the enclosing Walls, touching a thick petal with my tapered finger, one for each syllable. I walk rhythmically, battered tattered cloak folded under one arm.

Today it is warm and the sun is on my back like a peacock's fan. Hibiscus. Asphodel. I carry the Gardens with me, and name the flowers in infinite repetitions, even in my sleep the names trickle from my lips like blood, like rainwater. Delphinium, amaranthus, asiatic lily. Lotus, pennyroyal, poinsettia, marigold. Roses and opiate poppies and bluebells. The rain-washed flagstones bear the imprints of my sandaled and unsandaled feet, my pleading knees, walking the same Path again and again. Nephthytis, larkspur, foxglove, hyacinth. I do not pull weeds or comb the soil. I often catalogue, to pass the time, though it is equally useless since the topiaries and terrariums change like a dervish spinning. I note the growth patterns of hibiscus in the humidity of July. I commit to memory the cross-pollination of red dracaena and night-tulips. I twist moorland heather in my black hair. I walk in the green shadows of tropical leaves, in a contorted Babylon.

The gold which is no-gold on my fingers is heavy, weighting me to this desert place which has no great umbilicus of river, rooting me to it, binding my body to these very shades of blackberry blossoms. This expanding microsecond now contracts so fast I cannot even touch its saturnine rim before it vanishes like the up-spiraling smoke of a silver hookah. But even to consider this pinwheeling threatens madness, to engulf the howling mind that weeps over every lost instant, crying to the rings of Jupiter to slow and remain in the center of one fuchsia-breasted moment. But non-linear travel is forbidden here, in the realm of the sternest of all gods, and I swoon (have, will, might) beneath the weight of such endless forward movement.

I arrive often in a rosemary-scented Courtyard rimmed by manzanita trees, low and twisting. I have seen it perhaps seven or seven hundred times. It means nothing, not truly an arrival. The Sea laughs and beats a drum with blue-palmed hands down past the line of my vision, (but oh, I can hear it as it foams and thrills in my collarbone!) at the bottom of a convoluted Escher-like staircase, jumping and arching over itself, doubling back and spiraling crab-wise, chasing its long helix-body down to the edge of the tidepools. Into its stony flower-boxes and hedge-creatures I glide, still wrapped in my darkbody, leaving tattered scraps of shadow on the thorns as I pass. Didn't I want to be a dark woman in some *longagoothertime*? The Labyrinth has covered every whiteness with violet petals and the dark pollen of night-lilies. I have crushed the thousand gardens into a vial of pigment to hide myself from its eyes, painted like a pagan, chasing after deer on the steppes. I march like a good soldier on the shell of a Sea-snail. It goes on and on. The Sea is unseen, beyond the Walls, and I will never float within its blue.

4

"IT SNAPPED AT HER," A THING INTONED.

"Did the Door, and she fell in, *downdowndowndowndown*. Silly, running—why grumble, greymalkin, when there are violets about, and sweet?"

It was a pair of fat auburn haunches, chocolate and honey, fur like velvet gloves, long, eloquent ears pink as girlhood. It startled me, this new thing. An enormous Great Hare sat calmly on a patch of thick grass and wildflowers, as though guarding a corn-maiden's tomb. I marshaled language like reticent troops in my dappled head, so long had passed without another Voice but the echo of mine. Her nose twitched, staring with liquid eyes, chewing industriously on the lip of a daisy.

"Did the Door and swifter than I could. Was it a nice Door? Was it soft and delicious? Did it lead to a sweet thicket? Will you see its teeth when it comes like a hound? Silly girl-thing, why not stay and flower-eat? Wait and they will come. You will travel well enough."

The Hare stretched her long feet as though trying for a marathon. She nibbled at a toe, yawned. Nonplussed, I reached out a hand to scratch her head, and she leaned warmly into my palm.

"Where did you come from?" I touched, gingerly, her face.

"Away! Away and away and away and away! Do you know the Way? I do, I do, I do! I am the flower-eater and the grass-devourer. I am the swift sun-runner and the apple-thief. I know the secret. What are you?"

"I am the Walker. The Seeker-After. I am the Compass-Eater and the Wall-Climber. I am the Woman of the Maze. And no Door has ever caught me." The Hare wriggled her silky muzzle and ground her teeth in derision. A massive foot slapped against the ground as the air filled with rabbit-laughter.

"So certain. So full of titles. So proud. Did the Door and swifter than I. Inevitability is the color of water. Movement is a waste. They will find you. I did."

"Were you looking for me?" I asked incredulously.

"I looked for breakfast." A sprig of heather disappeared into her little mouth. "Breakfast beckons the strange and you are strangest of all. Eat. Drink. Why punish the earth with your girlfeet? There is sweetgrass and wild lettuce and savory roses—these are enough. Why can you not let it be enough? They are alkaline, syrup-filled, fine as baker's sugar, and they will coat our throats like warm toffee, like brandy and olive oil, and make us beautiful. The Way escapes you. It will always escape you. *Downdowndowndowndown.*" She snorted and stroked one long, brown ear. "I am the swift sun-runner. My feet are better than yours. Yet still. Still did the Door and brought me. Now I am here with the roses like buttered artichoke hearts and a girlfooted creature insisting on motion."

I drew aimlessly in the black soil with a tapered finger. Circles, one after the other, each as starless as the last. Downstrokes like bypass surgeries, heart beating like a bavarian choir. I could stay, I could vomit galaxies into this earth and never burn my throat with light, wearing scalpels like jewelry, wrapping my body in bloody togas, reciting my own eulogy with a mouthful of cat's eye marbles and agaric mushrooms, arm jutting out awkwardly into the world.

I touched her, her softness and earthlight. She laid her head against me, speaking with a barbed intimacy. "What is the secret you know?" I asked.

"Blue Door it was," she answered, "covered with stars-nine-pointed. Hiding in the raspberry brambles. It snapped at me, clapped on me just like a farmer's big hands. It leapt; I was not swift that day. Downdowndown. I don't run anymore, I am not prey. I wait, and swallow things when they come." She looked at me with brittle eyes, glittering full of the light of the sun on the violets. She was very big, staring straight at me, our heads level. "Stay with me and eat well. Fall through a hundredhundredhundred Doors with me. There are always roses enough. After awhile, even the falling is gentle."

By now my fingers were thoroughly tangled in her fur, sepia over onyx, swift over slow. I wanted her warmth within me like the Compass, to devour it and hold it still, to take her peace like a pretty ring. But pretty things are all beyond me.

Disentangling, I gathered up a few fallen petals, and met her limpid eyes through a forest of lashes, gently pulling back, and speaking low.

"I am the Seeker-After, I cannot. I must Go, despite the roses."

"There is nothing," the Hare assured me, shrugging her autumn-shaded shoulders. "That is my secret. There is no Way—only the staying still and the quiet. The waiting and the melting of a rose petal on the tongue."

5

MY ANKLE HAS SWOLLEN APPLE-HUGE.

As though I were incubating some warm and throbbing egg between my cuneiform bones, the pinch of white hands gripping me tightly during the anointment of the Styx. Humidity sighs orchids and seasmoke through my hair, the vibration of a string bass on the westerly wind, blowing off the invisible Sea in trailing puffs. The moon like a garlic bulb scenting the sky, throwing out starry pale green shoots, glowing between raindrops.

Here am I laughing like the Hare, my girlfeet pierced with honeyed stigmata. Here am I bright as a dueling pistol in the dawn, hobbled and kept still by strange circles turning beneath the skin of my darkbody. I cover my translucent feet with the hem of my skirt, so as to expose what they contain. that perfect Greek ankle, palpitating for the advent of a Serpent, the auroral revelation of a penetrating arrow. I have swallowed the Road, I have eaten death. Hard, coarse black bread crumbling on the teeth like fallout; warmth like oak-honey clogging the cilia with its liquid sibilance. I am awake, I am asleep, I am a somnambulist who each night presses herself between the Walls, in among tiger-spiders. I eat clay and drink dust beside kings whose names I have forgotten or never knew, because we have both refused the gods and their perfumed eyes. We stare ahead and calculate the burn rates of white dwarf stars to pass the time.

I dwell within this invisible ravage, the scald of temptation. Stay within the white wheat the silver and the star, stay within the Wall and the Garden greaves, folded into a rose like an exhausted bee, gold enfolded in scarlet, and sleep forever with a sugared violet pressed on my tongue like a coin on a corpse's eye. Oh, but it is beautiful, to sleep and to rest and to walk no more.

The radiance of true nothingness set against the glimmer of its threat. It would have been a breath of gold to lie against that great leaf-shaded flank, the prickle of sepia-silken fur under my limbs, those pupilless eyes above me like secret moons for all time in the shade of aster-breathing Doors with their sulfurous hinges and studded with heliotrope. They would rise like suns over our sleeping shapes, bodies curved into symbology, and we would fall a hundred times a hundred until the falling was all that existed, the tumbling of her lucent haunches and my hair trailing like kelp on the Sea. *Downdowndowndowndown.*

Wouldn't it be better than this, the Road cutting vision, the Walls containing shocks of self, bolts of tawny motion? The peace of the fall, the certitude, the gentility of surrender. Long railway of silence into the depths that Doors must conceal. How everything here becomes luminous through the illimitable veils of concealment. Seduction shivers through me, the obscene, serpentine promise of what is not known, navigated, charted. Not split like the trunk of a tree into what I have walked and what I will walk. Not the inarguable vastness of the Labyrinth.

But. I accept. I pull back at the threshold, shunning liminal space for the within-ness of Here. I go up the Staircase, and the world is still pressed like a dragonfly in ice. I never touch Edge or Center, never Entrance nor Exit, but remain somewhere inside, hanging pendulously among the trembling owl-winged scales embracing all those who fall.

It is late, it is early, it is dark, it is light. How I lust for light, all light. Did I once beneath the apple trees stand scrubbed clean and pink by the sun, white flowers trailing my heels, laughter shaking the red fruit from the branch, eyes pools of August skies? Is this the *alwaysnow*, under the yew trees with violet flowers bleeding into my hair, learning desert tongues from the moon and carving whitethorn sculptures of Rabbits and Doors. But the green softness of the wood under my silver knife excites me. There is nothing in my footprints, not even dust, not even the ridges of a usual foot. One feather-fanned mark in the Road drags more than the other, the thorn in my heel pulling back towards the little patch of grass, back towards liquid coffee eyes, back towards those endless roses. The alexandrine tooth of a hare embedded in that hollow where skin is a papery wing over quivering bone, thorn-chaining me into stillness. Checking my movements—black queen to e4.

I enter, near dawn, a twisted tower of ice, of glass. The Labyrinth here has fallen into freeze, the Road disappeared beneath cream-cobalt crystal, reflecting, refracting, eating the color of sky like winter soup. It reflects the small, silent colors of sunrise onto my deepened skin, blue over black, rippling, sighing. Fountains still in stop-motion, cresting wave of water arching through the sky, a cascade of diamonds. All the earth has become a diamond, a faceted jewel pulsing like a heart. Whiteness devours. I am caught in this freeze-frame, the same few seconds of film over and over, the same cold moonlight, the same tinkling piano, the same villain in the shadows, the same ingenue. At least it is white, under the veil of silver and blown glass that admits no imperfection. That banishes original sin. In this world, my lips are perfect, my skin snowy.

The beautiful darkbody flees in the face of all this hoary paleness—the Labyrinth has stolen it. I am bloodless—snow hair falls to my waist, pupilirisall vanishes into classical eyes of milky stillness, though my sight remains. The jet of my tongue shrieks into the air, a mouth of chalk remains. I am a long scroll of blank paper, all color ripped from me like a gown. I stagger with the violence of tearing. The flowers are a graceful gasp under the silver Sea. The elegant bannisters of staircases, gone to blown glass and aquamarine. Shall I go up? Shall I go down?

6

HIC MONSTRA DELITESCUNT . . .

I could not say, I could not say. Whether there are monsters hereabout. I have said that I am not exactly alone, but then, I am not exactly *togetherwith*, either. I have seen things, in the shadows, but who is to say? I dance on the leeward side of the mandrake Wall and a quarter of my iris rebels into violet, the Walls march in a phalanx and my body becomes quicksilver, shining as a trout in the river, illuminating the spear-leaves and wizard-staff stems, reflecting on my rippling skin the wormwood and the moonseed, the orris root and the milkweed. Who can ever know what I have seen there revealed? The shadows know, in their depths and scrying sleek. Whether when I in a fever cross a drawbridge made for children with smaller feet than I, a troll with ambergris eyes lurks delicately beneath the creaking wood. Whether at the Center-which-is-not of all of this rests a quiescent Minotaur, his horns resplendent with blood and ash, death in an amulet around his neck, eyes like shuriken, a great brass ring in his poisonvelvet nose. Whether his volcanic heart thumps in time to mine, whether he waits for me in the geometric darkness, to wed himself to the Labyrinth forever in the sacred ritual of my dismemberment.

Will I serve as a corridor between them? I fear a Minotaur. I fear hooves tramping in showers of the white blood of lotuses, crushing Franciscan bones under him. Hooves separating brow from skull, viscera of the "I" that is me digested through a Maze of four stomachs (for do not all we Labyrinth creatures carry the turning Path inside us. We carry so much, all of us pregnant with incident.) I fear a Lair of rattling sternums and tibia, prayer ropes and iron ore. But there is no Center to house a Lair to hold a Beast, so if one echoes in this place, he must roar his acidic throat to razors among the halls of where-I-have-not-walked, and stalks, a hunter like the rest. Some ways back I saw a pile of Doors splintered and broken like moldered corpses. They had a smell of rotted almonds and shoe leather. Am I to be as they are, cracked and bleeding in the jeweled hinges of a vengeful Gate?

"*Hic monstra delitescunt. Sed puella, puella, ubi abscondes?*"

Voice like a rustling of linden leaves, like sand becoming a pearl. My hand fluttered to my mouth in terror, hiding the shameful whiteness of my lips. She sat on a Wall of salmon scales, which clinked and jingled as she turned her perfect face towards me, eyes full of hawk's claws. Her wings reached back over the crest of the Wall and nearly brushed the ground, arched and pointed, of feathered ice and lapis lazuli. Her body covered in a skin of milky opals, clinging to her breasts and belly, her long arms and her bare feet. I could not speak. My blank statue-eyes were helpless, could offer nothing to her beauty. In her hands a slim rod of ash and spider-thread, she was fishing in the Road, a hole cut in the ice of a left-hand turn. An Angel of Ice-Fishing. She was smoking a long reed pipe, tobacco that smelt of cranberries and elephant-skin. And hauling trout from the Road in great silver heaps, flopping beside her on the Wall. Some leapt ecstatically towards her, not waiting for the line and bait.

I climbed up, clumsy and strange in my lightbody, full of cold and slowness. In the mountains of fish I found a resting place, leaning against the marine brickwork. Amid a corona of smoke she pressed the rod-end into a crack in the Wall. The fish still threw themselves at her opaline body, eyes full of her form. She curled her lips into

"*Hic monstra delitescunt, cara.*"

I looked up into her and choked, "You speak the language of the Doors!"

She breathed her jungle tobacco into my pale mouth. "Yes," she hissed, "Do you think perhaps I am a Door?"

I could not answer, tongue thick in my bloodless mouth. The Angel leaned into me, cold radiating from her owl-skin. She began to draw on my papery flesh in stark black chalk on my belly and lunar, heavy breasts. Her finger was cold.

"The key to catching trout is the lure," she intoned throatily, tracing a horse-shape on my thigh. "Today they are biting on dragonflies smeared in my blood." She exhales, long and critically, editorializing her drawing with smoke-rings. She began on a spiraling snake, just below my left shoulder. "Tomorrow it will be roasted cicadas. They are fickle."

"Sometimes I am a cicada, hissing and singing in the leaves of a tree by the sunlit water, thoughtless and wordless, a voice that is all consonants and tribal clicks. Sometimes I rub my legs together like a string bass, and the lake quivers." She listened intently to me, as if diagnosing a tumor hiding in my voice.

Slowly she took possession of me through the figures; antelope grazing across my shoulder blades, leaping salmon on the soles of my tattered feet, dragonfly-knees, flames searing up my arms, river-belly, storm-brow, tree-spine. A fleur-de-lis branded onto the nape of my neck. And a great snail shell winding around itself, blazing on the small of my back. My lips she paints with the blood of enthralled trout, but my eyes, still yet uniform perfect white. And I lie against the silver bodies, empty within my mosaics of wounded buffalo and women carrying water, all rock and dripping water, all darkness and sleeping bears. Claws clack on my stones.

"You see what a beautiful thing I can make of the whiteness," she laughed smokily, "this is the dream I insinuate, this is the discontent I plant like a seed of pearl in you, that grows like a cornstalk from my throat and fills the Void of you with little orbs of gold. I speak the tongues of the Door-tribe, and though I have no hinge and no bell-rope, in a way I am the Door that catches you, I enfold and take you to the world of faith-in-the-Center, of bone-desolation, of belief. I plant in you the conviction of the Monster, the Queen, the Castle, the Treasure. I destroy your nonchalance, I take your certainty of nothing. Now you will suffer, my pretty *puella*, for I give you in a casket whose angles are swords, the desire to find what cannot be found, the dread adoration of what is not. This is my gift to you." I trembled under her avian eyes, numinous and desert-savage.

"I do not want it. I am happy enough here, walking."

"You are the Seeker-After. Is that not what you said? It is not for you to be happy. You *accept*. Did that not also escape your white lips? The Labyrinth does not accept you. I am filling you up with Want like acetylene semen. You have been here too long. Did you not think the Doors had a function? All things do, even you, even I. It is a present. Make no mistake, there is nothing, no Center, no Monster, no Quest. But in your proximate madness you will believe it." She paused to trace a lion's tail around my toes.

"The Labyrinth is all. I will make a small place in the soil of you and bury the grafted seed of *Yes*. Is it not a beautiful gift I give you?" She beamed, a blue light that shook through her skin and hair, glowing corona and belt of nebulous ice-rings. Painted over with her hands I was frantic to escape the Angel, to continue as I had been, to Wander as I was meant, secure in the world I had delineated, whose moods and selves I knew.

"Please, Lady, I will not yield to even so beautiful a Door as you, I will not. I am the Seeker-After. Don't you see? If I found a thing, I could not seek. Don't change me. It is illusion, all of it." I lifted myself slightly on pale palms as if to run, to escape the advent of Purpose. More terrible than the roses was this awful constriction, this assignment of identity, eradication of personality within her impetus. It would fill me up until I choked and there would be no "I" at all, only the Center-that-is-not. My breath had stopped, squeezed by her python voice, a panic of screams rising up like vomit.

"I am not quite a Door, you know," she whispered, "nor quite an Angel. You will cry out for me before the end, if an end there is, can ever be." She plucked a many-colored opal, swimming in a borealis of light, from her navel. "You do not yet understand. You do not even know your name. Keep this always by you, and thus keep me close to your skin. I will be always with you, and in you, and keep you, and guide you."

She bent, heavy with her beauty, towards me in my wriggling silver throne, and kissed my slickly star-white mouth, warmly, full and musky with the smell of ice. The Angel bit into my lower lip, drawing deep rushes of marbled blood. Drawing back, licked hungrily where it had stained her chin.

And vanished. The ice receded from the Road, with no scar where she had drawn up her subterranean trout. I wanted to throw the Stone from me, but I could not. It was so warm clutched in my hand.

In my glyphbody I ran, wailing into the night.

7

DESPAIR.

I am blind. Still in my statue-eyes I die in my steps blooming red and black. The glyphbody flies apart, together. The Stone burns all through me. Talmudic Walls rise, recede. I dive, I dart, I runrunrun. I know the way to away and away. Infatuated by motion my feet make love to dirt, couple with jeweled stones full of corrosive oxygenblood, death of a thousand cuts executed on my own human haunches, never running fast enough to escape the threat of Purpose/non-Purpose. The Mazescape sloughs off its icy corselet as I scramble from the Angel's shade, but still I am the wasteland, white within white. Whales hunt for fat seals across the icy expanse of my torso, wolves gnaw at my ears. My septum is pierced with a barbed harpoon. I shudder in my own cold, watching my lips turn cream-blue, reflected endlessly in the glaciers of my transparent fingers. I am snow, I am stone, I am wind. I hollow myself to make shelter, scooping out shovelfuls of slush from my stomach, my thighs, my skull. I break open, holding this body together with screams. Perhaps when it is done I can crawl within the now-palace of stretched skin over the frame of icicles and become warm. Perhaps I will understand. Careening, pinwheel stride around a cul-de-sac, I kneel before a crumbling Wall—perhaps with bricklaid eyes it saw the birth of the Labyrinth in the *longestago,* squeezed from the womb of some unutterable hundred-armed Ionic bear-goddess with screaming eyes, covered in slime and dust, shooting its arms out into geometric monstrosity, eating worlds to make its new limbs and mouths and voices, fulminating in the shadow of gargantua, suckling at its mother's shaggy body until she died—

I push its broken bricks back into the Wallbody, weeping with mortar of tears and saliva, fingernails torn and leaking white liquid, blood of pulverized moonstone flowing through me burning, burning, burning, the witch on the platform of my diaphragm, flames shooting from her mouth into my veins. Everything is fire. I grapple at the broken rock and dust, cramming it into my colorless mouth, crushing it into nothing, tasting the sour pencil-lead and hashish flavor of it, the gore of an ageing Wall, muddy intestines spilled out onto the careless Road into my careless belly. In, in, in, the tawny supper of clay, salted by manic tears, through the mash of dirt crowding I speak in tongues; Door-tongues, Hare-tongues, Sky-tongues, Trout-tongues, sordid demon-tongues, flower-tongues, snake-tongues like nooses, tobacco-tongues and belly-tongues, darkbody-tongues and white-eyed tongues, reptile-tongues and black wine-tongues, girl-tongues and foot-tongues, pummeling tongues of non-being and cadaverous tongues of lunatic frogs, O blasphemy, blasphemy in my tongue of tongues with the Wall dribbling out the sides of my wretched mouth. O holy Meal of Myself, Queen of the Center-that-is-not, babbling up at staircases that lead everywherenowhere, monoliths gawking at the clowning moon.

Exploding frenetic devourer, I eat the Labyrinth and it eats me, each grinning with stringy meat dangling like earrings from a hungry mouth. Conquering, driving it before me through my body, chasing it, knowing that time will come for the kill, screaming into it, filling the world with a rape of sound. O send out your Doors and I will splinter them! Sacred gibberish of Maze oracles too full of self, Road blasting through my abdomen like a cannonball, paving me flat, pushing, pushing, forward motion, reversal verboten, it is one-way, the Way of Tongues, the Way of Body, the Way of the After-Seeker. Breathe, breathe, lungs, or the Wall will strangle you like a criminal. And so I draw a rasping, shearing breath, inhaling the revelatory dust into my fishy pink lungs, maidenhair cilia, exchanging air for earth. Elementals dance in trapezoidal patterns, and always within. I will not yield, I will not let the Labyrinth trap me into belonging. I have eaten it, as I ate the compass rose, and it sits in my belly like a thrashing mollusk, throwing out the shrapnel of its hydrochloric shell into my stomach-lining, into my howling womb Walls, into the deeps of my secret throats. Of all those infinite thousands of tentacled Maze-arms I have one fleshly sucker within me, a grisly victory. In the sign of this body thou shalt conquer, thou shalt slash and rend flesh, thou shalt Devour for it is thy nature, to Devour what is Sought. I am I, and no other. On my lips the Wall disintegrates, on my lips it dies. I refuse. I refuse these mewling seductions. I am I. I move within the Labyrinth, and it moves within me. If there is madness to be swallowed, I will swallow it. But for the crashing chariots of Purpose I cannot halt.

8

I WHITTLE THE WAXEN SURFACE OF TIME.

White crows cackle at the blackening dawn. Dewy air finds me curled in the wreckage of the Wall, liquid light hair streaming into the sky like a cloud of gangrenous butterflies. The morning so thick in my mouth, the pulverized brick on my tongue, ancient mortar like congealed vodka pouting at my uvula. Vagaries of the morning after paroxysm, ache of jaws recently frantic. (I contain an abundance of whiteness.) Still shivering in copious plagues. Penumbral lacerations and ruins of hallowed sylph-hips. I lie here, pressed down into the ground, unable to move, to pry open painted eyes and coerce action from opiate corporeality. Float in the dark, girl-creature, it isn't the sun on your limbs, it is the fire. Is there a tree heavy with peaches for your breakfast, waiting fat and friendly and golden outside the body barrier you cower in? Arboreal messiah, full of sugary seraphim, the grails of pitted cores? No, there is dust. Outside you, inside you. Dust. Toothless sky gumming your fingers like a grandmother.

I move. I have to. I am—there is no tree adjacent, of course. It would have been too docile, for the Road to have twisted and turned to serve my belly and its cat-howl, scowling empty. But it does not take long, no longer than a half-sliver of silver sun-glide, to locate a copse of cold green fruit trees. Under all juice flows down my lips, running the pigment of the Angel's art like watercolors. Impressionist, I stand tall and still within the sky-armed trees.

What remains when fire has filled the viscera and vanished? The oily tracks of naphtha, steaming black arteries, barren metallic smoke-smell, liver glazed like a vase, glossy and intricate. The lungs are blazed to crystal, and the long necklaces of veins strung with gleaming ligaments, each capillary popping clear of the flesh like a carnelian bead. What is left when the grimy veil of delirium has passed, with its greasy flames of green and blue? The Void, the Void only, that is the Labyrinth and that is I. When it is over, we remain, as we have *alwaysbeen*. The Others are ripples.

But I am troubled, I am haunted. Function, meaning pry at me like hungry children. There is power here, in my place within the life of the Maze. I am a terrible whirlwind, the eater of cities, but I choke on my own clouds and skirts of dust, my long ropes of sand. Wild roses on the Wallface, and the Void giggling under a veil of waving carpets of summer grass. And I, burning, falling, raw as bark-stripped pine. There is no sound where I step, for I am not really here, this shadow is not mine, I swear to myself that I am more than this, that transcendence exists somewhere, and a secret avalanche far off rumbles like the clearing of a diamond throat.

I am tired.

9

WHITHER AND HOW. SHALL I GO ON?

Do I dare to crawl on my belly through this pilgrimage of grass and earth? A pilgrimage with no Rapture at its dread terminus? Wear my knees to inkwells over endless Paths. Shaken by the spidery intrusions of words like snaking belladonna, I am not so firmly forward moving as I was. The clouds are threatening admirals, dusted in golden medals of sunlight. I have not heard the shuffling gait of a Door on my trail in days. It is strange, the ineffable silence. Do they no longer want me? Has my smell become less delectable in their nostril/keyholes? All around is barren, Walls of bare copper wire and a scalded Road, and I am the most blasted acre of this waste. I have seen scurryings in the corners, I have heard scratching feet. Yesterday a thrush shook its wings of rain nearby. But it would not speak to me, it turned its little brown back. I am verboten, nameless, null. There is a sliver in the pad of my ring finger, the reliquary of my own flesh cradling a breath of ash, tinged in blood and vinegar from lips of sorrowful countenance. In my earlobes thorns, my eyelids draped in shrouds with the imprints of a thousands faces emblazoned in sweat, a spear entering my mouth and piercing my skull at its base, obsidian arrowhead dripping in liquefied faux diamonds, the viscous substance that pools in my brain pan and slides from the edges of the wound, thick with hieroglyphic ideation and the terribly worrying diagnosis of blood-poisoning. Oh, yes, I feel it already, marching through the byways with alkaline toes. Sad to think I am so streaked in squid-ink poverty that I cannot even be devoured properly. She was right. I do not know my name. But. I accept.

A sound fractured the air, behind a Wall of diamond and boiling pitch, spilling onto the Road in a writhing swamp-hand, reaching, reaching. My scalded eyes rolled like slot machines, pivoting to follow, sliding to wrap the molten corners. I was not ready, not ready for another thing to disturb my madness, growing like a favored son in me. I could almost see its source, spy with my little eye—

"A MAN!" it cried out, voice bleeding gasoline, slow and egg-runny, wriggling towards me.

"WALKS!"

And I could see it then, scaled knee sunk into the pitch, mouth gaping like a cellar Door. A swath of green hyphenating the Doorscape, glittering coldly and savagely in the brittle sun, still slick with the waters of some distant marsh. His great tail slapped the air, thumped the earth with enthusiasm and abandon as he, a monstrous Crocodile, clacked his feral jaw and winked, launching full force into his sermon, quivering in every green claw, gesturing with fat scaled fingers.

"A MAN WALKS INTO A BAR! Hallelujah, child, hallelujah, I say! Say it up and say it down, say it east and say it west, say it *diagonal*, child, say it *out loud!* A MAN! WALKS INTO! A BAR! A! MAN WALKS! INTO A! BAR! A! MAN! WALKS! INTO! A! BAR! AMAN, child, sing it, AMEN, glory on high, walks into a bar, and do he ever walk *tall!* A man walks into a bar, my child, do you *hear* what I *say*? He walks and he walks *slow*, he walks like *paint drying*, my friend, but he walks straight up to that bar and it'll only be *the best brand* for this one with his five-day-beard and better-day-seen jeans! Oh, yes, girl, surely so, a man walks into a bar and don't he have the look of a *union man*, don't he have the look of coffee and cigarette break *on the hour every hour*, don't he look like *our kind of boy!* Oh, pour him that double shot! Pour him that twelve-year old *brand name!* How many apostles on that holy mount, my child? Oh, yes, my girl! *There were twelve!* Can I get an AMEN? Oh, pour him that apostle-scotch, barman, *pour that drink!* A man walks into a bar, *holy holy, holy!* Oh, he walks *long* and he walks *strong* and don't he walk *grand*, like a boot-barrel man should, and ain't that cigarette in his mouth just as white as your mama's wash-day, child, and don't that smoke *rise up*? Oh, way up *high* it's said that men they don't *walk* but *fly* but oh, my child, I say unto you that that man *walked* into a bar and he *drank that whiskey down!* Say it high and say it low but in he walked and *lay his money down,* in he walked and sat on that red vinyl, in he walked and *tipped that barman five dollars,* hallelujah, child, *five dollars!* And ain't that green bill *crisp,* friends and neighbors, ain't it *brand new,* ain't it *mint?* A man walks into a bar, in his holy *name,* and it is nigh on *last call* but he lays his money down, he lays it down and drinks it down and ain't that *just fine?* Ain't that *right as rain?*"

I arched a kindergarten-paste eyebrow like a flying buttress. The Crocodile stamped his feet joyfully, splashing my ankles with black grime. His eyes glowed like pools of crude oil.

"Do you hear me, girl? Do you *get* what I'm *saying?* Can you *grab hold* and swing it around? Can you *feel* it in your *teeth?* Can you grasp the *sublime* and *angelic* perfection of the Gospel of the Man and the Bar?"

I leaned on one hip, exhaustion covering me like a lead shield. "I heard. I hear. It is no different than the Gospel of the Hare or the Gospel of Ice-Fishing. Everyone has another useless revelation."

"But it *is* different. Can't you *see it through and through?* I have heard those Gospels and they are *false prophets.* They are *cheap copies.* Truth lies with the Man and Revelation in his Bar." The creature inched towards me, his fat green body swaying from side to side, black eyes roving over me like sweaty hands. "I'm not surprised. We Crocodiles are *spiritually pure.* We can hold the Gospel in *our mouths.* Can't expect a little thing like you to grasp the higher registers. Your mouth is too small."

"I try, I try to understand the manifest and the invisible. I Devour. I Seek, I Walk."

"Of *course* you do, precious thing, of course." He sidled up to me and pushed his emerald head up under my hand like a cat. "No one *blames* you. It's just not how you're made. White as paper you are—well, what's paper for but writing on? And the paper knows nothing about it, can't go about reading itself. Just so, you can't be asked to know my Gospel any more than the number of my scales. If I had hands I might scribble a bit on you myself. Such sweet skin." He gestured in a friendly manner with his slick reptilian legs. "You just keep on as you are. *Downdowndown.* You haven't found your true Author yet—not like my own radiant self and the radiant Man. There is one that will cover you in ink like a hand. Until then you're just a river without a bank, *rushing* and *crashing* and *flooding* with no ocean to devour you. To gobble you up. Wish it could be me. If you could touch but the *outer rim* of the golden meaning of the Man and the Bar, the first layer like a *crystal onion*, you would be *saved*. If you could only understand that there is only one Man, and only one Bar, and they walk into *each other*, and they are *the same*. These are High Mysteries. But no! No one expects you to be *pure* like we are, pretty girl. Why, no!" He looked at my hips smugly, his marble eyes preening. "But whether you grip it in your little white hands or not, a Man walked into a Bar, *and it was a fine day.*"

The Crocodile ambled away, humming a little, slogging through the sparkling pitch with the sun pooling on his back like thick rope.

10

I SEE.

Shoeless in the cunning morn, under sky's wet wings, blackness of the huntress-night faded to denim blue, old washed jeans hung out to dry in the rain-scrubbed air, knees torn open to reveal a blaze of dawn. Another day, it goes on and on, ever faster around a dying sun. Things have changed, they never change. Have I never seen another creature, Hare nor Angel nor Man nor Bar in the nevertime of my tenancy here? It is possible, I could not say. Memory is full of back-folds and hidden levers, my origami-crane mind, creased upon itself, blankness crushed into Form. It is equally possible I have seen and spoken and trembled before them a thousandthousandthousand times before. It flows together. I shrug underneath it, the dilated copper of the Road and the Journey re-settles on my muscled shoulders. I accept. If there is a new thing in this place, its newness may be mine. Longago but also tomorrow and Thursdaynext I lost the grasp of solid hand on happenstance.

There is something. It appears suddenly and without golden trumpets. It is not threatening, it does not speak. This is a relief. From the terrible cisterns of memory I excavate a name for this silvershimmer thing I find on the inner curve of a dead-end Wall. Mirror. Copper snakes raven each other around its polished surface, gnashing teeth like guillotines. Asphodel twines through their tangled bodies, pike-branches piercing the thick serpent-flanks. I approach, because it does not move or hiss. Deadwood-drift I on its silvered Sea, azure ether of reflection wreathes my face. And the hieroglyphs of the Angel's hand which seemed so radiant leaping like enthralled fish under her fingers are now surly and vulgar, wide swaths of grease staining, avenues of gaping black wounds, fury of childish lizard-scribblings biting into body, slime-tracks of some unimaginable worm, foul soup of rotten tempura tearing obscenity from unthinking skin. My flesh her possession she scrawled in wordless barnacled umbilici, each downstroke of pen a penetrating blade, spurt of reeking ink over breasts and belly, navel filled up with grotesque swirl of jet, hair streaked with toad-skins, the snowy peaks of curls hidden in sightless amphibian eyes, paints clattering over me like a kettle of festering squid, eating the white and pale with their horn-beaks, destroying, destroying.

I can see reflected her horrid watercolors seeping into me like poisoned semen, defacing the Walls of my womb with angry graffiti, splatter of mucus-paint and ravening teeth tearing bloody chunks away, like a crumbling Wall, vandalizing my uterine Wall with obscenities drawn in fouled india ink and tongue scrapings, the ravening hawk, the gaping earth. Streaking the mouth with the oil of octopus eyes. For only the eyes remain, horror-blank, the erasure of iris, pure white as rice paper and saki-cups. I wept and screeched with that ruined mouth, owl-rage filled up with razored feathers. Betrayed into monstrosity. *Hic monstra delitescunt.* Milky tears seeped from my blasted eyes like sap.

(—Dare frame, dare frame thy, Dare clasp—)

Mirror. Threads of voice and fennel like capillaries, invading my mind, refracted words from a beforetime I know has never been. Curse I all things. Mirror-eyes full of reptilian venom, green scales clinking like armor, full of unanswerable ecclesiasts. Despair rises up in its terrible bubbling laugh again as I fall, head full of hammering, onto the calm silver thing, clawing with ragged hands and spouting all-vowel gurgling rivers, my mouth a goblet of ash.

And the Mirror gave way, into tumbling and pale, into watery possession, sleek of covering mercury, perfect wash of purifying silicate, hydrochloric Sea burning slicing pulling skin from bone, ramora nibbling vermin from a great grey arrow of shark-flesh, warm pain flowing clear, fallingfallingfalling.

(—In what distant deeps or skies—)

The rush and foam of that invisible Sea aural licking at starving earlobe, thunder a ceaseless rhythm of time irredeemable, ecstatic Seaweed strangling gleefully, leaping goldfish sparkling into waiting mouths, open icy aquamarine descent through cobalt and midnight, phosphorescent tumbling girlshape in (at last) the Void of sight-without-seeing, in the oceansmith, in the blue, blue forge

(—On what wings dare he aspire—)

benediction of liquid gliding half-intoxicate eternal coffin-wrappings of cerulean manuscripts, the Water Verses. Ear over heel, *downdowndowndowndown.* Or up. Up or down, I could not say, I could not say. Lime skins cover me like garden snails, suckling gently. Turning and sizzling in the deep, bubbling skin like fiftyfiftythousand cauldrons, jostle of newt-eyes and ox-horns.

(—What dread hand and what dread feet—)

My hand like a white starfish among them, bouncing among the morass, the soupy opiate snowbank enveloping. Something different, not the Road, but the Fall, breathtaking Descent, bauble-perfect and giggling, the Fall surmising the world, surmising the Maze, surmising vandalized I in its blue-black wash. Crushed stuttering onto a silver washboard, strong brown hands pounding into cleanliness, all of us slipping, falling, drowning, throats coated in blue, nothing but blue surrounding in this incubatory downstroke,

(—What the hammer? What the chain—)

filled with turquoise yolk-fluid swimming inside this cyanic egg, swallowing the Sea obediently, fish flopping in the draft of foam. Fast as I can, speeding through indigo waves crested with elephants starry pale, transcendental fedoras filled with meringue

(—when the stars threw down their spears—)

seeing nothing through blank eyes injected with oceanic dye, deepening, deepening. I am still I, arms drawn like a bow towards the sun.

(—Dare frame, dare frame, dare frame thy, dare frame, dare clasp, dare frame—)

Down, down, down.

I fall and fall.

11

GIVE ME THE NUMBERS OF THE MOON, THE ROCK-SALT TRANQUILITY.

I wake with hardness, the bumps and trickles of cobblestone under my ravaged back. It has rained, I can still smell the earthy thickness of rinsed air. Still the Sea lies invisible, but it thumps loudly, much more loudly now in my breaking ears, a piano's lower registers broken and crushed to ivory paste. Still the Walls rise up, these new manifesting in streaked bloodstone, carved skillfully, not a glimpse of decay anywhere, antiseptic and darkly beautiful, springing up from a Road of polished coral like sunburned titans, draped with wilted windflowers climbing into nothingness.

Desolate circle of stone, with the Sea screaming somewhere unseen. There is a click and clatter behind me, behind me where the Mirror should be but is not, unsurprisingly, blank stone. Just a tunnel, after all that ecstatic ideation, just a passage from one sliver of the Labyrinth to another. How many times have I known it and given it voice but must remind my unlearning self: there is nothing but this.

The clicking repeats, a purposeful morse code of tapping the coral Road and I turn to recognize it, now nearly accustomed to Others and their erstwhile Appearances, and so accompanying my turning with a great, burdened sigh.

"Don't you sigh at me, landlubber. I am very fierce," announced an extraordinary Lobster waving a claw at me with imperious airs, a flamboyantly large crustacean snapping at the Sea air. "I sleep the sleep of manic frog-songs, reel in bright rings of my-and-your sulfurous selves, my claws click on lacquered women and sandpaper men, leave puckered scars on their pretty, pretty skins. I am a Meaningful Lobster."

His lithe shell was aquamarine and crowned by such deeply indigo claws rimmed in copper, drumming and clacking those fabulous non-opposables.

"Sigh, ugly human? Divine madnesses stream from my vermillion feelers, but only to be boiled and broiled and served to your slobbering lips with garlic butter and parsnips, followed by the delicate dessert of my soul, caramelized and en flambé, garnished with raspberries. Eh?"

"No—" I wanted to laugh at his indignation, his purpled face. But he blustered on.

"Who are you to sigh? You don't even know your name. You tumbled through a Mirror and blundered into my Courtyard. Very rude. You're getting everything dirty."

CLACK! His claws snapped emphatically.

I bent my head humbly to pacify the storming creature. "I am sorry, I meant no offense. Others are so often strange and terrible . . . "

He stood unmoving for some time, his stubborn brow coloring emerald with injured pride.

"They certainly are," he said pointedly.

But with a courtly gesture of his claw, he acquiesced. "Very well, I shall not Scratch you to-day." He clambered nearer to me, clattering on the slippery Road, little legs splaying out and correcting, until he sat next to me on a chalcedony bench. "I am the Rope-Cutter, the great Key-Maker, the Splitter of Bones and Eater of the Sea. In another life I was a Dragon, and I scorched the face of the world." All this he laid out in a low, confidential music, by way of introduction.

"I am the Walker and the Seeker-After."

"Seeker after what?"

I had no answer, of course. "I am the Woman of the Maze. I am the Compass-Eater." At this last his scaly eyebrows raised in impressed surprise.

"Compasses are difficult to catch," he nodded. "You are strangely colored, for a Seeker. I think you have undergone Assassination. Do you know the Way?"

I looked at my hands, the lined manuscripts of my palms, unable to speak for the frustration of tears. The Lobster shrugged.

"Neither do I," he admitted. "The Labyrinth has a surfeit of Ways, and all the Ways are its own. I cannot choose. I stay close to the sound of the Sea. It is the best I can do. I am very fierce, I do not like Others. They Disturb me." There was a long, pulsing, and pointed silence between us.

"What sort of Keys do you make?" He was such a strange, sad, frenetic little animal, flashing storms on his shell. He brightened immediately.

"I *told* you I am a Meaningful Lobster. All kinds. So few take an interest—it is an ancient and refined art, but makers are few in these degenerate days. Keys of baleen and Keys of dried mud, Keys of Door-meat, Keys of fishing-cages, Keys of rain, Keys of whitethorn bark. Keys of gold and silver and bronze and ivory, sodalite and beryl and amethyst and liquid rubies. Sardonyx and cat's eye and hematite. Keys of wolf-tails and Keys of iron pyrite. Keys of gardenias and camellias and rosewood, of wine bottles and Wallbrick and Roadstone. Horse-hide and sweetgrass and priest's collars, polenta and lizard claws and king's crowns, chess pieces and cheese wheels. Keys to Castles and Treasure Chests and Queen's Chambers and Cellar Doors, to Garden Gates and Serpent Cages, Witch's Huts and Prisons, Stables and Wax Museums, Towers and Armories, Tollbooths and Secret Rooms. Keys to Rivers and Caverns, Keys to Wind and Body."

The Lobster was hopping from one row of chopstick feet to another with excitement. "Do you want a Key? Is that why you came? It has been so long since I have had an order." My vision had filled with dancing Keys, all in a paper-doll chain, all promising Entrance, Passage, Motion.

"Yes, yes, I want a Key! But I have nothing to give you in return."

He considered, cocking his cerulean head to one side. "I will take a lock of your hair. It still has some of the angelblack of your Assassination on it. I could make a good, strong Key." I nodded assent almost at the same moment he reached up an enormous casual claw and clipped off a curl about six inches long. Tucking it away under his shell, in the same movement he produced a small Key made of a deep blue green shell. If it was possible, the Lobster blushed from feelers to tail, his body flushing a deep orange.

"It is my best Key," he whispered, "I made it from my own shell, my own claws. Under the seventh moon I soldered it with my blood." I took it quietly, away into my pack, but as I tucked it out of sight, a great, indignant screech froze my hand.

"Why does *she* get a Key? I ask and ask and get nothing but your

wretched shell turned against me and she barges in and you give *her* one?"
A mammoth Seagull pinwheeled before us, cawing and screaming in a
frenzy. "She's nothing but a *girl*. She doesn't deserve to go forward, or back,
or anywhere! You cannot give her one—give it to *me*, you vile . . . *Crab*!" The
bird spat this last deadly insult like a wad of tobacco, quivering with wrath.
The Lobster leapt up, flushing orange and snapping his claws.

"I can give my Keys to whomever I wish, *Sparrow*! You go away! You are
a rude beast and filthy—you eat rotted fish! I can smell it on you! I would
never make a Key for your kind."

"But why *would* you grant this to me?" I asked, bewildered.

The Lobster shrugged his jeweled shoulders. "I sleep the sleep of manic
frog-songs. I pity you. You of all creatures know there is nothing here, not
even Reasons Why. Yet you keep going. *He* thinks he knows all the Reasons.
Take it before I change my mind."

I nodded and thanked him. He gestured towards the spiral Road. "That
is all there ever was or will be. You have to go now, girlthing. Or the Gull
might try to bite us. *Isoganakereba narimasen*. I have to hurry, so do you.
And keep going. Downdowndown."

"No! It's mine, you can't have it! You'll lose it or drop it down a well or
some other wretched thing!" The Seagull wept and stormed overhead.

I rose with ache in my thighs, amid aviary outrage, ignoring him.

"You don't even know what its for—you'll never find the Lock. Even
at the Uttermost End, you won't know," he warned, gnashing his beak. I
turned my painted back to his protests.

"You are a very odd Beast," I smiled at the smaller and quieter of the two,
who was still blushing furiously.

Again, the jeweled shrug. "I am a Meaningful Lobster."

As I retreated from the bloodstone Courtyard, I caught my image in
the receding Mirror of his shell, framed in the squealing of the frustrated
Seagull.

I had gone entirely blue, from heel to hair.

12

I LOOK OUT OF MY SKULL AT ALL THIS INKY BLUE SKIN.

Lakshmi-flesh blossom, dark-soled deva. All evidence of the Angel's work—my Assassination—vanished into sapphires and crow's feathers. To my waist sea-colored hair rolls and slips, washing foamily up onto the shore of my now azure back, now period shoulders, now violet waist. Legs stalks of skies, cobalt lips, a seabed fulminating, birthing a bewildered undone on the canvas of my skin.

But the eyes, the eyes. Still blank and empty as a well, now blue within blue within blue. Another shake and smash of noses and eyes and hairlines, another stained checkered floor of cleft palate knights and thalidomide bishops. Walls like craven rooks, bursting out of an acetylene Road. Another, and another, and another. Is this set of walking beats different because a little blue-green Key lies nestled like an infant sparrow? I do not know what it Opens, so it is as though it does not exist. It has no Purpose. Yet I know deep as Self can go that Purpose is the worst kind of trick. I am in the fish, Daughter of the Whale. My mouth tastes of old tea water, these old questions recurring, spinning like bicycle wheels over and over, that same Queen of Spades click clacking against the spokes, the same black wheel and silver rim.

I thought I had worked this unto its uttermost end, had demarcated my world, river from stream from ocean from beam. I had encapsulated it, trapped it in my little coffins and lockets, figured it out. I did not exactly come here, and so there was no *beginningtime*, no entrance through some fantastic Gate. But it was a measurable moment ago that I was satisfied with the non-advent of nothing and its persistence, that eluding Doors had become easy enough, that I was metamorphosing into a kind of expert Labyrinth-Woman, I knew its tantrums and its dervishes. And now I tumble like a candle through the night, wax end over end. The Mirror changed me, took me in like a Door, but not a Door, a jeweled tunneling worm. But didn't the Angel change me before that? I have lost the threads. Memory is masked here, and days dissolve into ripples and smears of movement almost as soon as they pass beyond the moonrise, and so I could not say if I have been eaten by a Mirror before, but I think not.

There are advents and newness stalking me. I could be certain before that the Labyrinth shifts, but it does not change. Yet I am within something else now, a sequence of events, beyond sheer movement, pure and dazzling. It boils all around. the tiny pale blue hairs on my arms bristle like a boar. I am waiting for the portents to come. I feel them cackling around me like a copse of witches.

The carried compass sends out trails of sickness like medieval sunbeams, lassoing organs into green grassfires. The slab of north lacerating my throat, spilled mercury and spoiled stew east roiling in my belly, south-arrow crackling in my bones like kindling. It travels through me as I travel through the Labyrinth, navigating the turns and traps, inhabiting slowly, imprinting the landscape. I have eaten Direction, and it has eaten me. Oh, the yin yang cycles of self upon self, oh zazen clay of form upon shape, oh wheels within wheels within scarlet-flaming wheels. Oh, Ezekiel, what do you see in the glabrous sky, bound with glowing spokes? What is it searing and smoking, scalding the hermetic moon in a boil of stone? What do you see dancing in primate patterns over and over? *In this sign thou shalt conquer.*

How all we pretty snakes have a taste for our own tails.

CANTO
THE SECOND

13

IT HAS BEEN DAYS UPON DAYS AND STILL MY EYES ARE SLATES.

Crack the egg for the answer, the gold and the white. It lies within like the ascended scrap folded in a fortune cookie, malignant scrawl of notime.

Oh, Ezekiel, what do you see in the sky?

Answer: the Void. The Void and the Stone.

I have stumbled into another layer of within, the sky and its signs are covered by intricacies of stone. This that surrounds—no circular Wall but a great Temple carved into existence in the center of the Road, luxuriating in columns and steps of striated granite, studded with quartz like roused eyes. Exhales into the viscous air like a sleeping dragon. Circus ropes of thick vine lie net-like over the Walls and crumbling balconies, weeping fat tears of wet crimson fruit, which comprises my breakfast in this abandoned place. Sky like a dove's belly can be seen through vast cracks in the domed ceiling, crusted with flecks of ancient paint like flocks of birds. Copper bells gone to rust litter the floor, fallen in some antediluvian cataclysm. Mosaic with no picture to reveal, (as though any Revelation lies buried and smoking here)the stones of the floor have conquered their polish and lacquer, host to grass and occasional columbine. The wind prophesies in breaths of blades, slicing my inky skin.

In the shadows of the altarstone I chew my fibrous breakfast, savoring the musky juice, beckoning the strange. It is not long in coming. The air is stale, still, except for the Cossack-wind that gallops through on occasional pogroms. Oh, the scrabble and scramble of sequence closing in like hands on a fly. Where am I going, beneath this frenzied sky? Clinging to my knowledge that there is nothing, no Center, am I blind to the wheels of fire? Oh, what do you what do you what do you see in the sky?

I see the corner of the nave move silkily, shadow within shadow, suggestion of gesticulate limbs. I swallow the sliver of fruit on my tongue, peering closer, dreading the next in this idiosyncratic parade, this sequence. This episodic hermitage so full of opiate swans and painted mouths. How will it end, if an end is ever to be contemplated under an infinite train of Bo Trees and crusted snow, skipping projector illuminating this same arboreal testing ground over and over, the ascetic, the pearl, the slanting light? My turquoise fingers are sticky with apple-blood.

It is not long in coming, the breakfast-strangeness. Obligingly a creature darts out of its sanctuary, making for my tiny Bo with determined speed. A handsome golden macaque with a bodhisattva face, clever twisting hands, his gleaming fur bristled with excitement, clapping wildly and slapping his palms on the stone slabs. He stops short an inch from my face and sniffs sharp and greedily at my shimmerings of blue. I have not moved, and how we must seem like Temple statues, the Monkey and the Deva, sea-blue and still as time.

"Who are you?" He inquires on an intake of breath, words riding air like a camel.

"I am the Seek—"

"Ssst!" He interrupts me with a venomous hiss between enormous teeth. "I know all that. Who are you?" Each syllable punctuated by a slap of Monkey-palm against Temple floor. There is a long silence filled by a tabernacle of flapping birds over some distant Maze-territory, the slow, irrefutable crumbling of the Temple into divinatory dust, reading the future (nothing, of course) in its granite entrails.

"No one, I suppose." The answer was meeker than I intended. "I am my Wandering."

"At least you know it. I am myself, nothing more. And often not even that. I know my name, I found it in the belly of a sturgeon with a golden ring and salty Himalayan caviar. But I learned to ascend it in the hysterical ravage of the Turkish Baths at the Center of the Labyrinth." The Compass in my belly lashed out in epileptic grandeur and I choked and sputtered. "There is no Center! There is none, nothing!"

"Silly girl with no tail, did you think there was no Center just because you had not found it? I showed it my teeth, and it was afraid. Hoo!"

The little Monkey danced triumphantly, waving his arms skyward and stamping his long feet. I could hardly speak for the pressure of sequence. How great lay the Lie of the Maze if there was a Center I had never guessed to Seek? How could I guess the shape of un-knowledge from the depths of the Road? I rasped coldly at him, grasping his golden fur.

"Where is it? Tell me, tell me, please. I have to know. Where?"

A grin of jubilant savagery seized his mouth, and he rubbed his iconic belly. "I ate it. It was afraid. Hoo!"

What relief there is in the reassurance that the world is as you suspected. His absurdity revealed his lie. The Compass calmed to its usual pulse and the winds dried blue sweat from my brow. Madness knows madness, delirium draws its own. He was caught in the same narcotic web of enchantment and counter-enchantment, trapped in the same Golgotha of perception. I knew it for a Lie and was comforted.

"All is the act of Devouring here," he lectured, "it is how you conquer, it is how you survive, it is how you ascend. It is why you ate the Compass, and the Wall. This is a Labyrinth. Have you any doubt that its nature is *inside*? There are beyond a thousandthousand Walls. What did you think you had done by Devouring one corner of one? There are beyond a thousandthousand Centers. I ate one. Downdowndown. It tasted like a witch's nipple dipped in morphine. Delicious. I ate my name, which was a Center of a three thousand and forty forever Centers, but mine. And so I become another in a writhing nest of Centers. You do not know your name and cannot achieve that kind of mastery—you do not know the tracks of your prey. I ascended its fish-eggs and padlocks. Now I am myself, whole. I carry the Center with me, and everywhere I go is the achievement of the Quest. With every step I conquer the Labyrinth, the world of my birth-tree and my first-milk."

"But you don't, really. You trick yourself. There is no end to it. You can't leave it. So it makes no difference. You and I are the same. You just have a better Lie to tell yourself."

His eyes glittered shrewdly. "Darlingblue, it is all a Lie. That does not make it lesser. Is it victory to abandon a thing like a wounded wolf? Is the truest expression of mastery is to Abscond? Not the vital thing, no. I choose. We are *not* alike, because I understand these things, and you do not."

"You think you understand. It does not make it so. After all, it is all a Lie. Even you."

"True. Even the purity of crocodiles is a derivation of moon-mother tea ceremony and a falsity. You have your Labyrinth and I mine. And I have had the Temple where you have had the Road. You have been Assassinated—it is something to see. Nevertheless, I have been waiting for you. I see the wheels in the sky and the shape of approaching. Hoo." I shut my eyes, heavy-lead-bodied and grinding closed.

"I am weary of all this. I do not wish to listen patiently to your reed-mat ministrations and nod like an ignorant postulant. I must keep moving."

"Yes, girlbodied thing, and I am going with you. For awhile."

"You are not welcome."

"It hardly matters."

"I will not listen to you."

"I will not speak."

"The Doors will catch us both."

He said nothing. I covered my eyes with my hand. "I don't care. Come if you wish, Beast. Or stay. There is nothing new, even you."

I rose, striding towards the Temple steps like a wave. Lost, lost in *sequence*, in the hagiography of this opaque menagerie, it is, it was, it will be all slipping away. I feel the slide of earth beneath my bare and cyanic feet. The Monkey dove into my Path and planted his limbs like a portcullis. "You must do something before we leave this place."

Exasperated, I spit words like poison darts. "I do not need you."

This was predictably ignored. "You must give me the Stone."

"Why?"

"To demonstrate a Thing. You do not want it anyway, you ran from the Angel like a river from the mountain."

How weary can I become before I vanish? I handed over the Stone, because it is what I am supposed to accomplish, what has been written for me to do, what is required to silence him, to further the Road another inch, another mile, another winter clutch of nights like a basket of hissing eggs. Someone asks me a thing and I do it. I am only the object.

And into his little gold mouth it goes, sparking briefly with light glinting off his unsettling teeth. He smiled at me, a smile of perfect satisfaction.

"See? Nothing changes. I am not consumed with the finding of the Source, the End, the Monster. It was afraid. Now I Have it and it will ferment. It will drive you mad; already you are a little *loooony*. But without the blessings of madness you will not survive. Hoo. Only the mad can find anything under the sun. Now it has all begun properly, and you cannot escape it." He rolled his eyes and stuck out his tongue like a party favor.

"Why would you do this to me? I have never hurt you!" I heard my voice as from a distance, wondering tremulously at his green-flecked eyes.

"Another time, Darlingblue. Explanations are a waste compared with the metamorphoses we will find under a thousand spotted leaves. Come, come, come." His *hoo* was soft and warm while he took my hand blue as a Map in his leathery paw and half-sings:

"Let us go then, you and I, while the evening is laid out against the sky . . ."

14

AND NOW WE ARE TWO.

The Walls wind thickly in long, womanly curves now, covered with a fine thin bead of playing cards and syringes, sweated movement of clubs and hearts, binary black and red, down to the invisible sea. Step for step I am matched by golden feet, slide-swish down the Road at twilight, into the night, into the stars and the black canvases, into the pendulums swinging from a nervous sky, earlobes of clouds belly-heavy with listening. It is not unpleasant, to have company. He does not speak because I have not. Lunacy, if I have opened my veins to its beastlight, surrounds like a nimbus. I can eat the Center, and be whole. It is possible. Temptation has fled in her red shoes and gargoyle petticoats, ravening through a forest primeval, drowned in a sleeping river with the Stone around her neck, to weight her to the sandy bottom. No more the grotesque desire, the terrible Lie of Purpose, the seduction of Meaning. I have wrestled with the Angel and pinned her opaline shoulders to the red, red rock. He took it from me like a tumor and perhaps there is now some hope.

But they are all Lies, even Temptation. They whisper of Reasons, of coming and going, of Time, and of the possibility of a thing that came before. Dread dark bullroaring fear of a *beforethis*, frog-sounds in the marsh of midnight, dreaming of who I might have been before I Walked. It does not exist within me, my interior is the Mazescape of the Labyrinth, vein to vesicle to womb floating like a rough hewn-raft. I cannot locate it among the branching capillaries and smoky pneuma, I do not believe it is there. But I could not say. I cannot say anything anymore. Once there was no new thing in the Labyrinth, and I thought I understood. I survived. I cannot say anything anymore. I am not quite myself, not quite another. I draw the stars down upon my head with a sickle blade. I think he is right, that I am going mad. I do not fear it (*hoo*) but I think it is just behind me, on fox paws, printing patterns of circlescirclescircles on the dust of the Road.

What do you see?

Oh, what do you see but the salamander's back splayed out against the sky, the fire-lizard caught in a frieze of Death, the silhouette of scorpion and desert? I see nothing, it is all black, no turns, no hiding places, no Doors with handles of gold. No cloudwalls drifting across the hooded moon, her mask of wax and spittle of cicadas, her ululations, her hair of whistling bats. Wholeness, unbroken, clay pot filled with jasmine tea, warbling in its earthen goblet, satori-sky of blossom and grass harp. When I was in my darkbody how beautiful I was, how singular, how like this perfect expanse of charcoal smeared across half of all, how hidden and cohesive was I in my sweet-smelling nightskin.

We walk and walk and walk and there is no end. He chatters on, and I cease to hear, the voices within bubbling in my kettle-body. Cycling stains, marks of wood-stamps on my skin forced to open and receive, wedged open with an ash spear, my entire form slashed and drinking. And yet—

What do you see?

Wisps of logic, penetrating like armies with furred hats and shaggy horses when the world had ordered itself without. We build our Walls high as—

    (—*the topless towers of Ilium*)

We push our shield-line against theirs—bronze on bronze,

    (—*And will I combat*)

Gates bruising the clouds—

    (—*come, give me my soul again, here I will dwell*)

Our arrows pierce horse-hide and fire-mail—

    (—*yea, I will wound Achilles in the heel*)

Our horses gnash with teeth like tearing steel—we do not want it here—

    (—*I will be Paris, for love of thee*)

And the fire, how high the fire on the turrets, devouring—

    (—*Brighter art thou than flaming Jupiter*)

The dissonance, the half-knowns, I cannot, I cannot. I hold my head as though a Monster (the minotaur tossing his horns at my skull) were going to burst from my hairline.

Oh, for the blackness, the smooth and cool hand of that dark heaven on my face, I cannot disembodied drift deadwood between knowing and unknowing, I am being torn by hooks—in the gills of my seabody, the salmon silver gills breathing an air-that-is-not, slits in my flesh like gulping vaginas, *vagina dentata* and the masked knife, rifts and breaches, continental drift splitting my tectonic bones, pullingpulling apart, whispering intimations the voice within, hinting and grasping. Intimate, grave, the song, a frazzled beard brushing my cheek, and down I go into this pool of sick, this avenue of buoyant retch, heaving waves of bottlenecks and Chinese dinners, aluminum siding and bile-soured wine, bread crusts and fish tails and fulminating bananas, ox hearts and newspaper hats and diner menus, sheet music, guitar strings strangling plucked chickens, watery blood and pulp of novellas, hat-rims and shattered upholstery, shoe-heels and shoehorns and turkey livers, tomcats with semen-sticky red fur nosing in this vile flood of me through the Center of the Road, column of vomit floe of madness and dis-ease down those smug cobblestones.

The Monkey, oh, he looks at me with pity crinkling those black flickering green eyes.

(—And none but thou shalt be my paramour)

The sounds of that sibilant pentameter, those lisping lips worming over my throat, flickering screams of lizard-fire and the paradisiacal yammering of *truetruetrue!* His pity is a hammer splitting my skull, silver knob bursting through a firework display of blood and bone, spurting upwards, cerebral ejaculate, bang crash of fontanel puckering and blowing high as a whale's spume. The brain exposed, that Labyrinth of twisting pink flesh, wrinkled as an old man's belly, and it is really all belly, all gut, the depth from which it rises, madness and sublimity, from the Center, from the Devouring-Place, from the primordial swimming cauldron of murky stew-self.

I claw at the Road, ripping my fingernails and chipping teeth. I have fallen, *downdowndowndowndown.* The Monkey moves his long brown fingers over my forehead in a tender circling motion, calming, consoling, cooling the fever blistering the peaceful azure sky of skin. His voice is soft as rain:

"*Within the bowels of these elements,*
where we are tortured and remain for ever,
The Labyrinth hath no limits,
nor is circumscribed in one self place;
for where we are is the Labyrinth,
and where the Labyrinth is, there must we ever be.
Hoo."

I slept.

15

THE PANCREATIC MORNING BREAKS SICKLY AND YELLOW.

Again, the thumping body, the hang-over from delirium. This, at least, holds to pattern, grinding millstones in my grisly head, scarlet shame frothing and gurgling like spoiled port, grapes trampled underfoot, stains of burst fruit spreading like sin. As I wake the Monkey is perched bird-like on my chest, picking expertly at my aquamarine hair, grooming me as he would a member of his troop.

"It is poisoning you, the Stone, cyanide in your pretty blue cells," he informed me with some cheer as he mussed with my curls. I answered sleepily. "It was just a rock. I escaped the Angel. How can it hurt me?"

"Hoo, hoo, Darlingblue! *I* escaped the Angel when I took it from you. You are still within Her. She wanted you mad and gibbering, and you are obliging. It is all going so well. You did not swallow it, so you could not master it. It licked at you like a grassfire. I took it so that you could not conquer it, so that you would follow the path that lunacy has laid out in such profound bricks. If you were your singular body, you could not follow me, tread so heavily this Road. Only the mad are Seekers-After. You are burning, girlchild. It is beautiful to see. The Stone is Doubt. It is Pernicious. You ought to pay more attention, you know. You have lost your eyes and are changing bodies like ball gowns. Were you so malleable and myriad before She came with Her swathes of ice?"

"*Hic monstra delitescunt.* But she cannot be the Villain. There is no Monster at the Center of the Labyrinth, no Minotaur, no Beast. I know it. That is not the meaning of this place. And why would she harm me? Why would you keep me from deliverance?" He nodded sagely. "This is Assassination. You have no choice. It is a game that has been played and played before. This is the Way. There is no Monster. But there are many monsters hereabout, as there are many Centers. You are a monster, I am a monster. She was, and a Center, too. You should have showed her your teeth. Instead she is poisoning you like mistletoe on an oak, because you thought she was beautiful and you let her. Hoo. Now you are very sick, and you will continue to spend your nights speaking in the breakwater tongues of the Labyrinth and clawing at the earth until your bones weather to white on the wide lanes of the Road. Or possibly light blue. As for howandwhy," he shrugged wheat-shaded shoulders. "She Devours. It is the Way. Can't you trust that the tale unfolds as it should?" He was contorting his graceful fingers rhythmically, tapping my body like a piano.

"No, I can't. And how is it you know so much, Beast? Who are you?"

A long, slow smile spread across his features, widening the wrinkled face to a glowing jack o' lantern. "I am myself and no other. But nothing here is precisely what it is."

"Ssst!" I snorted, grinning. "I know all that. *Who are you*?" He laid one finger alongside that squat little nose and uttered his syllable.

"Hoo." The air was suddenly filled with his wild laughter, leaping across the Road and careening off Walls, cavorting and thoroughly enjoying his joke. Catching his breath, he giggled, "Oh, Darlingblue, that was lovely. If you are very, very good and promise not to strangle me during your funny little fits, sometime soon I shall show you my name, then will you know. Until then, mum's the word."

The Monkey was off on another fit of hooting acrobatics. "But you," his voice calmed, became grave, "are in trouble. I would like to help you, very much, very much. But I can't. My Medicine is not for you."

And so I was falling again, lost in the newness-which-was-not, lost in waves of golden fur and shining eyes, winks of I-know-what-you-don't and shrugs of self-satisfaction. Lost, not just strange and Wandering, but diseased and poisoned, asps worming towards my great indigo heart that very, very moment. My voice cracked like a clay pitcher: "Is there nothing to be done?"

The Monkey flicked at a gnat on his saffron pelt. "Oh, please, woman. Of course there is or I would have stayed in my cozy little Temple and let you blather on your way. I merely said *I* cannot help you. Hoo! I can't do everything, you know. We must find Her again, the Angel. And you must be entirely mad before we do, wholly Devoured, or there will be nothing to give her."

"It is a Quest," I said doubtfully.

"No, it is a sequence of events. You will not defeat Her with some Vorpal Blade, or win anything at all from Her. It is not the End, nor can we truly Seek her, as the Labyrinth carries us where it wishes, if it can wish. Will has no meaning here, like everything else. There is no meaning. There is no pagination. There is no index, no glossary. There is no first edition, no reprinting, there is only this battered, dog-eared *now*. There is no gallery, there is no photographic record, there is no grand entrance or dramatic exit. There is only the great nowbody roasted in its sapphire hide, and your great seaside eyes, widening in ineffably slow understanding, rolling weakly into darkness as you are eaten, piece by piece.

It is not a Quest merely because it has a beginning with me and an ending with Her. You are not going to fight, or act, or plead. You can get nothing from Her. She may not heal you, and you cannot force Her. But you must make a circle. You may never find Her. A Quest is Heroic, you are not. You are selfish: you wish only to Survive and Devour. It will not change the Labyrinth, or the fate of a fair-armed damosel. You are the damsel and the dragon, you are the prince and the witch, you are the captain and the whale. 'Quest' has no meaning for you, who Seek only the delectable end of your own rattling tail. You are the Seeker-After, so get on with it and Seek." He folded his arms across his chest.

"It is, really. You are tricking me into it, but it is a Quest, a Journey. I do not want it."

"Nothing here is precisely what it is."

"And I shall die otherwise?"

"Yes. You may die, anyway."

"And it will be quite awful?"

"Yes."

"And there is no other Road but this?"

"Has there ever been another Road for you?"

I paused. "But we cannot Strike Out and hunt her."

"No."

"Then how do the Doors hunt me?"

Again the slow butter-spread of a smile. "So clever, Darlingblue, so precise. How indeed? They are not like us, not our kind."

"They Devour," I remarked.

"How would you know? Hoo! You, the great Labyrinth-Navigator, the great Walker, escaping every Door like bread from the oven! Yes, they do, but not like us. The Doors are part of the Maze, not within. They can hunt you, and me for that matter, because they are conscious of you as the Road is; you are within them/it/all. It is all one. Such the terrible instinct to run, suspecting darkness and dread on the other side. But if you will not believe in a Monster or a Castle, why do you cling to your faith in that terrifically humanological fear of fire and black on the windward side of the Door? You do not really engage the Maze at all."

"You do not go diving into Doors, you flee, too!" I protested.

"Yes, because I do not wish to be Devoured in any fashion, and I prefer a Singularity of Possibles. I run because I know their danger. You run because you do not, because you are good at being hunted. Perhaps the best. So good you have never been caught."

"You're being very serious."

"You're being very stupid. Afraid to save yourself." I bristled in indignation and frustration. He watched, bemused.

"I do not wish to die on her command. So I am forced. Will has no meaning," I sighed. "But how will we do this thing?"

The Monkey curled up next to me, long tail waving lazily, curving like a question mark. "We will be as clear as the rivers of Babylon, and the sun will shine through us as through a clear glass. We will plant our feet on this long highway and the Labyrinth's currents will take us where they must. Or they will not. You never know. But we are caught up in a sequence, and these things usually find their way. Make no mistake, Darlingblue, we are Highwaymen, in our blue velvet cloaks, we are Dashing and Brave. And we go out onto the Road to steal and Devour. Numinous, rapacious creatures are we, and when we stamp the moon quakes."

His tail wafted like a kite on the breeze, weaving into a figure-eight. "But now, by the sun and the fabled shores of the Gitche Gumee, it is time for tea. Boil the water, dear, whilst I go and hunt for the well-known and elusive beast, the ferocious butter-backed cucumber sandwich. Hoo!"

He scampered off, disappearing behind a low gorse bush, yellow on yellow, smooth butter of fur and flower. It is all falling apart, leaving me to strike the fire in the shelter of an overhanging Wall, crushing nettles and dried roses from the Hare's Garden into a mild tea, pouring like a wife into my little clay pot, waiting for the returning pads of little golden feet.

I was saddled suddenly with a Companion and a Quest, and the witch's brew bubble of pale green in my hands. I knew now how far I had slipped since I lay helpless beneath the Angel's potent form, how close her white fingers lay to my heart, how much more quickly it beat now, now that the hooded beauty of nihilist ideation, the certainty of emptiness, the comfort of a Search without End was slowly being stretched by red-faced inquisitors, limbs pulled like taffy, plucked like harp strings. My head fills with the whipping birch-switches of that music, my arms and legs strummed roughly, that old E minor chord over and over. I can smell the simmer of the oil, molten bronze waiting for them to dip my body like an altar candle, to raise up boils and blisters like love-bites, fill my mouth with a liquid scream, gurgle of churning gold coating tooth and tongue. I will not confess, recalcitrant I, that all I have known is false, and that this Monkey is the master of all. I will not confess that I am a child and must be taught as though I sat at a little desk with a ruler and fat pink eraser, the smell of chalk in my nose (and yet where does this image come from, the twin-braided child with a heart-shaped face, staring into the wild nirvana of a blank green board?)

I will not confess, and whatever this is that grows inside me like a tumor shows me with boyish pride the rack and the thumbscrews, the eruption of nacreous fingernail and warm spurt of blood over knuckle, the melodious popping of joints on the merry wheel, crackling of bones like a winter fire. It is so beautiful to give in, it whispers, the voice of the Stone in my mind like a gilded priest, so simple and right, to let the welcoming arms of that promised madness enfold you, comfort you, nurse you like your own mother. Bend under the leather-handled whips, back like an ash bow, yield under the hooks and blades, allow us to come inside you and purify your soul.

It is pressing me, the Stone on my chest, the great slab crushing the ribcage of a relapsed witch, splinter of bone like rotted wood. I am losing, slowly, so that I do not even have the strength to resist this temptation, the temptation of Purpose again, floating like a blood blister before me, to resist the lead of the Monkey, the Trickster, drawing me into pursuing myself over a shapeless land. Too weak to stay my own course and continue in the velvet pleasures of Wandering alone and unfettered. I am losing myself, the self that is no other. If I knew my name, I could grip it like the edge of a cliff, drive my teeth into it and never let go. I could keep hold, and not slip. But it is hidden in the Book of the Hammer, and the inquisitors will not let me see. They are preparing a vat of acid, red as withered roses boiled for tea, sour as lime leaves. I can smell it, the mescaline-arsenic, the stabbing scent of metallic greasepaint and twelve-year scotch, and the pitch they will spread over my irisless eyes so that I will not see how they mutilate my breasts with mewling hands. It will have me, in the end, the Stone wide and bright in my mind's eye like a rotting moon, I will burn in the tincture that even now simmers in whale-skull vats.

Into my reverie bursts the Monkey, turning temple-creature with geometric arms full of sandwiches. Dainty white squares from what ingenious tree. But he grinds to a halt and widens his almond eyes to perfect zeros of surprise.

From scalp to sole my body had flushed to deep red; red palms, red ankles, red nipples, red hair to my waist.

And eyes, smooth and featureless, pools of blood-shade, red as roses.

16

"Hoo! Aren't you a pretty little rose, now! Can't leave you alone for a minute!" He bustled about, preparing a ridiculously proper tea service on the mottled quartz Road, now reflecting in infinite dusky facets my crimson flesh, torso like a ruby breastplate, carnelian legs crossed gingerly, fire-toned, as though one knee might inflame the other. Fire-goddess, Kali-boned, body of Martian silicate crushed to liquid glass. I touched my face, warmed under the new skin, scald of red, the still-blank eyes wide, wild and creased with fear. The Path seems to blush as it holds my image to its chest.

"It is getting worse, isn't it?" Tears like blood welled up.

"Come now, Darlingred, it's very striking. Drink your tea. You must not succumb yet, there will be more of this before there is less. I have brought you cucumber sandwiches out of the Wild, why do you not smile?" His own brown face was covered in crumbs. I drank with sullen lips, the bloodstone color of the Sea-Walls.

With a sandwich in one hand, held up like a pale green mudra, full of salt and taste of a watery delta, I turned my face towards the sliding honey of a late afternoon sky, light illuminating the scarlet contours of my firebody, woman-shaped flame sitting zazen on the tatami of the wide Road, knee deep in the latticework of tea ceremony, a primal streak of red against the sky gold as a temple-creature's hide. I am the Monster and the Prey.

"I am dying, dying in a clutch of painted swords."

The Monkey shook his head at the earth. A flash of color caught my eye; in the warm black soil a little Grasshopper twitched her pale green legs.

"She talks too much, friend Monkey," the pretty insect whistled, her voice fiddle-high. The Monkey laughed and let the little creature crawl up onto the shelf of his tail. "Yes, but we must forgive her. She is only a small Beast."

"How long will you walk the Road with her? How long will you let her think that fur is yours? I have come far, on smaller feet, and I am not so worn as she. Who has been dancing in her, that the slippers of she are so tattered? She is not very pretty, even with all her paint." The Monkey did not answer, but stroked the top of my ruddy thigh with something like fondness.

"It's none of my nevermind, of course," the Grasshopper chirped, "have to take company as you can get it around here. Two's better than one with Doors about, eh? But she isn't well, not at all well. You don't want to catch it."

She waved her antennae at me thoughtfully.

"I won't, little one, I won't. There is some sandwich left, if you would like it."

"Oh, thank you, I haven't had the strength to climb the sandwich-trees lately. Getting on in years and all." The Grasshopper marched over to the crust I held in my hand and perched on the pad of muscle under my thumb, chewing daintily. After a time, she spoke again in her piping voice, this time to the monkey. "Poor little thing. Listen, and I will tell you something. We insects understand more than you, so big you miss nearly everything important. The Road does not end, everever. Count your steps and the sum will number redemption. Like me, walking on thread, you will learn; traversing a thing you Devour it, watching a thing you move it, conquering a thing you are eaten by it. Drink from a puddle, you are rain, grip a vine too tightly, you are a Monkey, crease the night with song, you are a cricket come morn. In another life I was a Wall, in another a Rabbit with organdy ears. It is all the same. I think I can recall that I liked having bricks for bellies." The Grasshopper stopped, her tone thickening.

"And you are being tracked by a very big Door. The leaves are shaking with his progress. This is the help I can offer you, from my warm soil-bed."

The Monkey frowned and gently lifted her from my hand. "I had heard his prowl, but I did not want to frighten her. Walk carefully, little sister, I have seen birds about," he warned. The Grasshopper flushed pale.

"Well enough, then. Goodbye, redwoman. Look down as you go, you will see more that way. Downdowndown."

She scurried away in a jitter of opalescence.

17

Oh, golden Monkey, *darlinggold*, Companion though I would have none, can you see it? Walk beside me and guard me against the marauding Doors, (and say what you will, I shall not be caught) but can you *see*? The gold-skinned camels sluicing through the snow-crusted Road, their breath like pale puffing mushrooms in the grey air? Utterly confounded by the cold softness of this not-quite-sand, stamping in bewilderment and fear. Mercurial rivulets trickle from their wide footprints, and their muzzles crust over with a multitude of icicles. I can see, I can see them marching upwards, over the pass, packed with Bedouin blankets and tassels, humps swollen as for the first time they know water-plenty. Their trembling cries like blown glass, trying to be brave in the midst of all this terrifying whiteness. Poor animal, nothing is clear any longer, nowhere is home with beautiful gleaming dunes and a sky like liquefied diamonds. The heat that was your mother has fled and the idea of winter is slowly birthing Revelations of Ice in your chambered heart. The mirrored glacier is playing midwife to a shivering Apocrypha of Snow, written on your long scroll-tongue.

Is it a (vision), is it *hereandnow*? I could not say, I could not say. The men trudging beside their great woolly beasts, carrying woven leather leads covered in an elaborate wind chime of icicles. But in their left hands they hold a strange burden. Blue fingers drag in the snow, bruise the Road, covered in agate rings and hieroglyphics. Eyes show all whites, shimmering in perfection and exaltation, insensate and exalted, hecatombs rising in their lashes. They are carried by the rag-wrapped men, whose hands wrap tightly around the handles that protrude from bowed backs, black handles of painted glass, fused with flesh. Sublimity crackles in the places where slickness joins skin, that precious desert-mothered silicate sand scalded into clarity of form. Oh, where, where are they going?

They are women, women converted into carryon luggage, their curved handles as lovely as their curved hips, such symmetry and style, these ascended seraphs scrawled all from brow to womb with the Scripture of Hoar Frost, lifted to the frozen peaks to deliver their in-spired, in-breathed, in-gested prose, each in a separate language. The First in Romanian, the Second in Portuguese, the Third in Breton, the Fourth in Phoenician, the Fifth in Zulu, the Sixth in Maori, and the Seventh in English, the savage English of fire-tipped arrows and impenetrable forests. Will I find that I can speak that fire-English, that I can bear to hold it in my mouth?

The women are still bent, their noses brushing soft snow, voices swallowed by the mountain and the earth, words diving and arcing in the ground, wrapping the root of every tree in their rhythm? The camels leaping from the sharp heights into searing wind to carry the verses into the dark earth, loyal beasts carrying their burden to journey's end? Every glade and meadow that ever grows will speak with azure tongues in seven languages. Will I hear it? Will we be fortunate enough to come across the fields of violets and lingonberries that whisper of the Seventh Verse? Or will it be the yucca and agave of the Fifth, and lost to the shell of our ears that was formed only for the last and most subtle lines? Is this my Gospel, my false prophecy, the Myth of the Carried Women?

I must Walk By. Believe if I can that it was only the wind in your fur. Believe that it is only the madness coming on, a smattering of random and meaningless images firing in my brain, fading into un-reality and darkness. But how can I when I feel the oily leather of a handle breaking the skin rising from my back like the curve of a whale in the sea?

Can you see? Can you hear?

The Monkey's fletched eyes wrinkled nervously, flicking back and forth from my blood-skin to the empty Road. They, of course, are gone, and my flesh is whole. I cannot see where I am going, night waves like a rice field, the Road is a pavilion of ash. I am grateful for his dry, leathery palm in mine, after all. My humanity is difficult to coalesce among all these writhing phantasms, I am voiceless and paralyzed, visions of frostbitten camels trampling through my paved-over eyes, my breastplate of arctic hare, face of a spread-winged roc, laminate fire

(—*which here, in this most desolate isle,*
else falls upon your heads)

Oh, but they were there, and I heard the voices like feet crushing clouds into blue wine, I saw their hair brush the snow and their mouths hanging open, vomiting light into the earth

(—*I have made you mad;*
And even with such-like valour)

No, I will not believe it, I am still whole, I am still myself. They came to the mountain, the mountain accepted, I accept. The Verses came—staccato notes, and they spilled over the peaks like the ecstasy of caribou, they sand and spoke and it is only that you cannot hear

(—*Sometimes a thousand twangling instruments*
Will hum about mine ears, and sometime voices)

But where do I achieve these slashing words, slantwise through my mind like a magician's swords into the magic box, terrible and alien—from what black place could they issue if there is no *beforethis* to remember and reanimate? I could not say, oh me, but I must be I the central I, the lodestone, the trinity, the tripartite division! I carry the Compass, I know north from northwest (north lies the head, the kingspiece, the red screech of brain; northwest lies the right hand which writes the left hand knows not, amphibious inscription on the bones of a *homo erectus* with arms full of flint, still etching the cave Wall overandoverandover—

(—*Be not afeard; the isle is full of noises,*
Sounds and sweet airs, that give delight and hurt not.)

with a fatal buffalo, dressed in his finest brown and white)

I know this, I see it, the body becomes the lodestone and I, oh, I, have become the Stone itself, turning in a grinding orbit around a flaming sun which is also myself, dying my skin with the blood of that beforetime hunting party, glutted out onto the slick glacier, around and around, faster and faster and something is breaking in me faster than it is being built, something is splintering, offbreaking, the vivisection of confession before their ravening altars, evisceration in the rays of that whistling sun, and, oh, the sky is opening and I am dying because it is growing so within, roots

bursting out of my mouth, the thick rootandbranch of the Stone roars out
in a beam of white, and I am breaking, breaking, breaking

(—*The clouds methought would open and show riches*)

Oh, what do you see in the sky, high up high where I cannot go, trapped
am I here among the turn styles and empty way stations? Rice-fields planted
by centaurs speaking all those scriptures I have heard as the caravan
embraced the mountain? Are they there where you can touch their watery
crop? The jasmine-blossom of the moon, fat and morose above me, eating
the stars like escargot, popping each spinning pearl-shell into her milky
mouth? What do you see that I cannot, I Possessed and ground under by
those old smoking wheels within wheels bearing in their spear-spokes

(—*which Lie tumbling in my barefoot way and mount*
Their pricks at my footfall; sometime am I,
all wound with adders who with cloven tongues do hiss me
into)

madness.

Oh, I and all under the gallery of twisting night, what is becoming me? I
see your outline, the macaque-shape sliver of gold against the grey-lit Road,
and you cannot help me, cannot give me the redemption of nothingness, the
benediction of emptiness. You suffer near me, I suffer inside this woman-
skin, the shade of fire-salamanders, and both of us dread the night when
I am not precisely what I am. But here in the dark that brings delirium,
I am open and beating, my whole body become seven-chambered heart,
aorta like a rope of rubies, like a red, red Road. I can feel him coming, the
Monstrum, hinge by jamb. And in terror I approach the Beauty that dances
the steps of annihilation, the Maenad-self with the blood of cats dripping
off her Rosicrucian lips so that—

(—*when I waked,*
I cried to dream again.)

18

"OH, DARLINGRED, WHAT DO YOU SEE WHEN YOU ARE LOST?"

Out of my skull I blearily watch the world detached and departed. I drink from a fountain with a Minotaur pouring water from a maiden's beheaded corpse, as though the Labyrinth were creating itself to taunt me. No comet-track of the frog-kicks of voices whispering from before, no sprinting ideation, no speck of camel-hair remains. We are moving, expecting to make time against the morphing Path, expecting impossible things and racing against the night which will bring only progress towards mania and fire-vertigo. I brush a long sheaf of burgundy hair from my face, and stare at the Road, in this region fashioned of polished cedar.

"I see wheels in the sky and my own body cracking like a tree's trunk. And strange whisperings tunnel through me like earthworms."

The Monkey scrambled up onto my shoulder and stroked my cheek with great concern.

"I am so sorry, beautiful, pitiful girlcreature," his voice was warm and kind. "It is so hard for you." Garnet tears sprung to my Grecian eyes, spilling like paint.

"I am afraid that I am not myself any longer. Even in the day I stare out of my body, I do not inhabit it. And I can hear the Door following us, shuffling and sliding."

"Yes," the Monkey sighed, "I was hoping you had not noticed. She told the truth: there is a Door, perhaps a few hours behind us. It is very stealthy and patient. But I am more clever. I snuck up on it, to see what sort it was." I waited, while he hopped from one foot to the other in agitation. "Oh, my dear, it is a great, black Door, oval and light-eating, with a bull's head

knocker. It will not come before your next heartblink, but it will come." He
patted my hair and fussed with his tail, softly murmuring, "We have time,
little one, we have time. Hoo."

"I cannot think, Monkey. Tell me a story, or a riddle, or lecture me. But
fill up my head, I am weary, I am growing old." He paused, seeming to
ponder some great puzzle.

"I will tell you the storyriddle I think you need. I will tell you how I
Devoured my name. Long was the time I lived young within the pretty
stone arms of my Temple, and I was alone. I enjoyed alone, it enjoyed me.
I swung from the thick red-berry vines, and felt their length firm and sure
in my golden hands. I danced the altar, I sang the songs of my birth-tree
and my mother's strong fur in the choir, echoing all through the dome as
though my brothers and sisters were all around me in the forest. Hoo! I was
content. I did not think about the Center, I did not care."

"Once I was like that, too," I whispered sadly.

"We all are. And then there is a day when we are broken into, like a
rich house, and rifled through. Everafter we look sidelong over alabaster
shoulders and know that we will never be so pure again. Mine was a
pleasant spring morning, the rain fell like a grey sweater unraveling, and
I played in the yarn-drops as I was used. I was not myself then, just as you
are not yourself, but empty and happy. But that day, and not another though
it matters not which, a Snail crawled into my Temple to escape the wet.
He was very beautiful, with a great, grey double-spiraled shell like mother-
of-pearl, sparkling even in the dim stormlight. His body was like living
oil, goldensilver, rustling and slippery, large eye-stalks waving gracefully,
visiondancing.

I hooed in a more or less friendly manner, but he ignored me, moving
within his ponderous shell towards the thickest and most delicious of my
vines, slowly breakfasting on a fat leaf. I marched up to him and rapped
imperiously on that iridescent shell, whereupon his oilskin rippled slightly
and eye-stalks swiveled vaguely in my direction.

"Leathe me alone, thwiftfurry thing," the Snail yawned. "Of course, my
Darlingred, I was indignant, began to hop mightily and grow purple-faced
in a most unbecoming fashion. I insisted variously that he ought to be more
respectful than to gobble up my vines without a word, that he ought to
vacate the premises immediately, that he ought to know he was eating in

my Temple. Again, my only answer was the bored motion of glistening eye-stalks."

"Lithen, mate. I needn't take orders from thome thilly primate who hathn't got a name."

"I don't need one, you lisping mollusk. My mother knows my smell well enough, and the Labyrinth has no use for names. Hoo! Now run along."

He munched thoughtfully on one of my red fruits. "Doethn't it though? If you hathn't got a name, you aren't much of anything. Thith Temple can't be yourth, you hathn't got thome thort of *deed*, and even if you have got a document of thome fathion, to whom would it be made out? Tho the vineth are ath much mine ath yourth. Leathe me alone."

I was at a loss, and covered in snail-spit. He seemed logical enough, if one forgot where one was. My pride, which in those days was great as the vaulting Road, was wounded. I growled at him and bared my yellow teeth, but the Snail snuffled further onto the emerald vine. "And I suppose you have a name, wretched slug?"

The great Snail drew himself up to what I assumed to be his full height, his damascene flesh rippling in opaline waves. Across his broad chest a word floated uncertainly, but clear as your red limbs. It was quite sloppy, for a Snail cannot be very good at letters, but in its oozing alphabet I read distinctly: CALIBAN. He rustled and reduced slimily, with a triumphant little smirk. I stamped and hooted.

"Where did you find that?"

"Not that it'th any of your bithness, but I went though a green-and-clam-thell Door, downdowndown, and I found it, playing with thome ugly trout. It wanted to come to me. It'th mine. You can't have it. Go Away."

(Now, Darlingred, you must understand that Snails know very little about anything, and are quite slow and rather silly. I think now that he must have stolen it. He was too fat and lazy to Wrestle such a fine name. They are officious and greedy, and they walk the Labyrinth believing themselves its masters. Snails are tiresome creatures.)

"But why do you *need* a name, Snail?"

"It maketh one Important, it makes one a Creature of Influenth. It denoteth Worth and Thubthtanth, pinpointeth one's Plathe in the World. The value of name cannot be overethimated. It is one'th invitation to the banquet. My banquet today ith your vineth, becauthe I have a name and you do not." He crawled even further onto the vine, which of course caused him to lose balance and tumble to the stone floor. He was not harmed, really, but scolded me anyhow. "Hateful little monkey! Your wretched vine tripped me! No wonder you are thuch a no-account, foul-thmelling thcoundrel! I thall never come back, never! Beast! Ruffian! Rathcal!" This train of Snail-speech followed the opalescent moon of his shell past the threshold and onto the Road.

It mattered little, for by then I was not listening. I was fired like a field of dry wheat with the idea of a name, the desire for it. I cared nothing for being Important in the wobbling eye of a Snail, or my Place in the World, nevertheless, the need filled me like rising bread, a growing hole in my chest.

But I could not leave my Temple, the Labyrinth would swallow it whole behind me and I would never see its warm Walls and cozy altar stone. Already I had left my birth-tree and lost it, along with the bristled, hot smell of my mother's russet fur. So I laid a trap. Each day I left the Temple, just a bit, trailing a length of spider's thread, sparkling like a strand of a star's mane in the mild sunlight, to find my way home. I let the Doors catch my scent, let them pick up my trail in the blackberry brambles, leaving a bit of fur in the thorns. They would sniff around the Temple at night, creeping like mangy coyotes up to the vaulted entrance. But they are creatures of *outwith*, of the dark wild air and the external void, they would not come in, for the nature of a Door is a conduit, and they were lost like a wolf in a snare in the paradox of a Door entering through a Door, DoorswithinDoorswithinDoors. And I waited, watching them like a besieging army, fanned out like playing cards. I waited for the Door which would lead to my name. I was certain I would know it.

And I did. A very fine old wrought-iron gate, designs of baobab trees, banana leaves, and lush hibiscus, a heavy steel knob in the shape of a panther's head, complete with real fangs, stolen away, the milk teeth of some savage kitten. With a joyful snarl I leapt at it, trailing a length of strong vine behind me. Did the Door but no swifter than I, I looped the end of my emerald lasso around the massive knob, swinging wildly wide, entering the snapping Door. I shrieked and groped blindly, reaching out for the name, calling it, beckoning with my paws. I snagged something on my fingers on the backswing, slipping out of the Door's grasp, nearly losing my tail as it clanged angrily shut. I fled back into the Temple, clutching my prize, accosted by the cacophony of thousands of Doors slamming in fury and gnashing their hinges. Hoo!

What I held against my heaving chest was a gigantic sturgeon, swollen with silver scales and squirming in my grip. Her mouth gaped helplessly and its pupilless (so like yours, my own!) eyes blinked their transparent lids in fear. I did not lose a moment, but slit her Gautama-belly with my teeth and plunged my paws into the writhing black mass of salted caviar, searching, searching, searching.

With the last gulping heave of the great Fish's gills, I seized and pulled from her corpse the body of my name, all entangled with translucent entrails and strips of silver skin, scarlet and flowing moonstone, clinging to the shredded womb of dark eggs and golden flesh. It was furious, and began to bite at me with the sharp branches of letters. I knew I had little time and gripped the vicious thing in both paws, shoving it down my triumphant throat, the sweet tang of starfruit and water-moccasins. Hoo! It was mine, I held it within me.

After this, I began to understand things, as the Snail could not, since I alone ate with intent. I was wholly Other. I had Devoured a Center and it arranged my organs into ascension, made clear the Paths of the Labyrinth, and I ceased to fear it. I ceased to be myself, and yet I was myself, whole, and no other.

At this the Monkey began a slow grin that split his face, terrible and feline, punctuated by his long yellow teeth. He reached into his belly, pulling aside the golden fur like theater curtains, the skin and muscle Wall parting like an ocean, and behind it the dark and secret moon-shape of the Stone. He held open his body so that I could see, pushing against the oily flesh of his stomach like some misshapen fetus, the outline of his name in a savage jungle-calligraphy, still trying to escape the calm pool of his gastric perambulation.

EZEKIEL.

19

"I COULD NEVER DO THAT, EZEKIEL," I MURMURED AS HE CLOSED THE SHEATH OF HIS SKIN.

"I know," he said, closing himself as though buttoning a suit. "You are not strong enough. There are ways within ways. You follow the way of the mad. It is different." He shook his head at me. "But I am here, *hereandnow*, I will not leave you." The Road had slushed almost entirely to deep, rich black mud, and we were slogging through it one sucking footprint at a time. The Monkey's fur was streaked in dirt like war paint, my arms like ruby stalactites circled in bracelets of earth.

"Why are we walking? The Labyrinth will change around us, the Door will swallow us. Why do we not trust in it? I want to lay down, I want to Stop. It will carry us to her, or it will not. I don't care."

"We must keep up appearances, Darlingred. We cannot stop. Forward motion, endless if, but still we must."

"I don't care." I stared ahead, unblinking, scarlet eyes drinking in the wide marshes and waving reeds. "Once I was the Marsh King's daughter, and my wings were brown. I sipped at tadpoles with a delicate beak, scimitar-curved, and when I took tea with my father, I crooked my little finger like a scythe. I was a blade of flesh and nail, I was murky and obscene as the delta water." Dew formed in blood-droplets on my eyelashes.

"You are slipping away from me," he warned in a whisper. "No, I know it did not happen that way. But was there a *timebefore*, Ezekiel? Was there? Was I a child once, did I make mud-pies and leap two-footed into inkwells? Was there a yellow-clouded summer once when I skinned my knee, and felt the prickle of a father's beard on my cheek as he dried my tears? Did I love a boy once, with hazel eyes and hair like wheat in the sun? Was I a woman once and not this? Did these breasts like swollen apples ever feed a daughter or a son? I could not say, I could not say, there has never been anything but this, but oh, Ezekiel, what if it has not been *foralways*?"

I was crying, long, stringy hot wax-tears, coloring my face like a Christmas candle. Through the red blur, I could see the landscape changing, the mud drying into desert-cracks, gold streaked with spider-legs, expanding into the horizon, sparse Walls become cacti—filled up with their thick tequila-water, oozing from green shell like mucus. The Road nearly disappeared into the thirsty land, its track crossing back over itself over and over, fashioning from dust and sand a checkered pattern we strode, a weeping candle and a gilded djinn.

A terrible thumping sound came ripping across the land, searing and boiling the air, the sound of a Door opening and slamming shut hungrily.

Thumpthumpthumpthump.

It was the whole sky, eating all other sound. I clasped my hands over my ears, screaming to drown it out.

"We must move quickly, Darling. This place smells of tar and spoiled vines. He is coming! Hoo!"

"I am Sister to Rigor Mortis," I shrieked as though it were a mantra, a spell to ward off the Door. "I am the Wife of the Crucible. I am still, the desert moves." I felt a calm pool of darkwater within me, growing, a lake which had never known the rumor of waves. My fear was stopped up like a bottle of wine and speed flowed into my limbs.

"Quickly, Darlingred, quickly!"

We began to run over the flat land, the binary earth, feet trailing bronze clouds like wings. It truly felt as though I stood motionless, and the Labyrinth swing wide and long around me, a farmer's scythe whipping through grain. Blue and gold, sky and sand. And then nothing.

We halted like a sentence fragment, cut off mid-syllable. Silence reigned and the horrible clamor was gone.

The Road was garrisoned, bordered on all sides, attended like a bride. All around us stood limbs of glass, dismembered legs, arms, heads, blown glass like crystal, like sculpted water. They stood in formation, that old familiar (though how familiar to me who has known no othertime?) phalanx of the chessboard. On each side they stood, silent, transcendent, prisms through which the radiance of the sun-that-is-a-star flew like a wind. Facing Queens of women's torsos, full regal breasts and prince-bearing, horse-riding hips, Kings with muscles like breastplates, broad, bow-drawing shoulders. The Knights were shapely legs meant to grip the flanks of a war-stallion, cut off at the crown of thigh and the ankle, the slice smooth and perfect, revealing faint rings like great trees. Bishops stood as straight, powerful arms, perched lightly on fingers like insects. Rooks molded into feet, toes like transparent pearls curling into the desert Board. And the Pawns, severed heads all in a row like marigolds in the window. Each of them were beautiful, craggy faces of crusaders and classic profiles of a dozen Helens—

(—I will be Paris, for love of thee—)

I pushed the voice aside like a heap of armor. Their pouting lips full and slightly open, hair falling in glassine waves around slender necks, couching the crystal faces in a sea of refracted light. We gaped, I am certain I no more than the Monkey with all of his smirking knowledge, with all of his high-sounding name. The suddenly equatorial sun streamed through them in broad sword-strokes. I could feel his paw sweating in my hand, and when he spoke his voice was low and growling.

"I think we ought to be very quiet, and go around them. Follow, follow me." He began to creep along the perimeter of the glass figures, but even as he passed the line of pawns rippling voices pricked the air. A fractured unison, each delicate soprano tone following on the previous note.

"Stop. We know. We see. You are the Magus."

I froze before the mirrored unblinking eyes and tall limbs. "But I am not."

"Not you, womanchild. Him," they sang. I turned towards the bronzed figure of Ezekiel, who stood with bared teeth.

"We should go now. Hoo! I beg you, they will spoil everything!" The response of the crystalline limbs flew outwards like a sonic boom disrupting a choir of castrati. "No, No, you cannot! We know, we know who you are, we can see the flesh beneath your oystershells, we see your Path blazing ahead of you. You have returned! We knew you would, we did not lose faith. You must hear us!"

I began to tremble, as though the precise tonality of their voices had achieved a terrible resonance in my bones, and I was shaking into rubble. There was no change in the figures, the Queens' breasts still proudly rode the air, the Pawns' hair did not rustle by strand or lock. They stared at each other, the opposing armies, ever at the instant before battle, before the Knight slides on his severed ankle to his appointed square, never truly fighting, shattering, slivering, poised forever on the *edgemoment*, the *timebefore*. The weight of their anticipation creased the wind. Ezekiel snarled and spat, noises bubbling up from his throat as from an ancient cauldron, rimmed in leather and studded with iron slugs. He growled under that stream of sound, "Now, now, now, now. We must go. They will take you away from me." I knelt and held him, as he had held me, stroked his coarse yellow fur into silk, whispered and pressed my waxwet cheek to his shoulder.

"No, I will stay, I will hear. I have to. I stayed for you, Ezekiel, I stayed to hear you. Perhaps everything ought to be spoiled."

He seemed to calm, the smooth of rippling muscles under alarmed skin, ruffle of bird's wing ligaments and joints like mouths. He touched my face with something like tenderness, resigned and hopeless. But his flesh only leapt and hardened again when they spoke, fluttering in the wake of that sapphire music, thirty-two voices striking like a dulcimer hammer.

"This is our mind: the quill-hand is the noble, the tooth-hand indolent. The left foot knows the blistered sky, the right foot treads the leavened Road. This is what we see when we look through the glass-that-is-you. Separation and shattering lie like lovers below your fifth vertebrae. The right hand and the left hand fly apart."

The Monkey's shrill vibratory words cut through theirs. "You see? They know nothing, they are lunatics. You can learn nothing from headless pieces who can never Play." He spat like a woman's curse.

"Oh, my Ezekiel, but I am a lunatic, too." My face was an ocean, flowing in its own tidal reds, the effusion of tears eroding the shoals of my cheekbones. My mouth hung open, collecting the leaden drops, lips full and loose, gleaming with salt.

"Magus," came the glissando of the chessboard, "why do you hate us? We do not harm. We do not lie. We could never harm her, of course not, no, never, never." It was as though the pieces asked and answered themselves, though they spoke in that same fractured unison.

"That name is not mine. It is a lie." The Monkey smelted his words like a twisted blade. "It is, it is!" They sang gladly, "The falcon told us, with his leather hood, and the desert mice! You are the Magus, with hands like stars, who walks the sacred marshes with crane-feet, who ate his name. He who made us and has come again."

If they could have danced, they would have made their chessboard into a ballroom. Their glass flesh glistened and flowed over invisible bones like the currents of a hundred rivers. The long calves of the Knights wanted desperately to tremble, the fingers of the Bishops, arched like flying buttresses, lusted for movement.

"What else could it mean, that you bring her with you, excreting Want like sweat, she who will kiss the belly of our Queen, the Seeker-After, the Player?"

"No one brought me. I came on my own feet," I protested.

"All that matters, humanchild, is that you came. You came and you will make us whole, you will mend what he built, give with both hands what he held back from us. He knows you will, he knows. That's why he snarls at us, who never hurt him."

I looked helplessly at the inscrutable Monkey, his eyes like rosary beads, glinting dangerously between the shield-lines of crystal figures, his little copper body like a smoking hookah. I fell between their words, clinging to cliff-phrases, slipping on the algae of predicate nominative, tearing my fingernails to the quick. I could not understand.

"Ignore them, continue on. We must stay on the Path. Forward motion, endless if, but still we must. You know the Door lies behind us. They are foolish." He was already walking away, leaving me, expecting me to follow—how soon had he come to believe me a loyal child, an acolyte, a modest student with the moon-scalp between her braids illuminating humility! I straightened my scarlet spine and called out to his back, "Are you what they say? Did you make them? Who are you?" I whispered the last. His warm, autumn shoulders slumped, and he spoke to the wind, without turning towards me.

"I am myself and no other. But in the beginning, before the Walls and the Road, beyond the beforetime, before and after the name traveled through me, I was also myself. Do not interfere with them. They are, that is enough. Let it be."

I waited for a friendly *hoo*, but it did not come. In the press of the desert I was cold. I turned back up to the watery shapes.

"The tooth-hand is indolent. It does not speak. He carries the Stone, but it slithers in your veins like a sidewinder. As long as he walks beside you, you are not free. He keeps you mad for purposes none can divine. The right and the left. He conceals like a Door. He left us like this, and will leave you. But you can help us, you can, you can. With your red mouth you can show us the Way." They seemed to beg, to implore.

The Monkey had given up and leaned against a large adobe Wall some space away, chewing on a cactus-thorn lazily. His glance spoke of resentment, do-what-thou-wilt, bemused sorrow. I closed my eyes, swam in the fresco of light on my inner lids.

"How? I cannot help anyone. All I can hold in my hands is Death, red and bright."

"No, no, humanchild," the chrysalis-voice of the pieces whispered, faint with anticipation, "You can give us the great silver chariot, the reins and the moon-bellied mares. You can move us, you can Play."

Stutteringly, I began to see. "You cannot move yourselves?"

"We are the Game," came the bell-like answer. "We stand forever at the beginning-place, where he put us, stiller than rain, and we cannot move the smallest iris. We are forever tilted towards action, never within it, never thrilling to Purpose. We were made, we cannot be. We do not know what Game we are, we do not know our name. We do not know Rules or Stratagems. We see into the hallways of your bones, but we cannot see a Path across the Board. No one can be both the Player and the Game, no one can hold both ends of the sword in his hand and yet part the flesh of his enemy. No one can be both the Man and the Bar."

"You want me to teach you to play chess?" A silken rustle, smelling of mint and new basil on a grandmother's windowsill passed through them, sibilant and sighing.

"Chesssss . . . is that what we are? Are we *Chess*? Tell us what *Chess* is, child, tell us how it tastes. Tell us, tell us, and we will give you a thing you desire." My heart began to flutter like a sparrow within. "We will give you a Vision, a Vision of the *beforetime*. You may look into the glass belly of our Queen and see a landscape of *notnow*. We are poor oracles, our eyes cast not forward but backwards and within. But we can show you this small thing. Trade us for it, beautiful, blessed redwoman."

"There was no beforetime. I have always been here."

"And yet in the oracle's eye you extend both forward and back. Perhaps you are right. We have been known to lie. It does not really matter, of course. Your want speaks loudly and in perfect verse."

The Monkey was frowning now, but he was a gold blur in the darkness of my tears. I held on so frailly to the Road and the now, I feared to look even an inch beyond it. One madness had become comfortable—could I bear another? The serrated edge of unlearning my own singularity? But my Will had long ago become flotsam, curiosity a plank which had forgotten the shape of its galleon. If a thing was offered, I could not refuse. It was not the Way.

I sighed, drying my tears on my wrists, walking onto the Board, listening to the dull pad of my bare feet on the squares. The pieces seemed to lean in like glass towers, listening with their crystal veins. (But how do I know these Rules, how can I know them, who never learned them?)

"The King," I began, sniffing, "can move one square in any direction. But the Queen can sail the Board like a dreadnaught, can move anywhere she wants . . ."

20

The Board thrummed with its new word: *Checkmate*.

They were ready to move, leaning into the sun like wind sprinters, finding the shape of strategy in their glassy bodies. But they were honest pieces after all, and would keep their bargain. A high, clear voice like an amethyst trumpet trilled down the battle-lines, and this time it was the great Queen's alone, her powerful shoulders squared and assured now of her position, hips flared provocatively, thighs in a feline crouch. "Come, humanchild, come here." Her tone had grown leaves of command and the language had lost its surreality—she knew now she was royalty. I walked through the forest of erect glass, mirrored in the limbs, a bleed of woman through perfected flesh. They towered, crackling with silence.

I knelt before her, because that is what one does in the presence of Queens. Headless her beauty seemed more annihilating and lightning-edged, full now of new power and surety, knowledge that she was the key piece in the precious Game. Though she had no hands to stroke my face, her voice nevertheless caressed me like a favorite daughter, smoothing my hair and drying my face of tears like blood.

"Darling, it is not so dreadful as that. Oh, my dear, my dear one," she crooned, as though rocking a sweet-faced princess to sleep after a nightmare. "Look into me, now, into the canvas of my belly, see what you have purchased, yourself and no other. Look deep, *downdowndown*. It is yours, our sight is yours. Don't cry, don't cry, my precious girl."

I placed my hands on the vase-curved of her waist and stared into the curved mirror of her stomach, the crystal womb within, and a strange fog was there, forming into a scene, projected against her uterine Wall like an amorphous child, slowly sprouting fingers and organs like a night-lily. This is what I saw in the Queen's womb, with the anointment of oracular sight on my brow as I pressed against the coolness of her skin:

A girl and a boy, sitting lazily cross-legged under a pale green willow, picking at the grass. She is lying with her head in his lap, long red hair fanned against his knee. Her skin is not my unnatural red but like honeyed cream. She grins up at him, his eyes the color of an evergreen forest, of dragonfly wings, his corn-gold, too-long hair falling over his forehead. And she laughs. When she does her back, her throat arches slightly, and he blushes. He smells of wheat fields and fallen autumn apples soft against the earth, and it is a smell she knows like her own. Under the filmy reed-curtain of the old willow tree, they hold hands and talk quietly, shoes discarded like peach pits. The sun is low in the sky, warm and orange-gold on their young faces, their strong white smiles and freshly washed hair. The light spills onto their shoulders like water from a well. There are sharp-smelling rosemary branches braided into her hair, with their little blue blossoms, and the oil is on their brown fingers. The boy whispers something in the girl's ear, and she closes her eyes, lashes smoking cheekbones like bundles of sage.

They rise from the thick grass. They lean, arm in arm against the tree, that melting sun illuminating their youthful forms, her smallish hips, his long legs all rimmed in summerlight. Just before the image fades into the looking-glass womb again, I can see him tenderly brush a strand of hair from her face, full of uncertain care. And then they are gone. They know nothing of any aftertime, any night in the long line of nights ahead, and they are beautiful, simply. I cry after them, hands and face flush against the crystal-ball belly of the Queen. I choked and sobbed, clawing after the vanished watercolor, trying to hold it to me like a doll.

"There, there," the Queen murmured. "It is what you came for, after all. To know that you are more than you were. Poor thing. But you must go now, for we are ready to Play at last, and we are terribly excited." Indeed, she seemed to wriggle in her space.

Stumbling across the Board I blindly sought the edge, and as I passed the last Pawn with his flowing hair, I heard him whisper sorrowfully, "I think you were very beautiful when you were young—"

And then they were lost in a rush of light as a Knight leapt over the row of Pawns and the Game commenced, so swift and violent that a sharp-paged wind was thrown up by the whirring movement of the pieces. I could not even see them, only their phosphor-trails, streaming glasslight behind them as they looped threads of infinite patterns over the Board. Knight to take Bishop, Pawn to become Queen, Rook streaming across his straight highways.

"Well, now you've done it," came the reedy voice of the Monkey I had nearly forgotten, hairy arms crossed over his chest. "Do you think you've fixed anything?"

I sighed heavily. "I did what they wanted."

"Of course." He walked over to the edge of the Board, profile whipped by the Game-movement as by a speeding train. "Do you see what is happening, what you have done? They are Playing their Game, and they will Play as long as they can, every possible Game combination, every conceivable attack and defense. And when they have traced the leaf-Path of every Game that could ever be imagined, it will be over, and they will die. They will Shatter and Splinter and there will be nothing left but a mountain of broken glass. You were right, you carry only Death in your hands, and it is Death you have given them, its tiny seed wrapped in your crimson smile."

I wanted to feel pain, but there was nothing. They had asked, begged, even traded. If they died it was their fault. I could not pity them, it was not in me, if it had ever been. We all find our Way here, or we do not. It was not my fault.

"Surely there are many combinations," I said.

"Yes, more than you can hold in your painted head. But it is a finite number, and when they reach it they will die. As they were, they were immortal. They were missing a thing, and you have not given it to them. They can no more Stop now than they could Begin. You put them in motion, and now the motion eats them whole. But they are no more than they were, it is only that they have traded for a different stagnant swamp. The wretches would not be satisfied. Come, Darlingred, this is a graveyard now, with glass headstones, we should not stay to witness. I do not blame you. It hardly matters whether one thing in the whole lives or dies. But I warned you."

"What did I see?"

"An image, nothing more. Let it be. Oracles show, they do not interpret. If you let it grow in you, it will consume the delicate madness we have woven to lead us to the Angel, and all will be lost. I warned you. Forget the children and the tree, forget it all. There is no possible retrieval of even a single strand of his hair."

We walked out across the empty desert, with its ghost of Road, and I stared ahead unmoving, falling though I was standing, yielding not to the radiating image of the Queen's womb, but in the possession, entirely now, of the Stone within his belly, its promise of seizure and deliverance, and the moon like an epitaph in the black sky. I did not see in that half-light that my body had blushed to a deep, rolling green. I did not see the flush of fecundity, the sheen of willow-leaves covering the surface of me like a mosaic.

I walked like a jade statue, over the dunes and Away.

CANTO
THE THIRD

21

MY FINGERS CURVED LIKE RAM'S HORNS, BERYL-GREEN AND HARD.

Osprey-claws, and how the green, green willow branches of my arms do look black in the sallow moon! How sequence like a tumor pure and white multiplies in my throat. How I must swallow it, the thick mushroom flesh, swallow it all. *Downdowndown.* How that sensual slither of *must* snake-coils over my larynx, squeezing—how it all goes and I with it, no more than a wicker raft seeping water like cyanide.

I am Death, oh yes, with my pretty green eyes. I can smell it, oozing from my emerald pores, stink of blood and spent semen, mustard-gas and alleys thick with crooked, greasy pink lipstick, the musky scent of headstones slowly sinking into mud, fingernails disintegrating, bile rising in a thousand throats, sparrows with necks broken like slender arrows, rot of trees, rot of splayed limb, rot of stale whiskey in a rusted flask, worms suckling at breasts blooming like corpse-daffodils, the sickly trail of black milk trickling from a molded nipple. What you smell coming from you when you are Death, when you are dying, when you are exiting your own flesh, stage left, stage right, exeunt, exeunt. The left hand and the right fly apart.

The body becomes all things, the stage and the player and the entrance, the foil tipped in poison and the exit pursued by a bear, the return carrying a severed head, my own pretty severed head trailing cobra-hair and blood of jade, never to be monarch again, Medusa in repose at last. It is the mistaken identity and the lovers united, it is the climax repeated until it is the denouement, the soliloquy of folded hands and pointed toes, act twelve borne on the silver tray of a flat belly. When you are leaving it, how beautiful the platforms and stairs of the body seem, the trick Doors and velvet curtains, the skein painted pastoral and scaffolding of bones, musty costumes hung in the closet on ribcage-rungs, the proscenium arch seems to vault upwards to the damned, the orchestra pit down to the divine. It is all so graceful and well-conceived a creature, so realized a character, fleshed out in all its roles from ingénue to crone, so comfortable a body, so desired, when it is flying away from you like a migratory bird. It is everything, yet I cannot connect to it, I seem to move my legs and hands from a long distance. My sight, unblinking and yawned, remains, the beam of stage-light from blank eyes like grass on a grave.

I want to lean against a tree (a willow, bright and pale, and a boy with the sun in his hair?) and wait for madness and death, pretty sleek hounds worrying my meaty bones between them, gnawing the marrow and howling at the tree-roots. I care for Nothing. Indeed I tend it like a favored rose, nuzzled and cupped a motherly hand around its dark petals, breathed the sharp incense of its exhalations and coaxed them skyward with the ministrations of a patient monk, gardening into eternity with a luminous rake. I pulled out the green shoots of Purpose and Center, held off the marauding winds and ate their fruits, juice dripping from my chin. And now I have lost my charming grail, the woolen Nothingness that warmed me so well.

Am I green now, malachite and woven leaves over rounded shoulders and unpierced heels because of life or death? Because tendrils of red-fruit vines loved my skin, because the wide, furry leaves of violets and spears of rosemary are infatuated with my hair and my knee-caps? Or because mold and decay have dressed me in their ball gown with its plunging neckline, clad my feet in algae-slippers and circled my neck in grave-grass like a string of pearls? I could not say, I could not say. I am so tired, I do not care. And he cannot make me, the golden Beast with stiletto eyes, this little homunculus dogging my steps, snapping at my heels, vomiting words from his long-toothed mouth, vomiting truisms and riddles like tubercular phlegm-blood. He cannot make me, he cannot make me. I am too full of the fat black-palmed baby of my Death to allow him within me, I am too near the coughing morning of its birth. Its teeth join the needles of the Compass, snagging on my womb.

I am within my verdant body as it is within the Labyrinth. We find our Way. The sylph that is "I" is vanishing slowly, a daguerreotype dissolving under a spill of phosphor, image of eyes like stone wells seeping from the page. My body will remain, and the Compass within, magnetized, aborted daughter, but I will be eaten at last by the Labyrinth in a triumphant swallow—I will be a high Wall or a fair-thighed fountain. I will be remade into the flat expanse of the Road, my pointing arm extending into geometric perfection towards the horizon.

And the golden golem Monkey will keep swinging and hooing with his iconic smile, as content to preside over my dissolution as my baptism. As long as he can anoint my colored forehead with oil and announce me to the invisible multitude, corpse or Queen, it matters not. He hates a poor, doomed toy in the desert because it showed me what he would not, because it did not incline its head humbly toward his paw. I hurl my bitterness at his chest like a pistol shot at dawn. Pace off ten steps and fire true.

Ezekiel, Ezekiel, what do you see in the sky? A burning woman, a bullet fired from the mouth of a star, streaming green fire into the sucking earth.

"Darlinggreen," came his rasping voice like a silver spade in the soil, "You don't mean that. Hoo."

22

OH, I DON'T MEAN ANYTHING.

Whether you are here or not matters less than nothing to me. Sun-creature, I never asked you to come. You attach to my flank like a lamprey and want me to love the slow drain of my blood from the wound. Leave me to the copper bit and the foaming mouth, the pulverized teeth and the jaw of frayed wire. Leave me to drown in the rice-fields, when I have become blue again they will eat pearly slivers from the delicate dish of my mouth. Leave me to go mad alone. It is such a private thing.

"I know you are glad of me, it matters nothing what you say," The Monkey patted my bent head and I simply breathed. There was nothing else my body could manage. Under the curtain of my agate hair I could smell a strangeness growing like a bladed weed, sharp and thick, sweat and smoking bones. Ezekiel tugged on my glowing limbs.

"Visitor," he murmured.

Through strands and curls like living vines, through my heaving breaths ragged and strangled, I saw now a massive Bear, thickly-furred and broad-headed, lying on his side with a great sucking wound in his flank. He whimpered and bellowed at turns, black blood seeping onto the papery earth. The Monkey scampered up onto the mountain of his hip, examining the gash.

"It has always been like that," the Bear moaned. "It never heals. I have tried poultices of laurel and banana, honeybees' wings and birch bark, bird-marrow and Wall-dust. Nothing helps. It laughs at me, with it bloody lips.

But I have come to love it, now. It is warm and bright and pretty. It never fails me. Would you like to come and touch it?"

I said nothing, moved not an inch. The Monkey looked at me expectantly.

"If I put my hands on him," I whispered, "he will only die like the rest."

"You touch me, beloved Darlinggreen, and I am not dead," Ezekiel crowed softly.

"Yes, see? Perhaps not, perhaps not, girl," the mournful Bear brightened hopefully. "Come closer. I am very beautiful reflected in your skin." His wound did reflect black and red on my thighs, pulsing like a womb, open and quivering as if to speak. He stared at himself reflected and refracted in me, preening. I did not move, frozen by a manic disgust.

"Don't be afraid. If you are very, very good, you could have a wound, too. I would even administer it myself. My teeth are the color of the stars, aesthetically perfect. Orthodontia is so *expensive*. But see the results! Wouldn't you *like* to have them in your nice green flesh? Be sweet to me and I will make you beautiful, paint your belly with blood." He struggled to rise and come near me, but I backed away as best as my weak leafbody could manage, bile rising in me like the tide. The Monkey had also clambered off, and returned to me, protective and proprietary, grimacing at the beast. It kept on its imploring way:

"Don't run away. You haven't seen the pointillist masterpieces of my intestinal tract, the glory of my bruises, the majesty of my swollen tongue! You are very ugly now, girl, with no breaks in your body. All revolting solidity. Come, come, I will make you splendid, seraphic, *gloriana* in the highest! I will make you the Queen of Capillaries, Empress of Bones! Don't you *want* to be beautiful? I will love you forever, I will write masterpieces on your flesh!" I began to cry through my suffocation, drawing dagger-breath, loathing his nearness, the warmth of his mewling breath.

"Come closer, I cannot see myself in your mirrorbody any longer. You are too far off. I am being very generous. It is not polite to refuse."

I broke and ran, stumbling and weeping. The Monkey sprinted after me, trying to keep up.

"Come back! It is useless to run, the Door is on your heels! One way or another, you will be like me, and bleed! We will all be beautiful before dawn!" His howls echoed after us, choking my poor neck.

But he was right, I could hear it now, clanging copper pots in my skull—

(—*nam vos mutastis et illas*—)

Latinate clams clattering in the water, their vulgate symphony of clicking nails and meaningless morse code, which translated reads as a meaningless clam-tongue, pink and meaty. The Door-tongue, the Hinge-dialect.

I cannot run far enough, ever and ever.

The sea takes back its stones. My limbs crumble. There is black mud under my nails, secret and ashamed. Such a private place I inhabit, with no Rosetta Stone to help you make sense of it, of my ceilings and windows. I never asked for comprehension.

Mask yourself, Ezekiel, with that knowing look, and pretend you can read the scroll. Pretend you know what we are doing. What do you see in the sky? You cannot say because you do not see. I with my irisless eyes swallow the vaulted air under an eyelid. You see nothing. You would sell my bones for katana hilts in some furtive bazaar, my eyes for jewels in heraldic shields, my ears for pincushions, ninepence each. you would hawk my green brocade skin for upholstery, my knees for inkwells, my hair for quills, my lips for slide rules, my breasts for goblets. Abandon me to a thousand hungry Beasts, partitioned and packaged, given away like a bride, devoured and burrowed-within, until I am no more.

(—*In nova fert animus mutatas dicere formas corpora*—)

But the language of the Doors clangs in my swollen head like a busy dockside, I can feel it behind us, the black circle, divining our tracks with a velvet nose. Is it past the Board in the desert now? Has it come past the coffin-body of the Queen? Its strange trilled consonants move over me like diamondback snakes, the rhythmic phrases like the charmer's straw basket in the musky market, sidewinding somewhere in our shadow. With each pianowire strangle of sentence, a new lacerating chord is strummed in my thick-pooled brain, with each bevelled vowel, brightened under a glass cutter's knife, finds its mark and pierces me like a gold-fletched arrow, and the Door turns towards the church-bell tone of word striking flesh. In this way I can feel it drawing closer, the heat of its black body like a secret sun.

(—*torpor gravis occupat artus: mollia cinguntur tenui praecordia libro*—)

Oh, it bears down like a woman giving birth, the pressing, all those massive hands on me, pushing down into the swallowing earth! And among those thousandthousand hands can I not detect a bull's solid amber hooves? Can I not see ivory horns tossing above me, tips gilded with hemlock? The Minotaur at last, the *monstrum* lurking, the monster-that-is-not, hunting with powerful thighs my steps like crocus shoots in the spring, the Center of the Labyrinth that I know cannot be stealing along the Road, stalking me as though that Center were I. We circle each other, a fleshy yinyang covered in blood and dust and sapphires crushed like blueberries, seeking each other, spiraling like sumo wrestlers, stamping our fat feet in the sacred salt. And when one of us is perished, gored through like a potter's wet vase, will not that crusted salt be found on our howling mouth?

(—*pes modo tam velox pigris radicibus haeret*—)

Black eyed Bull behind me, lowing at the moon, fatal light flickering on his gold nose-ring, his blood shouting with the nearness of our meeting. As though that Center were I, as though I were what he sought, my presence in his belly the very completion of his bovine existence. As though it were not I that sought him, sought the terrible Center of death, as though I were not the Seeker-After, as though I were not aware of his breath smelling of sour mash and clay kilns, as though I were fleeing the inky ripple of muscle and not waiting for his milky teeth on my breast.

(—*in frondem crines, in ramos bracchia crescunt*—)

And still this hypnotic chanting in the confessional of my ear, the hissing syllables wreathed in smoky incense, the intimacy of his rust-red tongue lapping at my calves, a lover's searching fingers grasping for me in the dark. These savage incantations meant to bind me still as nightwater or to warn? He is so close now, the wild smell of his mouth is so near. Perhaps I will lay down on this Road, covered in soft leaves how like a bed, perhaps I will lay down and let him slam shut over me, his Bull's mouth clamp down at last on my emerald humanflesh. Perhaps I will not fight. Perhaps I would be more beautiful Devoured. Perhaps victory means collapsing in mid-stride, knowing the precise moment to give in. It is the fight which comes at the end of a Quest, is it not? Even a Quest-which-is-not. If I do not fight, there is no Quest. Perhaps then I will not. The Compass beats a steady time, a sparrow-waltz, ticking towards the north of my glacial eyes. It wants us Devoured, within that meaty belly; Compass-child Within me Within the Bull-Door, all of us together like a Russian doll.

(—ora cacumen habet; remanet nitor unus in illa—)

Come then, poor Beast, I am not afraid. You must admit I was a challenge; I have eluded you for such a long time. You do not need to ensorcell me with these murmured verses, black and red. I am still already, soft and quiet as a hedgerow in infinite fields like skies, dotted with lambs as with stars. I will sit and wait, draped in green, cypress-candle, palms resting on my knees in fertile quiescence. If I am yours, you are mine, wheelswithinwheels, and we will gobble each other up as though we were hook-nosed witches feasting on the plump calves of naughty children, gleefully sucking delicate bones and our long, greasy fingers.

I collapsed and knew nothing but a long expanse of blackness.

23

Fat raindrops like children's hands slap my face.

I rose cork-like into watchfulness. I could hear the slip-slush-thud of his hooves, of his sliding threshold still gritty with desert sand. He is just behind us, close now, our faithful and patient hunter never daring to disappoint. The Monkey tastes the rain with a long, cicada-seeking tongue.

"It's coming. It's here. Did the Door and swifter than I. Are you wakeful? Will you keep running?"

"*He*. He is coming," I murmured, swaying slightly.

"He, then. I am sorry for what I have not told you. Hoo, Darlinggreen, I am sorry. Get up, now, my dear, there is further to go. He is coming." Ezekiel stroked my olive hand and coaxed gently.

"Sooner or later, there must be a Door, there must be a Minotaur, even if there is not. I choose this Door, and no other. So I win. I will lay down at his threshold. What is eaten also eats. If I choose him, I will never be caught. I will win the Game. It will stop."

The Monkey shook his coppery head. "I will go with you, you know. I will always go with you, at your side, my Darlinggreen. Hoo." His gaze was loving and soft and forgiving as a glove sewn of feathers.

We sat for a time, listening for his approach and combing each other, my fingers twined in his fur and his rubbing my cypress-skin like oiled cloth.

"I do not know," he admitted, "what it will lead to. This is our first capture, the gaining of a Third. It is something new, for the first time in alltime, something new. But it is also older than all. It may take us to the Angel and her white lips, but it may not."

"I know."

"I am quite sure you do not. Hoo."

Silence. The sky overhead was a profound blue, blue as once I was, the cobalt flesh of longago, perhaps not so longago, but I could not say. I was melting, and I cannot say anything. I have come to this, I accept.

And then he comes over the horizon like a black moon, simply, soundlessly, dark as a pupil, gliding gracefully towards our little tableau, knowing that he no longer needs to conceal his movements. It is an elegant entrance, without trumpets or heraldry. The silver Bull's head knocker, a tarnished and terrible sky-gray, leers, diamonds dripping like saliva from his great teeth. He is so beautiful, coming towards me, coming towards us, slightly ajar as though his mouth were open in anticipation, the eyes of the Minotaur as blank and irisless as mine. My handsome Death, gargantuan, profound, and I am proud of it. I am its green-veiled bride, reclined and waiting.

The Monkey looks at me with warm eyes, squeezing my hand. But I am not afraid. It is leaning over us now, a devouring eclipse, breathing heavily and watching to see if we will run. I laugh softly, a glutted and velveteen chuckle. I am stretched beneath him, body curved into a crescent moon, with the Monkey nestled in the swerve of my waist like a glinting jewel. I can feel the Minotaur's mouth on me, his muscled arms gathering me towards his inevitable throat/threshold, the beaten earth littered with bones at the Center-which-is-a-lie, the dry fires of his digestion, furnace leaping towards me, to conflagrate and Devour my limbs in a rush of fire and slamming wood. How tender Death and the Monster can be, if you do not fight. I hold open my arms in second position, remembered from some mirrored room impossibly longago, to take him in and tear into his flesh as he tears into mine.

As the great black Door slams shut, he breaths a sigh of relief and release, a hot rush of that fermentfire air as he rasps his words in a rush, orgasmic larynx shredded by my jade nails as we fall, downdowndowndowndown.

" —*hanc quoque Phoebus amat. Carissima! Ederis!*"

24

RAIN OF RICE-CLOUDS AS WE PASS THROUGH HIM.

The thick throat full of bats and chewed rope flies by, and it is not so much *down* as *through*. Through the twisted body of the Minotaur, skating on bulbous intestines and pancreatic oil-paints, slicing his flesh with katana-limbs as I go, Devouring what flanks and flesh-handfuls I can seize, savoring the smoky meat, full of fennel and scorched crow's wings, his black blood dripping from my willow-chin as mine did from the Angel's. I enjoy now the biting and tasting as she did, the cello-bow slide of flesh into my belly. It is Power. With each sink of my teeth into him, his teeth into me, I hear him hiss like a kettle, the low comfort-hoo of the Monkey at my side, and my own triumphant wolf-cub yelps. What a lovely little concerto we make, the three of us in the dark. But as it is begun I can see that I was mistaken.

This is not the important thing, the *passingthrough*, the Devouring. My white-armed Death is not comprised of this sooty bullbody. There are many Detours. After all, something lies ever on the far side of any Door. And I could see it as soon as

(it   snapped   at   her,   did   the   Door,   and   she   fell   in. *Downdowndowndowndown—*)

we were inside, lying like a hearth and waiting. What lies inside a Door? What do you see in the sky? Only Another and Another and Another, a Door *toleading* within the Door *fromleading*. Doorswithindoors unto the end of the world, the disappointing climax of entrance, knowing that there is always one more, always another Wall, another step, another bridge across the doom of ages.

The second Door glows red as from a forge, a dull and angry light illuminating the muscled walls like a manuscript. It beats inevitable like a deer-hide drum in the distance. *Thuhthumpthuhthumpthuhthump.* We might as well be patient. *Thump.*

25

Such a simple thing, opening a Door.

And stepping through, such an accustomed sequence of muscles and fingerbowl-joints; habitual, thoughtless, even. As though from a lustral basin, I sprinkle sacred drops of the Minotaur's spinal fluid on my brow as we exit his Doorbody. (Have I done this before? Am I doing it right?) Anointed one am I. Dark to light we move, from the museum-arches of black bone to a dusty cloud of subtle gold, as though the wind had swallowed the last possible ray of saffron sun from a dying sky and choked on its beams, coughing out a cigar-puff of topaz-kindling into the little room where we stood suddenly, having stepped through a dilapidated closet Door, draped in rags.

The Monkey climbed cheerfully up my treebody and perched like a parrot on my shoulder, looping the long noose of his tail around my neck, a pretty tableau of gold against green. It took some time for our eyes to adjust, like waking up, peering and hazing. If I had had pupils they would have been struggling valiantly for just the right aperture to take in the little hut where we found ourselves safe.

It was her scream that brought me into focus, instantly aware of the new Walls, knotted shelves sagging with thick-bound books, the forked red of the fire in her hearth, flames feasting on the crisp pages of still other volumes, inexplicably interdicted and condemned to the stake. Tall, slender jars like sentinel herons, bundles of dried branches and herbs hanging like a tangle of roots from the ceiling, scenting the room with an unpleasant odor of rotted wood and rosemary. Thick brown pelts covered the floor, and in the corner nearest the fire sat a woman curled into a rough-hewn oak chair far too large for her frail frame, dwarfed by the high warped back, feeding another book to the fire. All this I took in like a breath, lined with the ragged razor of her voice screaming high, tearing, hawk-like.

The scream penetrated my body, coiling like an eel around the Compass within, spinning the needles, a twisting ribbon of tongue roiling through my ravaged flesh. Her so-human voice scored me like a whip, this realwoman, the first I had seen, without wings, without glass skin, just an old woman crumpled into her last chair, wrinkled and dog-eared, her house full of strange beasts.

Of course, it was not the same for her. I was not human any longer, my lithe serpentbody green as grave-grass, long arms like birch saplings, lips like anemones. And my terrible eyes, almond-shaped emptiness, plain green stones set in my chameleon-face. How awful I must have seemed to her, how grotesque, with my smooth-furred macaque brushing his tail over my collarbone. I emerge Monstrous from the Monster, my skin the dragon-flesh of nightmares.

And so she screamed. "Stay Away, Away! Don't touch me!" She fox-howled and spat, shaking as though possessed. Her long white hair trembled like an avalanche, black eyes deep as river-rocks. I reached out a hand to calm her, and she scrambled backwards in her huge chair, screeching louder than before.

"No! Don't come near me, you can't!" I recoiled from her, and whispered when I spoke. "I won't hurt you, I promise. I'm not anything bad."

"No, no, girl, I am," she hissed like the pop of a black book-spine on the fire. "Very bad, indeed. I'm sick, infected. If you touch me, you'll be sick, too, and then what will you do, hmm? Don't breathe near me, don't touch anything, just leave before you swallow my infection like a frosted cake. This is a plague house. Didn't you see the black curtains, the sign on the Door? Please go." She seemed to shrink into her chair, nearly weeping. I was stunned, transfixed by her hate and fear like sour black bread crumbling on my tongue. The Monkey picked at a knot in his fur.

"You're fine. I would smell it if you were really ill. Hoo. Sick smells *awful*," he said matter-of-factly. "No, no, I am Deathly Ill, I am Afflicted, I know it," she cried quickly, her piccolo voice. The wretched woman was shaking as though her bones were rattlesnakes' tails. Her breath came in great, tattered rasps, thin chest heaving. I walked across the small room and knelt beside the poor crone, leaning my emerald head on her knee, gazing up at her weathered face.

"Please don't," she whimpered, "you'll die, I swear."

"It's alright, grandmother, it's alright. I'm sick, too. Mad and Dying." She flinched at the contact of my cheek and her bony knee.

"Is that why you're green?" The woman seemed interested by the possibility of a new disease.

"I think so." I answered softly. The fire crackled behind us as she considered us. "Well, if you're dying anyway, I suppose it doesn't matter," she brightened, "But keep your pretty pet away, he'll catch it for sure." The Monkey hopped gracefully up onto the lid of one of the oblong jars and proceeded to groom himself contentedly.

"I shall keep my distance if you like. But you're not sick at all." He paused in mid-comb. "Darlinggreen, she isn't, I'm sure. But I can smell something else here, like mint in a rose garden—" He trailed off cryptically, smirking as he returned to his glossy pelt.

The crone chose another fat book off her shelves and began to rip the pages into long strips, stuffing them into her mouth until her eyes watered and her cheeks bulged. Painfully, methodically, she chewed and chewed, until she could swallow the pulpy mass of parchment. Black ink stained her lips and fingers. When she had eaten all she could, she threw the book-carcass onto the fire and reached up to seize another.

"What are you doing?" My serpentmouth hung open in confusion.

"I'm dying. Why should they live? I'm hungry. Why should they be full? Now they are inside me, and I can store up words like a camel stores water. I shall never run out." She patted her stomach, which was indeed swollen to motherly proportions. "Whereas you, my green-skinned dear, I think will be entirely spent before the end. Dry as a sand-beetle." She chortled throatily and returned to her books.

"Why do you think you are dying? You have lived a long time," I asked sleepily, warmed by the fire.

"I do not think, child. I know." She ignored Ezekiel's loud, derisive *hoo* and continued. "I have already killed a boy, already infected him and he is dead, moldering in the ground."

With this, the old woman began her story, told in a familiar sing-song rhythm, for she had told this tale to herself a thousand times before in her small dark hours, like a rosary. I reclined against her, my back to the rosy heat, listening to the vibrations of her reedy voice through the skin of her leg.

26

"I CAME OF AGE DURING THE PLAGUE YEARS.

Every night I would stand in front of my great carved mirror and raise my arm over my head, grip my shoulder lightly. I pressed oystershell fingernails into my skin, feeling for the embryonic lumps, the soon-to-be purple buboes I was certain were seething just beneath the vanilla smoothness, a smoothness waiting to play me false and erupt. I turned my head, feeling the night wind on my neck, blowing in through the frosted window. In those days the night sky seemed to me to be the great raised arm of some dark woman, her armpit and the first curve of her black breast, and the stars glowered, punctured lesions of plague ruining her perfect flesh, the great red autumn moon a blood-filled contusion.

I used to sit on the fountain-rim with a young boy in the Square, under the pale-cheeked fountain-statue of a beautiful selkie-woman with water flowing over her classical face, half born from her shimmering seal skin, her long hair like the very kelp-braided sea, her hands peeling the length of grey sheathing from her marble thighs. Her eyes stared blank and unblinking, (just like yours, my girl,) perfect eyebrows carved delicately. I sat on the rim of her fountain with a boy with orange-blossom eyes, a willowy creature without a name, and his skin smelled like a wheatfield strewn with the sweetness of fallen apples. He was blonde like the silken wheat and blonde like the yellow apples and blonde like the ocean sand. The boy had slender legs and a fine, aquiline nose, and all in all recalled a deer paused below a cypress tree, tensed in the moment just before bounding away.

When no one was looking I would lift my thin blouse, exposing in a blush-inducing flash the light brown of my girlish nipple, and ask him with a quavering voice whether he saw anything. His dark eyes flickered over me, appraising. Sometimes he pushed his fingers into my flesh painfully, sometimes he would just glance and assure me I was not sick. But every time he would smile and softly say, just as your pet says:

"You are fine. You will live forever."

I used to run away to a wide field full of long grass and dense hedgerows. Around my pale toes the soil was black and wet, sodden with March rain, rich and velvety, oozing under my heels, swelling beneath my arches. I was transported by the chocolate soil, its sinuous sheen. Crocuses pointed upwards all around like candles with young green leaves, unopened purples and whites. I would run far from the willow-framed square and its sorrowing fountain, far from myself, and pause there in the mud and silver-green grasses like Eve below the Tree.

I ran to expel the scream that roiled and churned inside me, the cry that threatened to rip out of my larynx and tear my bones. In those days I was a scream embodied, saliva and tears pouring from my shaking mouth into the earth. I did not yet know the color of apples or Indian serpents, only the tightness of quavering pink lungs, uninfected lungs, plump and blushing organs clear of any blemish in their polished interior.

Against a great gnarled oak tree, feeling the texture of its trunk like a second spine, I sat cross-legged in the late afternoons, roots extending down into rain-soaked deepnesses. Into the sky-mosaics of pearl and dove and dusky ash and cream-tipped waves of pussy willow softness I stared, tremulous with the fear that the color would never change, never shift or contort, searching for the black line of a bird to break the endless expanse, as though the breath of my soul depended on the shattering of the sky. I waited in my own incubatory warmth no less than the crocuses and dormant tulips, thick with the desire for change, restless beneath the unvaried veil of cloud, trying to move the long strands of cirrus-mist with the sheer kinetic force of my need.

The boy sat beside me, clasping my small hand in his small hand. His face was half-lit by the clouds, gentleness of elephant skin light playing on his cheekbones, so high and noble, the arches of medieval buttresses. I remember him always in profile, a dark-browed angel, the glint of quartz deposits in his marble skin, gazing steadily at the horizon as though the line of his olive-eyed gaze could penetrate the secrets that lay along the linear flow of sky.

I suppose I loved him, though he never asked me to search his body for lesions. I cannot even recall how many days we spent under the water-shadows of the fountain, in the grass-pillows of the field, though they seemed then and still seem innumerable. The coughing and retching of the world dissolved into the wind. But the examinations of flesh and sinew continued separate from the taut-skinned drums of pounding plague.

The fear of a flat-palmed hand sounding a low note across my throat flowed on faithfully. It became a game, even after the hottest forked flames of sickness had blown over and what remained was merely the mass graves, the pits with long, mushroom-colored limbs stacked within like the rotting bricks of a misshapen pyramid, the tangled once-gold hair of women like handmaids meant to accompany some monstrous pharaoh into the silver sky and the storm. Hollowed cheeks like jackals echoed loudly in those ashen faces, covered in squares of bravely bright green grass.

Later, when I learned geometry, every angle I measured with my clean plastic protractor seemed to be that of a bruised and broken elbow, the acute angles of riddled bones to haunt all the calculations I ever made.

It was only a game, for him to probe my neck and my arms with tremulous seriousness, as though some latent epidemic lay under my skin, straining to burst the confines of my body. His eyes trickled over me with such earnestness, such tenderness, as though my wretched skin might break. In the rainy sickle-bladed stalks of grass we laughed as softly as the susurring leaves, wrapped ourselves in woolen lengths of silence, watched whisperingly the sky and the trees.

We were young by the sea. The salt and kelp towers, foaming terraces, portcullis of coral and brine. Below the flowered balconies pounded the ineffable blue of the ocean, petals like rose-stained feathers drifting down onto its mirrored surface. The sea bore away the wind of the plague, carried it off into the soft cloud-drifts. The sea scoured us clean, made our skin perfect again. The stairs like a shower of peachstones down to the surf became polished and merry again, bright as brass banisters. The universe of our twinship, our two-ness, the low-population cosmos of our lives seemed slide back into the familiar leather gloves of health and flushed cheeks, of hair streaming in the flapping breeze and laughter like the songs of white pelicans.

Of course I never caught the plague. If I had, perhaps the boy would have stayed with me, feeling that I needed his clinical expertise, his gentle fingers, his eyes boring holes into my uninfected skin. If I had begun to perish beautifully, with a trickle of sparkling ruby blood at the corner of my beestung child's lips, perhaps he would have waited for me, knowing how I needed his clean fingernails and quiet voice, he would have stayed because he would have known how I loved him. He would have stayed and told me I would live forever even as the blood vessels burst in my rose-leaf eyes.

When he died I tried not to think of his body being the color of mushrooms. I know, know now forever that I passed the terrible knives of plague into him, that every time he touched me he took the disease out of me and into himself, purifying me every time his fingers pushed into my muscles and bones, making me smooth and white and clean, taking all the purpled darknesses that never rose up like tiny volcanoes into his fawn-limbed body, dying of the sickness I never contracted.

But I knew, secretly, that I was a carrier, and bore like infants the black strains of death within me, the only children I would ever have. That I would live forever by virtue of the demons I harbored, and bring affliction like a silent choking seafog to every boy that ever lived. Every boy I loved would cough up a glut of blood onto my white dress and apologize weakly before he collapsed into an ecstatic seizure of death. I knew always that I had killed him, killed him, killed him. I knew. I know."

27

THE WOMAN'S FACE HAD BECOME A JAGGED MOUNTAIN.

Salted tears coursed from every crack and niche, the secret erosion of her once-beauty and her bitter core.

"I know what I am," she wept, "myself and no other, tumors blooming in every pore." I cannot imagine we were a comfort, my blank stare and the Monkey's accusing indifference. Her tragedy had burrowed into her, and the crone before us was little more than a maze of empty worm-tunneling. I pitied her so, even through my own ant-farm form.

"Still, you are healthy, old woman," the Monkey mused calmly. "I can smell the warmth of baking apples in your skin. Why do you not simply give her what she wants so that we may leave you to rot in peace? I can smell it here. She will hunt it out. Hoo. Your story is your own. We cannot take it from you and we do not want it on our backs." I looked up from her warm knee with a start, at the visage of yet another riddle from the mouth of a primate, another thing I could not understand.

"What do you mean? What is it? What do I want?" He ignored me and the crone chewed long book-strips, avoiding my eyes. He slipped from the jar and trotted over to me, fur rippling in the firelight.

"Darlinggreen, I know you are angry with me because of the chess pieces, and because I am such a sealed box where you believe treasures and secrets are hidden away. But do not think that just because there is a friendly fire and a ceiling, because there are books here that we are not still within the Labyrinth. That a house is an escape."

At this, the woman cleared her moldering throat unfolded her limbs like creaky shutters and rose from her chair.

"Would you like some tea, girl? I have some nice willowbark tea somewhere . . . " She rummaged in her jars, profile caught by the palest of slanting lights entering a round window near the birchwood rafters with their garrison of black-beaked crows. She put the kettle on for tea in the half light of a hut filled suddenly with long shadows of the hearth and of dawn, filling the little tin vessel.

I watched her drawing water, most domestic and ancient of tasks. Draw water from the well, and the moon from the sky. Corn from the earth and a child from the womb. (Wise woman, wise woman, do these things with your strong brown hands.) The hut-which-is-the-world is washed in blue kitchenlight, in the small, smaller, smallest morning. There are no possible others, just us beneath the kettle-steam spiraling towards the ceiling like the trajectory of a strangely-fletched arrow shot above the burnished pot, a little copper sun growing red on the stove. And the tea-leaves where she will divine the only face of her beloved endlessly repeated in the blue, blue light.

As the water bubbled and she made tinkling domestic noises with mugs, I heard her mumbling like an incantation: "This is my house. This is my bed. That is my wine-glass which does not drain, that is my fruit-bowl. I have put those violet flowers in their vase, I have set the saki-cups and the tea-cups and the flour-cups on the table, I have cleaned the mirrors. I have swept the threshold and the closet-floor. I have tended the Library. This is my house, where I have cleared a space for my sickness to curl up like a cat. I am half-sick of shadows—I won't give it to her, I won't."

This last was underscored by the dreaming trickle of brew into a goblet, and her shuffling bare feet moving back to the fire. She sets one clay cup before me, shooting a gruff look at the Monkey, and kept the other for herself, collapsing back into her enormous chair/throne with relief.

"You get none," she clucked, "because you are a nasty little Beast who talks when he shouldn't." I drank, and it was bitter. Piquant leaves and rainy soil, the tang of acorn mash and copper filings.

With his large eyes like equatorial bats, the Monkey looked up into mine. "Look at these Walls, look at the Path from kitchen to fire, look around at the Doors and the Creature in her chair. Hoo, darling, it is the Maze writ small, yet and still holding you within. This is not your home, you cannot stay."

"But I am so tired, I want to sleep, I want to stay. I could get better if I slept."

The crone nodded over her pulpy supper. "Let the girl stay if she wants to, I have plenty of room. But it will not help you to sleep. I have slept and slept, until I could not dream, but it is no balm, it does not heal. You came here because you are sick and this is a plague house, where lepers like us must eventually find our Way. This is where you belong."

"I am too weak, grandmother, too weak. You are right, I am Sickness, I am Death. I ought to go no further. I deserve to be buried in your book-shreds and disappear."

The Monkey stamped his foot. "Hoo! Stop this! You are the color of my birth-tree, it cannot be long now. Come out again into the moon. You will heal, and she loves the smell of her own rot. How many times must I pull you along like a mule? You would not listen before, and you killed all those beautiful Queens and Rooks and Knights. Listen now, the Road is calling like a mating swan." He stopped, breathing heavily. "Please, do not leave me," he murmured, as though he did not want to be heard.

I pretended I had not. "Yes, I killed them," I wept with heaving breasts, "they were kind to me and I killed them."

"Hoo! They were not kind! They could have killed you with that terrible vision, they could have stolen you away! You barely escaped with your lunacy intact! You are separating faster because of them, your seams popping like an old mattress. And now you cannot even move your treebody from a filthy hut."

"I killed them . . . " I slipped into my accustomed, guilty sea, gentle and welcoming, flagellating my back with pilgrim's whips. The crone's eyes glittered blackly, her teeth flashing in the fire light and the growing morning.

"Stay, girl, with your body full of green lesions. There is nothing for you but your disease. It will be a good friend, it will be a faithful hound, it will love you and stroke your hands at night. Remember the Bear, and how his wound was a comfort, how it made him beautiful. It *is* beautiful to Stop and Rest, to recline and drink one's tea. I will be your mother and tend to your ravaged body as if it were my own. I will mop your brow when you fever, and wrap you in furs when you are chilled. I will lance your boils and clean the blood from your lips. I will rub your feet with oil and make you brews to calm your stomach. I will clean your vomit from the floor and cradle your head in my lap, I will tell you stories and kiss you goodnight. I will love you and check your soft skin for buboes, I will press my fingers into your flesh with tenderness. Stay and be warmed here. We are alike—we carry Death like a swaddled child, with her black eyes. We owe a penance. This is where you belong, here with me."

With her great gnarled hands like walnut branches she pulled a heavy volume from the shelf, bound in leather like silk, dust like gold plate over its cover. Embossed in silver on its surface was a great glimmering hammer, heavy and deadly as though it might truly crack open my skull like a chest of coins. She opened it and ripped a long piece of parchment, stuffing it into her wet mouth. The old woman, face kind and pitying, held it out to me like a Eucharist, pages opened and waiting, offering its papery throat meekly. I reached out a hand to tear a morsel from the thick spine, and saw the proffered page, and the word written across it like a brand on a bull's thigh.

KORE

I drew back my moldavite fingers sharply, my mouth parting like a pond beneath a ducks feet. I gazed at the Monkey, struggling to understands why the word was spinning through me like a drill tipped in yellow naphtha. He smiled, slow and wide.

"Yes, yes, Darlinggreen, you see. Because you choose a course once, because you choose one sequence out of many possible, do not think it is the only time. You must choose it again and again. Will you take this thing and dwell within forward-motion or take it and wrap yourself in woolen death until you cannot tell if you are a corpse or a woman? You will take it, but will you Stop or Go, and here is stillness, will you rescind it? Kore, Kore, you are the Maiden, the Maiden and the Monster and the Blade, the Sleeper and the Castle and the Kiss, the Apple and the Mouth, the Damsel and the Dragon, the Witch and the Spell. Wake now and take the name she hoards like a fat gem, the old lizard."

Between their gazes, one milky and rheumy as a new moon, the other black and fierce, I keeled like a ringing buoy. How long had I swum within the whale and known my Will was nothing, no meaning, capsized? It would sicken me further, I knew, to go on, to take this name, to reach out and make a gesture, drive me further from what I was when I was myself and no other. It would fly through me like a row of teeth, madness carousing and glad, faster and faster. She wanted me to take it and throw it into the flames, lose it forever, repudiate it and kill it. But I would not, of course, of course, because that is not what a Seeker does, what a Maiden does, she ever after eats the apple and the pomegranate and impales herself on a spindle, its sparkling tip emerging from the crown of her dappled head.

And so I extended again that brocade hand and tore the name from its book, in a long rip of infant thunder. Without removing my eyes from the crone's hungry face, I folded it in two and placed it on my tongue like a sugar cube, and closed my dark mouth over its edges. It melted like chocolate, slightly chalky and full of oil, the taste of gold ink flowing down my throat, coating my organs, liquefied manuscripts with the sweat of pale-eyelashed scholars permeating, incense and myrrh like waves, smoke of burning horsemeat and overripe peaches, the name turning end over end, falling into my belly, *downdowndowndowndown*.

The Compass needles tore it into frenzied pieces, and it floated on pointed toes into my veins, inseminating my body like a blown milkweed, vanishing into each cell as simply and quietly as closing a Door. It crawled in my fingers, flushing warm in my calves, the name taking hold and sinking like a galleon into my bone-reefs.

I smiled, though behind glimmered the mad lolling of a wolf's leer, I smiled.

I stood without a word and took the Monkey's paw, walking softly towards the next Door, round and rough-hewn. The crone snarled and called after me and wept all at once, her voice breaking open with sorrow like a fruit, pulling at her thin white hair, clacking her rotted teeth like guillotines. Behind us I could hear her ravenous, clawing at the books and shoving them into her. I could hear her strangling grunts as she pushed them into her throat with both hands, choking on chapters and indices, cutting her wrists with glossaries and footnoted, poisoning herself, verse by verse.

The wooden Door opened smoothly and elegantly, sighing a little, and closed behind us with a satisfied jamb-smacking, smothering her coughing gasps. As I stepped into the sunlight, I could see my feet below me, following each other down the Road, and each toe shone pure gold in the auroral grass.

28

I KNELT HEAVILY IN THE LITTLE MEADOW.

Scalp burning, eyes crackling thorn-violet, feeling a hundred hands on me, judging the Void that is me to be common and poor. Hair hung in a tangled saffron morass, seaweed drying on the beach, lost in gladiatorial sand, foam clinging to the curls and tendrils, smelling of salt and starfish. Walls surrounded the clipped green, covered in salmon-colored roses and lilies of the valley. The air cloyed a too-sweet perfume. The long grass-stalks full of milk lay restful and sweet, as though a woman's hand had smoothed a taffeta dress over her slender knees. The alpine virtue, the perfection and peace. (Which is illusion, it is only that it wishes itself so.)

And I was not peaceful in its center, (perhaps because I do not wish myself so. Is it wishing that makes the world, glaring and broken?) full of my own bubbling streams and thrusting trees, full of harsh-branched gorse and cattle-hides. And the Maze doesn't care, it is impassive and huge, it mocks and waits.

The Monkey's fingers twirled clockwise in my sorrowful hair, shifting from his terrible requiring self to the warm lickings of a mother lion in a flash. Curls now the same shade as his rough fur, burnished gold to my jasper waist, my warm-shaded hips. I was a womansun, high breasts with nipples like coins, mouth like a reliquary. I shone with faceted light, blinding, pure. My skin radiated. I could have warmed a hundred ragged-eyed children, huddled together on every inch of me, trying to cover me like a subway vent. My flesh crackled, an orb of dilated copper.

But my eyes are true, still featureless and blank, plates of gold armor set in my face.

"Kore, Kore, my Darlinggold, it is not much further. I see the sun in the sky and its light." I nodded dumbly, sleep pulling my head earthward, exhaustion creeping with her feline tail, sweat in arcane snail-tracks around my knees, my wrists.

"I am so tired, Ezekiel. You must let me sleep. She would have let me sleep. There is no "I" anymore, the scarlet letter to mark my position on the Map-which-is-not, the "I's" which cross within the hermetic "X", not unlike a Compass, under which must be buried something of value; I am only pulled along like a ship on a tether, pulled into port with a shattered hull. Please, let my poor "I" choose sleep without your prodding and gnashing teeth. I must, I must, I cannot . . . "

I was nearly asleep already, and as I laid my head down on the cool grass I heard him crooning his loving "hoos" like a lullaby.

29

IN THE DARK, THE DREAM-SELF BLEEDS.

Dreams of the interior, standing on a rib, balanced on one foot, looking up into an esophagus-sky. Catching as it passes the brief light of a boy with hair like cut wheat—and then it is gone, and I am falling into poison sweat-lodge dreams rubbed with white sage, with buffalo blood, with rattlesnake bile.

And, oh, I am under him again, the Stone with the Inquisitor's cragandjag face, and he with the rack under me, bending (as though for a shield) my spine into a circle, diameter twice radius, π^2, numbers marching like ants up and down my bleached bones, the queen and her thousand daughters perched upon black and white ladders and staircases that smell of opium, velvet slant of plush-lipped opiates, slant, slant, slant, slant of perpendicular bones, the geometry of bruises and burst lips. His marble mouth next to my ear, words like grave worms, like winged insects, like mocking plague rats. The Stone torments me:

Go ahead, Darlinggold, precious. Scream in the sunlight and scream in the moonlight and scream in the starlight and lakelight and cloudlight and fishlight and gooselight and rowanlight and dawn's rosy fingers, Rosicrucian dawn, Templar aurora, Maltese cross blazing across the sky like the outline of a corpse: In this sign thou shalt conquer . . . To the gold dust of the desert, to the streets of the Maze, feel the cool stucco on your burning back, feel the lick and tickle of the flames while we burn you, burn you, burn you, witch in the Holy Land, cat-woman, you smell like the sage-garden and didn't we see you dancing naked with the devil in the orange groves last midnight Thursday? Can't deny, can't deny, but my did

*the oranges taste nice, my didn't their juice taste cold and sweet, my didn't
he make music on that drum, didn't he make you a percussion/tympani,
beat on the copper bellied skin of your back, songs to wake the stones, blow
into your bones and out came symphonies?*

(—They cannot finde that path, which firste was showne,

But wander too and fro in wayes unknowne—)

*How can you deny your possession, your Assassination, with all those
jabbering voices in your head, pretty young thing? Aren't you the devil's
pan-flute, woman? Confess, confess, confess and we will merely strangle
you, and the hooded executioner will hide his erection from the crowd,
the excitement from seeing your lips burst open like sea amenones, eyes
go wide as though in the throes of orgasm, his hands intimate on your lily
throat, oh and he'll turn aside at the last minute so no one will see. Confess
and be saved. Or we'll we'll hang you from the hawthorn tree, burn you at
the stake like venison and eat your pretty limbs at a banquet attended by
twelve Kings and no less, twelve Queens to drink your blood from teacups,
for I say unto you that the body of a witch mortified and vanquished in the
name of God is yea verily as sacred as the body of Christ, and it shall melt
on our tongues like unto the very Communion wafer, and we shall feast
upon it as on the tender breasts of doves, and suck the holy marrow from
her bones. Our hounds will gnaw the severed feet and be blessed in the
hunt. the children will suck your knuckles like cherry candy. A burning is
always cause for celebration: the village eats for a week. Quick as a spring
hare you won't escape, we know all the best hiding places.*

(—Furthest from end then, when they nearest weene

That makes them doubt, their wits be not their owne—)

*Oh, ho! Indeed, you are far from salvation, from rescue and release. I
am the Path that pierces you, my body gores you like a matador, and how
I burn inside you as though you were a censer with all your pretty gold
finish. Never think there is anything else but you and I alone in the dark.*

*Oh you Salome-witch, with the blood of that glass-bellied Queen on your
painted fingers, dance here in the Dungeon as you danced in your heathen
grove, and we will merely crush your skull with a stone. We will take a
sliver of flesh from your dancing heels and plant the wisteria with them,
and oh! How purple they shall grow in the spring! Walked you on the desert
Road like the shadow of a hawk, but you can never, never escape it, it trails*

you like squid ink, trails you like a credit report, chases you like wolves after caribou, clings to you like jellyfish. We knew you when you came, we knew the moment your black foot touched Holy Ground. Perhaps we will only drown you, drowning in the Sea will salt the meat, and your lungs will fill up with scrolls before you die, the parchment will choke your cilia, papyrus in your ivory nostrils, (and tell us, tell us how nice the oranges tasted!) Aramaic letters smearing on the Walls of your esophagus; oh, how pure you'll be! HOLY, CLEAN, PURE, white the color of divinity, and you all stained RED, RED, RED, blackberry juice on pricked fingers, pricked like that famous beauty's finger, only you weren't ever a beauty, were you? Oh no, not with that dress, not with those shoes, not with that ratty hair!

Oh, you though you could charm even with that dreadful time-release skin moldering into all sorts of decayed shades, your stupid mewling mouth gibbering with black vomit on your lips, the vomit of your sickness, your unclean brain, cramped and filthy, and yes, oh, yes, precious, aren't you the Monster after all, deformed and grotesque, commedia dell arte devil with bells for horns, weak but ugly, oh isn't that you in the proverbial nutshell! Isn't that JUST PEACHY? Your little piglet haunches all scrunched up in your dank corner picking at the lice eggs of true reality and how they GROW on you like fruit!

Oh don't cry, little bird, don't cry. Aren't you a NICE GIRL after all with your lolling eyes and your mouth full of smoke and your sloppy eye-make up, aren't you really a NICE GIRL at heart, oh yes, of course, precious, we know, we know.

And we'll crust you in salt like a diamond dress, how pretty and NICE you'll be for the feast! All dressed up. With three fingers (for the Trinity, of course) we will scoop the mound of salt from your contorted mouth and remove your teeth to play dice with, and scrape it from your cheeks as though from a fat side of salmon. In the afterglow of your ascension we will dance and dance.

(—That path they take, that beaten seemed most bare—)

Oh, you foolish girl. I am beyond everything that you are. You should not have come, not have come, to the walls of the Labyrinth with its mosaics and cisterns like the vaults of heaven. So becoming with your clear eyes. Yet you could not see the Way. Come and dance for us, Jezebel-witch, Delilah-daemon, show us the calves famed in Gaul and Britannia Ultima, show us the white-armed dervish of the orange groves.

(—This is the wandring wood, this the Errours den—)

This is the end. You know nothing. Do not pretend. You are mine, my very own.

And in my dream, in my sacred madness I see his face how like a stalactite lit by the light of bat's eyes. The callow face of the Stone, cutting me like an obsidian arrowhead, surgically slicing, glutting himself on me, glowering, gloating. Now that I have chosen sleep he can have me entire.

Oh, but know that I will wake as dreamers do and you will slip back into the white pebble in a macaque-stomach, and I will lurch onwards.

Will you now?

Oh yes. I accept. Here and there, my body is all sweet flesh and curve, ready for the witch's oven, ready for the gingerbread hut, ready for the peppermint banisters and butterscotch windowpanes, the cinnamon-gummy rugs and white chocolate stairs. Ready for the black licorice whip oven grill and cotton candy pillows, the pumpkin pie floors and caramel apple chandeliers, the lemon-ice wash basin and the cider bath water. But I'll wake. And in the end, won't I make a lovely pie, cinnamon crust with a honey glaze, twenty-four blackbirds baked inside, to lend sugar and mystique to my bones? Won't that be a dainty dish to set before the King? When I lie souffléd at his bedside and he runs his tongue over my soft grape-flavored centre? Won't I then be the best dish the witch ever served to his Majesty under a silver dome?

Oh, we are just SALIVATING, darling, positively DRIPPING.

You will see. If I accept, if I do not fight, I will prevail.

(—'Yea but,' quoth she, 'the perill of this place
I better know than you—')

30

Hoo.

I am watching you sleep, Kore, Darlinggold, watching your eyes flutter like bees' nests, watching your breath whistle through the grass like a scythe. I am watching your coppery chest riseandfallriseandfall, tidal motion of your stomach concealing and cricket-breathing. I am watching your forehead crease like an envelope, lost in dreams I do not share, but can guess.

Oh, womanchild, I have walked beside you and I have chosen to, not because you were weak and needed my padding footsteps next to yours, but because I heard your voice echoed off the faces of every Wall, and came to you drawn as a furry-feelered moth. I dragged my Temple along the Road to you as though it were a plow, as though I were a black-shouldered ox, and I let you breakfast on its fruit. I let you kill my beautiful, simple-minded chess set because even in your delirium you dazzled above all their cut crystal. I let you go mad in my arms. I have pulled you quietly and surely along the Road, to give you what you desire, because you were bright and new against the mud-brick. Just as Maidens cannot help but eat anything they are offered, Beasts cannot resist the pull of Maidens, irrefutable and fierce. We lumber towards you out of our black corners and dripping dungeons, drawn and caught, even when we know it is so. Oh, especially when we know. And I came to you, you and no other, out of the grey of the Temple.

Soon it will be over, my Kore. Soon there will be a blue Door and a Key you do not think I know you have. We have played this scene so many times. Soon there will be a shaft of light through you like a lance and we will part, because that is also the way of Beasts and Maidens. I know. I accept. I have, after all, set this sequence in motion. But as you sleep I am filled like a pitcher with sorrow, because I love you and do not wish to see the last of your many-colored shapes against the sky. But it is the course of these things, and I will follow the tale I know to be ours.

You shift in your sleep and I know it is because of the Stone, the Stone I carry inside me and thus keep close by you, so that it can do its work and change you one last time. You did not want a sequence, but I have given it to you, you were content, and I have given you pain in a silver bowl, for as I love you it is also my nature to harm you, to torture you, to push you along the Road that passes through me and present you amid fanfare with new twists and snarls, with new bottomless wells and dead ends, with Angels and Hares and Lobsters with colored shells. Without pain, there is no progress. Though you cannot see it now, though I am only the little golden Monkey who nuzzles your face, I am also the Stone and the Inquisitor, the Camels and the Carried Women, the Man and the Bar. I am the Voice that Recites verses inside you, from a place you will never remember. I am even the Road itself. I adore you and I worship the presence of you within me, yet I have borne horrors to you on my back, given them like presents. It is the Way, and I have fulfilled it.

I have brought you this far, through the acetylene torch of Walls shrieking a beckoning call, drawing the orange streaks of your soul towards it, to absorb into itself all the cardinal colors, to bring together the reds and yellows and white-heats and oranges, to conflagrate in some Compass Rose which lies at the center of you though you cannot believe in a Center. Nothing grows in this place that cannot carry its own water, the cactus that blooms at night, the single lemon-yellow flower. And you carry seas inside you, the salt and the tide of blood and plasma.

So you walked and became purified, and ascended poles that dwindled skyward like fabled towers covered in thorns, the sky opening like a womb to enfold, envelope, encase, entwine, entreat. The burning blue furnace of heaven, where the world is battered on a white anvil, poured molten into a Labyrinth-shaped mold, spattered with red sparks that become stars and iron-oxide rich soil. You turned your salt-crusted face upwards, creased eyes and parched lips, hands blistered from making corn cakes on the searing rocks, toes calloused from walking through caves with the dark, seductive rustling of bats overhead and the maddening smell of water within, you raised your eyes to the vault of sky, and I saw you like a first revelation. You are so beautiful, Kore, Kore, my Darlinggold, painted with metallic dye, extended arms thinned to thread by hunger and ascension.

The balance of one foot on the pole, like a parchment-colored flamingo, will be as it ever is upset by your arms in second position, and you will falter as you must, feel the hot wind rush up from earth and down from heaven, and as you step off into space, into unknown and unknowable, flesh carved with hawk-claws and pictographs, shaded by the great image of the desert snake etched in sunburn on your back, and I will vanish gratefully in a puff of raven feathers. Their Plutonian violet-black will float in a sudden hush down to the red rock below, and I will leave you to do this all over again, for that is also the Way, the cry of events sounding again and again like the tide, full-throated. We have walked together before how many times and will again. So it is not really farewell, though each time my heart tells me that it is. You cannot teach the body to know the lay of the Maze, it will insist always on its own telling. You will not remember me in my golden fur, you never do, with your shivering eyes, and next time I will not be a Temple-Monkey. But you will be a humanchild, fevered, forever and ever, for it is your tale in which I am the villain and helpful guide and the scenery and even the shuffling prop master.

There is no end and no beginning. There is only we two, alone in the dark, for always.

31

SHE WAKES, WITH SAND IN HER EYES, FOR IT IS THE LAST DAY.

It is a silver sun, full of diamond sunspots and a nacreous corona, beatific, filling the sky like a supernova. The Monkey, fur made into jewels by the brilliant light, makes her a last breakfast of robin's eggs and wild turnips. Terns wheel overhead, with their lonely cries, watching the gold woman and the gold animal go about their morning tasks. She washes her gleaming face in a fountain, water trickling off her features in sweet rivulets. Her blank eyes have become beautiful, have become hers, and they are polished like copper pots. She eats the steaming turnips and salty eggs slowly, not entirely knowing why she savors them so. The Monkey grooms her (savoring himself this last contact with her wild, coriander-scented mane) and she allows his touch on her bronzed hair, calmed of her night terrors by his deft fingers.

They are near a long Wall, stretching lazily beyond sight in either direction. It is made of living vines and long tendrils of ivy, tangled together like the woman's hair, over and under, over and under. Here and there a fat white blossom opens and shuts with a flutter, like a hand. It is well-kept, tended by some loyal hand. There is no stone beneath, the Wall is entirely leaf and stem, entirely alive, displaying its green like a lady her colored fan.

It is the last morning of all mornings until the next, with its cold light and misty breath, the last grooming and the last fountain-washing. Her limbs creak slightly as though she were truly made of gold, a molten statue-woman walking far from her pedestal. She is pure now, in her lionbody and named, and her flesh is liquid light where the sun strikes her, striding like a flame-deva down the Road which is sullen, ashen, carrying Direction inside her, so *that she faces herself on all sides. The Monkey clambers up her smooth back and takes his place on her glittering shoulder.*

Is it indulgent, perhaps, to take a moment to admire them, their pairing, their shapes against the tooth-white sky, the comfortable lie of his tail around her fleur-de-lis neck, the confident rhythm of her bare feet, the precise matching shades of her skin and his pelt? Is it a distraction to give them this last tableau, this last snapshot under a spring morning, under a willow tree with her eyes laughing?

Let it be. We must make allowances.

CANTO
THE FOURTH

32

FORWARD.

I move forward. There is comfort in my feet, pads thick as rain-boots. I woke up, after all, with the Monkey murmuring over my head. The Wall smells of ambergris and its flowers are weighted like suicides. Hunting the old emerald self, dingy facets of a forgotten sapphire elbow or garnet knee, merrily we go along hunting the sloughed shells of me on this corpulent Road, we highwaymen looking to rob ourselves. Once perhaps I was a streak of charcoal painting the Road like a cannibal, but I could not say. My mind is a laundry line, flapping white wings as a rinsed sky, drops on a tin washboard. (But are there welts on my back, measured kisses of the rack? Oh, yes.)

Here we go round, here we go round and what do I expect from the svelte malarial dawn but another suspense of hours? There is comfort in a tail around one's neck, I suppose. I walk looking down, trying to see what the Grasshopper saw, the prim insects that once were Walls. Trying to see the next step on the Path, trying to see where in these muddy tracks the spider-leg pinpricks twist, trying to divine subsequence as though it were water. (It is as though a thing has been taken from me, now that I am named, now that I am gold. I slip, I cannot hold a thought.

But I am not concerned. The sun shines through me like a sieve, I cannot hold the ragged tuxedo tails of my dream, I slide easily along the Path, a little chipped-paint boat. I cannot think, I can hardly feel my body, the only weight being the fat rose-green Compass resting as solidly as a breadloaf in my spacious belly. I am made of air, suddenly, constructed of my own breath. Because of a name which somehow takes as it is given? Because of a border, a limit, a Wall which walks with me, cradling close.

Call me by name and inchoate I will sidle up to your princely thigh, call me by name and be made an alms-cup, be made mendicant on my Temple steps, be beggared and crippled because I cannot be a word, only a word, a tongue-curl which is me, a flick of lip, a syllable or two, certainly not three, and is this me after all, chained to the sea floor by a creeping sound, vermin of aural combinations? It is not so pretty a madness when it is named, then it is a patient, wrapped in white and pinned to a butterfly board. Then it does not blaze or consume and I am not, I am named and still as Stone, it is not what I wanted, what I came for, no, not what the contract stated, but I will take it with grace—)

"Do you smell it?" The Monkey sniffs the air, alert and aroused, face banging into the air like a hickory switch. "I smell the chlorinated honey-grim, I smell the hominy and loam. Hoo! It is the End."

I looked where he did, and saw nothing but the linear Wall stretching like a cat's claw, and the tallow of the horizon.

"It is an empty day, Monkey. It is a day for walking. I do not think we will find anything. It is a day for Skimming Over, cream from milk."

The Monkey bit his lip and ventured a resigned little chuckle.

"If you like. But I can smell sap and plum sauce. We are Nearing."

"Oh, stop," I sighed, "Can you not speak to me outside of riddle-realm?"

"Should I speak of the Bear we abandoned to his beauty? Should I speak of your visions? Should I preach the Gospel of the Man and the Bar?" He paused like an insect on a leaf. "Should I speak of how I do not wish it, after all this, to be the End?"

"Do you not?" He looked earthward, blushing if a Monkey could blush.

"No. I am accustomed to you now. I should not be surprised. It is always like this, and I am always sad. Hoo. It is the smell of the sky on your shoulders that does it, that roots me to you at the last of all possible moments. Let us try to be quiet. Words spoil everything."

And so we went, softly and methodically, Monkey dozing off on my shoulder and politely remaining smugly silent. And of course I could not see what was ahead, could not see the terminus, the road sign marking the last detour, could not see its nailed boards and blue shadow until we nearly tripped over it.

"I told you, I told you," hooted the Monkey, clapping his little hands. "I smelled it miles ago! Humangirl, your nose is a poor servant. The End! The Uttermost End." He danced a little, though less happily than he once did, when in the delicious throes of proving me wrong.

It was nothing more than a little Door, no higher than my wedding-band waist, arching to a delicate point at its crown, like a Bishop's miter. Deep blue, was the Door, expanse of India ink, flowing tempura-thick over boards knotted and hewn with a dull axe. Vaporous frescoed stars floated around its rim, edges blurred and fading into the expansive blue, giving each a pale aureole, a vague corona. I felt myself falling into the color, as though it were truly a lake and if touched would ripple outwards from my finger. But there was no knob anywhere on its ornate surface, and it did not leap out or gobble us where we stood. In fact, it had not even been following us. We had stumbled on it quiescent and still, and even now it made no move to seize us.

"Why doesn't it want us, Ezekiel?" I marveled, slightly disappointed.

"Do you want it?"

"Well, no, of course not, it's dreadful . . . but . . . I cannot quite say . . . yes, I think I do. It is Not Like the Others."

"No, my Kore, my love, it is not. It is the Last Door, Your Door, and this is the last day. Not the cream but the last dregs of milk. And I must leave you to it." He smiled wanly and scratched his elbow.

"You are a slippery little thing. You come when I do not want you and go when you please. You drag me out of the crone's hut only to leave me here, when I don't even know how to open a Door I shouldn't want ajar. I am nearly dead, if my jaundiced skin didn't advertise it, and you will go and leave this bird's wing Door as my headstone."

I wept a little, but it was cursory, the shedding of such valuable tears as my own metallic drops. (Collect them and be a sultan, be a banker, be a thief of forty) I knew it all along. When long, long now before I lay beneath the radiating Angel I was alone with her, in her arms so cold they burned, and it would be so again. I am the Maiden, and when the Maiden faces the Queen it is alone, so no one will see that she thinks the monarch beautiful and worthy of love, even as she seizes what is hers from those white arms.

"Hoo! Darlinggold, if you think you have been carrying a Key all this Way for any other purpose but to open a Door, then you are a silly girl and you do not know how these stories go. It is the Uttermost End. Everything is simple from here on out." I tried to hide my surprise that he knew of the Lobster's little Key, which I still had nestled in my pack.

"As for the rest, at the end, you are always alone, it is inevitable. The Maiden goes on, the Beast stays behind and catches tears in his whiskers. But as I have tried to tell you, even this is only an event, not a true end. It is the borderland of a sequence of events, but there is no revelation to be had. There is no conceivable end in this place, it goes onandonandon, past the last permutation of a chess game, past the last rose that ever grew. 'Last' and 'End' are meaningless here, and when you go through the Door you will find nothing more than the Road stretching on, *downdowndown*, past where you thought it must end. I have played my part for you, within you. Now it is done and I will go back to what dark corners Beasts originate from, and you to the cloistered courtyard that all Maidens find behind the last Door, even if it is not truly the last. But perhaps it is, after all," his eyes twinkled. "I have been known to lie."

"There is still so much I do not understand," I said softly. "I do not even know, truly, who you are." He threw his skinny arms around my neck and stared into my marble eyes.

"Oh, my darling, I am myself and no other, no other unto the nexus of all possible endings. Look deep enough into my eyes and you will see Roads and Walls extending infinitely, in my pupils lie every twist you have ever walked. I am secretive, I will not give you answers, but there they lie, scattered about like shrapnel."

I swallowed thickly, seeing in those black pools all the miles upon miles, the spurt of a thousandthousand fountains and the right angles of hedge Walls, and the wide Road, extending its massive Avenue like an artery into the body of the Monkey, knotting and turning and opening onto itself, another thick snake breakfasting on his tail, sautéed and served with tea.

"Good-bye, then, Beast," I whispered, awed.

"Good-bye, Kore, my Beauty, my Darlinggold."

"Oh, Ezekiel, what do you see in the sky?"

"Air. Air, all around, like wings."

He covered my face with his hand briefly, tenderly, and I could smell the wheatfields and fallen autumnal apples on his leathery skin. And then he was gone, vaulting over the Wall in an artful leap, tail disappearing over the wild green.

33

I TURNED, CREAKING LIKE A HINGE, BACK TO THE DOOR.

So blue, so blue, and I could hear it panting slightly under its veneer of silence, struggling to wait quietly, like a good girl, and fold her hands under her legs. And I stare, into and at, unable to move when at last it comes to it. It seems such a large step, the span between two sparkling feet.

I draw the Key out of my pack where it had lain since the millennia past when the Lobster clattered. And it too had changed, once the indigo of his baroque claw and my impressionist belly, it had shivered into gold like an autumn tree, nearly disappearing into my palm creased like a map of some lost continent. But the surface of the Door lay as smooth as a child's mouth, no Keyhole marring its oceanic sheen with black.

(—*For the straightforward pathway had been lost.*

Ah me! how hard a thing it is to say—)

Keen and bright the unmarred surface, and I without a guide to point the way with a finger taking up the sky. The Door seemed to laugh, to shake soundlessly with mirth at this hapless girlthing trying to enter its starry girth. (How am I to do this alone, who avoided the Doors so well and gracefully for year upon day?) How to elude one, simple. How to penetrate a laughing fence, I could not say. I am weak and blurred, contours entering themselves and diffusing like the perfume of the harem, My ignorance like a fat jewel, something I could grip in my hand and turn over, marveling at the workmanship. I am playing that same old four-string chord, stretching my sapling fingers to press down on a neck like I was strangling a goose.

I am old, old, now, no Maiden but that very crone with her diseased bones, her desiccation, her bleeding liver, her cataracts. Full of lack, bursting at the perforated edges with emptiness, pressing, pressing

(—*So did my soul, that still was fleeing onward,*
Turn itself back to re-behold the pass—)

pressing in like a tourniquet, and it is her blood that gushes wantonly from my body, sick and congealed. I have progressed, the effort is so tiring, so full of weights, hanging on fish hooks from my beaten breasts, pulling the flesh earthward, to entice the worms. How do I open it? Does she lie on the other side, all lithe paleness and un-mad, un-sick, un-weary? Liquid Stone, airy and full-lipped, surrounded by her throne of flapping fish? I cannot compel her, ever, so full of every Compass ever minted, and I with only my chubby-cheeked one, so pitiful in my belly, shrunk into a corner of acidic solace,

(—*And never moved she from before my face,*
Nay, rather did impede so much my way—)

all quivering magnets and wild needles cutting. I cannot excavate from her womb the fluid of a grimacing umbilicus to heal myself, I cannot put up scaffolding over her snowbody and chip her down to the size of a pill I can swallow and become. I cannot even open her docile Door, her little lapdoor, pink-tongued and eager. I cannot

(—*Thou art my master, and my author thou,*
Thou art alone the one from whom I took—)

for will I once in the cloistered cobbledstones be hers again, to write on, to be carved, to be marked by her terrible black tongue, to be her shuddering paper? I have no long yellow teeth to show like crescents suns, how without a Monkey by to scream and gnash, will I keep her from scrawling over me againagainagain?

But the Door, (did the Door and swifter than I) the Door waiting for its answer, its correct walk-on-three-legs-in-the-evening magic words, the sibilant slip of a Key into its body.

And though its body is smooth and coherent, perfect polygon of gleam, mine is not, battered and meringued I, with pores like chasms burned there by my claws and ragged voice and I have always lain open as a book, read and skimmed and coffee-spilled, left spine akimbo. Because of the ease of sliding a Key between arm and rim, between the ulna and the radius bones, between the socket joints of my legs. Because I can be pried open like a window.

(—Behold the beast, for which I have turned back;
Do thou protect me from her—)

And so if the Maze has twisted in me, bone-Key hair-Key meat-key opening my chameleonbody to it and all its fingers and all its mouths and all its teeth, so may I twist in myself, (all things ending in the body) and open the Maze.

I took the Key in a shimmering hand, caught into fire by the afternoon sun, netted into a sphinx's paw by shafts of pikelight. Well wrought the delicate shell, serrated edge of claw forming the Key ridges, where it would fit and swivel. The Door seemed to hold its breath, chest swollen with amphibious lungs full up, peering to see if the correct sequence would be followed, the correct procedure observed, if custom and usualhow would dance as they were used, hand in hand.

Holding it like a blade I stood statuesque, arm outstretched like an orator to deliver scathe and curse.

(—Thee it behooves to take another Road—)

And I plunged, delved, dug, stabbed it deep into the brittle surface, oh and the severing blow of fracture and slither (*ininininin!*) into the soft place between my coin-breasts, where there is a fine down like a gasp, and oh, the grinding as it chews inward, the molten gold blood sluicing from the sucking wound which is so like a mouth, so like the opening to a jeweled womb, so like an iris. (*Ininin!*) Rushing blood warms the Keybody, it is deeper than inward and I cannot see for the pain, the pain of opening which is always present at these little penetrations—

(—Forth issued from the sea upon the shore,
Turns to the water perilous and gazes—)

See how soundless, accommodating, finger-crooked, the Door moves open a sliver, not enough to bite and tear, but enough for me to slip inside, like a Key. Its breath winds out like a thread soaked in gasoline, sour, tonguing the skein of air between us, searching for me, for the blood it smells. See it wait, still so patient, expecting that if I will not step I will certainly fall if I bleed just a little more. (*Ininin!*)

But, oh, oh, see that the blood is not gold any longer, any longer, and how I have side-shifted the spectrum one last (but it is never the last) time, one last chloroform masquerade, one last ball with slippers worn through, one last night on the town under all those lights! I have flashed trans-parent, trans-lucent, cut glass, clear as the rivers of Babylon, and how the sun shines through me as though I were a goblet at the feast! Oh, how the clouds reflect milky in my brow, in my Grecian eyes, my singing foot! Fled color and now there is only light, light, light. I am made of light, brooks and streams, hair cascading like snakes from a glass-blower's pipe, pure and clean and clear at last, but it is never last, never last. I can move in any Direction, I hold all Direction within, and oh! See now it lying prettily within, the Compass with its thorn-needles and bouncing glacial norths! My little child, my little dusk-daughter so nestled in the glass belly, flushing all your greens and pinks, indignant at the disappearance of flesh. I am glad to see you, little one! Where shall we go, where shall we go? Forward is the only remaining place, I'm afraid, we must suffer to be eaten again, *ininin* and down, here we fly and fall. Into the Door at neverlast, slip of light we!

(—I cannot well repeat how there I entered—)

And I step within, hush inside, whisper through, and there is a vanishing, of a perfect crystal foot as the deep azure of the Door closes with a coquettish latch.

34

"I SUPPOSE YOU THINK YOU'VE ARRIVED SOMEWHERE.

That you have won a thing, that you have *passedthrough*, achieved a fetching Grail."

Comes her voice like a grinding Stone, on her fishing-Wall as I knew she would be, covered in her opals like eggs, watersurface-shimmering, wings curving over her long back to the icy earth. The wound and the Key had together vanished from my glassy sternum. Her court of mercurial trout heaped themselves still along her white thighs as she exhaled that same noose of nettle-smoke, watching me with eyes like gutters trimmed in icicles.

"Hic monstra, hic monstra, *puella*. I suppose you think you have come all this Way and found me out, found a Lair, found a wicked, wicked Creature, a *femme fatale*, a Villain."

I sucked in my breath, blood ticking in my temples, and replied, "Angel, I have come through a Door. I suppose nothing more than that. But it did not capture me, I chose it."

"And now," she hissed, "you think I will wave my magic rod and reel, and heal you, you who disdain my frescoes and chuck my lovely navel-Stone down the gullet of a Monkey. Wretched girl, ignorant glass-piece, for your pleasure I will do nothing."

"I did not think you would. And I cannot make you do it."

I walked slowly to the foot of her alabaster Wall, through the familiar pale of her courtyard.

"I have no artifice, no companion, nothing to seek after. I am here blown clear as the southern sand, offering only myself, and you know you have been expecting me." I smiled my most charming smile.

"Why do we not at least fish together awhile, since I have come all this Way?" I held out a crystal hand to her, crossed with lines like longitude or—*(in this sign thou shalt conquer)* to be helped up onto the slippery Wall.

"You have come no distance at all, girlchild."

But she hefted me up and by her side, handing the rod to me, and smoking resentfully. "They are biting on Grasshoppers this afternoon, young and crisp," she added. The Angel puffed her pipe like a squid sluices its ink. The fishing line trailed down to the icy Road like a web, into the neatly cut circle and frothing Roadwater. I held the arch of the rod gingerly, not knowing what next to say to her who regarded me with a catlike stare.

"Ask yourself, infant, how many times we have sat thus, among all these writhing fish. Ask yourself how many times we will yet smoke together under this tumor-white sky. And still you think it is an act of moment for me to heal your pathetic little death. You always do. I tire of patching you like corduroys." She exhaled from her carved nose.

"I have sat with you but once, Angel, when you gave me this sickness like a slice of cake."

"Yes, of course, dear. I am terribly wicked. And this *petite* scene has been played only once, only once. Why, we hardly know our lines! We must practice, a thousandthousand more times, until we choke on their dust."

I fixed the rod into a crack in the Wall, ignoring the thrashing pulls at the line.

"I have gone mad for you, as you wished me, as Ezekiel said it must be, lost in marshes and under red robes, I have lost my eyes and eaten my name and it has all been because you could not let me be, you could not let my walking lie, you wanted me and so I have become what you wanted. Why do you mock what you made?" I stared blank-eyed at the repetition of Wall-rims endless to the horizon and further on.

"It is my entertainment, to watch you flop and gasp like one of my little trout. You would not rob me of that, my *puella*, no. Do you not see what you have achieved? Completion, End. At least a facsimile of it. It is so beautiful. And your singularity is the best of all. You cast a shadow neither sunward nor back, it is only *alwaysnow*, for you. That is enviable. But you have done it without Purpose, without intent, and so it means nothing. You still and always understand nothing of what I could have given you. I would have made you a Hero, you would have been made entirely of blaze, and eaten the Labyrinth in a swallow, so great would have been your need. As it is, you have found your Way to the End, and you do not even know it, because you would not accept the Quest. The function of a Quest, my function, is merely to make the End significant—you squandered me."

"But it would have been illusion. Nothing is the reality, the absence of Center and meaning. I carried it like a shawl around my shoulders. You would have laughed as I drowned naked."

"How vivid. Cling to your little cliffs, if you must. My gifts are vast." She bent her archer's mouth around the ivory pipe. "Oh, humanchild, must we do this, must we play this game where I am a frightful Witch and you are the brave Maiden? Don't you want to play something else? I am very nice, you know. Put your mouth on my wrist, it tastes of peppermint. Wouldn't it be more fun? Why don't you be the witch this time?" She smiled for the first time, teeth like a row of soldiers, leonine and seductive. I felt my old helplessness roving.

"I am dying and you speak of games. How long do you think I can sit at chatter before nightfall when I will be mad again? Give me what I came for." The Angel shook her sapphire head.

"Oh, all right. You are such a stubborn little caryatid. You must always have it *precise*." She cleared her throat dramatically and fluttered her razor wings wide.

"I will *not!*"

I spread my hands, hopelessly confused, lips parting in anguish, unable, at this last which is not last, to comprehend her animal mouth. She moved close, trailing her fingers from my waist to my chin, slowly, tattooing cold into my flesh, her dark eyes drawing those same snail-patterns inkless on glass skin.

"Oh, pretty little thing, we all play our parts for you. Do you like it, precious *puella*? Are we very good at what we do? Do we satisfy each and every night when that red, red curtain goes up? All of us glossy little ducks in a row? Do you love us, dearest, darling, only? Will you clap, clap, clap? Shall I bow at the end as I yield? Oh, Darlingglass, will you laugh at *all the right parts?*"

She laughed herself, deep in her throat, an intimate rumbling as she lay her silky head on my terrified chest. "It is all an act, my own, but it is all there is. All we have, you and I. The rapiers are real, the duel is true. But you never see the stage, tragicsylph. I suppose I cannot ask for that much. I am a witch forever, and you will fear and never love me."

"Please," I whispered through loose and prismed lips, "take it out of me, take it out, let me be whole."

"You are close to the skin, now, beautiful, close to the rim, dancing out beyond its edge. You could put out your smallest finger and see the pattern. But it is not, after all, the Way of things. Come, come now, you must play your part, too. Threaten me, put your hands on my throat, tell me you will surely kill me like a brave and good Maiden ought to, if I do not wipe you clean as a window."

She leaned upon me like a divan, smiling her disturbing kittenish smile, bewildering and lithe, full of snow. I put my hand tentatively over her mouth, shrill cold screaming lip to palm with the contact, and her eyes twinkled with mirth above the flesh-hyphen.

"Just stop laughing at me and help me. Or I . . . I shall. I shall throw all your fish back into the Road and shovel in the hole. I will snap your pipe and your rod. And . . . I shall Devour you piece by piece down to your last feather. I can do it." I spoke in measured beats and though I didn't really want to harm her, I understood instinctively that it was the Way. That was clear now, clear as I was.

"Oh, *brava*, darling," she said, muffled by my hand which I removed without expression. "It is so very hard to be strong when you need something from someone."

"I want to be well. I am not your mouse to bat between paws. I want to be as I was. I shall go if you do not, and whiten to dust among the poplars and whitethorn. and then you will have no one."

The Angel's face flushed with her pearl-blue light, her corona pulsing once, twice.

"Oh, Darlingglass, don't get upset. This is all pre-determined, after all, written on the whalewalls in indelible ink, at least more indelible than mine. You cannot blame me for wanting to drag it out a bit. You are such lovely company. Kore, Kore, after all is done and done again, there is no end and no beginning, there is only we two, alone in the dark, for always."

She leaned forward in a cloud of yucca blossom tobacco and ambergris, her face filling up my vision like a moon, and touched her lips to mine. I shrank back from her glacial kiss, breathing in gulps.

"My dear, this is how it is done. The Kiss that heals the Maiden, removes the thorn from her thumb. I gave you your delirium with a Kiss, and I take it back, as you have commanded. It is the Way. You have been such a good girl all this time, right on cue, will you allow propriety to keep your death snuggled up inside, just below your heart, safe and warm?"

She touched the skin of my sternum, where the Key had thrust, and leaned in again. This time I did not shrink, but allowed her snowdrift lips on mine, pressing like a vise, crushing the blood from my face, and the delicate bones, pushing her face downward (*downdowndown*) drawing me upward like a bucket from a well. Chewing lightly on my lower lips, still connected thus, she whispered, "At the other side of a Door lies nothing but another Door, and another, and another."

Each "another" was punctuated by the press of her diamond teeth on my mouth. "I am the Door that catches you, and you must step through me, limb by limb. Come in, come in, my Darlingglass, it is the Way. Hoo."

Her eyes were shut and in the sheen of her high cheeks I could see my reflection, irises large and green as sugar cane. I moved forward, only slightly, only slightly, an intake of breath, and I slid through the scrim of ice, I breathed through her skin, passing through her body and the wriggling trout and the ice caves like Temples, through the river-network of her veins, where fish upon scaled fish spawned towards her great silver heart, booming cavernously,

(*thumpthumpthump*)

and I passed the threshold of her bones, and I passed the barrier of her spine, (*ininin!*)

and I breached the Wall of her muscled back, flowing through her in one long inhale. I went through her like a pane of glass.

My last hand disappeared through her torso with an exhale of smoke, smelling slightly of apples strewn over a field of cut wheat.

35

Such a simple thing, opening a Door.

Stepping through, the familiar series of movements, the old village dance. Feeling the rush of air as it shuts behind. So simple and sweet, to be whole in the dark. I understand now. I accept. The revelation is complete only here, in the soon-gone second, with nothing but blackness all around. This has all happened before. It will happen again. I can see myself stretching forward and back like a chain of paper dolls, walking through echoes and shadows of each other, held and rocked to sleep by the Labyrinth, which is constant and adoring. I understand. For one instant, I see the pattern before it is consumed again like a burned photograph.

There is only one Man, and only one Bar, and they walk into each other, and they are the same.

And once through there is, of course, only another Door, a little flame pulsing civilly and softly. And so I fall, again and again, end over end which is not. *Downdowndown.*

CANTO
THE FIFTH

36

LOOK CLOSELY. THIS IS NOT THE WAY.

Up or down, I could not say, I could not say. I ate the severed halves of a Compass Rose seven-hundred-and-negative-eight miles back, covering the yellow red meat with lime skins and choking it down. Now it is Within. So I could not say northwest or south, only the veil-fire *that way* and the moon-forest *this way*, this turn or that turn, round the oleander Wall rippling underwater or over the mandrake Wall salivating on my hand as I execute a three-quarters pike half-caffeinated flip over its thick shoulders. My body is bound with guitar strings, nipples like fawn's hooves strumming E minor chords and finger-picking a Path through resonant briars, redolent of the desert bellies of blue lizards. By now my feet are worn through, holes like mouths gaping and smacking in cathedral soles, pounding, thrusting on the Path like a drum-skin stretched into incandescence, finding that old comfortable rhythm that by now I know so well, that I invented out of dust and the sweat beading prettily on my own calves.

It is all familiar now, after the passage of constellations and the ingestion of the Compass Rose, holding now that flaming cross inside me, *in this sign thou shalt conquer*, north-brow south-hips east-wrist west-thigh, in this sign thou shalt walk until the end of days, in this sign thou shalt blaze and burn, in this sign thou shalt stride tall through this Place, this happy Garden of Lies, in this sign thou shalt eat berries and lie under the moon, and let it tan your skin silver.

I carry Direction inside me like a child, a watery infant daughter of a circuit of dawns, connected by the fibrous strength of my spinal fluid and thread sun from the enamel of my teeth. She, in all her diamond gills and sunfish fins is anchored in my rich belly, wrapping her precious little Compass-form in my umbilicus like a mummy, and so I am her sarcophagus, too. Her mother and her coffin.

And the directions never change, magnetic north is always at the crown of my mercurial head, south always at the arch of my holy foot, for I carry the Rose within, growing like a Vedic moon. O serpentine I, having a tail fat with scales linked like opaline chain mail, and thus no way to give birth to this precise little cat-child, kept inside an adamant muscle wall. It pushes against my ribcage, stretching the skin of my lifting belly. Amphibious and infertile, webbed into frozen fecundity, Great-With-Child, never Birthed, never Mother. Trapped in the swallowing, breasts heavy and pendulous with milk, unable ever to feel the tug of that small mouth against them. Ever huge with the weight of oceans, of a thousandthousand mountains, halted in freeze frame like an urn. Ambrosial blood swimming between us, the eater and the eaten and the eater again, sucking at the soil of the womb like a clear-petaled lilac. And in this habit of motion-forward, I have learned:

The Void of the Labyrinth does not exactly stretch, or exactly coil, or exactly twist. But it *snarls*. A bolt of belligerent lightning-silk angrily unraveled, corded, torn, circumnavigating itself in a rattling feint, coming apart and crushing in. And it changes, like the horned moon, cycling without pattern. Walls mutate like film noir rape scenes, tearing at pearl skirts with mud-brick fingers that leave stigmatic bruises.

Roads. Oh god, I cannot speak of it, but the Roads have filled me entirely, stuffed and crammed into every corner, oozing out of my body like icy caviar. They are my avenue-bracelets and my fat sapphire street chokers, my gold scarab short-cut armbands and my boulevard harem anklets, they are my cobblestone coin belts and my alleyway-agate earrings. Long Paths criss-cross my torso like ammunition belts, and the innumerable dead-ends pierce my breasts beautifully, hanging pendulously, swinging with laughter, slapping triumphantly against my bronzed belly.

And. There are here tremors of Doorways. They appear in the morning like dew-dampened butterflies, manic and clever. They travel in packs. At night the hinges change from right to left, or vanish completely. Some are no more than flaps of fur, iridescent in the light of the Walls, or sweeping veils of gauze and silk, long curtains like a woman's hair. Like my hair. Some are hard and ornate, carved with a fantastic code of Arabic and Greek, letters drawn in a paste of crushed diamonds and the hooves of a drowned horse, written with the elegant tip of a black cigarette holder. These have heavy knockers and bulbous knobs, brassy and baronial, in intricate shapes; I have seen a knob like a griffin's fierce mouth, open in a scream with her tongue made of rose quartz, feathers fanning out magnificently in silver on the face of the Door. And a falcon-claw knocker all of amber, the reptilian talon, the three terrible nails ending in their razor points, all wrapped about with the leather of bondage, the flying trails of a hunter's bird cascading down the polished Door, ending in a large lacquered ball with which to strike and enter.

But they are not beautiful to me, any longer. They cluster whispering and break and dance in and out of vision. And they hunt. Like sleek foxes they creep along the places where the Wall meets the Road and wait. They will glide up silently and swallow you as you lie beneath a sighing willow, or stalk you through three dozen twists and turns of the Labyrinth, seizing you as you come upon one of the long boulevards. They are savage creatures, and hungry. On what do they open? I have learned only to avoid them, and I could not say. I did not exactly *come* here, and I will not exactly *go*. I have always been Here, I have always been about to escape. I have never been *arrived*, always *in transit*, slowly digested by the Road with Doors snapping at my heels. I will never tell the tale of:

"One day I woke up and I was here."

But perhaps it was so, I could not say. Then equally perhaps I shall one day fall asleep and be not here. If this is true, what came before has dissolved from me, lost like milk teeth. But I think, rather, that it has always been as it is, and there was never a *beforethis* nor will be an *afternow*. I am accepting. This is not a thing to be solved, or conquered, or destroyed. It is. I am. We are. We conjugate together in darkness, plotting against each other, the Labyrinth to eat me and I to eat it, each to swallow the hard, black opium of the other. We hold orange petals beneath our tongues and seethe. It has always been so. It grinds against me and I bite into its skin.

I accept. It is not always unpleasant under this particular cubic yardage of sky. I once (will? never?) thought in miles and leagues, counting my measured footsteps with my abacus-lips. I once chanted the low, quiet black magic of numbers and distance, of meters and kilometers like coiled snakes in baskets. I wrote over my whole body with sap, calculating how many times my feet had abused the earth, how many times the stones had gnawed my toes. No more, I have forgotten numbers. I washed the sap in a marble fountain of a serpent-woman spewing clear water from her gaping mouth, that despairing cavern. And I walked on, my pack secure on squared shoulders. I accept.

I am not exactly alone. There are Others. Of course there are the Doors, and they are company of a brutal sort, but I glimpse now and again a flash of golden fur or tinfoil tail in a stream. And I hear rustling in the nights that is not the sibilant gliding of an impending Door. I could not say what creeps and whispers through the branches and down the threaded Road, but I hear it, and I am not afraid.

I am the Seeker-After. I am the Dragon and the Damsel, I am the Castle and the Dungeon, the Mad and the Madness. I am the Man and the Bar, I am the Sword and the Flesh. I am the Player and the Game.

I am the Walker and the Maze.

YUME NO HON:

THE BOOK OF DREAMS

AUTHOR'S NOTE: The chapter headings are taken from the Japanese calendar of the Heian period, which are in turn adapted from the Chinese calendar, which is made up of 72 divisions.

The chapter "Rotted Weeds Metamorphose Into Fireflies" is in part adapted from the Enuma Elish, a Babylonian creation myth.

The world of dew
Is the world of dew
And yet, and yet—
—Issa

THE EAST WIND MELTS THE ICE

Put a truce to any thoughts of departure. I am she who glides through the sky when the snow is falling fast, the lady of frost and darkness. I am a ghost, which is not to say I ever lived. I am a memory, which is not to say I ever died. I begin at the moment the ice on the river begins to crack like bones of glass. I am a silence written on pulp-mash paper, in ink drawn from village-wells.

Inward is the only conceivable direction. All arrows point within. So too, this book, which faces *down* and *in*, along the sallow thread of my tongue, into darkness and out again.

If I were to tell you that I am an old woman-hermit, who lives on the side of a mountain I cannot name in the year of the ascension of Taira Kiyomori, this would be true. It would, of course, be as true to say I stood outside the Theban wall whose mud-bricks are the color of pages and asked riddles with lips of verdigris. It would be as true to say I drove six brown horses around the walls of a burning city, that I gathered my husband in fourteen pieces and knelt in delta-silted river reeds with my arms full of his flesh. It would be as true to say I invented the world last year, from coffee beans and plantain leaves mixed in my veins. We are a body of Contradiction, flesh-full and fleshless.

But perhaps I am just a mad old woman squatting in the wreckage of a pagoda halfway up the mountain, mending my sandals for the seventeenth time and scraping in my bean patch, waiting for the new green shoots to slide out of the earth like stars. Perhaps I am only she, Ayako of One-Name-Only, who each night brews a sour tea of dandelion roots and watches the stars slide out of the sky like bean-shoots. It is possible that I only dream her, her rags and thin hands, her snow-cold calves and breathing eyes. It is possible I have never been anything but her.

If I do not dream her, then these are *my* hands deep in the soil of the Mountain whose silence booms in her heart as though it were an empty hall. If I do not dream her, then the others are a mist on the wild goose's wing , the dream of my lion-haunches and terrible teeth.

I wish to be dreaming her, so that I may call these others true.

LARVAE BEGIN TO TWITCH IN THEIR COCOONS

(To be alone is to work at solitude. It is very difficult, a lifetime's work, like the building of a temple. The first years are the carving of steps from camphor wood and the bodies of infant cicadas. Desire is still present like a moth—he flits onto your hair, your thigh, your smallest toe. He sits so quietly, small and brown, intricate as leaves. And you are not truly alone, because he is there, slightly furry against your skin, breathing.

The next years are the erection of a great Gate, red as poppy-wine, with guardian statues of jasper and knuckled silver. Now you are learning, you have begun to fashion your solitude with skilled hands, to chisel away at all that is not loneliness, to dwell in seclusion as you would in moon-white larval flesh. Desire has gone, but Need remains, and you look down the path for the shape of any human at all. Soon you begin to dream that they come. Your joints have begun to fuse, to make an utterly separate beauty.

The interior hall comes next, in shadow and rough-cut incense. You had thought yourself a Master already, but in these years like flapping crows you begin to scream, and your screams become the temple bells of perfect bronze, and you clutch their silken ropes, caught in the great work. These are the maddened years, when you have only the strangling Self. You are a pre-suicidal mass. There is no release from it now, and you begin to sow seeds in a little garden, understanding for the first time that there are no endings for you.

After a bushel of winters tied with chewed leather, the roof is laid out, corners dipped in boiling gold, arcing up towards the sky, which has begun to speak to you. You have polished and cut and painted with hawk's blood the edifice of your solitude, and it shines so under the dead moon.

And you are the icon, the holy relic to be housed. Your bones have calcified into sanctity. You are the created thing, unfathomably apart, clothed in antlers and rain-spouts. There is nothing now but you and Alone, not even a body, which long ago hushed itself into the snow-storms. It is completed, your *magnum opus*. A fontanel has re-appeared at the crown of your head, pulsing gold and silver—you are an infant again in the arms of the empty air.)

I have been alone for a long time.

FISH SWIM UPSTREAM,
BREAKING THE ICE WITH THEIR BACKS

The dream-pagoda has five floors. It is red like dripping wax and in my cloud-body I have not climbed to the top. I think I meant to, once, but the cycles of fat salmon spawning took my smooth limbs and left juniper twigs. I huddle, or she does, the dream-Ayako, on the first level, against a wall that was once lacquered green and blue.

I cannot tell if it *is* me curled on the damp earth. The gray spider perched on her dusty wall seems equally myself. I apologize, it is what happens when the loneliness is built up and frescoed in costly paints. Solitude becomes populated with a legion of selves, each laid on each like stacked frames of film, like pig's ears in the noontime market, or the floors of a pagoda that once was red. The original is lost, just one of a thousand thousand silvern copies, scattered upwind.

Laying over the dream-tower is the dream-wall. It is brown, glum-grained and jaundiced by a Sun which frowns under her straw hat. Dream-men pressed the earth together to build it, and now it is my Nest. In this copy, which is not Ayako but comes from her like a long braid which begins at her crown, I can feel the bristle of fur like a bronze brush on my thighs, the jut of morphine-wings on my back. It is the dream of the lion-haunches, which is familiar as a shoe.

A Boy comes to the dream-wall. He is smooth and brown as an almond tree, with wide-set eyes and a cruel mouth. His hips sing of palm-oiled pleasures and I like him in a moment, because his beauty touches me like a hand. My paws are deep-padded and hungry—I breathe his smell in sheaves, smell of cinnamon and burned bread. My belly yearns for him, knows he is meant for me, will swell inside me like a black apple. I am certain of him, of how he will feel inside me, how his sweat will taste.

But he is waiting for me, and I oblige, for the dream-body knows the thing for which it is intended. Riddles, and games, and adulation.

"What is my name?" I ask in a voice like the sound of the Mountain gnawing his knees. The Boy looks at me with a quixotic raise of his brows.

"That is not a very good riddle," he replies, and I let his voice slide through me like spiced honey. He is worried, now, for he must suspect that he cannot possibly guess the answer among the possible answers that spread out in his brain like a Euclidean plane. When he attempts it, I can hear his tongue thicken in his mouth.

"You are named Truth, for only Truth can loose what is bound."

And it is a good answer, better than most can dredge from themselves, pulling their words up like wooden well-buckets. My belly exults.

"No, beautiful boy, dream-within-dream. I am called She. She who travels when the snow flies fast. She who devours with woolen teeth. She who asks. I am all possible shes. There is no other She born under any mockery of a moon. I am the she-Wolf, the she-Axe, the she-Belly. I am the destination of that which is He. I cannot be guessed, and I am never known."

And then the dream-boy was inside me, in my throat and in my lion's stomach, whose ulcerated walls pulse in time to the flooding of rivers. My teeth drank him, and I slept in the corpulent sun.

Woman rises out of no-woman, and Ayako stirs in her sleep.

RIVER OTTERS SACRIFICE FISH

Metamorphosis. It is a long line of bellies, chained together flesh-wise, circling each other in a blood-black smear. The sparrows pick cold red berries from the mud, the hawks pluck the sparrows from the sky. The fish swallow grasshoppers, the otters gulp down the fish. The world eats and eats and eats, and stomach to stomach it embraces itself. Hawk is Berry, Otter is Grasshopper. Woman is Fish and Sparrow.

Ayako sees this as she watches the new sun tiptoe on the river. She understands it, for she, too, has a belly which longs to pull creatures into it. The I-that-is-Ayako knows that dream-bellies also connect, along a strange umbilicus of tamarind bark and snow-pea shells. In the half-shelter of our ruined pagoda, I can see the stars, the constellations rotating in their angular anatomy. Over my/our flaxseed hair the kimono-sleeve stars tumble like lost feathers. The river whispers arcane spells, thick-voiced and gurgling with pleasure at the face it holds in its ripples, which is mine. The dream-face, with eyes of new apples, for in dreams, all eyes are green. The River and the Mountain split me between them—they have a treaty which is re-negotiated regularly. Codicils are added, addendums and appendices drawn up with rustling laughter. There is no time here—Thursday has been killed in his sleep. They can afford to wait.

It is a small dream, this. It follows the seasons and eats orange kabocha squash boiled with wild greens. And into the dream occasionally some black-eyed boy or girl comes, to bring me a sack of rice or a little box of tea. They come from the dream-village, which has not the gentility to know it is a dream, because they pity the old woman on the Mountain. And I long to ask them riddles they cannot answer, I long to hold them belly-to-belly. They go back down the Mountain with innocent feet, back to huts and *miso* and smoked fish.

Because in her body, I hardly speak at all any longer. The rusted brass hinges of my voice have gathered dust. I put my/our hands to the soil of the garden, and can feel the heat of growing things, meant to be soon inside my body. The Mountain marks me, knows I am meant to be in *his* belly, etching his shape against the sky-that-is-not, pinioning the woman, the cobbled personae, the dancing cranes and bobcats and lizards and singing monkeys and squirrels to the slivers of dreams pretending to be stones. He gathers his blue and green and white to consume me, he gathers the gray and the gold. His chortling streams and the meadows lie restful and sweet, as though the moon-goddess had smoothed an emerald taffeta dress over her slender knees. He is impassive and huge, he mocks and waits.

Inside her/me the dreams are burning, falling, raw as bark-stripped pine. There is no sound where they step, for it is possible they are not really there, that these shadows are not theirs, that she is not doubled and tripled, tumbling backwards through bodies like scalding water.

And some secret avalanche on the far side of the Mountain rumbles as he clears his diamond throat.

WILD GEESE GO NORTH

I dreamed cannon-winds shot through my belly; each strand of wind carried talons and curved beaks which tore my flesh. My navel was cut out like a coin, my mouth was filled with dead leaves. I dreamed that I was the first belly. I dreamed my flesh dark and star-sewn. My womb bore up under a five-clawed hand, slit down a scarlet meridian, and black daises grew from the skin of its depths.

I dreamed it was Mountain who passed all these canine winds into me. He put his slate-blue mouth to me and took a breath that serrated the edge of the world. I felt his caves erupt in me, his glaciers and his footholds. I dreamed it was River who held me still, gripped my forearms in his hands like otter's paws.

I dreamed that I cried out to Moon, but she had been eaten whole.

The winds were in me and marauding, the teeth of Mountain nursing at my womb, and he filled me with migrating birds, he filled me with blade-wings that carved pictographs on the inside of my bones, where I could not read them. I dreamed that Mountain shook with pleasure as he emptied all his stones into me, the boulders and the pebbles and the granite flanks, and the sharpest wind which blows at his peak.

When I was filled with stone until I was too heavy to whisper, and wind until I was a body of breath, I dreamed that Mountain and River tore me to pieces with their teeth. They put my throat and my breasts into the sky frothing with whitecap-stars, and my thighs into the glistening rice-fields. They put my arms into the sea that boiled with serpents, and my hands into the desert, palms downturned.

And between them they ate my womb on silver plates, and called it perfection, called it their precious-sweet, their horn-of-plenty, their best work. They sugared it with marrow and lapped with agate tongues.

I dreamed I was dead in them, I dreamed I was scattered over the rims of earth.

And I dreamed that when he had swallowed his last, and I was a spot of blood on his beard, Mountain began to laugh.

SEEDLINGS SPROUT

The I-Ayako is satisfied with the progress of the beans. They have not broken the scrim of soil yet, but she can hear them wriggling beneath, like butterflies. She is worried about the turnips. Next year she will have courage enough to ask the dream-villager for some wheat to plant. She looks now to the crocuses peeking up their candle-tips. They will not keep her alive, but they are so sweet on her little pink tongue.

The wind is still cold when it comes down from the Mountain after its prayers on the peak. She would like to say it is a kimono that she pulls around her thin body for warmth, but long ago it abandoned its pinks and yellows and seems now little more than a blank cloth flung upon her.

My/her mouth aches like a shut box. I want so to speak, to moisten my lips and make my own wind-ablutions, add my verses to the Mountain's long poem. I am afraid it is broken, its tumblers have shattered in the winter freeze.

Thus one evening I went to sit at the foot of gnarled old Juniper near my pagoda and told him my story, which sprouted from my throat like a plum-tree. I do not know the juniper's name, but he is a good listener, and the moon rustled his branches while I spoke in a cobwebbed voice.

"When I was a girl and had a fine brocade *obi* and soft sandals, I lived in the dream-village. (I suppose it is possible that this is only a vision like the others, but I am here, and so I must have come from a Place, and one place-tale is as good as another.)

I had seven brothers who were all very wise and brave and they protected the huts and the market and the temple. But then came terrible men with their bodies covered in leather and iron, who swung long swords against the wind which screamed as they bit into flesh. They killed everyone, even my poor mother with her hair like a spider's best web, and they burned the temple to the ground.

I hid under a wheelbarrow for three days, until they had gone and the dream-village smoked black. I was very afraid. I wandered among the ashes of the bodies and wept.

Near dawn on the seventh day after the men had left, a Sparrow came to me with a fat red berry in her mouth. She ruffled her fine brown feathers at me and spoke: "Go and see Mountain," she said, "he will be your village, your father and your mother and all your seven wise brothers." Her fluted voice drifted off and, dropping the berry at my feet, took flight eastwards, towards the craggy toes of the sacred Mountain.

And so I took what clothes I could, a leaky water-sack I could mend, and the fat red berry and I went up the Mountain, following the path of the Sparrow.

It was evening again when I found her, perched atop my pagoda, picking at the ruined paint with her little gold beak. I waited for her to speak again, eager for bird-magic, but she did not. I held the berry out to her in my small white hand and she caught it deftly as she flew back to the village, leaving me to the tower and the Mountain.

It was difficult for the first years, when I had no rice or tea, but Mountain provided for me cherries and plums and chestnuts, almond milk and cold green apples. After a time, people returned to the dream-village and children began to come to me and bring me little presents. Since I am a ghost, they wish to appease me.

And so we sit together and watch the origami-clouds, our dream-village of Mountain, Tower, River, Juniper, and I."

PEACH BLOSSOMS OPEN

They are suddenly here, floating on the trees like a cloak of butterflies, a blush creeping through their white petals. Suddenly the pagoda has beautiful handmaids which shower it with pale silks. There is warmth hushing through the sky. I lie under the trees with their flower-veils drooping low and I dream that in the afternoon I can see the eyes of a dream-husband in the blossoms.

I lay dreaming on the long-haired grass, legs brown and smooth as a sand dune, arched at the knee at the same angle as the tip of the Mountain, as the line that divides the sun-stone from the moon-stone, the shadowed side from the light. My toes wound in the reeds, tiny emerald rings on the dream-darkened skin, set with the diamonds of milky toenails.

See what in what regalia my dreams clothe me! Violets brush the small of my back with lithe, sugary movements. The scald of blue above me like a velvet gown, cut low on the horizon of my breast, clasped with clouds at the shoulders. See how it covers me in veils and layers of silk, rustling against my now-royal thighs with secretive grace, how it moves against me and strokes the skin. And the gnarled intricacy of these roots of a mountain ash for my Crown, jeweled in sap and leaves yellow as papyrus. What sovereignty my dreams supply! I am clothed in sky and bough, crowned in arboreal splendor. I laugh softly, let the wind imbibe my voice, the tonality melt into nothing like the wax of a candle-clock.

Lying so I looked up into the wind-braided branches of the dream-tree, its skin brown as the paint-pigment, the pale green of leaves against profound cerulean, the pink shimmer of flowers glinting like voices. They gleamed in the molten light, bright as blood, bright as the Dog-Star in the deep-blue days of summer to come. And slowly I saw, in the interchange of colors, red, green, brown, blue, white, that two of the blossoms were not blossoms, that their shade was not rose but the familiar olive-gold of his eyes, the dream-husband, staring blankly down from the branch, become the season's first fruit, snagged on a splinter of rose-tinged wood. Heavy-lidded, still rimmed in the kohl I mixed with my own fingers in red clay pots until the tips became black as cat's claws. I tenderly darkened his eyes that past dream-morning when he broke into pieces. I ran my fingertip over the fringe of eyelashes, letting my lips brush the iris as I move from eye to eye.

And now I lie under those eyes, against a tree which may or may not be on Mountain's flank, on the banks of the reed-jeweled river. I watch dream-crocodiles warming their bellies in the sun, regarding their mates with a fond reptilian eye.

I dreamed I had no trail to follow, that he left no blood-path. The dream-husband, the dream-brother, left me to scramble after him and clutch his body to me like a penance. I wandered, merely wandered, like a caravan-woman, my hair tied up into a crimson veil to keep the smoke-black length off my back. I did not speak, except to the hawks which flew at my shoulders, and they were silent.

But I also dreamed that beside me ever walks she, the second, or perhaps third self who knows none of this. I wander in her like an echo.

THE SKYLARK SINGS

The sun pealed out a hundred bronze bells smattered blue by a bleeding sky.

Standing in the sacred "I" of limbs caught to torso, of *alone* on a mossy stone with the stars combing my hair. I have smelled the sizzle of my curls. I have clawed and screamed but no one would venture close enough, no one's arm ever lengthened to cup this body like a grail, and the Mountain gobbled my voice like krill.

They are pathetic, my solitude and my dreams, they are sodden and grotesque, dripping their shame on the summit path, the filigree branches, the gossiping reeds. The river roses tangled in a smear of obscene red as the dawn spilled like milk over the tops of austere trees.

It is Water-Carrying day, when the Ayako-body walks down to the River and fills its shabby clay jars. The running stream asks me wordless riddles, the lark punctuates his versifications with small pipings. I kneel and my knees creak—I sadly recall a time when they did not. The newest sun of a thousand warms my back like a winter dress as I lean into the chortling brook.

"Tell me a lesson about water, River," I murmur, for River has always been my tutor, less stern than Mountain in his dreaming heights. And when River speaks, his voice is yellow and blue, the fringe on an emperor's sedan chair, rustling imperceptible gold into the wind:

When you put your white foot into me, I part for you. But when you drink, though it is cool and sweet, you part for me.

"River," I say, "tell me a lesson about earth." And when River speaks, his voice is green and gray, the mist sloughing down into the valley.

If you plant your meager bed, perhaps a bed-tree will grow, perhaps it will not. But in the ranks of beds and trees and planters, only Mountain abides.

"River," I whisper, so as not to disturb the harp-tongues of the lark-flock, "tell me a lesson about wind." And when River speaks, his voice is white and rose, the air stirring new blossoms.

When wind touches the water-birds, it turns them the thousand colors of snow. Yet it does not change you.

"River," and now I am almost asleep again, my lips scarcely move to make the words, "tell me a lesson about fire." And when River speaks, his voice is tinged with red, its edges flushed and hot.

Flame travels on strange feet. Its heart is never twice the same.

And down by the dream-river, among jars of mottled clay, I sleep and write these lessons with the others on the tablet of my wax-flesh.

EAGLEHAWKS METAMORPHOSE INTO DOVES

There is a dream-sister. She is all red, even her nipples that cut open the flesh of the sea. When the sun rises over our islands, which lie like a beaded necklace on the green waves, she drinks the light in a goblet of vines. When she sleeps, she sleeps in the curve of my waist, which is also red.

I dream there is no loneliness, I dream that she drinks my sorrow up like the dawn. This is the fire-dream, and I know it, for my limbs burn. I recognize the necklace of orange wedges and crab's eyes I wear, I recognize the bird-bright throat of my sister.

It is the fire dream and I am going to die.

I dream that it is River once more who holds me down with his turquoise hands, and my sister's arms are full of stones. One by one she brings the black rocks down onto my body, my sky-skull, the fine bones of my flaming feet. My lava-blood spurts like semen from throttled skin, leaping out as if it hated me. She crushes me under her vitreous stones, under her talon-hands, under her grunts and screams like a skewered boar.

I am not afraid. My bones grind to dust with joy, frenzy, the marrow liquefies ecstatically. In River's strange-nailed grip I writhe and laugh, tiny flame-hiccups erupting from my bloodied lips. She rains down on me white-eyed quartz, basalt, feldspar, granite. She stuffs my mouth with dream-coal like an apple, and I can feel the seraphic pleasure of my teeth cracking. She is releasing me, and my flesh gobbles her stones as greedily as a child.

The dust-stuff of my bones River gathers together and mashes with rice-paste and goat-fat; into this he pours plaster. He makes of me an island chain, rounded as beads of sweat bubbling to the surface of the froth-torn sea.

And I rise out of my bones like steam—they are nothing but mute earth, now. I am a naked fire, with breasts of naphtha and sardonic knees, I am beyond what once was the red of flesh and the dream of the sister, the crab-iris of my pendant and the blue molars that River sunk into my neck so tenderly as the last rock rushed down and bit into my brain.

In the dream I am free, I range out, flitting from place to place, faceless, formless and wild, painting my scalded heels with ocean. The jellyfish pout in the harbor like little mouths, translucent and pure, swallowing nothing.

All paths are taken—I fan out over possibles like hair on lightless water; my matchstick-braids swing wide and encompass heartless mountain-architectures, skulls and steppe-altars, the shape of a crone scraping circles into the sand.

I am a body of flame, without steel-jointed bones. The dream-sister released me and only the fire remains, the fire and the voice, my voice, that ever-owl-screeching voice, banshee-bright on a hundred infant hills that are the old body, that thump like a suffocating trout, tail to the starry south.

THE SWALLOWS RETURN

"Why do you not go up to the second floor of the pagoda?"

I leapt up from the rush-bed of River, the hair of Ayako-I tangled up with twists of milky grass. A great Mountain Goat stood before me on hooves of pyrite, his shaggy wool twisted gray and white, snow and stone, colors of the roots of old things. His horns were monstrous, swept back from his mossy brows in pearl and jaundiced bone.

"It is not so very far," his voice ground, like a stone moving aside to reveal a cave. It was not surprising that he should speak—when you have built your solitude-temple as I have, many things speak which should not.

"I cannot get to the top. My feet are weak and stupid, now. My knees are like paper boxes." The Goat seemed to shrug in his tangled skin, his black eyes shifting shades from jet to coal to the roof of a smoking temple.

"I did not say you ought to reach the top. But the second floor is not so great a feat. Why not unfold your knee-paper and climb? If there is a tower, there must be a climber, else why would the tower stand?" With this his hooves clattered on the stones and he was gone, up the side of the mountain where the wildflowers grow all dewy and bright.

Ayako is refuge. I am profound within her. She is the simplest of dreams, perhaps my best one. She trembles and is hungry for fish and rice, she fears storms and has silent flesh which rustles like a robe. I am afraid for us, that if the I-that-is-Ayako ascends the red tower, I will become lost in our/her dream-women, and I will not be able to tell the dream of the lion-haunches from the dream of the belly-winds.

But we had young turnips and mustard greens in our befuddled stomach that day, and these things make bravery.

So I-in-her stood in the center of the pagoda, in the crosshatch of shadows and strewn stalks of sun-leeched grass, looking up through the ruined levels, rising and rising like angular suns. I found a foot hold in the wall, and a ledge to grip, and thus worked my way upwards. There had once been a fine painting on the pitted stone, I could still see shabby colors in the cracks—a bull's head, a burning horse, a woman giving birth beside a river.

I was a column of sweat by the time I pulled myself through the mildewed floorboards and into the second room.

In a corner long ago conquered by fierce and noble spiders lay a leather wine-sack, an intricate moon finely wrought upon its surface, and it was filled with goat's milk, which was sweet and warm.

THUNDER LETS LOOSE HIS VOICE

When you come to the sun-wall, you expect a Question. A Riddle. But because you do not know, cannot know, which on is peculiarly yours, all Questions are asked. Only when my scarlet-dripping mouth opens around the divine interrogative does one Question gain ascendancy. Before I speak, all the Questions that ever were lie under the possible quiver of my leonine tongue. And so, because any Question may be there, soft as a Eucharist, all Questions *are* there.

Equally, all these Questions are answered. (This is the logic-dream, intersecting the dream of the lion-haunches at consecutive right angles.) Before you speak, all answers jumble themselves behind your acoustic uvula, a traffic in conceivable responses, as though they fled from some dark monster for whom no answer exists. Before you speak, you could say anything, and so you have said everything.

Further, before you ever came to my dust-bricks and the slow slide of my paintbrush-tail, all the Questions and Answers have been uttered, rejected, accepted, stuttered over, well-orated, and guessed at. You have been eaten, regurgitated, defecated, decomposed. I have been slain, flayed, skinned, vivisected and displayed on your mantle for generations. You have killed the king and married the queen, blinded yourself and died in obscurity. I have picked my teeth with your metatarsals and sunned my belly on the grass. It has all *occurred*.

And yet, before any of them have occurred, it is possible that all have occurred, and so they all have. There is no reason for us ever to meet. We have already met. I am in your belly, you are in mine. We are a many-colored *ouroboros*, merrily chewing on each other's scales. My riddles are answered. I am content.

And yet you keep coming, to find in me the snarled yarns of a thousand and one imaginable universes of envowelation and verbiate gesture—words and words and words, a tower of possible vocabularies, a geography of lingual variation.

It is possible that women are like this, too. That from a single source they dilate into all possible women, like a flame changing colors from the center outwards in wide bands: white, blue, yellow, orange. It is possible that all women are one woman, who has already lived, died, conflagrated and drowned.

It is possible that men are also connected this way.

Despite this, I love because it is my nature the dream-taste of all possible flesh on all possible tongues.

THE FIRST LIGHTNING FLASHES

The milk was warm and thick, better than the throat-that-is-Ayako has had in many years. In the early days I used to pray to Mountain to send me a little goat I could love and who would keep me warm with her wool, whom I could milk. Perhaps I could even strain cheese from the milk. Instead he sent rabbits and squirrels to eat. But I did not complain.

And strangely, with the sweet milk circling my teeth I was completely Ayako. I was within her tightly and hotly, blooded and fleshed. The dream-women fled and I was the white singularity at the center, open, iconic. Self flowed into self and all things flowed selfwards. The milk seeped through me in ornate patterns, a complicated knot work separating fractal-bright in my veins, which in themselves separated and separated further like winter branches thinning into twigs.

I was truly alone for a moment, and the temple was whole, gilt-edged. Incense sighed from my pores. I forgot the lion-dream and the fire-dream. I forgot the dream-husband and the dream-sister.

The phosphor-stars shone through a hole in the distant roof, and clouds drifted over the moon like mendicant's rags. And under their house-blankets and mist-curtains I was Ayako, and no other.

But soon the wine-sack was empty, and sleep brushed my ears with her ash-lips.

THE EMPRESS TREE FLOWERS

In my dream, I begin to plan a revenge. My breasts and my thighs conspire.

Mountain cuts an alpine range through my torso, tumescent summits swell up horribly, boils of dirty snow. River is rewarded for his complicity, he flows now directly into the mouth of my womb. I am his banks, I am his delta, I am his floodplain. His fat throat giggles as he encourages himself into frothing rapids along my cattail-ovaries.

But inside the dream of the belly-winds, the revenge-dream begins to form like a gilled fetus, in a *satori* of suspended animation, poised on a curious tiptoe like a Neolithic messenger-god. I am horribly open between them; they have polished my skin like banisters so that they can live inside me, playing checkers on my painfully elongated spine.

Quietly, I start to gather clouds across the black line of my collarbone, to hide the star-areolae from their sweating glances, from Mountain and River, who hold my battered legs open. I take the stars away, I rob their treasure house of all those white jewels, I let them laugh and drink from me like tavern-thieves and all the while I am robbing them of all possible skies.

I turn the dream-oceans dark, shade by shade. They deepen like a bruise: yellow, blue, indigo, black. I spit pigment into the waves, onto the new islands that have burst up in the west, onto the silent continents. I stain everything black. There are no harbors, there are no ports.

But there are villages. River coughs, Mountain smokes his pipe, and between the saliva and the smoke I find thatched roofs in my knee-pits, marketplaces in my sternum. They sink wells in my tear-ducts. I suckle a generation of water-diviners.

I hear them whispering, where a tributary winds up the cloud-side of Mountain. They are planning a Palace of my teeth. Molar-turrets, incisor-halls, portcullis of canines. When it is finished it will block my throat and I will never speak again. They send in canaries and cartographers to map the veins of usable enamel.

But they work slowly. I have time.

MOLES METAMORPHOSE INTO QUAILS

A hawk sat that evening in the pink flush of sunset picking at grass seeds, not looking up or down, only at the seeds which will now never sprout. And possibly I, too, the Ayako-body and the fire-body and the wind-body and the lion-body and the wife-body, germinate together in some dread aviary stomach wall, fed only by blood and bile and the occasional field mouse, growing dark and strange, with limbs the color of pupils. In the mirror of gastronomy I do not recognize a woman, only flesh, only bone, only the swift-scarlet ventricles of quickening tongues. I see only multiplicities. My feet are rooted in this unimaginable belly, as are theirs. Toes disappear into fluid, into soft veins and pulsation, into rhythms inconceivable, irredeemable, and un-patterned. In the belly of the hawk I am silent, in her thick body I am still.

I climbed down from the tower—down is always easier than up. When in doubt, head downward. By the time my joints have accomplished it, a weak moon has drifted out of the black like an afterthought. I made my small cooking fire on the familiar earth near the crumbling *torii* gate and boiled a thin stew of bamboo shoots and young potatoes.

After a time, the Gate seemed to loom larger and I spoke to it, my second tutor, whose architect was ash, a body that had long ago burned out like a cigar.

"Gate," I said, "tell me a lesson about cooking-pots." Gate did not turn towards me, but her voice was thick, paper-pulp fashioned into a mouth.

They evolve like drawbridges, they open and shut.

"Gate," I mused, "tell me a lesson about tea-cups." Her voice ran like paint, trickling down her red flanks.

They are the nature of empty, there is nothing in them but that you put it there.

"Gate," I bowed this time, for Gate is much gentler than River, "tell me a lesson about chopsticks." Her words stood still and vibrated.

Enough of them together line a passage down to the belly-throat, where all things occur.

"Gate," I whispered, "tell me a lesson about hunting-knives." Her voice fell on me like a shiver of pine needles.

They are origin.

Hot stew simmering contentedly in me, I curled against her once-beautiful wood and the constellation of the sea serpent coiled overhead.

THE FIRST RAINBOW APPEARS

She is my dream-self, my night-self, she is my deep-self, she is my obverse, my androgyne-self despite her full lips and curving limbs, my hunter-self, my archer-self, my earth-self. The self-that-is-wife. She is the god-self that must rest within like a child when I eat beneath the Gate. She is embodied and unbodied, the Saturnine sliver of me that haunts the corners of my elbows, eyelids, and sits fecund in her smoke-lodge creating universes from pine needles. That swallows the world whole like a golden-bellied snake and excretes mythos like sweat from her crystal-scaled skin. The dream-body walks the desert on feet cut by thorns, with scratches on her palms and date-juice on her lips. She is made of earth. But within me walks the unscathed and unmarked, and she is made of light.

I dream I have smashed clocks and pocket watches and sundials and bronze-orbed pendulums to feathered-glass razors, pulverized their round faces into metallic dust. I dream lilies grow from the inner curve of my skull. I dream I can see the muscles in my/her back slide and move beneath her foxglove skin as I moves beyond it, into the next self that dissolves into seafog when I strive to see the one after, to see myself in her body, sheathed in her hair, to unite with her, to be a whole. I walk in the brittle sun and she waltzes under the arctic blaze of the north star.

I/she found your jaw today. It cast a shadow, delicate and wavering on the water, the shudder of a waxwing shaking rain from her feathers. The shadow eclipsed the water, and the water eclipsed the stones, stealing glimmer from the stream and silt. Deep in its fingers lay a row of perfect moon-teeth embedded in pink flesh and a ridge of perfect bone, torn and bloody as a trout in the jaws of a hawk.

This is the dream of the sister-wife, and in it the silt-body becomes a narcotic, a morphine that encourages nothing but forward movement, denies the lateral progression of these beggared forms. She is sheer color, needle-wings of every irised shade. In her morphine river I drift like a raft of yellowed reeds.

FLOATING WEEDS APPEAR

I have used the last of my tea. The dream-village boy brought it last summer folded into a square of yellow cloth, holding out the wrinkled green leaves to the Ayako-I with trembling hands. He was in awe, to see a living ghost, with her flesh looped over bones like knitted shawls, and hair that brushed the back of her heels like a kiss. His eyes were so wide, offering his tea as though I/we were a statue, a wood-woman covered in gold leaf, worthy only of terror and service. I imagine they draw straws for it, the honor, or shame, of bringing me these small gifts.

But I have used the last of it, and I must wait until summer to drink my tea again under the slow-blink of starlight. Perhaps it is just as well—my teacups, rough hewn from River's fleshy clay, do not stand up quite right. Some of the tea is always lost, the sour green liquid sits at an awkward angle and sloughs out when my fingers brush the rim. My fingers, my dream of fingers, are not so graceful. I lose the tea, down my chin, out to glass, onto the earth. I cannot keep it all in my mouth. I am too small for it, and the cups too poorly made.

The wine-sack, too, is gone. I woke, forcing the Ayako-eyelids open as early spring sunlight pried at me greedily, and it was gone. I think perhaps it is wrong for me to miss it. I think I should be content with what Mountain brings and ask for nothing else. Then again, perhaps it is not me.

I warm water in my little pot and pretend I can taste the sharp star-points of tea in my throat. It is enough, but somehow, it is not.

DOVES SPREAD THEIR WINGS

I stand in my cloak of embers and stir the dream-earth, my skin-scald medieval and slant-eyed. Sage, peppermint, wormwood are scorched beneath me—I care nothing, nothing at all. Rain like inkwells pummel my sternum, my haunch. Away from the islands that River made, the ion-trail that is my flesh sears the sky.

There is nothing here but the fire-dream, the savage flesh and the stern destroyer, nothing but death under the wide elms, the staunch oaks, death under my own eyes bleeding gold paint, my frescoed mouth, flooded with tempura and cobalt-poisoned blood, the lead of murder-pipes.

I choke, I cough up a wreck of wood pulp and iodine, I drown in my own fluid-flame, in the churned death of volcanic paths, the whirling leaf-self which dervish-scours all in me that would lie well in beds of birch-bark, in beds like paper, where books like this one, which is not mine but *hers*—the dream-hermit, where books like hers are written in sweat, the manuscript of elongated muscles illuminated in diamond salivations.

I am a vessel of salted meat, eyes glazed over by an abundance of nights, a surfeit of dream-visions wherein I touch human breath. There is a film over my dream-body, a veil which cannot be touched or torn. My heart beats seven times and stops, ventricles covered in thick gasoline. It is only in the stopped heart, the deadened pulse that I can discover any revelation, that any ease is to be unearthed.

I am already blackening the soil, already devouring the root systems of baobabs and dandelions, already seething in my half-living skin. Stamp, stamp, stamp, beast rampant on a verdant field and I am nothing but a heraldic smear, blood on stained glass—the sun refracts through me onto the faces of the faithful and I am again only skin, only surface, only the fur and lip of a woman.

Seize this chimeric body, this betraying flesh and it will always and only escape.

I am a tooth, a body of teeth, and I pierce through as though the world were made of water. What else can I ever be but this black-eyed eater of men? What patchwork breasts can I offer up to the screaming stars that will ever satisfy their dark tongues? My back flares wide and strong under the sky, under the moon with horns like mine. Alone I corrode the earth, alone I carve shapes into the path. I walk uncloven, and open my woman's mouth to swallow darkness until my jaws crack.

I search for a city, I search for walls. I search for the dream of flammable materials.

THE HOOPOE DESCENDS TO THE MULBERRY

The boy who brought tea had clean fingernails. That is how I knew he was a dream—what villager can keep his hands clean after working in the rice fields, at the butcher, the blacksmith, mending the well-rope, spreading pitch on the bottoms of fishing boats? So I spoke to him, since dreams are my peculiar surrogate family, I felt I had the right. That it was my duty to address the dream and call it by name, so that it would stay and join all my other dreams in their agate-toed walk. After all, I had no boy-dreams.

He was very pretty, with unkempt hair and limpid eyes. His narrow hips seemed to jut a challenge, though I am long since the days when the hips of men pointed to me. He extended his offerings to me, trembling—he was the fear-dream, then, the dream of cold sweat. I liked watching his hand shake, as though I could curse his line with a glance and a muttered phrase. I liked the quiver of his brown skin.

A sack of rice, a woolen blanket, and the beautiful-smelling tea leaves, which sat in their yellow cloth like oblong jewels. I could see the whites of his eyes, terror-moons lodged in his skull. I readied myself for the great effort of speaking with the throat-and-belly instead of the mind-and-heart. It is altogether a different skill.

"Boy," I said, and I was ashamed of my broken voice, creaking like a brass hinge, "tell me a lesson about the village." I waited eagerly for the dream to speak. I loved my lessons, I was eager for more than River would give.

But the boy only gurgled in his throat, an animal, horrified noise, and with a yelp threw down his bundle and ran back down the Mountain path. Behind him a dust-cloud rose up like an eyelid, and closed again.

Ghosts are not supposed to speak. It is considered impolite. And now I must wait a full year to try and catch the villager-dream again.

SPARROWS SING

I flex my gold-shag paw under a drumskin-moon. It is easier here, in the lion-dream. All that there is on the Mountain is solitude, each of whose notes must be plucked on the harp-strings at just the right time so that the music of my disintegrating self will arc over this land like a temple ceiling, and with as many colors. That is not concerned with me, with asking and answering. In considering the whole, one possible woman is not enough. Only in groups, in clusters like cattle-stars, can they bee seen for what they are.

I ought to remember the name-riddle. It is a good one. The boy who called me Truth still swims within, a seven-gabled fish. Between Questions there is not much to do but lie on the wall, devouring grape-pulp and mashed cardamom, resting the muscles in my back. I have a peculiar anatomy, being a winged quadruped, and the weight of wings on my thick-knobbled spine gives me pains. The city doctors will not come—and who can blame them? If I asked them which roots and roasted leaves would be a salve to me, their saliva would dry in their mouths. If they answered incorrectly I would be within my rights to swallow them whole. It is the nature of things: any Question I utter must be answered with blood—mine or theirs.

This is the dream of science. In this feline body I am bound to examine myself, as though I were a butterfly skewered on a wax board. *Maculinea arion.* Save that I am also the slim silver pin and the thick wax and the hand that affixed these things. When I look at my flesh it looks back.

This is the dream of separateness. I am not the city I guard. They fear my scythe-claws no less than my mausoleum-tongue. I am sub-urban. The hermit-dream lies with her boiling visions somewhere higher than her city, a superior altitude that forgives her this geography of the unreal. I am beneath and outside my city, I circumscribe it, I keep out the unworthy. We are on the outer edge, beyond the pierce-reach of copper compasses.

Momentarily, I am the men I eat.

But that passes.

EARTHWORMS COME OUT

I have become accustomed to the second floor of the dream-pagoda. A few centipedes, with bodies of jointed rubies, have made my acquaintance. The floorboards have fallen through in places. Dust and flecks of paint hang suspended in the air which is often gold these days, under a haze of low clouds that suggest the sun.

Ayako moves more slowly now, as though she/I cannot connect to her body. I hope that when the dream of the villager comes again I will be able to catch him—I think another dream might cure the creaking of her bones. I hate the sound. The other women do not creak.

Everything is full but this body—the rains have brought worms wriggling into the mud, and River's fat pink fish are full of the worms I have dropped into their throats. The trees are made of flashing wings. My little garden teems with thick young shoots, pale green and dark, promising that I will not starve come winter. But the body is empty. I hardly live in it at all these days. The sun makes it lazy and I drift into the dream-women with diagonal ease.

A gentlemanly brown Moth flits in and out of the pagoda. He wears his creams and fawns with the grace of a salaried courtier. He sits in the shadows and lets his antennae waft with the breeze. Often he will land on my hair or my sandals, (which require mending again) and his furry belly will rub imperceptibly against my skin.

"Moth, tell me . . . " I whisper in a voice like an autumn frog-song.

"Yes?" he hisses, rubbing his paper crane-wings together.

"Nothing."

CUCUMBERS FLOURISH

This morning, before the dream-sun could report me, I swallowed one of their villages.

I simply drew my knees together and it vanished, caught between my moss-bones and my vine-skin. I felt the roofs splinter and pop against me, the cattle scream and the temple bells shatter. My thighs exulted, trembling with a shivered joy. I tried to conceal my sighs of delight as they all crushed inwards and were finally silent.

When my knees fell back, there was no trace. Mountain and River did not notice. They are busy with the Palace. They have called the ocean creatures together to fill a great jade vat of ink, in order to inscribe their names over the Gate, and the History of the World. River rests the vat on my belly while he blows smoke rings at the scaffolding which has by now obscured my jaw almost entirely.

I am wasting. I begin to wonder if the villages would sustain me. If I only swallow a few at a time, perhaps they will not notice. They have set the red sun on my steps, and he is now my gold-chinned jailor, arcing over me, back and forth, dragging his great clunking cloud-chains behind him.

There is much activity on my body, and they have poured the foundation of the Palace from a blood-mash of cartilage. The miners tap, tap, tap at my jaw through the night, piling up teeth like cairns, piling them up in wheelbarrows and crates, in baskets and slings. I have heard Mountain suggest seventeen balconies. River plans a tower from which to view the History, when it is finished.

THE BITTER HERB GROWS TALL

I must confess that there is another dream. It is the dream of the silent girl. It is very small, and the I-that-is-Ayako is ashamed. It is not nearly so grand as the others.

In the dream I am wearing gray—very soft, cat-like. I am washed in blue light. The dream-girl is alone, for all of the dream-us is alone. We come from Ayako—we cannot be other than she, and she is alone beyond dreams of solitude.

Her dream-hair is drawn into a knot at her neck, but strands have escaped and blow darkly against her shoulders. This dream does not move. She does not change. The heart in her beats very slowly, and she wets her lips from time to time. After a pass of her delicate tongue, the lower lips shines silver. That is all.

She peers out a window at a long expanse of trees, which whisper to each other in the night, passing along what rumors there are that concern trees. In front of her/me is well-made paper, stacked together neatly, as if we meant it to stay; all her pens lie motionless in their pots. She has rings on her knuckles, and she taps them against the paper, making a thickly muffled noise. But other than this she does not move, and the paper is blank.

I do not know why she sits at the bottom of the Ayako-belly like a solemn stone. But she is there, and in their orbits, the dreams seem to turn towards her as they pass.

GRASSES WITHER

I found your clavicle, white as a wand. The grasses are beginning to turn brown at the tips now—not much, but a little, the gold before rot sets in. In the dream of the sister-wife, they seem to wave like tiny hands, the hands of children drowning. It called out to me among the reeds, plaintive and small.

I dreamed that I wanted it, the long chalky expanse, lying in the red soil like a hyphen—the sentence of your body unfinished. I wanted to put my mouth to the ulcerated predicate, to complete you with my tongue and lips and teeth, to bite you off and continue the flesh of you down into my own. In my hand it looks alien, an infinitive from a foreign language covered in bone.

I dream that I hate the owner of the bone. The dream-brother, ghost-husband. I collect him like marbles over half a desert, I crouch in the silt-ridden delta until I have sunk to my knees, grub his filthy bones and chunks of flesh from the earth, to pile them together in a grotesque cairn. When I found his intestines I had to loop them over my arms and around my neck, where they hung slimy and stinking, a mottled serpent-noose. They tried to drag me under.

It is what I was made for. The dream-search and the spill of his organs like egg yolks on glass. I hate the smell of him now, the curdled scent of his veins turned inside-out. It is all over me, gesticulating in my pores, his foreign sweat.

Yet I want the clavicle. It is smooth and clean of flesh. Dreaming within my dream I put it to my lips and play his collarbone like a macabre flute. My cedar-dusted fingers press into the marrow and low notes exude, sibilant and lurching down its barometric octave. Music throttles itself and serrates the wind.

Wherever the sound touches, the grass separates into dust and falls to the starving earth like a handful of torn pages.

I dream that he is death in death.

BARLEY RIPENS

I-Ayako has become ill. I watch her retch by the River with disdain. Her body heaves like a blown sail when the wind changes. I hate that she is old, that her skin is no longer beautiful. Below, in the valley of the dream-village, shocks of green writhe like demoniac oceans—the barley comes of age and the I-Ayako adds our body's sloughing to the earth.

My hands are not mine. Fingernails half-grown, jutting out like moons buried in a black-soiled field. I am only this lurching body. I am only this. These.

Yet, I begin to wonder about the body which hangs on me like torn clothes. If she dies, what will happen to us? Is there an I-above-all? An ideogram that is me and I and Ayako and all the dreams together—is there a divinity of first person? A prime mover of our limbs? We are afraid that she is failing us, that she will keep lurching into the water, vomiting and vomiting until she empties herself completely and we too have gone out of her by the throat-road. We are afraid the cramping body is the only real.

If she dies, will we simply blow apart, pine needles in a swift wind? Do the dreams possess location? Are we locative, dative, ablative? Where is the language of Us? What linguistic calculation could be made which would result in our variable, our presence outside of the Ayako-equation? We are cross-multiplied, we are exponential. She is not.

I am Ayako, and since she cannot answer, I cannot. When she/I drink our tea-less water, it falls into the flesh with worry edging its taste.

But in the morning it had passed, and our belly was calm.

MANTIDS HATCH OUT

I dreamed of a great maze. It turned underneath me, left and right and over itself, a great snarl of brick and mortar. It was painted and at each turn a color faded into its mate, so that the whole expanse curled like some impossibly complex sea serpent—perhaps if I had lingered I could have read some forbidden language in its knot-work. I could almost scry its subterranean tongues, reaching into the earth—down, down, down.

It had a physiology, a throbbing anatomy of stone and pigment. I could mark the pathway of its blood, through arterial thoroughfares and bile ducts, descending organs, kidneys, tangled intestines. It was a body, whole and complete, but one which contained the bodies of others like stacked dolls—strange-skinned creatures with blank eyes, and in the shadows a great black bull tossing his horns. I dream it lies below me, its skin touching my skin, like a prone lover.

I put my dream-lips, my flaming mouth to it. But I am a virgin, I have not done it before, so of course, the fire spreads too quickly. It blanches the twisting walls, blackens the creatures to skeletons, doors to molten piles of knob and hinge. I arch my back and my breasts brush the bull-horns and the great wooden gate—they shatter into pyres. My toes curl at its angular walls, my incandescent womb opens and shuts, clamping at its architecture, clutching wildly at the maze. I am a holocaust, breathing heavily and writhing over my adored labyrinth, twisting my legs around its girth. I am the inferno, clamping my body over the adulated—and who could find the blood of my virginity in the embers of this city?

Everything is red now and I dream my own laughter is a scorch-mark, my thighs tightening on the maze-roads send them up like cheap matches. My belly lifts up and a rain of naphtha-sweat gleams on the already engorged flames—and I am laughing, laughing, laughing as I burn divinity into this place.

What could I ever be but this black-eyed eater of cities?

When I leave the dream maze, still full of my heat and sweat, I can smell the flesh of the bull cooking, smoky and sweet.

And I search again, for another, for the beloved, for the bed-notch, for a city who will sing my love out in unmeasured lyrics.

THE SHRIKE CALLS

"What did you want to ask me that day?" the Moth mused in his thick voice, rubbing his forelegs together lazily. I sat with him in the shade of the second floor, escaping the early summer heat.

"I was going to ask you for a lesson," I answered. "Gate and River tutor me. More often when I was young, but still, from time to time."

"I am only a Moth, I know how to eat wool and seek light. If you want to know these things, I can teach you."

"No. I am not sure there are answers which would have meaning for me any longer. I am a bad student. I am too weak to be the wife of Alone."

The Moth shrugged. "Why do you not go up to the third level? Perhaps there is something there which would have meaning for you."

I-Ayako looked up through the slatted floorboards, the slant of unassuming light that filtered through to land, moth-like, on my open palm.

"It is so far. I have only just come to this level."

"I do not wish to stay in your pagoda. I have heard rumor of a beautiful flame in the city, and I go tonight to meet my family there. So I cannot tutor you. I do not have the time. Ask the third floor." And with that, the Moth spread his stately, cream-spattered wings and flitted out of the tower.

It was a far more difficult climb than it had been to the second floor. The walls were smoother and bore less paint. I tore three fingernails in the ascent, and when I pulled myself, almost weeping, onto the next knotted floorboards, my hands bled freely.

The angled room was bare except for a few forlorn grasshoppers and a small statue which stood in the far corner. Time had erased its face from the stone, but it stood, calm, seraphic. Gray featureless rock stared out at me and there were no sounds save the cries of prey-birds circling.

THE BUTCHERBIRD IS SILENT

I dream that I can string the Questions and Answers together on a long line of catgut, like little wooden prayer beads, or a thread drawn through thick leather. I dream I can see them all around my shaggy neck, sparkling against my fur. I hold the heft of them in my paws, matched pairs like chromosomes, *AB, CD, KL, XY.*

I hold a plethora of halves. Each time a man comes to gain entrance to the city, he completes a set and my collection grows. It is an art, and I am skilled at it. Perhaps at the end of time I will truly hold them together like a great necklace, a grand unified theory of interrogation. Each time their flesh touches my tongue with dark and secret flavors, I inch closer, my books tilt towards balance.

A boy came wandering with heavy-lidded eyes, the droop of the lashes that can only mean extreme enlightenment—or opium addiction. His fingers were long and pale, funereal, with fingernails I imagined would taste of ripe dates. I began to quiver with anticipation and desire.

The boy brushed hair of a watery shade from his forehead and looked languorously up and down my body.

And yet it is stupid and simple. I ask him to calculate the relativistic mass of a single photon. He blinks stupidly, he is flustered, he cannot answer. The ritual has become almost mute—no arcane spray of ash over their bodies could cure them of their pride. They all think I am a beast, a monster with no mind, able only to spout my riddles by rote.

I must explain to him, painstakingly—for I must supply the Answer if he cannot, it the least courtesy I can provide—how the mass of a particle is proportional to its total energy E, and involving the speed of light, c, in the proportionality constant: $m = E/c^2$.

His expression reminds me that occasionally there is beauty to be found in blankness.

And yet, another pair of wooden beads is drawn together, the oil from each mingling, and the weight of my necklace increases. It is for the city planners to worry that the population does not swell, that traders avoid the walls, that no beautiful foreign brides are brought with almond eyes. I fulfill my duty, the coupled words are spoken, and I increase.

This boy sat heavily in my belly, tasting of iodine and oatcakes. I am exhausted of this work, and yet it goes on. I am bombarded by photons with cruel masses, with high cheekbones and stiletto heels. Light sits heavily on my lap, an old whore as bored as her customer is disgusted. But it is the disgust that keeps it going. Disgust, at least, is tangible and real.

If there is a monster there must be a man, or woman, to approach it. It is the way of things. Perhaps when I have brought together all the beads, it will cease to be the way of things. And then I will rest and let Thebes be damned.

DEER BREAK ANTLERS

I-within-Ayako could not breathe. I could not move. Tears rushed from my eyes like a spring from a rock wall, streaming down my cheeks, mixing with sweat and grime from the climb up onto the creaking floor of the third level. My throat was a boulder against a tomb, my limbs a sudden dark wax, flooding into each other, under and around the radiance of the stone figure. I could not think. My mind was empty of everything but it, even the dreams, even the dreams.

Its face, luminous and round as all the suns I have ever known, stared out, beatific, sorrowing, without eyes or mouth. The sorrow penetrated me like a hand, holding my heart, holding all of me that can be moved by beauty, holding me like the mother that died, spilling over with forgiveness. Nothing I had ever done or been or imagined myself mattered, only this ancient stone whose name I could not begin to guess. What god had it been meant to show? I did not know, could not know, but for a slow blink of the sun's eye, it erased every shadow I had dragged behind me like a tawdry merchant's cart, its one broken hand gracefully bent into a mudra of seraphic gentleness.

It made me a child in braids and a poor dress, crawling into my mother's lap and pressing my face into her warm skin. I sobbed against her, my bones cracking open and my deepest blood pouring over her absolving hands. I died away from the dreams. I and the stone were the whole universe, for a moment that stretched out in all directions, an infinite plane of liquid jewels, she was all things, and the smooth gray of its faded eyelids filled my vision with a great burning. All of me was on fire, incandescent, my legs, my mouth, my tears searing as they coursed, rivers of naphtha scalding and cleansing. It was inside me, purging me of all that was not light. I was made of gold, singular, my skin kindled and blazed, I saw nothing at all before me but endless plains of its light and mine flooding together like tributary and river, river and sea.

"Stone," I wept, my face swollen with tears, "tell me a lesson about myself."

Stone considered for a moment, and began.

CICADAS BEGIN TO SING

The cicada lies in the earth for seventeen years. It is warm and dark there, it is soft and wet. Its little legs curl underneath it, and twitch only once in a little while. What does the cicada dream when it is folded into the soil? What visions travel through it, like snow flying fast? Its dreams are lightless and secret. It dreams of the leaves it will taste, it composes the concerto it will sing to its mate. It dreams of the shells it will leave behind, like self-portraits. All its dreams are drawn in amber. It dreams of all the children it will make.

And then it emerges from the earth, shaking dust and damp soil from its skin. It knows nothing but its own passion to ascend—it climbs a high stalk of grass and begins to sing, its special concerto to draw the wing-pattern of its beloved near. And as it sings it leaves its amber skin behind, so that in the end, it has sung itself into a new body in which it will mate, and die.

The cicadas leave their shells everywhere, like a child's lost buttons. The shells do not understand the mating dance that now occurs in the mountains above it. The shell knows nothing of who it has been, it does not remember the dreaming self, that was warm in the earth. The song emptied it, and now it simply waits for the wind or the rain to carry it away.

You are the cicada-in-the-earth. You are the shell-in-the-grass. You do not understand what you dream, only that you dream. And when you begin to sing, the song will separate you from your many skins.

This is the lesson of the cicada's dream.

BINDWEED FLOURISHES

I dream that my wrists are bleeding. Mountain spat basalt and bound them. River discovered the village was missing and in his rage tore open the walls of my womb. It lies gaping and red, the marks of his fingers black and terrible. My womb is screaming and they call it music. River says that I am beautiful now. That he will cut more of me open to reveal such beauty. He is planning an expedition to sound the depth of my spinal fluid.

I have had to release my storm clouds and let the oceans lighten. Mountain crushed me under his weight until I yielded. He ground into me grinning and panting. They have poured the foundation of their Palace directly into my throat—mortar and burning pitch, and no I have no voice but the mute growling of my deepest mouth.

I dream that it never ends. There are so many hands inside me now, rummaging in my flesh as though it were an attic. I am vandalized.

They are almost ready to begin the painting of the History in the first Great Hall. I cry silently as they balance the jade vat on the hollow of my throat. River holds the pen as he held my arms, and when he lays it down to rest, I can see it bears the same bruises.

My jaw is broken. The Palace was too large and the first gables shattered the bone. My teeth were scattered like seeds. The villagers scurried to gather them up and return them to River, their rightful owner. But now it will be perfect, and the blood that drips from my earlobe can be used as paint. There is, after all, no sense in waste.

River has only just finished the inscription of their names. That was his proudest task, and it took a long time.

HOT WINDS ARRIVE

I stayed with the statue as long as my belly would allow. The Ayako-body is demanding, however, and soon enough I did not wish to disturb it with the growls of hunger. I descended in sorrow, not knowing if I would have the strength to climb so high again.

I devoured a mash of wild carrots, beans, and mushrooms; I pulled down ripe plums from the branches heavy with green. Mountain provides. The dream-pagoda was inside me then, a bone like any other, and I confess that I had already begun to think on the fourth floor, though I knew my mewling flesh to be to weak to attempt it.

River washed me clean of tears and sweat and blood and dirt. He held me very tenderly in his current, as if I would break into five thousand pieces and float out to the sea. But I did not speak to him, though I could feel his disappointment at not being asked for a lesson in the summer, when he is at his best. River is such a proud creature. He loves display. He had an affair with Moon once, because she shone so prettily on his waters that he fell in love with her. It ended badly.

I had nothing to ask him, my eyes had glazed over like gray water. He became sullen and his banks pouted. I thought of the Stone and how its face had vanished. If none one sees a face, perhaps it is as good as vanished. Perhaps I have no face, either.

The sunlight was thick and hot, pooling on the earth like coils of molten lead. It sat heavily on my eyelids and began its long work of darkening my skin. Off in the Mountain-cliffs, the first cicadas open their amber throats and start to sing, their scream of ecstasy wrapping the air in a soprano fist.

CRICKETS COME INTO THE WALLS

I dream that I can smell his flesh in the cinnamon-breath of camphor trees. I dream it stops up my nostrils like the spices of the dead. I am mummified by him, each sliver I find takes its correspondent from me.

It is his cheekbone, after all, still hanging with skin and blood like a curtain, drizzling fluid onto my skin. It reeks of river-waste, of rotting crocodile. And yet, I hold his face in my hands again, the high arc of his noble bone-structure, beauty being the mark of divinity.

I dream that the smell of his divinity gags me.

The rains are coming and then it will be harder. His slick-sided flesh will slip from my hands and into the mud-which-swallows. He is my dream-beast, the brother-husband vivisected, the body which was whole now in wet clumps, like hair from a woman's brush. And the smell of it, embalming my body to drag it down with him into the *satori* of dismemberment. I am clay, and his fingers worm their bony lengths into the cracks of my joints, each part of him seeking its mate, but only its mate, having no care for the whole. His cheekbone calls out to mine, begging cartilage to rip from the wicked face.

I am his food. He eats slowly, conserving strength until he can come together again and wrap himself up in river-reeds, in necklaces of ibis-talons, in beast-heads which can be changed to suit the latest fashions. Today it will be Hawk, tomorrow black-tongued Jackal. How beautiful he will be, when the dream is over and he is bodied. My name will be written down in the book of the dead in gold ink, curled vowels and tender penmanship. There will be an asterisk, which notes that I took his place.

THE EAGLEHAWK STUDIES AND LEARNS

The air is still. It cups me like an older sister's arms and I become slow, languorous, heavy. Mountain has put on his best green, deep and savage, and there are birds circling his gnarled head. Soon, I think to my Ayako-self, the boy will come from the dream-village. Perhaps he will bring me a little chicken whose eggs I could eat. Or even some rice-wine in a clay bottle with a pretty yellow cork.

I haven't seen the moon in weeks. The constant heat-haze, as though from a well-rolled cigarette, prevents it. I am unconnected, removed from light, from the luminal braids that did not tumble down to the fennel and sage, basil and wild mint of an earth where I might have stood if I had not listened to Sparrow and been adopted by Mountain.

Perhaps instead of the fulmination of selves in my heart, I would have made daughters with eyes like plum blossoms. Perhaps I would have had a son with clean fingernails. I would have owned five kimonos, each with a different flower-pattern along the hem. Cherry, lily, chrysanthemum, orchid, peony. There would have been bleating goats and a rooster, even, perhaps, a fine brown horse. There would have been a husband to share a bed, and I would never have built the master-work of my loneliness with such care, the care of a swordsmith or royal architect. I would have kept a little songbird, and learned to play the *koto* with graceful hands.

The moon shines on the woman I never was, on the house I never owned, on her hair like moving water.

ROTTED WEEDS METAMORPHOSE INTO FIREFLIES

I dream that this is the History of the World as River wrote it and Mountain spoke it:

When in the height Heaven was not named, and the Earth beneath did not yet bear a name, all things were Dark and without Law. Into this came Mountain and his brother River, and they brought Light to the World. Mountain saw that a wicked and hideous woman held dominion over Earth, and she was the Mother of Chaos. Mountain saw her, and knew that she was evil, and resolved to deliver Earth from her grasp.

And so in the fullness of Time, through great strength and cunning, it came to pass that Mountain, though her form disgusted him, let himself be seduced by her, for she was also a Harlot. And when he came to lay with her, Mountain contrived it so that River could enter her chamber and bind her at the arms. When the demoness could not move and cried out in her extremity, Mountain drove all the four winds through her belly. He severed her inward parts, he pierced her heart, he overcame her and cut off her life; he cast down her body and stood upon it. And the lord Mountain stood upon her hinder parts, and with his merciless club he smashed her skull.

Mountain shouted his triumph, but the People did not hear, for they had lived in Terror.

So that she could not return and do further evil, Mountain and River devised between them a clever plan. River cut through the channels of her blood, he split her up like a flat fish into two halves; one half of her they established as a covering for heaven; from the other half they fashioned the earth and all its districts. Mountain fixed a bolt; he stationed a watchman, and bade them not to let her Waters come forth. Only River would hold Water beneath his sway, and only Mountain hold Earth. They saw that their Work was Good, and Rested.

This is how the World was made, and how the Men of the World were liberated from the dominion of Evil. So it has been Written, and let no one doubt its Truth.

Dream-tears trickle down my cheeks, and pool on the wheat-bearing valleys below.

THE EARTH IS MUDDY AND THE AIR IS HUMID

The rains have begun. It rained for five days and five nights, battering at my skin even through the slats of the pagoda-floors. Even on the third floor (which is not, after all, so difficult to reach) I cannot escape it, only lie curled around the faceless statue and murmur to it senselessly, words that are all vowels.

And then nothing but the same white haze for days, as though the wind smoked opium, until the belly of heaven opens again and the fat droplets splash down and turn the earth to a sloshing storm of mud and torn branches. Poor Juniper looks bedraggled and his branches have lost their fine berries by the bushel.

Wind conspires with water and I hide away from it. The green on Mountain's flanks looks almost obscene under the footfalls of rain. It is has a glower to it, a strut. Even the cicadas are quiet, a wing-quivering audience for the sky.

Once, when the I-Ayako was younger, we danced in it. Our toes pointed east and the great thick drops fell down onto skin which was perfect, cream-pale and smooth. those were the days when dreams stayed dreams, and did not encroach on the daylight like cities on the forest. Our/my hair spun around me in a long fan, my toes wriggled in the soft mud. Those were the days when I loved my lessons, and I laughed wide-mouthed at the pearl-silver sky:

"Rain! Tell me a lesson about dancing!"

Even the bamboo sways when the wind visits.

In those days, the voice of the rain was young and sweet.

THE GREAT RAINS SWEEP THROUGH

I dream I range over the seas, above the hyphen of rain clouds. I see my dream-sister on the bone-islands, her hands in the chalky soil, trying to force her crops to grow. River tries to help her, he flows around her, through her sugar cane and orange trees, through her banana groves and her copses of dark-leaved mango. All of these have withered and turned black, and I can see her beat her red fists against the earth-that-was-me and weep terrible tears.

She has set up a temple, fine and white, with a shaded veranda—heaps of hibiscus and palm fronds pile up the altar. There is a thickly sweet smell as they rot, trickling a sickly red juice onto the clean floor. She preaches there, and calls herself the fire-god who kindled the first flame when the world was dark. She tells River she never had a sister, that she was an only child, that mother and father loved her too much to have another. She demands that she is beautiful and that pigs be roasted in her honor.

But still, her groves will not grow. My bones would not let such a thing occur, that my sister would eat the fruit of my body. Still, the dream-rot spoils everything she touches.

It is no matter to me—better that she destroyed my flesh, that I am now naked of it and a flame alone. But I pity her. She rages, scarlet hair flying behind her, clutching handfuls of the bone-soil and ripping her breaths in half. I care little; she is a mewling puppet stuttering in her temple, her aspect mawkish and dull. I am grateful for her stones, which made me the lover of cities, which took my flesh and left only the fire.

I shrug garnet shoulders and move on. It is of no concern.

THE COOL WIND ARRIVES

The sweat on my neck has dried. I eat mustard greens and the beans which by now are thick and lantern-green.

There is a kind of contentment to be found in the dream-hermitage—it comes only when the solitude-temple is built and the hermit is interred there, but it does come.

It is in the earthy tang of harvested vegetables.

It is in the smell of the mildewed pagoda-floors.

It is in the little bells of River singing by, and the heft of silence under Mountain, who carves his shape out of the void-that-is-sky.

It is the ants milling redly home with prizes of berry and sap.

It is pale petals stuck to the bottom of my left sandal, dew-damp and wrinkled.

It is Moon touching River tenderly, her hand heavy with the memory of their lovemaking.

It is the dark, earthy taste of persimmons and the fire-orange of their skin.

It is the sound of herons washing downstream, the sound of their blue feathers rubbing together like cricket's legs.

It is the song of the plovers in the scented trees.

It is the shade of the pagoda at noon, the shapes that its shape casts on the earth.

It is the thick-dropped rain playing in the mud.

It is in bare feet that tunnel in loose soil, and the hum of cicadas which is like monks repeating their syllable endlessly into the hot nights.

But it is easily disturbed.

WHITE DEW DESCENDS

I dream that this time it is a girl. She comes to trade her water-jars in the great market, and indeed, they are skillfully shaped, with elegant spouts and handles that curve backwards like the necks of water-birds.

It is all the same to me whether her hair is the color of a burned oak or of the fire that burned it. But like all my postulants, she is beautiful. She smells of alfalfa and licorice. I feel a question-bead slide down the strand, and its passing sounds a baritone note, deep and wide as a bell.

"Monster," she speaks first, which is unheard of, not *done*—"may I ask you a question first?"

I dream that I consider it. Of course, it merely prolongs the ritual. But she is lovely, and it will not save her, so there is no harm. I nod my golden head, and the sand-choked curls of my mane tumble forward.

"What walks on four legs in the morning, six in the afternoon, and none in the evening?"

My dream-laughter fills the desert and I am sorry for a moment that I will have to devour her. I want to caress her cheek instead, and feed her from my own mouth, as if she were my cub.

"Why, I do, child. For in infancy I walk on my four paws, in maturity I add my two wings to this, and in old age I creep on my belly and use none of these. That was a good riddle, girl. I shall remember it."

Disappointment rakes it fingers across her face. I can see that this was her plan, to win her entrance by becoming herself the monster, and reversing the natural order. But such plans are not to be. The face of the coin cannot be its reverse. I am to far beneath the earth to be troubled by such small movements.

"And now for mine," I intone, in my richest voice. The girl squares her feet as though she is to recite a verse, and shakes her hair like a broom tangled in cobwebs. "If n is a whole number greater than 2, prove for me that there are no whole numbers a, b, c such that $a^n + b^n = c^n$?"

I dream that my smile is fat and sated, knowing she cannot answer and that the sweet smell of her skin will soon be inside me.

The girl's eyes fill with prismatic tears. She understands. Any answer she might make would be a fantasy of foolishness. And instead of stuttering a guess, she simply walks to me, puts her tiny hand on my flank, moving her fingers in the thick fur with a thoughtful grace.

The dream-girl lies down beneath me, willingly, and exposes her white throat to my mouth. Her tears slide off of her cheeks and onto the dry sand, onto the strands of her hair.

I dream that I weep as I swallow her.

THE EVENING CRICKET CHIRPS

Everywhere, on every high stalk of yarrow or fennel, on every low branch of camphor or juniper, even on the outcroppings of the dream-pagoda, the cicadas are leaving their shells.

Each one is perfect, unbroken, clinging to the stalk it has chosen with total abandonment. They must know such rapture as they wriggle out, and the grass rubs their bellies while the whole sky sings.

I think on what the Stone taught me as I watch them. I can never quite catch them at it, I only see the translucent shell cast off, with delicate mandibles and a diamond thorax. Some strange-eyed goddess has cast off her jewelry, and my meadow is full of sparking gems. The sun shines through them and they become little lanterns attending a nameless festival, swaying merrily from their stalks while the wind gossips with the flowers. They have sung themselves empty; the melody took their souls. The dream-shells remain, little urns empty of ash.

There was a moment when I wanted to gather them up and burn them in a pyre, to honor their lives under the ground and wish them well in their mating. But I could not. It seemed wrong to touch them.

They are familiar to me, as though each of these carapaces is a mirror rimmed in bronze, to show the lesson of the cicada's dream: that I am deep in the earth and dreaming, and it is the seventeenth year.

THE EAGLEHAWK SACRIFICES BIRDS

River has seen my tears; I dream they anger him. He washes up roughly against my face to clean them from the skin which is still beautiful and green. His whitecaps like scalpels cut the salt from my ducts, trying to stop them up entirely. But he cannot do it.

He calls on Mountain, who fashions blinders from his shale rock, and places them over my eyes. I cannot see to the side, only straight down the ridge of my nose to the half-built Palace. It is coming along, now, since they painted the History. Great crimson turrets rise up, exactly the shade of my lips—and in fact they have sliced away layers of lip to make a deep-colored pigment for the portcullis. I am being torn down to the bone, and it must come soon, if the conspiracy of my limbs is to come at all.

This is the architecture of affliction, the cryptogram of the palace stairs whispers that no freedom is possible, no surcease can be salvaged from the flotsam of my quarried body. Boils erupt on skin that once did not bear up under the roots of houses. This is the dream of desecration, the dream of the palace building. This is the first body, which foaled all other bodies in an unimaginable stable. It can be seen as though it were tattooed on a woman's stomach—the line of bodies, connected like a chain of paper dolls, from the one the Mountain harmed to the one the Mountain loves. A shock of limbs move between us, rimmed in light.

In my own body which is not my own I palpitate and sweat great oak barrels of Chianti. I weep Retsina and bleed a late harvest Riesling. The drops well on my fingertips like rain—small lips fasten to me, drawing the vintage from my pores. I sit in a basket of lies like oranges and pears, building, too, the architectures of pain and vengeance.

HEAVEN AND EARTH TURN STRICT

When I was a child and Ayako only, the village had a great number of silkworms, and the women wove with radiance. The fat little grubs ate such beautiful things in order to make silk in the ovens of their bodies— white mulberry, wild orange, watery lettuce. They were coddled like tiny emperors. Perhaps my gentleman-Moth was once a silkworm, for when the time came that they metamorphosed into moths and had mated, the worms were forgotten and shooed from the house as a nuisance.

I can remember one autumn when they all became sick, for the mulberry crop was sour and fouled that year. They did not produce the pure white fluid that dried into the fine thread which then could be wound into a delicate rose-shade, even dyed indigo or emerald. From their translucent worm-bodies came only a thick black fiber, which was not even or pure, but knotted and bunched in places, so that it caused the poor things great pain to expel the viscous, wet silk. In my child-dreams I heard them screaming as their ashen bellies were torn out by masses of dark, coiled rope.

It did not dry properly, and so the women burned it all in a great heap with the bodies of the silkworms which had died giving birth to the death-thread. When they caught flame the smell of flesh and cloth burning was like white cardamom crushed in a china pot.

The ashes blew away with the next wind and the silkworm colony healed itself.

Yet I have always wondered—what marvelous, secret things could have been woven from that wet, black thread, the thread that smelled so sweet burning?

RICE RIPENS

I dream that I am kneeling on the riverbank, vomiting into the clear water. In one hand I hold his leg, severed at the knee, and tears have mixed with bile and silt-water to make a horrible stew.

I can see on the kneecap a tiny white scar where he cut himself shaving, and I kissed the blood away. I remember the copper taste in my mouth, the taste of his inward self, his red blood swimming in me.

And now I have a surfeit of his blood. I carry it in buckets and in water-jars balanced on my head. I carry it in wine-sacks and water-bladders, in thatched baskets and even in my cupped hands. I did not think a man could have so much blood, even him.

I dream the brother-husband with his sundered body. I dream I see him in the moon which drives the sky before it like chariot-horses. I dream the corpse forming around me, the *homunculus* of his disparate parts, graying and moldered, and I have no thread to sew them.

What sort of golem will rise up out of this collected flesh with *emet* tattooed on its palm? Will I have to whisper in his wizened ear, wet and wrinkled as a newborn, some arcanity to bring it surging together? Will it love me still?

I dream it will not.

I dream I will not see the golem-husband whole.

All my eye can see is my own shape hunched over the river, emptying my own body of itself.

THE WILD GEESE COME

Feet crunched on the pebble-path to my pagoda. The heart within the Ayako-body leapt up like a fish flashing in the sun. The dream of the village-boy has come!

And he did come, walking up the Mountain path in a simple shift with a polished walking-stick, carrying a leather pack on his shoulders. He was not the same boy—I did not expect it—but he was handsome and strong and I was eager to speak to him.

The boy caught sight of me and a look of horror stole into his black eyes. For a moment I saw myself as I must have appeared to him: an old witch-ghost in tattered rags with horse-like hair that stuck out in black and gray bolts, filled with twigs and leaves and river-reeds. My bones were visible beneath skin that was too pale, and the hands which reached out to welcome him must have seemed like death-claws.

I do not know where she comes from, the crone that sneaks into the house and steals girlhood away.

Hurriedly, the boy lays out his gifts on the damp grass: a sack of new rice, tea leaves folded into a blue cloth, a pouch containing dried lentils and a chunk of pork fat. It was a treasure—each year the gifts were better, and within my Ayako-heart I was happy, for I knew this meant my old home prospered.

I called after the boy as he turned his feet to run—but not too fast, lest the ghost be angered—back to the village.

"Wait, Boy," I rasped. This time, I was sure, I knew the way to trap the dream of the clean-finger nailed child and make him stay. He would help me take down the timbers of my solitude. "Let me tell you a lesson about the Mountain."

He paused. The young can rarely resist a lesson. They pretend to loathe them, but in their secret hearts a good lesson is sweeter to them than winter cakes. He looked back to me and whispered, his voice full of terror, "All . . . all right."

I crept up to him, the first human I had spoken to since the men with the iron clothes burned the village. "What you see is not Mountain. It is the dream that Mountain dreams."

The boy squinted skeptically in the late afternoon sun, which rumbled a pleasant orange-gold.

"Are you the Old Woman on the Mountain or the dream that she dreams?"

"Your guess is as good as mine, young one. I am old, and I live on the Mountain, so it is possible that I am she. I possess three floors of a pagoda and a bean patch. What do you possess?"

"A colt, which will one day be a horse," the boy replied, "and a black rooster with yellow eyes. The rest belongs to my father and will be mine when I am grown. But why do you possess only three floors?"

"I am too weak to reach the top," I admitted, ashamed again for the bulging veins and jaundiced fingernails I also possessed.

"Then why not just try for the fourth? Four is more than three. Perhaps then your guess will be better. My father teaches that the more a man possesses, the wiser he is."

I laughed quietly, and the chuckle was a hoarse and empty one. "Then your father must be very wise."

The boy looked strangely at me and I saw his heart decide to speak no more. He bowed and retreated down the Mountain, with the sun on his back. I did not have the heart to try to stop him again.

SWALLOWS RETURN

Into the belly of the sun, my eyes burn to white oil and threads of flame spin down to the earth. I dream that my hunger gnashes its own heart, searching for a city as beautiful as a tinderbox, a city to lie over and sigh into its towers.

I dream that the autumn has passed while I danced in the laps of a dozen mountains, throwing my hands through their rooftops. In the fire-dream, all things burn under me, and the scorching of all things smells sweet.

On the horizon, I can see a great wall. It is a hundred shades of gold and its gate is strong. A wide plain stretches before it that might have once been green, but pitched battles have stained it red and black. It is a city by the sea, dark as wine, and sleek black ships line its harbor like suitors. Warriors are pressing against the wall, a bronze wave breaking on stone. Its towers are coquettish and tall, slim as girls, beckoning.

I can smell incense burning desperately in temples, I can smell terror-sweat in seven hundred bedrooms. I can hear the dull thud of marching men, and the squall of the dying. I can hear women weeping, and the rustle of their dresses on marble floors. The great wall whispers that it would welcome me, that it would show me new pleasures of which I had not yet had the courage to dream.

I feel my mouth water, and drops of oily flame begin to fall from my body.

Soon.

FLOCKS OF BIRDS GATHER GRAIN

This time I spent an hour stuck between the third and fourth levels, limbs splayed like some distended, helpless spider. There were no more footholds at that height and the distance between floors had seemed only to grow. Excruciatingly I inched sideways, my hips aching, to a thick vine that hung against the wall.

Touching it, I breathed deeply and trusted my weight to its length. Instead of a spider I then hung in the cavernous tower like the rope to a grotesque bell. And slowly, hand over hand, I raised myself up along the green stalk until the fourth level passed beneath me and I could see the tracks of ancient footprints in the dust. I let go shakily and stood in the center of a room which was almost intact. I had come through a large hole in the floor but other than that chasm, the wood was smooth and deeply oiled.

And in the center of the grained wood lay a book.

It was strangely bound, not in a scroll as I knew books to be, but clasped in a leather casing which was not black, but dark from the sweat-thick attentions of many hands. It had no design or picture, it had only the clutch of cream-yellow paper within its jaws.

It bulged slightly, a fat heart on the upbeat.

On the cover it read in yellowing ink:

This is the Book of Dreams.

THUNDER SUPPRESSES HIS VOICE

What is a Riddle? It is not merely a word game, or a puzzle, or a even, truly, a question. It is a series of locks which open only onto each other, in a great circle that leads back to a Truth—and this is the secret I tell you now on the great wall of Thebes: the Truth is always in the Question, never in the answer. All conceivable truths are in a single question. If I ask a boy-child to tell me my name, I have already told him the ancient truth that a name holds power. I have told him that I am more than a monster, for I possess a name. I have told him that in names lies the path to freedom, not only of the body, but of the ineffable Self. All this I have told him, before I ever demanded such a simple repayment as an answer, if only he could listen. There is not nearly so much gold in the answer, which is nothing more than a word.

What is a Riddle?

It is a box full of satisfactions. It never fails the questioner or the respondent. When it is opened, there is a soft intake of breath, when it remains closed, breath itself is stopped.

And on this box is written:

This is the Book of Dreams.

BURROWING BEETLES WALL UP THEIR DOORS WITH EARTH

I am afraid to open it. A closed book is beautiful, because anything can be written in it, and so everything is. All the stories that ever were—love, honor, death, lust, wisdom—every word written is contained inside it as long as the I-that-is-Ayako does not reach forward to open the cover and reveal what *is* actually written there. It can only be disappointing. Perhaps that is why it bulges, so full of what it *could* be. The curve of potential, like a pregnant woman's belly.

An open book is ugly, it is splayed open like a whore. It can only be what it is.

I am afraid of it, I do not want to touch it. It does not fill me with light like the Stone or the goat's milk. What do I need with a book of dreams when dreams people my body as though I were a capital-city?

WATERS DRY UP

River is worried. He sees that my dream-tears continue, falling with more speed, pooling around my shoulders in a salty ring. River is usually the first to understand. He will not tell Mountain until he is sure he cannot punish me alone. He set the sun on me to dry them, but the tears are alive now, they run their course like the mewling children of River do, heedless and wild. They come and come and come.

Within myself, I am smiling.

He himself tries to wash them away, frothing under their weight, blue on blue. But they sink within him and he cannot move to stop up my eyes like wine bottles. I am heavier, heavier by far. My salts scald and bruise him—I am warmed by his screams.

He sets the wind to dry them, but they can only soak up the thick waters, and send them earthward again as rain. The dams begin to swell up with my sorrows, the sea is black and deep. Great storms erupt on the hipbones of Mountain, drenching his gray skin with borrowed tears.

He set the glaciers on me to freeze them, but they are hot and thick, rolling over my body in a great gray slough, over my dark-treed belly, the skin of boughs that covers my secret womb, and on this skin is written in the sap and tears:

This is the Book of Dreams.

WILD GEESE COME AS GUESTS

I dream I have found the last of him. In the deep river currents where no reeds grow it floated like an abandoned cradle. I am ready now, to take the river into me. I do not want to, but now there can be no more delays, and I can see the colors of the water changing. I am draped in his body—intestines, blood, leg, clavicle, cheek, eyes, jaw, scalp, hands, skin, spleen, heart, skull. I am dressed for the ball, for a second wedding, for the insensate ritual of taking my dream-husband's corpse into myself.

I know what is coming, what the river will leave in me like sandy deposits in the delta. I am resigned, I want it done. I want to leave it on the banks and never think on it again. The hawk-headed child looms large in my vision. I can feel its feathers already prickling the walls of my womb.

I stifle revulsion as I clean the last of the dream-husband's organs in the cool river, which has inundated the valley and given life to the amaranth crops. I am the body of the sky, and I will give birth to light from light. I cannot tell if it is still a dream. If the child I will take from his mute body will be a dream-son or if he will be real. I am the amaranth, and I am the river.

I hold the last of him in my hands, mottled gray and shot with hardened blood. And on its length is written:

This is the Book of Dreams.

SPARROWS DIVE INTO THE WATER BECOMING CLAMS

Metamorphosis. It is a long line of bellies, chained together flesh-wise, circling each other in a blood-black smear. A book is a belly, too. It is full of dark, nameless things decaying into each other, dissolving in acid, jostling for position. Kingfishers dive into the water and become women; women dive into the earth and become books.

What woman was this book before it grew its leather wings? I do not want to disturb her, to open her and pry out her secrets with a knife.

I was breathing heavily, trying to escape the book without moving. Perhaps peace lay in it, perhaps not. I did not want to know. I wanted my bean patch and my first floor. I wanted River and Mountain sleeping beside me in the dark.

I knew then I would not open it. I knew my story, I did not need the book. I would not harm it, its capacity for infinite wisdom, by reading what was truly there. I was not sure, I reasoned, that I *could* read any longer.

But I could not stop looking at it, the vulgarity of its bulging cover. I wanted it, like a barren woman wants a child. I would leave it, let it remain quiet and alone, as I have been for so long. Let the scholars in Kyoto pour over pages until their eyes dribble onto their cheeks. I took my lessons from Gate and Moth, Goat and River, and Mountain, above all my patron Mountain, who held me in his arms and whispered lullabies.

I stood before the book. I was the anatomy of a *no*. All of me cried out in rejection of the black heart of the dream-pagoda.

I had to escape it. Up. Up onto the fifth floor, where there would be no terrible book to make my sinews tear themselves like so much paper.

CHRYSANTHEMUMS ARE TINGED YELLOW

I dream that I begin to seduce the city. I touch its walls lightly, with a fingertip. I brush my lips over the ramparts. I am better now, I know how to make the fire last. I know how to take my pleasure from a city.

Before the Gate a dream-battle is raging. Armor has fallen in the dirt made mud by the glut of black blood, bodies are piled up to be burned. Two men are slashing at each other, their faces turned into masks of beasts, theatre-clay with fleshy ribbons. The rest of the army looks on, waiting on the outcome. The only sounds are the cheap, hollow ring of swords, the dull thud of blows landing on leather-wrapped shields, and the hush of my body moving over the bricks of the city.

My nipples dip into the fountains and they are dried, my hair falls over a siege tower and it crashes to the frothing earth. I laugh and laugh. What they battle over is already mine. I have claimed it.

And on the great carved gate is written:

This is the Book of Dreams.

THE WOLF SACRIFICES THE BEASTS

The fifth floor was perfect. I simply climbed up a ladder which had not a single rung broken, and stood in the center of a room with no cracks in the floor, no pockmarks on the walls—even the paintings were untouched. They showed strange and terrible things—a beast sitting atop a low wall, half lion and half eagle, with the face of a woman. A woman tied to the earth with a green-walled palace built in her mouth. A woman standing in a river much vaster than my little creek, with the severed organs of some nameless man draped over her body. A woman whose skin flamed red, sighing onto a city which caught flame from her breath.

And in the corner stood a small Fox, beautifully auburn and cream-furred, with pert ears and a gentle snout, sitting on her haunches with an expression on her face which in the world of foxes must have passed for a smile.

"Why did you not open the book?" she asked softly, in a cultured, harmonious voice which rustled through the room like a veil blown from the shoulders of some pretty child.

"I did not want to disturb it," I gulped, suddenly ashamed at my cowardice.

"If I brought it here now, would you change your mind?"

I considered it, thought back on the dark oils of its cover. "No. I would rather you tell me lessons. I would rather Gate spoke to me under the stars."

"But there are no lessons in it. Only a story."

"My story?" I whispered.

"In a way. It is the story of your dream-women. In it are written their names."

The Fox scratched at her cupped red ear. "They have no names. Only the hermit-Ayako has a name," I protested.

"It is only that you do not know their names. But if you do not open the book, you will not finish the dreams, you will not reach the sea. Do you not recall what the Sphinx said? All women are one woman. If you do not seek out the shells they leave behind, you will not shed your own." The Fox trotted over and stood before me.

"Who are you? Why are you here at the top of my tower?" I rasped, my voice dry as rice in the sun.

"I have many names, as you do. This is my pagoda, I have always been here. I am the Stone, too. Once it bore my face. I am Mercy, I am Compassion. I am the flowing water that carries you. You cannot step into me twice, and yet, each of your footsteps drags four behind them. I am nothing more than a door through which you will pass. I am here to show you the End."

FOLIAGE TURNS YELLOW AND FALLS

Outside the dream-pagoda, leaves drifted down with thoughtless grace, green, gold, brown. The air had sharpened, swallows sang down the sun.

"Is this the dream of the Fox? Or the dream of the Fifth Floor?" I asked.

"In all probability. I have no revelations for you, only the peace that comes with understanding. You did not strive to reach the top of the pagoda—you fled to the pinnacle without thought of ascension. Because you did not seek it, it is yours. You dive into the water and become a clam, a pheasant, a book. This is about metamorphosis—this is about solitude. Look how you have built your temple! Look how high and bright the spires!" The Fox laughed, a deep sound in her throat like skin being stretched over a drum. "You must listen to the dream of the Sphinx. She tells the truth—she cannot do otherwise. Her body carries the physiognomy of true things—only a true answer will ease her hunger. Thus, she is emptiness. Not the expanse of pure emptiness in which wisdom grows, but the gnawing absence of knowledge, that which burns."

"But are all these women me?" I begged, confused.

"All women are one woman. You are the I-that-is. They are the I-that-is-possible. Open the book, and follow the voice-threads where they lead. Out of the black silk harvest they came, and they are yours. You have a responsibility to them. The multiplied "I" can not be reduced back into itself until all its light-paths have been followed. The Sphinx would say this has already happened. If it has, it should not be difficult for you."

And the book lay between us, bulging and dark, promising. The Fox retained her beatific face; I opened the cover with a careful hand and read these things:

INSECTS TUCK THEMSELVES AWAY

If all women are one woman who has already lived out each of her infinite possible lives, if all their stories are already told, if, in fact, all possible events have already occurred, the one infinitely copied photon has completed all conceivable pathways, then we approach not only the unfortunate conclusion that all Riddles have already been asked and answered, but must accept that we reside in the Wasteland of Quantum Exhaustion.

"Do you like that, Oedipus? I am delivering a paper on the subject at a conference in Alexandria next month," the dream-Sphinx mused, and Prince Oedipus picked his teeth with a sliver of bone. He is bored.

In the Wasteland of Quantum Exhaustion, the woman-who-is-all-women would stand at a central point, one of her possible selves would be a commonality around which other possible selves would revolve. Of course, each of the women in then in and of herself a commonality, and thus there is no center per se to the system, only an infinitely expanding series of centers, which negates the idea of a center altogether. As we all know, a center cannot be within the system and govern it simultaneously.

On the other hand, the wavelength of each potential self is determined by its distance from the fulcrum-crone. But if we understand any of an infinite series of women and ur-women to be fulcra, the wavelength of each self is also infinite, both infinitely short and infinitely long, infinitely red and infinitely blue. Instinctively, these selves seek each other out and merge, unable to comprehend the depravity of their conviction that a single woman can serve as a hinge around which they all turn. The resulting sea of constantly merging and disengaging selves resembles the primordial mitosis-swamp—the infinite female, treading water in a mass of pure, white light.

"I don't think you are listening to me," the dream-Sphinx said crossly. "Have you solved the Riddle yet? I think I have given you plenty of time. What goes on four legs in the morning, two in the afternoon, and three in the evening? It isn't even a very good Riddle. You should have heard the last one."

Suddenly, the Prince's rather dull face lit up with revelation.

"I do!" he cried, leaping to his feet, "I do! A man does, I mean."

And the Sphinx smiled.

"Don't congratulate yourself too much. It isn't the Riddle after all, that you have conquered, but the Riddle that conquers you."

Oedipus did not even do her the honor of eating her, but rather stabbed her with his dagger and watched her die with the peculiar satisfaction of aristocracy. He left her corpse to the flies and the desert-birds. And her body was the color of the dream-sand, which even as she bled began to cover her in gold, and preserve her bones as relics.

As she died, the dream-Sphinx uttered her last Riddle, which is, of necessity, unanswerable.

Of course, Oedipus, your story is already told, too. The King is dead, the Queen is dead, your daughters and sons are dead, and you are blinded on the road to Colonus. This is as easy to read as an answer in the back of a mathematics textbook. It has already been a hundred times over, a thousand. There can be no free will in the Wasteland. We are all bound up together, belly to belly to belly.

When one possible woman dies, it is as though a shutter closes, and the light from a certain window is snuffed out. There are many, many more windows, and really, since the window had already been opened and shut an infinite number of times, since in potential it occupies both the states of Open and Shut, nothing changes at all. Is this process indefinite?

WATER BEGINS TO FREEZE

"I do not want to, Fox. Just tell me my lesson. They are mine, I do not like to see them written. They are my own, no one else's."

"The more you possess, the wiser you become?" Fox asked, with an arch expression. I blushed.

"I did not say I was wise."

"This is the way. Each by each, night falls and the rivers freeze over, the black branches gather ice, the seeds sleep in the earth and dream the peculiar dreams of rooted things. The cicadas stop singing, the crickets die. You are not separate from this. Stories end, riddles are answered. If there is no end, no story has been told. Though the answers to a single riddle are infinite, the number of correct answers is finite—there is but one. I am the answer to you. I am the second bead, that which completes your question."

Night had stolen up the side of the pagoda, twisted dark fingers into the vines, and now shone blackly across the floor.

"Then the I-that-is-Ayako is the true thing. The others are false," I concluded with sorrow.

"In the end, silk-child, does it matter which is which?"

"To me, it matters," I pleaded.

"When it does not, then you will be wise." The Fox licked her paw and gestured towards me. "Turn the page," she said softly.

EARTH BEGINS TO FREEZE

There is an old circus trick: a girl lets a serpent swallow her whole. Beautiful people pay their pennies and see a woman become the apple of Eden, devoured by the grinning dragon, writhingly slick with olive oil so that when the tattered red curtains shut, her partner can haul her feet-first from those hinged jaws, a grotesque, hermaphroditic birth enacted every night at seven and nine o'clock sharp. This act requires both the serpent and the girl's consent—neither can perform it without the other. The old serpent lets herself be abused by the lovely woman and the crowd, but in exchange, she enjoys the bliss of reliving the meal over and over again.

In the audience, perhaps a mother will whisper to her child, "That was how the old stories say it was in the beginning of the world, when Tiamat, who was Queen of the Watery Abyss, was destroyed and the earth made from her flesh. She was swallowed by the serpent, too."

But I was not. I was the serpent and the girl. Mountain was the circus-master.

Now it is quiet. I have covered Mountain. I have covered River. I have flooded the hallways of the Palace and erased the History of the World. The ink itself has dissolved in me until no creature can taste its sourness. I spat the castle from my mouth when the floods came.

The salt-flood of my tears cleansed the world—the abyss is on the face of the earth now, and at last there is quiet. The waters rushed in and the dams broke with a sound like matchsticks snapping, the foam hushed over my belly and my hair floated on the waves like a silver-knotted net. There was a tumult of sea, the great salt waves erasing villages, temples, towns, capitals. It made everything clean, transcendent, pure. When the Moon rose up over the surface of the earth and saw the New Sea, she exulted in her diamond carriage and cried out with her voice of spun glass.

I battered Mountain with waves and forced River to join his water to mine. Mountain is merely buried, his voice shut up in a blue casket—River is within me, and I relive the meal over and over, with delight. He twists in my belly with delicious fervor.

There is flotsam everywhere, but that will pass. Seabirds call out desolate songs and search for aeries that have long been swallowed. They roost now on anything that is buoyant—cradles, spinning wheels, stable doors. That will pass, too. The world will be made again, no doubt. It is the way. The process is indefinite. It is made, it is dismantled, it is made again. Perhaps this time I will make it, and write my name in crushed jade.

I am peaceful now, the peace of the full belly. I look out over the sea and watch my wounds heal themselves. Flesh knits itself to itself, slowly, slowly. I am still missing many teeth, but I have confidence that they will turn up. I can afford contentment, I have bought it dearly.

Half of my body is still hung in the sky like a trophy. I lie on the earth-that-is-me and stare into the sky, which stares back. And we rock ourselves to sleep, we two, in this infinite mirror.

Softly, Mountain rumbles beneath me.

PHEASANTS DIVE INTO THE WATER BECOMING MONSTER CLAMS

In the dream of Ayako, she touches the book with tender hands and the Fox watches her. In the dream of Ayako she is washed in moonlight scented by the sea. It is becoming very cold, and Mountain has drawn over himself his old snow-cloak. In the dream of Ayako, her hands are terribly thin and have begun, in places, to shine blue and indigo.

In the dream of Ayako, the thought has begun to form in her that none of the women are real, that even she is a shade, a vision. Perhaps the villagers are right to think her a vengeful ghost. Perhaps the village is not real, either. She had, of course, long suspected that the boys who brought her rice were dreams. This thought was like the grain of sand that forces the oyster to make a pearl—it pained her, and yet the fist of her soul closed around it.

Perhaps the dream at the base of her soul was true—the silent girl who did not move. But perhaps not. Ships existed that had no anchors, perhaps even that had no sails or oars. It was possible that she existed with nothing at her core but ether, nothing but a dark swirl of air.

In the dream of Ayako, the Fox lies down beside her in the weak light, her red haunches glittering. She is very lovely, with her grand tail. Ayako thinks that the Fox must have found a great many succulent mice to keep her this fat in the swift-snowed winter.

And because Ayako is lonely, she reads aloud, simply so that she may hear the voice of a human, whether or not she is real.

THE RAINBOW HIDES

In the ninth month of pregnancy the fetus is nearly fully grown. It has gained a great deal of subcutaneous fat and can normally breathe outside the womb at this stage. The mother will experience anxiety and discomfort in the weeks prior to birth. The fetus sleeps for the majority of its tenancy in the womb, and experiences REM sleep, an indication of dreaming.

I kneel in the deep water to give birth, to finish the course he decided for me. In a dream did I mount the golem-husband and take the child into my belly. In a dream did I swell like a bow drawing and feel the hawk-headed son stir in my womb, felt the hard press of his talons against my flesh. Feathers serrate the uterine walls, and the metallic beak kneads my flesh like meager bread. In a dream did I set the body into a sarcophagus of jasper and agate, and let it sail into the south on the great currents.

And now I kneel in the silt, attended by crocodiles with their pupilless eyes, and my body drains out of itself—water and blood and pages of dedicated verse. I have lost the dream-husband, even his desiccated flesh is lost to me. I replace him with the dream-son and hope that I am not asked to sew his bones back together with the threads of my hair, as I have had to do with his father.

I cry out to the desert and my voice is eaten by a dearth of wind. My belly cuts itself like a flayed fish; a bloody-eyed child crawls out and shakes amniotic fluid from his feathered hair. Sobbing, I reach for him over the ruin of my body, clutching my son with the moon between his brow, little Horus, who will make the world over again.

I fall backwards into exhaustion, and my blood eddies out into the Nile. It is promptly devoured by a school of infant catfish, and the sun begins to rise in the west.

HEAVEN'S ESSENCE RISES UP AND EARTH'S ESSENCE SINKS DOWN

"This is the last woman," the Fox said, and I knew it was true. I was not the last woman, of course. I was not the first. The I-that-is-Ayako is a hinge which opens and shuts strange windows, who dreams she is more than her flesh.

"Words are redundancies, after all, my girl. Mountain abides. River changes. The cicada sings its time and is silent. All these things can be known without a single word. You have been glutted with words, but I have opened up a drain at the base of your heart and soon you will be empty as an amber shell. It is not altogether a sad thing."

I, and all the dreams of myself, looked in one body out the window of the pagoda, at the striated skin of Mountain, gray and quartz-white, as though he had been weeping. The blue-gold light of dawn crept up his flank, pressing his velvet nose into the stone. The sky had dropped its hazy veils over the valley, and to sit in the center of the morning was to sit *zazen* in the center of some vast pearl. The trees had all become bare again, and my garden was a patch of black soil, concealing the dreaming seeds.

As I turned the last page of the book and began to read, Fox extended her rosy tongue until it nearly touched my face.

And on it, like a jewel, was a single, perfect cicada shell.

WALLING OURSELVES UP, IT BECOMES WINTER

The man who was killed they called the breaker of horses, and the one who killed him dragged his body behind a chariot around the walls of the city. The sweat of the brown horses ran thick and fast, and the fire-goddess drew back from the holy city, so stunned was she by the madness of two men. The charioteer had driven himself into a frenzy—his hair flew wildly as a ship's loose sail, his teeth gnashed, his knuckles were white on the reins. Women tore their hair and begged him to stop, but even as the wheels splintered into wedges and two of the horses dropped dead of exhaustion, he would not cease.

The city trembled at the sound of the careening hoof beats, and the fire-goddess bided her time.

But I lay over the city and it rose to meet the movements of my crimson body—I only had to wait a little while. It crackled through my fingers and the mortar itself exploded into flame, the towers thrust up into me and fell back scorched to dust. I laughed and wept as my skin covered the walls and courtyards, the markets and temples. The wind whipped along the ramparts and the flames arched towards the pure white sky. The swords themselves melted to a bronze wine, running freely over the cobbled streets.

I lay in the center of it, curled into myself like a yin-yang, pulsing with heat, smiling into my belly and reveling in the surrender of the city to my love. Soon it would be a smoking black ruin, a diorama of ash that had once been called sacred.

But now was the best time, when I shot my flames into the windy towers and consumed the flesh of my body and the flesh of the divine city with one great, red mouth. This was my finest work, my masterpiece, the conflagration of cityflesh and horseflesh and manflesh. I could smell the hair of consecrated virgins sizzling, the paint bubbling on their altars, blood cooking into the walls. Over and over the city swore itself to me, gave itself over, abandoned its body into my arms. The tombs that ringed the citadel like a pretty necklace became pyres, and within the spiced smoke I suffered my scarlet paroxysms of luminosity.

When it was over, and the city lay steaming black on its high bluff, when the sea thunders it funereal march, I watched the last timbers cave inward, the last sparks gutter in the dawn wind.

I bent my roseate face and kissed gently the blessed ruin before turning away.

THE COPPER PHEASANT CEASES ITS CALL

In the dream of Ayako, there is a pagoda-tower. It is empty. There is no wine-sack. There is no statue whose face has been erased by centuries. There is no Fox with kind eyes. There is no Book. There is no hint of what has or has not passed within it, only the jagged hole in the roof through which unimaginable stars have shone, and which now lets through the first shafts of winter light, falling like snow through the tower.

There is an old woman, curled up like a child, on the floor of the uppermost level, whose rags flutter in the breeze. The sunlight makes her skin translucent, shows the blown glass of her bones and the delicate network of stilled veins.

There is no breath, and her lips are the color of the frozen river parting to receive her steps.

THE TIGER BEGINS TO ROAM

In the village, the boy whose lot it had been to bring the ghost her yearly offerings of rice and tea lay awake in his soft bed. He had dreamed that he was a prince, and a strange beast had asked him a riddle. Tomorrow, he would go and see the dream-interpreters.

The boy studied the pattern of the roof-wood. He is quiet, so as not to disturb his father and sisters with his fanciful dreams, which, after all, mean nothing. His father always told him that dreams were the province of the poor and the mad.

Outside his window, a squirrel left small footprints in the snow.

LICHEE GRASS WITHERS

In Kyoto, a scholar had fallen asleep in the midst of his scrolls, with his spectacles pushed up over his brows. In the cold morning, crows drew their wings close. Sleeping trees stood like soldiers at the gate.

Through an open window, a handsome brown moth fluttered into the room, landed lightly on the smooth hair of the sleeping scholar. It paused, as if in thought, flapping his wings with deliberate grace. It seemed to consider something brought on the snow-scented wind.

When the scholar's brow furrowed, deep in dreams, the moth lifted away from him, and out into the gray dawn.

EARTHWORMS TWIST INTO KNOTS

At the foot of the dream-pagoda, the great red *torii* gate bent low to the ground and cracked under the weight of snow. Her scarlet paint shone horribly bright against the pale earth, as though blood had been spilled. She lay there like a great heart burst open, and the sound of her falling broke the genteel silence for only a moment.

The splintered posts which still stood straight later wounded slightly the foot of a late-migrating magpie.

She would be buried under the ice until the spring, when the cicadas would come to mate in her shadow.

THE ELK'S HORN BREAKS

On Mountain's east flank, a shaggy goat with massive horns chewed the tough winter grass. Snow caught in his fur in long matted strands. He balanced on the rocks, searching for the sweet moss he liked best in the winter months. It was difficult work, pebbles slipped into his hooves and down the cliffside, rattling like a shaman's staff.

As the clouds drifted over his back, he looked down towards the little valley, and thought briefly of the girl who could not climb her tower, how he pitied her, and how her hair smelled of cinnamon.

UNDERGROUND SPRINGS MOVE

River refused to think on it.

Slabs of ice moved lazily down his current, grinding against each other as though they were carriages in the city. The fish dreamed and the trees bent low over the rippling stream, a thatched canopy.

If it was true that she could not step in him twice, then she had not stepped in *this* River at all, he reasoned. Perhaps, then, he had never known her, and therefore should not weep.

WILD GEESE RETURN TO THEIR NORTHERN HOME

The silkworm colony of the village suddenly ceased to produce their fine white thread. From the morning of Ayako's last dream on the Mountain, the generation which were then thriving in the house of the silk weavers produced nothing but a thick, viscous black fluid, which did not dry properly, leaving a strange, knotted coil. For seven worm-generations after this there was no good silk in the village, only the black cocoon-stuff. In the dreams of children the silkworms sang as they birthed it, and whispered that they were weaving a shroud for the death-festival of a ghost.

The boy saw this and was troubled. For no reason he thought of his beast-dream, and wondered what riddle would have this scythe-silk as its answer.

The villagers burned the dream-thread in the spring, and the smell of it lingered into midsummer, clinging to the temple bell-ropes and the granary doors.

MAGPIES NEST

The bones of Ayako still dreamed, but her lips had flushed blue and her body was cold. She had dreamed herself out of her shell, and it remained like a pale gem, slowly becoming dust on the highest floor of the dream-pagoda. She/I/we had composed our song, and moved away from the cocoon-tower to open our throats in the mountains. We left the meadow of shells-within-shells, where we lived within the body which lived within the pagoda which lived within the Mountain.

Perhaps one day there will be tower-shells and Mountain-shells glittering, too, on the grass.

We are finished. Our smile is beatific and mouthless. We have no more body to puzzle us, and our voices multiply in infinite combinations, through the trees and stones and snow:

When one possible woman dies, it is as though a shutter closes, and the light from a certain window is snuffed out. There are many more windows, and really, since the window had already been opened and shut an infinite number of times, since in potential it occupies both the states of Open and Shut, nothing changes at all. This process is indefinite, and cannot be charted.

THE PHEASANT CALLS TO ITS MATE

The dream-bones of Ayako were not found until the next summer, when the boy whose lot it was to bring the ghost her offerings could not find her. He had not lost the lottery this year, but had traded a bowl of rice and three jade beads to the girl who had, so that he could see the old woman again, and ask her about his dreams.

When he climbed the pagoda and discovered her small heap of pearl-white bones, he was overcome, and wept for the woman who had told him about the dream of the Mountain. He could not decide what would be the correct thing to do with her bones—for it was now clear she had not actually been a ghost, even if she had since become one. So he gathered them up and placed them with some incense and the sack of rice in one of Mountain's secret clefts.

Until he was forty, and appointed, through his father's influence, to the royal court at Kyoto, the boy brought incense and rice to her bones at the death of each summer, faithful as a wife.

He would dream of her often, even in his city apartments hung with curtains he had ordered made from the black silk thread of that terrible year. And in his dreams she was young, a child, hiding under a wheelbarrow. She peered out, whispered to him that the fire-goddess had fallen in love with the village.

The dream interpreters would not speak with him.

CHICKENS BROOD

The I-that-is-Ayako tells you these things. It is my lesson, and I have told it. River heard, and Fox. Gate and Juniper listened, and Moth heard rumor of it.

The you-that-is-Ayako has heard it, too.

THE EAGLEHAWK FLIES FURIOUSLY HIGH

There was a storm the day the boy interred my bones within Mountain. The rain curled down to him in spirals, and the air crackled with the potential of lightning. The stones could hear the song my bones sang, the slight, susurring song of the discarded body. I felt them press in to hear, and the juniper trees bent to catch it.

THE WATERS AND SWAMPS ARE THICK AND HARD

Alone, with the mist creeping in like a pale-mouthed thief, Mountain wept.

THE GRASS-CUTTING SWORD

A field of mustard,
no whale in sight,
the sea darkening.
—**Buson**

0
IZUMO

Descent is a peculiar behavior.

There is a sensation of being dragged by the glisten of the bowels. There is a sensation of being pushed at the crown of the skull by a lead-etched palm. There is a silence, and there is a detonation of air, a detonation of sudden light. A new fontanel beats nebulous and netted at the place where tectonic bone-plates converge, a gauze of flesh pink and shimmering, a trembling crevice where before there was only wholeness.

I set these symptoms down for those who might descend after me, for those other red-chested *colossi* expelled by the sun-woman, cast out by her bronze hands, the boil-blaze of her justice. For it is certain my sister will find fault in others as she found fault in me; some blue-black kernel of my nature which, buried at the depth of sinew, scratched against the red-gold bead of hers.

But I am magnanimous—I grant that our two natures could not inhabit a single heaven. I forgave her, even as she burned against my fog-limbs, even as her ribcage irradiated mine with its feathered fire, even as the salt-sea was dried from my mouth by her banishing blow.

After all, we are family, she and I.

Of course, I thought of none of this then. Then, there was only the air and the light, and the fall through tiers of star and ether, the light of her golden heels receding above me, and the earth below, green and checkered with watery rice-fields, their squares made radiant by the reflection of my descent. I understood nothing but the sky-roar and the grass-beckon: I did not even comprehend my name—the last brassy exhalation of Ama-Terasu obliterated it from my mind, and replaced what had been my name with a devouring whirlpool, black and spinning—and it was this, finally, which cut me from heaven as a spleen is cut from a diseased body.

One hopes it will cure the patient, but one cannot be sure.

The grass-leaves of Izumo were the first I ever touched with feet enfleshed. It was there my heel-pads first bent and crushed green things, there I first opened up my lungs like windows and breathed the air of the world. I was naked, my hair unpinned. I was a man, and my knees were knot-strong. I was surprised, of course. Mine was the first descent of all the Kami, I had neither map nor report of a wild-toed predecessor to direct me on my way—and so all things were bright and sharp, painful in their novelty, colors that scalded my eyes, as though a pan of steaming water had been flung at me. I believe I might have stood, knowing nothing but that I *had* fallen, but not what or whom had done the falling, until the moon flickered and snuffed itself out, had I not heard a terrible sound: wails and ululations like the keening of roosters who know they are to be slaughtered for soup.

I followed the terrible sound until I came upon a long river, winding through the quiet fields in the pleasant way that well-tamed rivers will. It was unremarkable as rivers go, its water more or less greenish-brown, its current neither quick nor sluggish, its span perhaps that of four or five men laid head to foot. Having by now seen many rivers and their tributaries, their deltas, their silt and their sand, I think it was rather paltry, but it was to me on that first day the most beautiful of all possible rivers, sparkling in the morning like a stream of jewels tumbling down to the sea. So enraptured was I that I forgot the piercing cries I had sought, and stared transfixed at the splashing eddies, struck dumb with admiration. And so it was only when the shrieks ceased, as if cut off with a choking fist, that I looked up, startled from my dream of perfect rivers, and saw the first humans my incarnate-eyes had known.

Like the river, they were neither lovely nor hideous, but plain and peasant-colored, quite aged, clothed in simple kimono the hues of which were not unlike the earthy shades of the river-bank where they knelt, tearing their hair in unworded grief.

Green and brown their clothing folded; green and brown the river ran.

They looked from me to each other, and back to me, some strange calculation clicking away in their furtive eyes. Their wrinkles fascinated me, etching their skin with rippling lines like hiragana, and I admit I spent some minutes trying to read the secrets of their senescence, the withered psalms written on their tired limbs. I was like a babe in those first hours—

everything enchanted me, absorbed me utterly, until the next wonder tore my attention violently from the first marvel. And so it was that I was deep in the study of their wrinkled cheeks when one of them, the male, spoke to me—the first voice to flood itself into my ears.

"O, Lord of the Wind! You have deigned to appear to this old man! I have done no deed worthy of such an honor!" He pressed his brow to the cool grass, and the female swiftly did the same, as if answering some unheard cue, crying out as she did so, though her quavering voice was muffled, since she spoke into the blades:

"Susanoo-no-Mikoto, Heavenly Ocean-Father! How we have prayed for this day!"

It was at this that I knew myself, the utterance of the crone scrubbing aside the scorch-black of my sister's rage, allowing me to see the walls of my godhead, the ceilings and floors of my name, my being, my history. It is always the peasants who know what they see—they are not befuddled by opium or intellect, as the city-dweller so often is. It took them not a moment to see past the gloss of my hair and the beauty of my new flesh and know that they were in the presence of the Sea-God, the sibling of Heaven, the seed of all storms. In the palaces of Hiroshima to the south, I would have had to tie on a great blue mask with a demoniac grimace and a nose like a bludgeoning club, trailing rainclouds behind me like a woman's robes to make myself known. But this woman needed no theatrics, and calling me by name she gave me my name; and naming me she made me myself, and myself, named, knew for the first time the tang of exile, the shiver of loamy air untinged by golden vapors.

The taste of sorrow is the taste of broth which has grown a skin and begun to attract mayflies—it sticks in the throat, fecund and foul. Did I even then love my sister, forgive her, long, perhaps, for her ember-bronze arms slung round my shoulders again? For the taste of her cakes in the evening, the perfect seams of the robes she wove in the days when she was inclined to gift-giving? I worried the question between my jaws like a meat-ribboned bone.

I decided I did not. Let her have the skies—the earth would lay itself out under me like a wife. And what new storms would I make when I was my right self again! Typhoons like spinning sunflowers would flutter against these sands, winds and seas as I had never before attempted would rise up like carved columns under the roof of heaven. She would not restrain me here, not if I could find my way from this heavy flesh to my old radiance.

I was disturbed in these pleasurable thoughts by the peasants, still kneeling at the river. It was strange to me that they had not gone, having served such divine purpose as they had already done, but still they wept and beat their chests, their throats open to the rainless air. I was compassionate—it is easy to be compassionate.

"Why do you weep?" I said softly, with infinite grace, putting my hands, knuckles raw and new, to the poor couple's heads.

"It is our daughter, Storm-King," the man said bitterly. "Kushinada, whose hair was dark as ink pooled in the belly of a crow, whose skin was pale as new-sewn silk! She was our only happiness—one by one, our daughters have disappeared into the air, but she, at least, was left to us, fair enough to marry an Emperor, if she cast her eyes to his throne! But she would not look so high, for our girl was humble as a mound of straw, and asked for no more than to cook simple rice-mash, and fish-eye soup, and serve weak tea to her poor parents."

"And where has this marvelous daughter gone?"

"Gone? She would not *go*," said the mother indignantly, "she was meek, meek as a deer startled by the moon's weight on a maple leaf. She was *taken*, taken from us by a beast with eight heads—it will swallow her as it swallowed our seven daughters before, and now we will never see our Kushinada more."

I considered this. Maidens are prone to kidnapping, and the loss of theirs was no more or less tragic than the scores of sailors whose brains I had dashed out on the brine-pink reefs—but Kushinada seemed to me worthy enough, and to kill a thing is always pleasant work. My sister never understood that, but destruction is a peculiar skill, and I longed to practice it, to know if its flavor was different in the skin of a man.

"If you wish, I will go after this beast, and bring the maid Kushinada back to this very river, to make your rice-mash, and your eye-soup, and pour your weak tea for all her days."

The ancient couple fell again upon their faces and wept.

"We dared not pray for such an honor as this! Surely nothing can stand where the Tide-Lord rises! We cannot pile up the jewels a god deserves, or weave for him a robe fit to be worn at the throne of his sister, the Queen of Heaven!"

The woman wrung her robe between her hands and spoke through teeth yellowed and grinding. It was then that she baited the trap they had cleverly set with their fine words and high praise for the virtues of the missing girl.

"Bring her back to us and we will give her to you to wife—she is the best of all women. Her limbs are young and will please you; she will make your rice-mash and serve your tea, and smile only when you permit it."

I laughed, but that gurgling belly seethed at my sister's name. This body could not turn from such bait, even when the teeth of the trap were plain.

"Tell me what sort of beast it was and I will disappear it, I will pass over it like a cloud and it will be no more. In your virtue, you called me by name, and I will repay it."

The wife looked at her husband and shook her silvering head. "It was a serpent—but it was not a serpent. Its heads were terrible, and each different. The husband of our other daughter said that he could not keep his eyes on it; they slid off of its skin as though he were staring into the sun. It seemed to be plumed in fire, yet its body was wet and slick as a worm's, mottled green and brown, with patches of blue, patches of black, patches of gold, patches of slime and flame. Its eyes were red, sixteen pupils like black chrysanthemums, and it had a tail for each head, thick as a woman's waist. Its body muscled and knotted in the center, with its mass of heads and tails spreading out before and behind like a doubled fan. On its back grows a strange snarl of trees and grasses, and some say there are eyes along its spine, blinking. Yet it does not slither on the ground like a snake, but has legs like a bird—save that there are four—gnarled with muscle, green as bile. It drags itself along the ground by these legs, and from its belly a great font of blood flows, and stains the land."

I bowed only slightly—in acceptance, not deference, you understand. I thought nothing of the beast itself, only wondered vaguely if that blood would be warm or cool flowing over my wrists.

They fussed over me, insisted on piling my hands with rice-balls—the last of Kushinada's excellent cooking—and draping me with their own rough robes. They tied sandals onto my feet and belted my slim waist tightly. Only when I was thoroughly uncomfortable did they let me go, directing me southward, into a range of mountains lying on the earth like a severed jaw, its jagged teeth sawing the sky, crusted over with ice. Beyond Mt. Hiba, they said, the beast snorted and feasted its nights into day. Beyond Mt. Hiba, Kushinada lay naked on a stone table, her sweet skin ready to be carved into meat for each of the eight slavering heads.

And so I went out from that first river, that first knot of grass.

Behind my heels trailed wisps of grey sea-fog, curling into the summer air like ink dissolving into water.

EIGHT

Call me Monster.

I am exactly as you imagine I will be. Green on black on green on black, whicker-snack in the dark, slapping binary scales—greenblackgreengreengreenblack—against cavern-aurochs, against shaggy reindeer and whizzing arrows and cicadas like wet brown seeds, against walls, always walls, caves within caves upon caves, against granite, basalt, maiden.

I am Eight. We are Eight. Lying on my side, if you prefer the symbolism. Eight heads, eight tails, eight snakes susurring against each other like auto-asphyxiating lovers, joined at the torso—circus grotesque, unseparated octuplets in a jar of formaldehyde, jumbled trunk a snaggletoothed muscle with the brawn of a circus strongman, and all the bells ringing, ringing, ringing in the gloam. Eight-all-together rattle eight diamond heads, heavy and flat, a clutch of serpent-castanets, and oh, the music I-and-we make, music for the maidens, music for the midden we made of our caves, music for the bones, the old rolled bones, rooster bones and buffalo bones and fox bones and tigress bones, bones like bellows and bones like cudgels, bones like whistles and bones like pillows.

Oh, the music, oh, the bed of bones.

I eat light, vomit scripture. Eat maiden; retch hymn. Eat hero; hawk meadhall. The natural reptilian digestion is alchemical: eight chambered stomachs bubbling like beakers, intestines looping between, above and below, logos-calligraphy whispering recipes between celestial spheres swollen with bile and flesh. Our body is proto-Ptolemaic, constructed all of hoops and circles, perfect circles, without beginning or end—mouth, eye, neck-elongate, poison-sac, egg. We swim in ourselves, we chew our tails, we exude diamond-slime and drink it from puddles in the pocked cavefloor, our every process is filthy with beatitude, we are exalted by excrement, transfigured by mucus-mandala. We have to eat, after all.

꩜

You will, no doubt, see us and cry: It is a snake, and horrible to see.

This is because your processes are redundant, revolting—eat maiden; shit sludge.

But we are witch-doctors, we are medicine, and all around us the maidens waver like ghosts chained to a lakefloor, coronal, illuminate, perfected into daughters of my flesh (greenblackgreengreenblack) breech-angled, nestled in the sandy soil of our tapering body. We carry them like daughters-strapped-to-the-back, we drag them along like sacks of corn, corn-women, gone down into darkness and up again, down again and up again, and there is no asphodel like the cilia of our viscera, there is no pomegranate like our colossal heart, sixteen-chambered, ventricles lines in white fiber, seeded in bloody rubies, slowly erupting, slowly retreating.

That there were eight of them you might call providential, if you believe in that sort of thing-but I don't imagine you do. What use is providence to a god? Of course, tradition demands seven only, seven brides for seven brothers, seven maids for seven monsters. But Kushinada, Kushinada, she was the false Pleiad, the Eighth, and her hair was so black. I am not ashamed—her sisters cried out for her in their cradles of snakemeat, the Eight-all-together ululated in our stony crèche, we all beat the earth with our bodies and ate up her name in her absence: Kushinada, Kushinada!

Family wants family, and I have all these mouths to feed.

Seven-eighths is no good; we want the whole set, perfect little dolls lined up in a row, and how pretty their birthday-obi gleam in the filtered algaelight this cave allows. She sits with her legs crossed on the mound of bones, sits like a student doing sums, and looks up at us, at the wallowing serpent, the slime and sere, the strange sister-shapes moving beneath the un-molt. We make this tableau each morning after breakfast, girl and creature, primate and reptile, evolution in miniature, titans terrible in contemplation of our splendor.

Every evening after tea, she pulls a scale from my throat, great and clear as a shaving from the emerald at the heart of the world, and with delicate lips—pink, so pink!—she nibbles at it, cake-sweet and swarthy with the taste of trees, and swallows with relish. I do not know yet what she can make of me in that strange pale oven of her body—much, I suppose, depends on it, but I-and-we are patient; love makes us so. This is the school of snakes, and she is my best pupil yet.

You recoil, but you can't deny it's compelling—this folkloric blueprint, handprint, angel in the snow, and oh, I certainly could not have made such a shape, not with these whips and flails, tongues and tails. You must have done it; any angel of mine would be an oceanic horror, waving its unspeakable heads at a punctured moon. This has arms, legs, an anatomy so simple and profound you cannot even recognize it as a single body: snake, cave, virgin.

It is your prurient nature which makes such things into miasma, it is you who holds up a glass and views her and I, our stainless acts, through the darkly of your clutching, it is you who lie on the grassy floor, redolent with oil and full of someone else's food, and tell the mustachioed man-god-father that you dream, you dream of the great eight-headed phallus looming over—is she smiling or screaming?—a schoolgirl in her best dress.

You dream of the cave's moss-veiled crevice, and the girl vanishing into it, and the snake vanishing into her, around and around and around, and you do not know why it reminds you of your mother.

Look at your angel in the ice, arms fanned out like spying stares.

It has your stink all over it.

I
HOKI

Walking is unpleasant. The muscles of my calves bunch new and raw like *fundoshi*, and my toes are flattening with use.

It is undignified.

My throat forces me to stop and soothe it at filthy wells lined in algae as thick as under-robes, but the water only runs out of me again, oily, seeping up through my skin like ink through rice paper.

I have had to piss several times; sour steam rises from the wet grass. The whole business is revolting.

Prefectural monks rub their heads furiously when I pass—they have not heard of the dragon, certainly such a blight would not befall their villages, blessed as they are of the Kami (and if I were in my right state I would haul seven or so typhoons from my left pocket to splash away those smug, simpering smiles—oh how I miss my limbs of thrashing palm trees and splintering camphor!) but they are assuredly grieved that the poor family of Kushinada, whose hair even here they have heard was as dark as ink pooled in the belly of a crow, should be made to suffer so.

Give me rice, brainless holy, and get back to your kneeling—the sun does love to see you scrape. As for me, my stomach will not shut up, and wants fish. It is not used to itself—ridiculous sack of meat which is always too empty for its own liking. I once had innards of pure light, intestines that served only to translate wind to sky. Where did the other body go when I fell from the floor of my sister's house? Is it caught in the clouds, in the slats of her golden *tatami*, light tangled up in light? I want it back, I want my storm-tongue and my oceanic muscles, unfolding like wings, black on blue on silver—she cannot have it, she has no right to keep it from me and leave me with only this stinking, mewling flesh dripping its slime over the earth like sacraments—why cannot I wring my hands and be rid of it as I would any other putrid mire?

The bitch always stole my things.

Even pride of the eldest—who ever heard of a girl born first? But there it was—she came sliding out of Father's eye like golden pus, and the pillar of the world was lit up with her, Mother-Below was lit up with her, the sky was lit—everything went up like a torch tossed into a barn, a barn perfectly contented to stay a barn and keep its straw unsinged. Only Father saw her for what she was: a silly girl preening in her shining hair, who would never amount to anything more than a paper lantern.

Then came the moon, sick-silver, oozing from Father's other eye like a wet and shell-less snail. There he was, our paternity weeping luminate, his face made into a gaping wound . . . my brother sloughing light from one fringe of lashes and my sister bursting from the other divine cornea . . .

What a relief I must have been—the rush of cold water and darkness, the mere and the gloam, the wind drying stray drops of effluvia on his open mouth. Out of his nose I came, and from whence should I have come but the curved nostril, in my sharp air and exhalation—I came up from the crystalline lungs like a waft of smoke and curled from my Father with a grace sun and moon could not begin to imitate.

Or I was sneezed out, snot and phlegm, a waste of leftover junk, a tickle in his nose that had to be expelled, but was never meant to be a child. After all, I am not made of light, like the others. The sky does not want me. What use am I? This is what my sister took pains to tell me every day of our youth among the jewel-islands, Shikoku and Ogi and Tsukusi, Iki and Awazi and great, bulbous Honshu, curved like the edge of a spoon. So my brother told me every evening before bed, with his white sneer gleaming.

Only Mother-Below did not worship their light, did not pile up psalms at their feet like jointed toys. She knew I was the best of them, she knew I was beautiful, too. Mother-Below, Izanami-no-Kami, the Inviting Woman, who did not shame me for having the misfortune of being born from a hairy nostril.

She is here, somewhere, between Izumo and Hiroshima, under the paddling feet of monks robed and roped, under the hills fat with loam, there is a crack, a crevice that leads to her. I am the only one who bothers, of course—sun and moon have better things to do than lay lilies on their mother's grave, grander tracks to trace than the one that arcs ever downward into the wreckage of Mother-Below, into her belly that should have birthed us, into her arms that still hunger for us, even battened as she is into the dark. They don't care—the sun tosses her red curls over one shoulder and promises to have one of her red-faced girls light incense next week; moon takes his snuff and asks if Father isn't good enough for any loyal son.

Only I love her.

Only I glimpse tufts of her hair caught between the river and the stone. She needs me; she loves me; she hates Father as I do, and all who take the beautiful things of the world for themselves and leave the rest of us with dreck and jetsam and fallow fields.

If we were brought, my sister and I, before Mother-Below, and Ama-Terasu smiling in all her summer-bought beauty, with hyacinth in her hair and white arms burning, Mother would choose me, I know it.

I know it.

And so it is not wrong, not really, to seek after that ineffable *her* while I hunt the dragon and the tea-scented haunch of Kushinada. Mother would not begrudge me a wife, and what man could take a wife without presenting her first to his mother? Filial piety demands no less, and in the end, how hard can it be to discover the signs of a serpent dragging girls through the dirt-drifts of dead cicadas, spurting blood as it goes?

The sun on the rice-pools is like a disapproving eye, reflected over and over. The night is so warm, so warm, and it is pleasant, if only to think that the heat comes from her, from her furnace-ribs, rising and falling in the distance, and her breath stealing over the water like sleeve-hidden hands.

FIRST HEAD

I am the first body/daughter./

The name my lower intestine whispers/the sound of the taste of myself on a tongue mine/*not mine*/is Kazuyo. I was born first of eight burdens under brittle stars/*my throat emerged first of eight gullets from the mother-dark-and-wet when the sleeve-stars were high*/and a roof of thatched cypress bark.

It is quiet in the length. My cells are/*its cells*/are my cells/*are its*/cells are my cells/*my cells my own*/its/*mine*. Meat on /*meat* /I am translated, child into *serpent*/worm.

When I was myself/*when I was myself and did not hold a girl in me like a steel pin in my hip*/and did not wear a coat of monster, I lived in a village, in a house, and the mats on my floor were neither thin nor fat. I was born in winter, in the dead days after the last snowfall but before the ice of the air shows any crack. I was a small infant, blue in the face and hung like a criminal from my mother's womb by the noosed length of my own umbilicus. My mother said later that it looked like a shell-less snail lying over my tiny neck. And like a weed-stuffed garden pest, it was cut and thrown onto the refuse heap, its silver scrap reflecting the moon as though it too was pregnant, swollen with light it was meant to have delivered into my little navel.

And so I was born without the light I ought to have owned, with a stomach curiously empty from the first moment I drew ragged, gap-ridden breath. The earth ate it, slowly, with teeth of grass and stone. In years hence a persimmon tree grew out of that heap of cast-offs, and we re-planted the little sapling—so carefully, as if it were a baby itself, in warm red soil. My sisters used to play in it, pelting each other with orange fruit whose meat smelled of spices we would never purchase to scent our skins.

I remember that now, in the dark, grafted to smoke-flesh/*hanging from me like a necklace I bought long ago and lost in a drawer*/like that old dark wood—my sisters throwing sweet scraps of my birth-flesh at each other, staining their dresses with sugared oil/*the heartwoods of my throats playing catch-me with their own pulpy wombs.*

When I was a girl I gutted the fish my father caught, and their intestines slithered over my fingers, over and under, like weaving silver—their eyes went into our soup, for which the we were modestly famous, and rest of the village came to our stall in the marketplace at festival time, to slurp up the murky broth with all those sightless eyes floating in it, eaten staring at eater/*and it is always like that, you know, the thing which cannot help but be eaten ogles the thing which will eat it, and always, always, the moist eyes are beautiful, their dark centers salty and sour*/but the fish eyes, the fish eyes were too soft for my taste, runny eggs dripping their iris-ichors on my tongue, the black soup that stank in our house all year/*Yours, Kazuyo, were smoky and sere, persimmon-dusk, and they rolled over my tongue, so soft—do you remember that, how you saw me as I swallowed you, saw my uvula bobbing over your limbs as you fell into me?*

Hush, now. I have not gotten to that part yet. (And I/*you*/say this to the self/ *notself* which is not myself/*but is myself, my selves, my daughterbody and my snakebody all wound up together like yarn*/the self embedded in green muscle wall/*hush, self, hush, quiet, bones, blood says be still*/the self of/*cell-to-cell*, I say this to the eater which is eaten which is eater again/*and hungry.*)

The soup of eyes brought men to our threshold, men with chickens hanging limp like claw-stemmed bouquets in their hands, with rice balls like diamond rings. They came to get the eye-girls for their own, to fill up their bellies with salty-sour tear ducts on off-festival days as well, and we were lined up, eight in a row, only I even old enough to boast breasts. Our heads bent like black daffodils, nodding mutely at the earth. They looked at our teeth; they tested our jaws and our water-carrying muscles, the length and dexterity of our stirring fingers. And, as they will, a man indicated that I was sufficient to bear his children and clean his house and boil his broth for all the rest of my days. He was not ugly, nor old, and his eyes were very black. I thought, idly, what they would look like staring back at me from a bowl of soup/*only ask, daughterflesh, and I will fetch them for you like a pair of buttons to shine your breast*/hush, hush, I've told you. This is what virgins think about when their wombs are sold.

It was midwinter, I think—in truth I cannot recall, but it seems to me from the vantage of these copper-blooded innards that the trees were bare and bone-rattled, that the sky was impassive and pale as a face. /*It was midsummer, you silly girl, and I watched you walk out under the eaves from a bower of green, and the sun was beating my back with switches of yellow light. So much green, so many leaves, all my heads lolled out of the trees and you saw nothing but bobbing fruit.*

It doesn't matter.

*I wanted you then, like a husband, in your clean white wimple. Only I didn't know how to be a husband, it is not my natural state. All I have are these mouths, these mouths and these tongues and these coils, and they all cried out for you that hot, still day, and I thought you were very beautiful in your dress, and I wanted to eat you, but I wanted to love you, but I wanted to eat you, but I wanted to love you/*but I wanted to/*I wanted/*I wanted to love you.

The man who was neither old nor ugly took my hand and led me from the threshold of my house, and the sun was neither yellow nor grey, and I looked back over my shoulder at the persimmon tree, which was very tall by then, tall as a standing serpent, and if something moved in the branches I thought nothing of it, only that it was empty of fruit, that the bark of my afterbirth was barren as a rotted root. *I wanted to/*see something of myself in the wood, something of my umbilicus wavering in the grain, something silver and unnamable which was my own flesh grown sap-ridden and forked. But there was nothing there, and I left my mother's house, and all my sisters, heads still bent like a tidy row of carrot-flowers, with nothing for a trousseau but the thick white linen of my headdress and the secret of the soup of eyes nestled next to my heart.

*It was on the beaten road south-winding from Izumo/*it was near the temple/*it was nowhere in particular but somewhere between these when I/*when you/*when the empty-we-I came reeding by. Do you remember, is it round in your mind like an orange fruit/*it is round in my mind like a floating eye/*I remember how your hair shone like a braised pig-stomach in the summer/*it was winter/*in the summer which was so still, and so warm.*

And you/I/said to me/*you/*as if you did not see the man who was neither old nor ugly at all/*I do not want your soup of eyes. I do not want your womb hung up in a tree, to give me persimmon-babies every fall. Come with me/*

go into this/*and I will show you the place where monster and marrow and maiden*/and meat and bile and voices/*pool. Come away from this man who is*/neither old nor ugly/*young nor beautiful, and I will love you better than he*/I will love you better than he. *Be my soup of eyes, be my festival morning, let me drink you down with due reverence, let me press your irises against the roof of my*/my mouth *until their sweetness bursts into salt, and all will be well*/I will be well/*and all will be well,* /and you will be well, /*and all manner of things will be*/well, in the dark, well and one.

I/I/do/I/I *will*/yes./*yes.*

You swallow like a child, milk-desperate.

II
YASUGI

Mother, Mother, I mourn.

I claw at the clay, the red furrows reek in the earth like kanji, ideograms of grief, need-glyphs. Mother, let me in, move aside the stones for me, for your poor boy who loves you. Mother, I cannot find the way down, I cannot find my way under the mountain—open a canyon for me, a cave, a door. Where are you? Why do you not answer your son?

If I kill a dragon for you, as heroes are wont to do, if I damp the soil with blood, will the stain become a gate, a hole, a passage into Mother, into the dreamed-of hell?

I am the only one who mourns her. The rest have all forgotten. And yet, and yet. Am I really her son? It is not an easy genealogy to parse—would she open the ground for me if I were not her son but a lover, a suitor, an ardent and earnest creature seeking only to lay his head on her knee? I walk in the woods like a wild innocent—could I not lure her out with this purity, worn on my breast like grass-plait?

Yasugi is a knobbled field spackled with huts, and clouds roam over it like clapping mollusks. Mt. Hiba dresses itself up in blasted rock, red as rusted blood and pitted like a crone's breast—it protrudes, it leaks a sickly milk of clinging snow. I am tired—I am hungry. The soles of my feet refuse to harden, but bleed openly, crack, gape pale and womanish on the grass. I have asked at sake-houses and bath-houses and fish-and-rice-houses after the passage of a snake, a monster of any sort, even a particularly tall or lumpish man. They know nothing, they see nothing. They are so slow, so dull I can hardly stand to smell their breath, their bandaged thumbs—if my descent-body disgusts me, theirs buckles my legs with retching. If I were my right self I would bring the waves up, blue and black, over this whole valley and scrub it clean of their crawling and crying. They nibble the suckers off of white and fleshy stalks of squid, and suggest I go further south, to the city. They know everything in the city.

South, south, ever south.

The sun slaps my back as if it loathed me specially—which, of course, it does. What sister misses an opportunity to annoy her brother when he is least eager to be annoyed? She knows nothing of Mother, she cares nothing for her, she drives me south to the city, the wretched city where there is no Mother, there is no Monster, there is nothing but fat men sweating in steam baths and dead, stupid statues draped in garlands of sweet-potato blossoms. They write precious little poems, delicate as eel-fat, and call themselves brothers of the sun, because it is a winning image, evocative enough to ply a pink-kneed girl behind their screens. But the sun is my sister, and rides my bones hour upon hour, and oh, how she burns, she burns. There are no eel-poems about us, only lightning, and wind, and red, red heat on a man's brown back.

I hate her, Mother. Why could you not have sown me alone in Father's flesh, like a persimmon tree growing without saplings in a prairie? The things I would tell you are not for her flaming ears.

I hesitate to recall it; I do not wish it to have been. I came across a shrine yesterday—I suppose it is the fate of the Kami to be forever plagued with monks and shrines. They stamp the landscape like ant-farms here, lumpish tunnels arching over well-planted fields and bubbling through the shimmering squares of floating rice, worming through the world, digesting it and exuding it from their pasty bodies as if earth could be offal.

But, like any ant-commune, they have great stores of food, and will occasionally part with crumble or wash when a man passes by and asks after their statuary. I did not mean to imply that theirs was in any way spectacular, but ants will be proud of their collected corn-cobs and strawberry stems. It is, however, a singularly uncanny sensation to look up at a statue of oneself, snarling and dancing and stomping, yes, I swear it, eight small snakes.

My breath was lost, unsure which way to blow, frozen under my own face, and my skin seized as if run through with rain, for oh, oh, since Izumo I have often thought—worried, suspected—that I am walking through a story that has already occurred, and here, here are the relics of it, here are the stations of the holy, here are the oft-walked pilgrim trails that repeat a journey I made long ago but am still making, but have not yet made, and yet the ants—the ants! The ants, they seem to have catalogued my every step, and swathed the grass-impressions in bronze, and held festivals to mark my left foot falling in Yasugi. Little librarians, and their scrolls have already illuminated my killing of the serpent, the thin-spun beauty of Kushinada under its coils—all of this is in their greasy hands, and if they know this, if they know my family secrets, do they not also know the way down to Mother, and if I will find her, and the shade of her face in the dark? They must know, wretched things, it is their business to know, they do nothing *but* know—I am chronicled, chronicled, and soon I will not exist at all but in their scrolls and their mute clay statues—

I wanted to talk to them about this, to close up with them behind geometric screens and ask them how the story goes from here, ask them if they think, perhaps, I was in the wrong when I went to my sister's house, if what I did there was wrong by their ant-measure. Their little white-capped heads must belong to oracles, scryers, magicians, if they could have formed this terrible statue from raw dirt, tunneled it into being—I wanted to hold them by their throats against their moth-eaten reliquaries and cry: *who am I in this body? How long will she punish me? Where is my mother? Where is the snake? How do you know these forbidden things, you stupid, mewling men?*

But in the incense-pregnant shadows of the interior rooms—lined with gold statues in that same eerie pose, foot raised over the squirming nest of heads—they only piled my hands with rice balls and salted plums, raw salmon and cups of soy-broth, smiling inanely, heads bobbing like lolling daffodils.

"Who am I in this body?" I asked, having devoured four plums and a quantity of bland rice. The monks scratched their heads beneath white caps and looked at each other like a gaggle of birds at seed-time. They smiled pleasantly and spread their hands.

"You are *musuko*, you are our son—all men are sons of the gods, all men are sons here, in the house of the gods, and beloved."

"That is not what I mean," I answered gruffly, clutching my chopstick as if to break it.

"What else could you have meant?" Their clean, white smiles did not falter. They did not know me, my blood chortled—rice-gobbling peasants know me by sight, but men trained to worship my kneecaps cannot recognize their god when he walks through their door. This is useless, said the blood, useless and comical, if it were not pathetic.

"I think you do not know half so much as your statues," I sighed.

"Most likely," they agreed heartily, "this temple is dedicated to Susanoo-no-Mikoto, Storm-God and Deathshead. It was he who came last from the nose of Izanagi in the beginning of the world, when the Great Father had finally rid himself of the foul dust which emanated from the body of the witch Izanami, who dared speak—"

I would like to say I did not bellow like an ox in heat, that I did not lurch out of my cushion through the scented air and smear rice and salt-plum into the noses and down the throats of the monks, just to *shut them up*, to stop up their stinking breath, greased with lies, that I did not screech my mother's holy name while I tore at their sun-colored robes, shredded their ridiculous hats, claw at their soggy skin, skin that already smelled of death, of putrefaction and again, again, of lies, that I did not rip the cat-gut that strung together their *looping* beads, and laugh when the pebbles clattered onto the floor like rain falling on copper rooftops.

I would like to say these things.

But under the gleaming, muscled knees of that awful statue of myself I bound them with what prayer-twine were left, back to back in a ring like soldiers in the grass, and panting, seething, sweating salt through these meat-pores I never asked to own, I began to read those fools, those orange-swathed ant-farming fools, I began to read to them their lessons under the tamarind trees throwing up their branches into the black-bustling sky like frenzied arms. Did they quail? I did not look, I did not care. No one listens to me, but these mouse-eared men would. If it is possible for a god to be filled with the evangelic, I boiled over, and they were the scalded stove, and they would hear, they would hear me, or I would open them up and spit scripture into their grinning throats.

"Listen to me, *listen to me* when I tell you: this is how it was in the beginning of the world—"

SECOND HEAD

Men, even gods-in-men's-skin, believe passion means (to adore, to lust, to be exalted through love.) *They are foolish. Passion means to suffer. It means* (to endure great sorrows.) *Passion is the grasp of blister-ridden hands, breaking its thumbnails on the floor of heaven.* (Passion is fear, like a peach tree planted in the navel, when your sister comes not wandering back over the cicada-emboldened hills.) *It is hoarse, needling, the great iron vat in which flesh becomes oil.* (It is eyes floating in murk, eyes crusted in salt like tears.) *Its pelt is deep-shaded, like love—red and black, wine-dregs and sour mash—but it is* (not) *love.* (But then, then you said it was, when you opened for me.) *Passion cannot weep. The tracks of once-liquid sorrows run down its face, jaundiced and leprose-rose, a warm line of marrow-dust pooling on its collarbone like the burst bow of a violin.* (Passion cannot weep, but oh, oh, it cries!) *Passion hollows bones to flutes and seeds the flesh with baobabs, baobabs and women like baobabs, dark and deep in the muscle walls, growing like recalcitrant children, gnashing their agate teeth at intestines of twisted ivory.* (I gnash, you gnash, we gnash at each other and eat each other and swallow and excrete each other and look at our passion, look how it gleams, look at the peachstones of our suffering in these caves!)

I am the second body (daughter.)

Quiet, quiet, second children do not speak. The neck behind the neck of the primary tongue is less than nothing, less than scale, less than true (less than true, less than firstborn, but I never understand you) *myself* (when you) *we* (are like this, old snake.)

   I pat my belly and you are within it, second daughter (second sister, second length of ropy emerald musculature) *and your name is embossed on my innards like the brand on an iron kettle. There is one belly; there are eight heads* (there are seven of us) *soon, my* (own, here in the dark) *self in self* (and have we yet learned to love the dark, to call it our mirror, to call it our flesh?) *We are thrall to it, it serves us. And you are stoppered up in our body like a cork, and I am full of you all the moon long, and I too want to be called by my name, but your names, Kameko, your names crowd the* (our) *my mouth like krill.*

(Have I not called you) *us* (by your name) *as we are?*

Call me Suffering, call me Fire, call me Gullet, call me, call me (what shall I call for, this city of dead girls and snake-guts, streets thrown over throat and thorax) *meat smoking in piles* (yes, call you city of the dead, city of wraiths in wells, city of reptilian meat smoking in piles) *second daughter, do not speak* (second head, what shall I call you?)

Call me Kameko (call me) *you* (by my own name) *for that is the nature of the filled throat. I still have them* (us) *inside me, all who have ever been eaten, pushing at my phosphorescent ribcage, blue and brown and green eyes blinking in aortal seizures* (but they are your eyes now, we who float in the bitter broth of you, and do you not love our eyes? You said you loved them) *the serpent-heart forgets, it is strange-gilled and fickle* (as if a girl's heart is air-hungry and constant under every possible sun) *but the Belly does not forget* (it bakes us) *itself* (like seven round cakes, and when we are finished, oh, we all have black serpent's eyes) *the coils heave and flail in the same sacred dance, helplessly repeating their susurrations in the sand. Flesh bears a thousand marks, a thousand fingernails, a thousand teeth. Every time it is the same time, and the body recalls all its usual acts of passion, all the expected responses, secretly weeping* (crying) *for all those it loved once but can never devour again. To endure passion is to burn and bleed the black of all voids.*

(I was only a child; I didn't know anything about devouring. You could have let me be.)

A child, yes, only a child, but I suffered for you.

(After my sister went into you, like a finger slipping into a ring, her husband, who was neither fat nor poor, returned to our house where the smell of frying eyes wafted from the pans so sweetly, and I saw his mouth water. He said that Kazuyo was gone, and he would not say, but he trembled, like a worm sighting a crow overhead. He demanded another girl to replace her—his loss would have to be answered, or he would call the magistrate and inform him that we had breached our contract. He was quite red in the face, and I thought, strangely, of the persimmons blowing into each other outside the house, flesh into flesh.)

Men are foolish. But they are beautiful, (he was neither beautiful nor old) *and they suffer so. They do not understand the nature of the Mouth, which is* (to ingest, to carry within,) *to draw the Beloved inside. I am the sacred Mouth, my body, my heads only hold it, like a many-colored reliquary, eight together in one, cradling the wide lips which open to encompass the conflagrations of all possible skies. Give me a wine I can bite, a human child I can drink.*

(Quiet, second head, do not speak. You have had these things, and they have had you.

And he had me. I stepped between my mother and the soup bubbling away, and offered myself with head bent low, offered myself to this man whose face was neither pocked nor greasy, and he pinched my arm for the muscle there, and said he would take me, and a pair of black chickens to make up the difference between a first and second daughter, a first and second choice.

But he insisted, you know. He was a good buyer, he knew how to tell if a horse is older than it seems by the hooves and the gums—he insisted on my virginity that very night, in case another serpent should befall his new wife, and he be left again having paid for nothing but a lump of blood and lymph left lying on the dry grass.

He asked me if I was born when the persimmons were thick on the branch, like my sister. Holding my arms over my small breasts as though they could protect me, I answered—no, I was born under the plum trees, when they were dark and pink with flowers. My mother was carrying the well water up to the house—and here he took my belt away—and the bar was so heavy on her shoulders, like a yoke—and here he took my robe—and she stumbled—her belly was so thick with me, thick as an uncut melon.) *Yes, it is like that, when I am full of you, of your voice and your plum-laden scent, and the well-water rolling in you*—(She fell forward onto her taut belly—and here he opened my legs with hands neither calloused nor small—and her thighs were wet with the water of the well and the water of her child—and here he pushed inside me with a grunt like a boar nosing for mushrooms in the loam—and she did not weep at all, but squatted in the garden and pushed her baby out among the quince and the mustard weed. My toes tangled in the raspberries, and I have never walked quite right—and here he stiffened and rolled off of me, and his hair smelled of oil and eyes.

"Soon you will carry my water, and give a child to my plums, and then you will be happy" he whispered, and fell asleep. He neither snored nor spoke in his dreams.)

Happiness (enlightenment—father says happiness is suffering, and enlightenment is a soup with no eyes) *can only be reached when you have eaten the world, when you hold it inside you like a content child, rocking slowly on the drift-currents of your blood. He thought you would be content when you held another creature in you—he thought you were a Monster, like me, but you were nothing yet but a girl with wet linens. Still, it never works, it is never enough. I cannot rest until the Mouth is sated, yet it can never be full.*

(He wore my maidenhead on his sleeve like a bright button, like a charm, to keep him safe when Kameko walked the road that Kazuyo walked. He called me his turtle-child, he called me his mare, and the sun was very high, like a pinprick in the air.)

Men believe that Beauty will keep them safe. That nothing beautiful is to be feared. And this is how they come to me, innocent, pure as ethyl alcohol, unknowing and sweet, dragging Beauty behind them. Their faith in the order of Man and Monster is profound. They never expect me (us) *to be beautiful, never expect the colors of my* (our) *flesh, never expect that Beauty calls to Beauty, never know how the sheen of your hair calls to me.* (How the sheen of Kazuyo beaming from your long, swan-bright neck like a lantern lit only for me would propel me into your stunted, clawed arms.) *And under the lights of my skin they gasp, their minds blown clear as glass, in rapture, in* (passion.) *They lust* (for me, for the snake, for the thing we make together in the dark?) *with a clean and singing strength—and lust, like passion, erases all but itself, imprints only its own image on the sweat-kissed eyelid, repeated like the refracted light of a star. Their stars become my eyes, boiling white and deep.*

His eyes were full of sons, and you were so beautiful, limping behind him.

And when you were empty of all but the sight of me, (but the sight of my sister, laughing behind your eyes which had neither pupils nor irises), *we began our too-brief courtship, under the high, wild cries of the migrating terns.*

(Like nested dolls we are, the snake and the maiden and the ninth daughter floating in me, gills like crystal, eyes without color, awash in the salt-soup of my) *our* (body, tiny as a needle, dreaming. It is not unlike a serpent, all Mouth and Belly, suckling at the womb-walls of this long throat, woman choked with woman choked with woman, and I) *if there is an I* (un-maidened and un-mothered, and where are the plum-trees who would hear my daughter's first cry?)

It is all one flesh, that monstrous swell, curve of globe beneath the Skin, heaving and tossing with an ecstasy that has taste and smell—quince and mustard and rotted persimmons.

III
ONOGORO

This is how it was in the beginning of the world: a churning sea, and no earth, and a great bridge hung in the world: a churning sea, and jellyfish macerating themselves into starry foam on the wave-tips. In the beginning of the beginning of the beginning, of the tips of the beginning of the waves. This is how it was pillared in black, and it was so black, and its suspensors were strung with light like *mala* beads, and jellyfish crushed themselves into raw foam on the tips of the world. A bridge hung on the tips of the waves. This is how the bridge was pillared in the beginning of the world: on clouds, and mist, and the depthless sea.

It was all confused, then, the air and the saltsea, and the darkness.

In nothing, some part of nothing seemed to flow into a space that was *her* and a space that was *him*, and his eyes on the undulate sea were as the hand of her flesh on the glittering suspensors, at once through the void, the void seemed to flow into her, and in the briefest beginning of the beginning of moments, the shadows were perfumed.

Izanami and Izanagi opened their eyes on the bridge that spanned heaven, and the feet of Izanami on the floor of the jeweled bridge were strong and pale. Her hair was as black as the nothing, and the void seemed still to cling to her, into her and out of her and into her and out of her. The eyes of Izanagi, in the days before flame, were the brightest objects of all objects in the span of space. The dusk sat on his shoulder blades like clothes, and he said nothing, and she said nothing, and they were the first of all things in the world.

Steam rose from their shadows.

Together, they pulled one of the suspensors down from its anchor, and the sound of it was like a harp breaking, and the lights were upset, red and gold and green, but in the hands of Izanami, who rolled the strand like a stalk of fennel against her thigh, it became the *Amenonuhoko*, the jeweled spear of heaven, and it was the third object of all possible objects.

Together, neither one before the other, they plunged the spear into the churning sea, where there was no earth, and the spray wet the underside of the bridge, and their faces crusted with the salt of it, and the light-grime of the bridge, and altogether salt and spray and grime were tasted for the first time, on the first tongues. Under the light-clotted spear a thing became bulbous and green, and, after a time, it became an island, rich of dirt and loam, and there were dead jellyfish scattered on its shores like shipwrecks, for they threw themselves against the hard earth as they had thrown themselves against the sea, and discovered first of all creatures that land and sea are not the same. On this island was an empty house, an empty house with a great pillar in its center, and shadows were on the long grass, the long grass and the jellyfish like a smear of diamonds. And this was the place called Onogoro, and it was morning there. Stepping down from the creaking, starry bridge, Izanami and Izanagi's feet squelched in the first mud of the world, and the smell of it was so new, like skin.

As they walked up the beach-head into the house, the jellyfish kept up their suicides, for the lesson of land and sea is a difficult one to learn when there has never before been any land, nor any sea, nor any jellyfish at all.

When they entered the great house, they saw that the floor was many-tiled and green as turtles would be once turtles were conceived, and on the wall, which was blue and black as the bridge had been, was written:

The Room of Eight Footsteps.

The letters were scarlet and gold, and Izanami wondered at them with eyes raw as peeled apples, while Izanagi was concerned with the pillar rising up out of the tiles like the trunk of a tree—save that Izanagi did not yet know what a tree was, so the word hung in his mind like a uvula of amber. He gestured to her, and she pulled herself away from the ember-lettering.

They touched the pillar side by side, neither before the other. It was smooth, dry, cool—and yet all these words crowded in a parade through their hearts, for smooth and dry and cool had never before been, and their scent was searing.

Izanami and Izanagi walked around the world-anchoring circumference of the pillar, in opposite directions, like planets orbiting some stony sun. When they met, Izanami, whose hair blew back and brushed the floor like reeds scouring it in summer, spoke first of all the things that ever spoke, and her words were the first sounds, save for the terrible, soft rasp of jellyfish on the sand.

"Oh," she cried softly, "what a beauty you are."

Izanagi frowned, and the corners of his mouth were like books burning. His brow furrowed and he looked through her, as though she were part of the wet detritus of crystalline flesh down below the bluffs.

"You should not have spoken, first of all the things that ever spoke. It is not right that a woman's voice should echo in the void before a man's. I should have been the one to open the silence; it should have been I."

"I am sorry," Izanami whispered, perplexed, and looked down at her feet, still grimed with the light of the Heaven-Spanning Bridge.

"No matter," said Izanagi through teeth clenched first of all clenching things, and with the flail and clutch of a newborn, fell onto Izanami in the shadow of the pillar. She tried to open for him, gracefully, but in his eagerness he crushed her foam-cooled thighs together, his knee awkwardly thrust into her muscle, and livid bruises bloomed there like chrysanthemums. His breath was on her neck as she tried to smile placidly beneath him, tried to keep any further words, any further cry, pressed under her tongue. Her body was caught into a pillar, calf to calf, arm to waist, and the pillar was bounded on all sides by the shuddering body of Izanagi, who quivered in the darkness, and could not find the way into her.

On the green-tiled floor Izanagi stiffened, and first of all spilt things, his seed pooled onto the tortoise-floor, useless and pale.

Outside, the soft slush of the jellyfish went on. He would not look at her.

Izanami pushed her long hair from her eyes and smiled sweetly, said things which in the long days of the world would become usual, but Izanagi would not be comforted, and his brow deepened into its furrow, and his eyes were haughty as they looked on the only woman on the shores of the churning sea, and it was cold in the perpetual morning of Onogoro.

THIRD HEAD

I am the third body—daughter—*Kiyomi-of-the-dogwood-smiling*—Kiyomi who was never good for anything. Kiyomi who could not make the soup. Kiyomi who could not stitch her own sleeves—*Kiyomi who tasted like mulberries and snail-shells, Kiyomi who dog-snarls*—Kiyomi who disappointed her mother, who shamed her house—*Kiyomi who lies curled in my heart like a slippery eel, suckling at the walls of my blue-green ventricles.*

—Festival days are hot, even in winter. Bound up, tied in, veiled and flowered: ritual clothes itch, and in my life my obi has never lain straight—I watched, and the Mouth salivated, even from behind its shield-wall of hills. All those girls lined up stiff as poles—and we stand all in a row, looking down, offering the loveliest side of the bowl to the men who come for the soup of eye and hymen, the soup of plenty, borne by virgins—*I suppose then I might have been able to stop, to seek out other girls who were not of a height and thickness, who did not link hands like a chain of perfect ducklings in the water, who did not look into each other's eyes with a silence like a child they had conceived together, without even the glance of a man to seed their single black, invisible womb*—but even in that row of bent heads like bobbing bluebells, I was a blight on the delicate flowers of the dresses, in the flavor of the soup—*but seeing the rest of them like that, six little maids all in a line, as though waiting for the door of myself to open and let them in, I could not turn away from them*—I alone of my sisters was no virgin, and my mother said the house stank of my sex—*six sisters with their suckling silence between them, and something in the turn of their mouths told me that they would want the jaw and the tooth.*

—Mother said I had to serve, even though I could make nothing but sludge of the delicate, fishy broth, and had sat by while my sisters learned stew-craft, sat by and pinched my lips to bring the red up. And he touched my finger as I passed him the soup-bowl, a breach of etiquette severe enough for banning, if I had cried out, but I was always bad, always, and I said nothing, did not even blush—*I only saw the cut on my belly after the turtle-girl pulled me over her body like a shell*—he saw what it was in me which would not turn away from bare flesh, the knotted leech in my stomach which slept,

slept until that finger brushed my finger—*after Kameko. It was still thin then, but it throbbed when Kiyomi was near*—slept and did not know it meant to suckle blood-bright and gasping at any teat it was offered—*in my nest behind the mountains, it throbbed when Kiyomi was near*—and so when the moon peeked out he took me behind the shacks under the white and stinking dogwoods, such beautiful cloud-blossoms, but their scent like wet fur and saliva—*I dragged my belly after the third girl, with the second girl still writhing*—and he picked me up like a bundle of rags, my back against the rasping tree trunk, my legs hiked up round his waist, bruised by his bony hips—*dragged my sliver-belly over the grass*—and I whispered:

"Did you know I was born under these trees? The smell made mother sick, the smell put its thumbs in her nose as she pushed me out—*and the cut throbbed its three syllables: Ki-Yo-Mi*—and the green pollen dusted my fists, dusted my tongue, dusted my hair still clotted with blood—*it was still thin then, and it stung when I saw the third girl, the grass, and the red.*

"Kiyomi," he gasped, "be quiet. I don't care about the dogwoods."

And he pulled from me amid a shower of green pollen—*the Mouth once it finds a delicacy, demands more of the same, and I could smell the pollen on you, quiet Kiyomi, the pollen on your mouth, between your legs*—he came again in the morning to ask for my hand and I laughed, I laughed like goats bleating, and I would have nothing of him, for I already knew the sound of his gasps, and that he did not care about the dogwoods. Mother said I was a demon-child, fit only for demons, and would not let me near the soup again—*fit for demons, yes, for demons, for serpents and worms*—she closed me into the rear room and laid me out on the bedroll. I was not afraid, for this was mother, mother, and mother would not harm me, but she held a bowl of foul smelling paste—*green pollen, and sap, and intestines from the little garden snakes*—and with a mouth like cut paper she opened my legs and smeared it into me, whispering that I was a whore, a whore and I would learn to be a good girl, for she did not raise whores in her house—*even later I could smell the little dead snakes, their little dead venom-sacs, I could smell their musk like family*—and oh, it burned me, oh, it scalded the mouth of my womb, still wet with the festival-man, it bubbled within me and mother waited, blowing on the sickly stuff until it dried, and I tried not to cry, I tried not to cry but the tears spilled down, and the bed-roll was wet with salt and paste and I said nothing to her but could not look in her eyes as she held my legs open—*you were still marked with your passion when you came to me, his fingerprints and hers*—until the smear had done its work, and I felt nothing at all there but the echo of the burning, as if I had once, long ago, born a child made all of fire—

In the well of my—our—*throat I*—we—*too still taste*—feel—*it.*

—When the man who was neither joyful nor sorrowing came back from the road to his village, came back with no Kameko, no Kazuyo, I did not care. I mourned my sisters but it meant nothing to me to go into that man's arms, I told them all I would happily go, with a smile and a proper girl's bow-and-shuffle. And I took him into the dogwoods—*I care about the dogwoods, your dogwoods, Kiyomi*—no, Mouth, you tell us what we want to hear, every maiden's dream, to have a monster all her own—*you are no maiden, and without dreams, except of the burning, and the dogwoods*—I took him into the dogwoods and let him lift me up against the stubbled bark, and the green seal broke and I thought I would die of it, I wept into his neck but he did not stop, I cried out and the moon looked blankly back, and the fire was in me again, the fire-baby shoved back inside me, and I bit my own hands to keep from biting him—*I bit your hands to keep from biting his*—and he was pleased with me. He kissed my damp cheeks. He took me by the hand when morning came up the road of Kameko and Kazuyo, the dust-dirt road over the hills, the snake-road, and when I saw the snake I was no more afraid than when I saw the man—*I held you all in me, and it was, for a moment, perfect, as you bore up beneath your passion, and disappeared into my heart. You were all through me, and the dogwoods were full of fire*—and the burning was by then so great that I fell to the ground before it and begged it to cut me in half—*so beautiful, and foolish, they will come, always, dragging wives behind them like quail, and I will teach them about passion, and we will suffer together under the trees and the stars*—to eat up the flames and I together, I did not care, I did not care, a whore never cares—

IV
OHOYASHIMA

Mother did her best, you see.

But with the dew forming like infant pearls on infant oysters, clinging to his matted thighs, Izanagi seized the pillar which had been Izanagi by the rope-taut length of her hair to the pillar which was stone in the center of the Room of Eight Footsteps. With the dew forming like infant oysters choking on their litters of pearls, clinging to the only woman yet in the world in the fist of the only man yet in Onogoro, he hissed at her.

"We will do it again, we will do it again and you will not speak unless I speak to you. We will walk the eight footsteps as though there had never been another eight, and we will do it in the proper way, and I will fill you up with islands like this one, and you will not speak, you will not speak, you will never tell anyone about the other eight. I will speak for you. Walk, woman, and fasten your mouth to itself."

Izanami walked. She placed one delicate foot before the other, eight times, as before, and she kept her eyes on the weeping floor. The dew made the green into a churning sea, and she thought of the bridge of heaven, and the light singing down the suspensors, and first of all things which lament, she mourned the loss of the perfect and silent bridge.

At the eighth step, Izanami and Izanagi met, and Izanagi cried out so loudly that the jellyfish paused in their flagellate, and their bodies fluttered up in the echoes like wings.

"Oh," he crowed, "what a beauty you are!"

Izanami stood still, and her eyes were full of pity as a basin catching rain. Her gaze did not falter or change as he pushed her against the wall, her shoulder blades scraping at the scarlet-gold paint which lettered the lacquer. She did not look away in modesty or try to encourage him as he lifted her off of her feet and sunk his teeth into her, sunk his body into her, sunk an island chain into her womb as he grinned into her unsweating skin.

They were already awake inside her when he pulled back from her, let her body slump against the wall. Dirt and worms and long grasses, camphor and plum and snails and milking goats, rivers full of silver silt and mosquitoes hovering over the shallows, spiders flinging their webs over their arms like winter sweaters, pelicans with their gullets fish-bulging—she swelled up with them in the little house on Onogoro, and the jellyfish sluiced into each other on the beach, wet, suddenly, with the first rain of all things that fall.

Izanagi was not there when the first of them was born. He was digging in the translucent corpses, shoving the pale, shapeless forms into his cheeks, sucking his fingers dry, slurping at their feeble, still-wavering tendrils. To him, they tasted of his first breath, and he licked his lips hungrily as he swallowed them down.

And in the house of the pillar, Izanami squatted on the tortoise-floor, biting her hands to keep back screams as the Ohoyashima dropped out of her in a knotted chain, like a necklace popping from her flesh, bead by bead, and she wept, first of all creatures that bled in birth. Awaji fell, already cracked with earthquakes, then Shikoku, so small she hardly felt it clatter from her. The Oki islands came next, shimmering like drops of her own sweat, then Kyushu red with volcanoes, and this scorched her spotless thighs with streaks of black like footprints. Iki and Tsushima emerged amid a thousand blades, and Sado swaddled in green. Then Honshu, and the inlets, the streams and the wide peak of Fuji opened the bones of her hips, and the crack of the bones was terrible, terrible and quiet, echoing only in the empty Room of Eight Footsteps.

Izanagi entered as Honshu left the womb of Izanami in a clatter of blasted rock, as it was carried away with the others on the churning sea, beneath the bridge of heaven and away. And so it was that he saw none of their first children, and only later walked on their fields and bones. But he saw their first limbed child, he saw it slither from her like an afterbirth, silvery and spineless, its piscine hands clutching helplessly at the air, the colorless blood languid within it, as though it were merely a sack sloshing with water.

Izanagi saw it with delight and went to devour it, for in its shapeless mass it looked like nothing so much as the pathetic, directionless jellyfish of which he had so much pleasure.

"No," hissed Izanami, "it is our child, our firstborn, and I have called it Hiruko."

Izanagi snorted. "That soft and stupid thing is no child—not any child of mine, if it is alive at all. You ought not to name the clots that squirm out of you, any more than you name your excrement, or your vomit. Let me eat it, and I will fill you up again."

And Hiruko reached out to its father, gills opening in its skin like cracks in opal. It whimpered, and in its infant cry Izanagi heard jellyfish dying, dying, and his own belly gurgling with their weight. He drew back from the silver hand, his throat squeezing itself like a fist.

"It is my child," said Izanami calmly, her black hair hanging over her face, "it is beautiful, and if you eat it I will unhinge myself to eat you. I have borne the earth within me; you will be no trouble."

"It is a punishment," he growled, "a curse, because you spoke first. It is a monster, a leech that has become fat on your blood—stamp it out, stamp it out, and atone for your wicked mouth. Crush it with your feet, woman, and your next child will be whole, it will come from my words, not your twisted, rotted exhalations."

Izanami held her child to her breast, and its nacre-mouth fastened to its mother—Izanagi watched in revulsion as the first milk of the world flowed into that tiny, boneless body, he could see the white droplets moving under its skin, which flushed in strange colors as it drank. If nothing else about it could be said to be healthy it drank as though dying, as though the breast locked between its toothless gums were all the world, and the sweet sounds of its sighing and mewing, slurping and swallowing filled the house, as such sounds would come to fill houses like habits.

"Throw it to the floor and crush its skull," Izanagi screeched, and he tore the leech-child from its cradle of arms and milk. A bellow he could not imagine would have come from such a pitiful chest tore through his ears, and Izanami clawed at him, tearing away the flesh of his arm after her child—and thus the second being in all the world learned to bleed. He took Hiruko, wailing its gruesome song to the grasses of Onogoro, out of the little house and down to the beach—and Izanami was close behind, her black hair streaming like serpents behind her, and she did not scream, but her mouth curled like a wound.

Into the sucking morass of thin tentacles and curving, transparent bells, he cast the leech-child's silvery body, and its awful cry stopped as it sank into the striations of corpses, its eyes confused and stricken, vestigial eyelids opening and closing without understanding. The other bodies closed over Hiruko, its limbs little different from theirs, one more who could not tell where the sea might end.

Izanagi took the only woman yet in the world by the arm and hauled her back up to the house, to the Room of Eight Footsteps, to the tortoise-floor now grey and slick with tears and blood and seed, and into this he threw her, and fell upon her, and though she made no sound beneath him, he whispered obscenities into the hollow of her throat as he filled her this time with a son, a son she could already feel flaring red and orange within her, and he too could feel the heat of it pouring from her even before he pulled himself off of her body.

He was gorging again when she bore it, and there was sand between his teeth, and the ruined diamond slush of the creatures dribbling from his chin. He would not have gone to see the new child at all—the feast was waiting, after all—except that something bright and hot swirled up from the house of the pillar, and he turned his head to the top of the bluffs, where first of all things in the world that burned, the little house vomited smoke black as Izanami's hair into the clear sky.

"Kagu-tsuchi!" came a howl from the blaze.

He ran up the sliding sands, half-curious at the beauty of the strange gold thing eating his house.

"Kagu-tsuchi!" came the howl like a tree-trunk tearing in two.

Izanagi stepped through the shattered door, which had once been carved so prettily, as if to welcome them, and saw the only woman yet in the world standing on the tortoise-floor, her body wrapped up in red, in orange, in blue and white. Her flesh bubbled on her bones, and her once-swelling belly sagged as if it meant to fall from her; her thighs were burnt black and crisp, and the smell of the meat of her filled the hall. The hot, ropy light pulled back her lips from her teeth, her lids from her eyes, and what stared at him was a skull, save that her hair still streamed back from it, as though it had all along been conspirator to the flames.

In her hands she held a flashing, flaring thing, its limbs splayed out and full of the boiling scarlet stuff, tongues of it licking around his chubby infant's arms, his mouth full of it, his eyes too bright, too bright, burning already in its head.

"*Kagu-tsuchi!*" she snarled, thrusting the inferno-child at Izanagi. "This is Kagu-tsuchi, this is Fire, it is born to us, it is your longed-for son, from your pure and perfect words! Take him, take him and may he burn you out from the inside, may he hollow you like a gourd, as he has done to me."

All around them, the house buckled and creaked, the fire of Kagu-tsuchi lapping hungrily at its mother's breast, at his mother's feet, at anything that would burn. Happily he nursed at the floor and rafters, at the ruined words carved on the holy wall. Izanagi held out his hand to his wife.

"Come out of this place," he begged.

Izanami threw back her head, burned clean of flesh, and her voice sent the roof into conflagration. Her body opened as if on a hinge, and out of her blazing bones tore a child of green and forked branches, her mouth a cluster of bleeding berries, and this was Hani-yama-hime, who was the growing earth, and then a splash of water which did nothing to dampen the orange flames still lapping at the belly of Izanami, and a sopping, blue-skinned daughter descended from her mother: Midzu-ha-no-me, who was well-water and puddles and lakes, and her fingers dripped with scum and algae. They rolled on the smoking floor, and Midzu gurgled as she slapped out lazy sparks with her wet and plump hands.

Izanami held her son to her tightly, and flames poured from her blackened womb, from her shriveled breasts, it leapt out of her mouth, and Kagu-tsuchi laughed, patting his mother's cheek with a flaming hand.

As she died, first of all women in the world to die, she thrust her son into Izanagi's arms, and her knees buckled into ash beneath her, and her body blackened the green-tiled floor.

Izanagi ran from the holocaust-house, his arms full of children as of apples, and Kagu-tsuchi giggled in his arms. Midzu-ha-no-me started patting at her brother, dowsing his flames in places, while he struck back at her, trying to set her afire. Hani-yama kept her wooden arms far away from both of them, shuddering. Izanagi dowsed his son in the churning sea, and the flames beneath the baby's skin banked to glowing embers, warm and cheerful. Midzu splashed happily, and her sister drank the waves with soft sighs. He drew his son from the water and stroked his cheek. The child turned his face towards his father's finger.

All around them, the jellyfish curled at the edges like pages and turned black, shriveling to smears on the water, and then to nothing.

FOURTH HEAD

{Her belly had grown into a globe, swollen with her fourth daughter's kicking life and round as a toy. She was become the moon, circular and symmetrical, a vast pale mass, pulling all the pulsing life of her youth into the new planet of her stomach, into the little red limbs floating inside her,} *floating, floating, within me, within her, circle and back, circle and back, into the interior churn, the water, the streaks of fat and lymph and blood, familiar as houses* {adrift on an inland sea, a thing which would be me, which once had gills and transparent skin like a salmon, that once swam in the universe of her body, but now pushed at the edges, outgrowing the space, impinging on tender organs and galaxies, stretching the tanned skin. She had become the Kaya-bird,} *my Kaya-bird* {her chest bright and out-thrust. Her movements were those of elephants, lumbering crocodiles.} *Ours are the movements of nesting, and the surfaces of nameless eggs, and soft, slithering things over the forest floor, and there is never any release for us, but we manage, don't we, Kaya, we manage.* {She could no longer bear the pinch of shoes on her feet, and walked barefoot through her house, marveling at her own metamorphosis into a snarl-toothed hippopotamus.}

After the third, my skin was hot and crackling in its boil of color. Even my toes had gone blue as rocks on the floor of the sea. My eyes were still shut, slick and pale against saffron eyelids. Each of you made me heavier, warmer, as though I was incubating you. And the cut, the cut along my underside had widened, flushed redder and wetter, and begun to drip onto the thirsty ground.

{But still, the baby did not come. Eight months and she was simply enormous. She could hardly move.} *Gashed and daughter-full, I can hardly move, they hardly move within me, it was summer and everything was so still, so still.* {She felt as though she contained cities, river barges, farming communes. She could feel the corners of the rice-fields pressing on her left side, carved temple-reliefs on the other. In the centre swelled a sanguinary Fuji. Snow swirled at her peaks, dense jungle crowded her base. Once she had been lithe and small, delicate, even, not this glutted thing.}

They told me you were the middle child, the prettiest save the last, and that you never listen. They told me about the tall weeds, and your little, wiry hands.

{In the beginning, I think, she had dreamed about this child, that it would at last be a son, dreamed of his dark eyes and soft skin, how his laughter would sound. But by that summer she merely prayed for release, for the end of her enormity, the end of the sensation of being filled to the throat, a sack of rice packed as tightly as possible, sent to market with tufts of white flying out of the bindings.}

They told me your sweet lips were famed in the province, and that the man who was neither sweaty nor pimpled secretly wanted you, even as he opened their obi under the stars.

{It was a Tuesday, dawned hot and blue, that she decided. No one was in the house, the doldrums of summer having boiled everyone red and driven them into town. She took a scythe from the shed-wall, the one with the smooth black handle. She marched out along the beaten dirt paths to the weedy fields like a general approaching his cavalry line. Stopping in the center of that yellow sea, she began, with long, sweeping strokes, to cut the gold-green stalks of thorny grass.}

They told me you were the middle child, and that you never listen, but they indulge you, because of your rosy lips, and how they came from the weeds. Will you not touch the wall of my throat, pretty Kaya? You can tell your birth-story over and over, it will not make you less dead.

{My mother loves me. She will cut us out, one day.}

Your mother forgot you as soon as the man who was neither fetid nor foul woke without his third wife. How many girls do you think she could lose before she no longer held you precious as the soup-eyes? Mothers forget, it is what they do. They cannot always be expected to be wet at the teat and smiling. And the prettiest girl, even the prettiest-save-the-last, does not always make the best soup.

{She panted with the effort of having me,} *all mothers do* {sweat ran down her face and back like delta-silt into the ocean.} *All mothers sweat so.* {The scythe rushed through the tender plants, her brown hair flapping like a nightingale's wing in time to the strokes. She told me that imagined she must have looked like deathshead, this young woman with her great scythe and plain black dress, weeds falling before her like ranks of soldiers.} *No, darling, I am Death, and I bend the weeds, and I hold you inside me, and you are my child, and nevermore hers.* {Death with long-lashed eyes,} *eyes in soup, eyes in children, eyes in me* {gliding through the fields like a shadow,*

Death beautiful and terrible, with her gentle face and singing blade. Only the great curve of her belly called her liar, called her not-Death; she swung the scythe high, grimaced with the effort of the swing; her arms burned. She was no doctor, to induce labor peaceably in a clean room, but gave herself to the strain of her muscles in the sun. With a downward stroke she felt something move inside her, like a stone grinding aside.

It was the weed-trees for you, then, the little saplings not yet grown. {She fell to her knees in the sweet-smelling earth, strands of grass stuck to her hair.} *And with the cicadas in your ears from the moment of your birth, you never learned to listen.* {I was born small, but my lips were perfectly formed, and so pink.} *They tasted of orchid, of orchid and crabgrass.*

{The sun was hot so early in the day when we woke and Kiyomi was gone. The man who was neither lovely nor soft took me by the wrist—his hand went all the way around my bones!—and his face went blotched and black. He accused my mother of cheating him, said that he would burn her house and poor father's fields if he was not given the wife he was promised. He said the others died because mother did not give proper obeisance to the gods; it spared him because he was pious} *I spared him because his blood smelled of oil and shit* { he took me there, that morning, into the rear rooms, and I cried, oh, I cried} *poor Kaya-bird* {I screamed and squealed as he tore my clothes, and he stopped up my mouth with his *tabi* and my tears soaked it through, and he pulled the bloody veil of my sisters' weddings over my face and his breath came in hitching gasps, frightened, mouse-chirp wheezes.}

I was sleeping when you came, but your sobs, your sobs were like thrushes singing {He dragged me from my mother's house and she did not cry—I called back to her over and over—why are you not crying?} *You ask too much of mothers, to weep over every child they lose.* {Mother, why won't you weep for me? And my father looked at his feet, mumbled that this was the way of marriages, sometimes, and one doesn't approve, but when the grandsons are underfoot no one recalls the ceremony.} *He fell to his knees in immobile ecstasy when I reared up from the waving weeds, holding his arms out,* {and I stopped crying, for at least this I understood, understood I was no different, that the man who was neither young nor old was still dripping from between my legs and this was no shield, a wife is no safer than a maid} *and I sighed into my Kaya-bird, nuzzling your new-beloved face with my own, crooning to you in the Mouth-dialect, knowing you would understand it, hear the new chorus behind the lower registers, for you were open and pulseate, and I was ready, hungry for your form to fill the void I carry like an egg within me, ready to be full of you, like a pale moon, and heavy.* { I held up my arms like a child waiting to be picked up, and the colors of the snake's mouth, oh, they were brighter than festival lanterns, and in the wavering throats like weeds I saw my sisters' mouths opening and closing like anemones, and I smiled, I smiled as you took me in, I was only frightened for a moment—} *He was weeping, shaking terribly—he understood, perhaps, what passion is. He hated my flesh and loved it, he cannot possess it, but it is possible he desired it, desired the thing glutted with the bodies of his wives, and knew that he was weak, that I could possess him, and their purity was no shield.*

{I} *you* {can hear} *me* {you, always, even if I do not like to listen. Sometimes I} *you* {touch the gullet-flesh} *my body* {with my} *your* {tongue, like an icicle, and it burns me} *it thrills through me*

{it tastes sweet, like the old soup.}

V
NE NO KUNI

Izanagi was alone on Onogoro.

The jellyfish had gone, somehow, learning at last what was and was not ocean, or at least, failing their lessons elsewhere. The strand was silent, and the ruins of the house of the pillar rose up like broken black jaws on the bluff. The pillar still stood, blasted and tall, and it seemed to laugh at him.

"Izanami!" He called to the cinders.

"Izanami!" He called to the empty shore.

"Izanami!" He called to the churning sea, and to the Heaven-Spanning Bridge, whose girded underside he could still glimpse, on clear days, far up behind the blue of the sky.

First of all things that are left behind, Izanagi could not think where she might have got to. He put Kagu-tsuchi, and his sisters to bed in the rushes and asked them what happened to women when they burned—they being the source of fire, and the death, and there being no one else to ask.

Kagu-tsuchi did not know. He sucked his thumb like a match-head.

Midzu-ha-no-me did not know. She sucked her thumb like a faucet.

Hani-yama-hime did not know. She sucked her thumb like a stalk of grass.

With the shadow of the bridge thin and receding on the shoals, Izanagi lashed together the trunks of eight young trees, and taking a lock of his son's hair to light his way, tucked the three bright-eyed children of Izanami's flesh away in the charred shell of the house with the last of the jellyfish to give them suck. On his raft of trees, the first widower of all things bereft set out across the churning sea, across the foam and the tipped waves, across the violet water and the black.

When he ran aground on Honshu, his beard was tangled and clotted with salt. He marveled at how Honshu-his-child had grown, how the acacia had brambled, how the mountains had grown braids and top-knots of snow. How the stones had rolled up from the barrels of earth. And he wandered.

"Izanami!" he called to the bloody-flowered acacia.

"Izanami!" he called to the top-knots of snow.

"Izanami!" he called to the stones from the barrels of earth.

And it was the stones that answered.

"Here," they murmured in their grinding, "here."

Izanagi pushed stone aside from stone, slate from shale.

"Here," they sighed, and moved from their loam, "here."

Behind a certain stone, there was a hole, tangled with roots and sifting soil, tangled with the dead-skin bells of mushroom and the sinuous movements of centipedes retreating from the light.

"Come in," sighed the centipedes as their ruby tails vanished, "this is Ne no Kuni, the Root-Country. She is here, she is here."

It was small, only wide enough for his shoulders, for his own hips, and it was open and dark as a mouth.

"Izanami?" he whispered.

No answer came, and thus, second of all things that go under the earth, Izanagi wriggled through the scrim of mud into Ne no Kuni.

In the Root-Country, there is no light. Even before there was land, there was light, and Izanagi crawled through the sludge trying to taste the dark, to breathe it, to understand how so complete and utter a thing could have come to be without his knowledge. The darkness grew around him until he no longer felt the wet earth stroking his limbs, but was simply over-hung with it, like curtains and veils, and he could see nothing, first of all blinded things. His feet squelched in a kind of softness underfoot; his hands groped in a mist like breath. There was no sound but himself and the darkness, which seemed to draw into itself and out again.

He pulled a comb from his hair, fashioned in the days before Kagu-tsuchi from pieces of the tortoise-floor, days Izanagi recalled as happy, when Izanami was quiet and fat with islands. He fumbled in the black with the curl of his son's hair, and lit the edge of the green comb. Fire flared out of the prongs, white and gold as a blanched sun, and the tile-teeth burned slowly down.

In the sudden glare, he lifted one foot and then the other out of the yielding ground; in the sudden glare there was no ground but flesh; in the sudden glare there was no air but the thick fumes of decay spiraling yellow and gray; in the sudden glare there was no Ne no Kuni, there was only Izanami, spread out over the gloam like a shroud, her body become the Root-Country. He was deep in her, in the pooled, moon-shot morass of her stomach, stretched now into a vast and planted field, wavering with untold grasses, with straggling trees clutching at her navel like dead hands. Her breasts rose up stiff and capped with black ice—clouds and cracks clustered at their peaks. Her arms lay out straight as highways, pocked with moldering wells and sinks where her blood had become brackish rivers moving sluggish and sere through the hollows of her elbows. Her knees had split open, and the flora of the dead already bloomed there, asphodel and dragonfruit and oranges like leering faces. Her thighs and calves spread off behind him; he could not see their end. She was gargantuan, the landscape itself, and her skin was broken so often, still streaked with scorch-streaks, that the red curve of her liver rivaled her femur for color-ghast, and her broken ribs rose up in jagged, thin-tipped stalactites. Her heart did not beat, but sat huge in the center of the world like an anchor dropped into an unguessable sea, cut by wiry meridians, its ventricles swollen and spider-blown, congealed and flayed and burning still.

Izanagi's lips curled back in disgust, and he vomited onto the navel of his wife—but the sight of his trickling sour seeping into her flesh caused his dry throat to retch again, and again, pushing against itself and finding nothing more to give to the country of Izanami.

Somewhere behind the ice-caps of her teeth, a cry began. It hurtled up from the depths of the rocks of her bones, it shook the hand-roots of the trees worming at her sternum. The roof of the Izanami-world shook, and strands of her hair, which he could see now had made up the great darkness stretching over him and over her. Great, ropy shafts of it tumbled down, crashing onto the wet-flesh earth, sending up sprays of stilled, clotted blood. The cry grew until he knew it for the voice of Izanami, and amid the spray of long braids slashing through liquefying vertebrae, Izanagi, first of all things that feared, ran from the bellow of his wife towards the tunnel which had emptied him into her.

"OUT! OUT!" it snarled, and shards of cartilage shot through with starlight and mosses cut through his back like shrapnel. He scrambled up through the mud and the skein of roots, through the centipedes laughing "Here, here!" and the stones gurgling dryly around him like swallowing throats.

"OUT! OUT!" the cry shook the dirt from the tunnel, and it sifted onto the face of Izanagi, it drifted into his eyes, his nose, his mouth, until he could not breathe, nor see. He choked, first of all things in the world to suffocate, and he was filled up with her, her voice stopping his ears like wax, flakes of her skin closing up every open part of him.

The stones moved aside like water and with a cloud of sweat and dust Izanagi was thrown onto the long grass still clutching his burning comb—though it scalded him, he held it before him as though it were his only dear thing. There was a sudden detonation of light, and he sprawled, prostrate as a penitent, on the green earth, beaten down by the sky and covered in the detritus of the Root-Country-which-is-Izanami, soaked in her dead-sour ablutions, clammy and shuddering.

Yet still, the cry barreled up from the weed-massed crevice, and he covered his hands with his face as it serrated the air:

"OUTOUTOUT! OUT OF MY GRAVE, OUT OF MY FLESH, YOU HAVE NO PLACE IN ME! EATER OF CHILDREN, EATER OF DEATH, GLUTTON, GLUTTON, GLUTTON! GO WITH THE CHILDREN WHO ARE TOO BIG FOR YOU TO EAT, GO WITH HONSHU, GO WITH KYUSHU, GO WITH KAGU-TSUCHI. COME NEVER HERE AGAIN, I WILL LET NO ONE PASS. I WILL DEVOUR EVERYTHING YOU MAKE, I WILL DESTROY EVERYTHING YOU SIRE WITH THAT SICK, MEWLING BODY. IN THE MOMENT THEY DRAW BREATH, I WILL BE THERE TO SNATCH IT BACK. THIS IS MY WORLD, NOW, IN THE DEEPS AND THE DARK. KEEP TO YOUR HALF, SPOILED BY LIGHT. GO, GET OUT, GOBBLE UP THE WHOLE WORLD IF YOU CAN, BUT COME NEAR MY COUNTRY AGAIN AND I WILL BURN YOU, BELLY-OUT, AS YOU BURNED ME."

Izanagi scrambled back from the gales of the voice, which stank of putrefaction: mushrooms and oversweet fruit, spoilt fat and dried blood.

"I would not come into your disgusting country again for any price," he sputtered, trying to scoop the offal from his eyes, scrape it from his tongue, "and I can sire worlds faster than you can lay them waste! You will see how many sons, how many islands, how many blazing boys will come tumbling out of me! You can't take them all, and for every thousand you claw to pieces I will bring fifteen hundred out of the ground. You should not have been made, there is no need for you—you are a leech-child like that monstrosity you spawned, and you have as little strength, as little beauty. You cannot banish me from the dark—I banish you from the light, and no one will care that you are gone, when the world is as full of my children as the beaches of Onogoro with jellyfish!"

The stones said nothing, but rolled back into place like sliding screens. The voice was gone. The earth glared back at him, baleful and silent.

Izanagi turned from Ne no Kuni, half-blinded, and ran from the soundlessness of the cleft—he followed the green smell of water to a babbling stream and finally cooled his eyes, his nose, his throat, and his burnt hands. He dropped the comb into the water, and cleaned first his left eye, dropping a clump of dust and dried flesh from his lid into the cold river.

He could not be sure, but he swore that the clump glittered, and shone, not at all like rotted flesh, but like gold, and fire.

He cleaned then his right eye, dropping a clump of dust and dried blood into the cold river.

He could not be sure, but he swore that the clump glittered, and shone, not at all like dried blood, but like silver, and light moving on still water.

He cleaned then his nose, and with a great breath blew a clump of dust and pulverized lung into the cold river.

He could not be sure, but he swore that the clump darkened, and thundered, not at all like the terrible cry, but like rain approaching from far off.

And in the water three things opened their eyes: the first clump flared out in a spiral, with hair red as the flames which ate the house on Onogoro, and she was Ama-Terasu, and she was the sun, and her eyes seemed to both rise and set at once. The second pooled out in a slow circle, and his skin was the color of the river, and it was difficult to tell where he ended and it began, for he was all over silver light, and he was Tsuki-Yomi, and he was the moon, and his hair was grey as clouds. The third clump seemed to fall apart and come together several times, a dervish whipping the water into foam, and its hair was storm-black, wet with salt seas, and his feet were ringed by jellyfish like newborn diamonds, and he was Susanoo-no-Mikoto, and he was the storm-and-wind, and he was me.

FIFTH HEAD

It is sad, that this part never lasts | It is sad, that this part never lasts | *the held gasp before events tumble towards the base of my belly* | when you do not know whether becoming no-longer-a-maiden will be terrible or marvelous, whether it will be all whiteness and the smell of clean skin, the way it has been in your heart | *When she is lovely and young and her flesh is full as a moon, the soft snort of a horse in the first morning of winter,* | whether it will be different for you, when so many sisters have gone ahead of you, and you are plain, and not like them, who had faces like winter fruits | *the smell of her heart beating, of the sweat beading on her throat,* | whether he will whisper in your ear:

"Kyoko, Kyoko, I love you," | *Kyoko, Kyoko, I love you* | "I do not care that you are plain." | *I do not care that you are plain.*

| I made the soup best of all, and I only wanted to keep making the soup until I was old and bent over the pot like a letter. The fifth daughter cannot ask for more. | *Your hair was matted under the poor, beleaguered veil* | My hands always—do you know how eyes smell? | *yes, yes, like copper filings, and green stems stuck upright in salt* | —smell of eyes, of burnt iris. It made me happy, to breathe that smell in my bed at night. I covered my face with my fragrant hands. My mother gave me the bed closest to the fire. | *I want the poise of this to last, when I stood over her, flashing violet and scarlet* | she gave birth to me in the storage room, among all the grass jars of eyes, pupils peeping between the woven reeds, watched, watching, and all those fishy, sweet things watched my dark head emerge from my mother, watched her first milk fall into my mouth, and they applauded with their feathery lids | *before she has looked up from her shamed posture to see that I am beautiful after all, beautiful enough for both of us.*

| The sound of blinking was so soft, softer than my mother's hand smoothing my wet hair. | *Kyoko, Kyoko, you are so quiet within me, and closed, like a crocus, like a candle. O smooth wax heart, this is marriage, meat and maiden, and me around you like a closed hand, and me bleeding from the belly like a new wife, slit open, oozing blood onto the earth like a bedsheet* | She said when the man who was neither sallow nor dark returned

with that same veil dangling from his broken hands that this was enough, he had had four of her daughters, he would have no more of us. I hid behind the screen and was relieved; I could stay and wash eyes and boil water, I could stay with my mother and all the grass-jars would watch me while I moved through summers like water slowly through a canyon. | *marry me, marry me, Kyoko, and I will rock you to sleep through a thousand thousand summers and you will sleep on a bed of my body, our bodies, sister to sister like a ladder into the earth* | But he was penitent, he was sorry, he was bereft, widowed four times over, and give him but the plainest of the daughters left to her and he would not take that road again, but stay in this very house, dedicate his fortune to theirs, and they would all be safe, safe together, and they would burn incense on four graves forever, and there would be sons, yes, and the pot would keep bubbling in its way. | *I want to hold the swelling of your body in my own coils, to circumnavigate your tiny limbs.*

| She frowned, my mother, and her hand fluttered to her belly like a memory. She led me quietly from behind the screen, and tucked my unruly hair behind my ears. She patted my cheek. She told me to try to be a good girl, and with thin and bloodless lips whispered that marriage was a joy, a joy and a wonder. She put my hand in the hand of the man who neither laughed nor wept.

"Kyoko, Kyoko, marry me," he said. | *Kyoko, Kyoko, marry me* | "Marriage is a joy, a joy and a wonder, and I will put honey under your tongue." | *I will put you under my tongue* | Will it be all whiteness and the smell of clean skin, the way it has been in my heart | *it will be all whiteness and the smell of clean skin, and you will be clothed in me like a dress, and I will hush you to sleep, plain little Kyoko* | you will hush me to sleep | *I will sing you to sleep.* | I dreamed through my wedding-blood, you know | *I know. You* | I | *were* | was | *waiting for me* | you. |

I came whistling down the way | down the way, down the way | *I came whistling down the way to my true love's door* | I left the window open and the wind was warm | *My colors came filtering through rice paper, and touched* | my face, woke me from my husband's arms, | *softly as a woman's fingers.* | I could not move, could not breathe, | *could only widen your soft black eyes and try to take all of me in,* | the shimmer of a thousand rainbows across your breast, | *the dark promise of my blue-black stomach, heaving and swelling for its promised Kyoko. I have eradicated all human women from this* bed | already I was confused, I could not tell if those colors were snake or sister | *already it was becoming confused, the voice of my throat of my belly of my lungs of my tongue was not my own, was becoming* (ours) *was becoming theirs,* | the rooster screamed once, but not again. | *I am the truly pure, and your mock marriage dissolved into love when faced with the multitude of my skin.*

| Serpent! | *Oh, Kyoko, when you raised up your arms!* | Monster! | *Oh, Kyoko, when your hair fell over his cheek!* | Oh, Monster, your eyes were so bright, so bright, as if they glowed from within a jar of grass! | *If he could touch the part of you that first glimpsed my flesh,* | moons within moons moving under that silver-green skin | *flesh you should have abhorred but cannot* | how could you | *I* | think I | *you* | would abhor | *this body of bodies* | myself? | *he might be able to crush it, wrap it in seaweed and boil it into something sweet and small.* | I have always been sweet and small. | *But even if he could tear you from my ruby flanks and run back to the fire-lit hall with you under his arm, how could he live, knowing that for a flashing instant you had loved a Monster? I sometimes wonder if he let me take you, Kyoko* | after Kaya | *after Kiyomi* | after Kameko | *after Kazuyo, because it was easier than suffering that humiliation.* | After all, there are always more of us left to take. And I had never seen such eyes, such living eyes, staring at me as though they were all the eyes I had ever stirred into salt. |

The Mouth quaked for you, | I quaked for you | *it did not wish to wait for contemplation, as though the man were an altar and I, penitent on knees I do not possess.* | I bent my knees for both of us, on the thin bed-roll, and your eyes, | *open to bursting, and as I took you into me you cried out,* | Serpent! | *ripping the leaves from the trees.* | Monster! | *filled with you,* | swallowed into myself | *writhing,* | your eyes were so great above me, multiplied, floating, | *floating* | floating over | *you* | me, | in | *you* | me, and there was nothing else, only me, | *us* | in the dark, and four strange hands reaching out through the | *meat-and-maiden,* | four pale hands drawing a mouth | *Mouth* | over me like a veil and helping me to step up, | *step up,* | into the fold.

It was all whiteness, | *and the smell of clean skin,*

| just as I had thought it might be. |

VI
HONSHU

When Izanagi had cleaned himself of children and, dragging them behind him like quails, run from the cleft of Ne no Kuni, the face of the world had changed. The Heaven-Spanning Bridge was not even a shadow in the sky, and the way to Onogoro had been lost in the churning sea. Even the jellyfish had gone far below, helpless to avoid the great islands' motion—for the children of Izanami groaned with her rage and moved together to huddle their heads against their shoulders, all in a line, like mourners, and hide away from her cry.

It was because of this that Kagu-tsuchi and his sisters had been able to step from the silver beaches of Onogoro onto Honshu, and Kyushu, and Awazi. They grew quickly, and Kagu-tsuchi became so bright that the islands could not bear him, and taking stick-limbed, stone-browed Hani-yama-hime who rarely smiled as his wife, he hid himself away in her, and was seen after only in flare and flame, sparkling fleetingly on the face of the world like an eye opening, then closing again. Closed up in each other, they had a wonderful child, who was called Waka-musubi, and in her hair grew the first silkworms, and the first mulberries, and out of her navel sprouted five grains like secret flowers. Midzu-ha-no-me, pleasant and laughing, laid herself out over the body of her sister, and glittered in pond and lake, stream and pool, golden in the light of Ama-Terasu, who had lifted her yellow skirts and climbed up to take possession of Takamagahara, the high celestial plain. Her brother the moon kept to himself, and took peacefully the lesser part of Takamagahara, which was black and filthy with stars.

Izanagi washed deities off of himself like dirt. The children of his children began to double and triple themselves like jellyfish thrown up onto the sand. The world was becoming filled, and only I remembered Onogoro; only I remembered Izanami.

Of course, Mother kept her word: in the midst of all that birth, things died quietly, in shadows, and went down to her, settled in huts of the dead, nestled in her belly, her sternum, her kneecaps. And for everything that died, Izanagi caused more to spring up. In this way their marriage went on and on.

I wept. In my clouds like cups I wept. The waves swelled up to meet me, eager, adoring, and I did not think they were beautiful; they stank of salt and fish guts. I looked at the earth, merrily rutting with itself, and I hated it, I hated its green and the light that made it green and the laughter that came from well-gods and bucket-gods and cloud-gods and spider-gods and mouse-gods and cicada-gods and cut-wood-gods and whole-wood-gods and seed-gods shaking in ecstasy as one topped the other topped the other, producing maggot-gods and mushroom-gods and seawall-gods and market-gods and gambling-gods and sulfur-gods. In none of them had the name of Izanami created even the slightest vibration, a bee's wing or gooseflesh rising.

Izanami! Poor Mother so wronged and so burned by wild and ungrateful children. Midzu was not enough—but I would have put out her flames, had I been born first. I could have rained down water of any sort she wanted. And I made Father tell me about her, over and over as I grew and the clouds around my wrist became more and more black. He did not want to speak of it—he could make children without her, didn't I see, it didn't matter where she rotted like a fat fungus, green and horrid. But little by little, like knotted rope pulled from his mouth snag by snarl, he gave me my Mother, couched in curses.

And I wept. I sent my clouds over the giggling, groping ground and flooded out the well-gods with my tears. I made the land dry up in great grey patches, where I would not let the rain fall—no rain should fall while the Mother of rain is a bed of spoiled flesh under the stones. I dashed the bucket-gods against their wells, and whipped the back of the cloud-gods, I chased the spider-gods and the mouse-gods and the cicada-gods into cracks and crevices, trembling in the wet and sudden cold. I cut the whole-wood-gods and sealed up the cut-wood-gods, and I scattered the seed-gods on barren rock. I drowned the maggot-gods and smashed the seawall-gods with my ugly, dog-earnest waves, I bankrupted the market-gods with washed-out crops, spoiled the games of the gambling-gods, dowsed the yellow fumes of the sulfur-gods with freezing mist. The mushroom-gods took no notice; springing svelte and sidelong from the grey flesh of the Mother-below, they were blind to rain or sun, and cared for nothing.

The land blighted, and that, that I thought beautiful, as holes opened up and fruit rotted on the ground, as green went to ashen and the smell of meat left to flies wafted through the wind, as the stupid, mewling, crowding earth began to look less like the greedy, gorged Father-face and more like the beautiful, ascetic Mother-corpse, then, oh, then I found it beautiful.

And while I sat cross-legged in the center of this new, tenebrous wasteland, while I sat happy for the first time since I opened my eyes in that murky stream, seeing all around me reflecting Mother, always Mother, her blight and her blear, Father came striding ford by fallow, and as Fathers will do, he slapped my face with the flat of his palm, called me child and woman, blubbering and weak as worms. My cheeks burned and I tried to be ashamed of my grief, but could not find reproach within me.

"You didn't even know her," he hissed, "you're nothing but her shit and my snot spat out into a dirty little creek. You're no one's son. If you love that dead cunt, go after her. Go to Honshu and push the stones aside until you can clamber inside her—isn't that where you want to be? The place that would never abide you? Go to it then, and if she doesn't chew your eyes from your head, rule there and never come out of the dark again. Leave us, leave us alone, no one here can stand the sight of you, not the well-gods nor bucket-gods, not the cloud-gods nor the spider-gods, not the mouse-gods, the cicada-gods, the cut-wood-gods nor the whole-wood-gods, not even the seed-gods, nor their children, the maggot-gods and mushroom-gods, the seawall-gods, the market-gods, the gambling-gods and the sulfur-gods. If you cannot manage to find a camphor tree to lie beneath you and squeeze brats out of her bark, go under the earth—at least we will not hear your wailing there."

I was proud, and I would not let him see me bolt for the sea and for Honshu—but when he turned to go and scrape another god from the sole of his foot, I ran for the strand and the surf, and the waves panted with joy, padding up to me with their foam dancing. The sun of my sister shone on them, and her gold skirts trailing on the water made me pause—if a man can be said to be worthy of his Mother, he cannot shun his sister, and Ama-Terasu was more truly my sister, herself scooped from Mother-detritus, than any of the god-rutting multitude. Should I not go myself to Takamagahara and see her blazing face for the last time on this side of the sky? Her fiery sleeves stirred me—I cannot say why, nothing she has done before or since has stirred me so much as a spoon would—and I resolved instead to ascend the stair to the high celestial plain, and be a brother to her before I went down to the dead, down to the dead and the dear.

The pale-headed monks trembled; the night had grown cold and they shivered in their idiot-skins.

SIXTH HEAD

Look on my colors, the vermillion and the cobalt, the oxblood and the saffron, the ripple emerald cutting through orchid musculature, silver scales hissing over tangerine, fuchsia streaks and peacock underbelly, the jade and ultramarine of my tail-tip. Look at the blood, at the leak of me, how wide it has become, a wound like a womb [Have I then no colors? Is there no obscene blue to the haunch and heft of Koto] *your blue is my blue is my blood is your blood* [is my blue my own, still, the blooming blue of my hip against the carnelian waist] *we are all so bright with each other. We shine through skin, through skin, and through my* [our] *mouth comes all this many-daughtered light.*

[I thought I would save them. The last two.]

You came to me full as a sail, and the moon on your wrists was like a bracelet, like a dowry. Where did you come from—this endless procession of silver-shoed girls? [Where does any girl come from? We come from each other, over and over, mouth to womb to mouth to womb] *In what moon-coated vat are you made, under what mottled sky?*

[It was sad for them, I suppose. They were already planning supper with roasted meats and parsnips, cold apples and broiled hawk. They were already peeling the eyes for that damned soup, that stupid, terrible, salty soup I ate every day of my life from the scoured floor of winter to the rafters of summer.]

But not too sad, I think.

[No, not too sad.]

You were utterly like your sisters in every way. [Yes, I suppose we taste the same in the end, but to our mother we were distinct, you know, at least as distinct as plum from cherry blossom] *Which is to say slightly more purple than pink, but still a mute, speechless flower, indistinct only from mice or spoons, but not, my love, not from other flowers.*

[Sometimes it is so cold in you, and the walls of your throat press in on me] *press out against me* [like a sarcophagus, and it is as though I am dying again.] *But you're wrong, you know. You didn't taste the same at all—you were distinct, not as plum from cherry, but as lime from orchid from woodpulp—* [and which was I?]

You were sour, and bitter, bitter as birch. Your brow was clean and brushed with that same dark hair, your eyes smooth and featureless as meadows undisturbed by deer. You all had the same purity. [Well, that is what virgins own, you had to expect it—wasn't that why you came rustling down from the hills over and over, into Izumo and into us, because our purity burned from us like soup overspilling its pot?]

But it washed off of you like flung silk, white and thick, full of salt, once I closed around you, once I closed over you like a wife. [Well, that is what virgins lose.] *I think you hoped that it would harm me, the bright bolts of it would penetrate my heart and stir my innards to ash.*

[I hoped nothing, nothing save that you would leave my sisters in peace. When the man who was neither old nor ugly returned to our house, even my mother's shoulders sagged like sacks of rotting melons, and she knew that she would have to lay out her next girl's hymen on the supper table.] *This girl comes to my glade and not even her fingers tremble. I am still empty of her, but they ululate within me, in recognition, Kazuyo and Kama. But she is a blank scroll, radiant in her simple and tragic grace.*

[There is nothing to say about my wedding night. He had a true claim for once—Kama had been taken from our house, from his very arms, by who knew what bandit. We owed him another, there could be no argument, and the magistrate would certainly give him his due and more if we, if I, if anyone balked his will. Mother spat after him, and he pretended that he felt no speck of spittle on his neck. He was in the right, his back was straight as he went to pull me out of my little room. As before,] *as before I took them* [he took me as he wished, as any magistrate would give him, and there were sliding screens, and belts, and I imagine his breath smelled much the same when he crawled inside me] *as you crawled inside me as I crawl inside you as we are in each other and there is no breath at all, only the sprawling, crawling interior of us, of sister and snake* [and I am sure the wetness was the same, and the soreness. I looked over his shoulder at the quiet shape of the house and thought of Kameko standing at the soup-pot. I thought I could smell her on his mouth, I thought I could feel her pressing down on his back, pressing down on me, pressing and staring out of his eyes, the invisible carcass of Kameko that he came dragging behind him, with her childsblood on his belly.] *Far off I smelled you moving off from him, his insensate body swathed in the sweat of two women, and within me,* [within my sisters] *the sleeping Mouth stirred—eyeless, atavistic, pure. It began to pant,* [I crept out of the house in the night, sure that I could feed the snake and it would be enough,] *that is not the way of it—do you eat a handful of cherries and then want no more for cherries through all possible winters?* [that I could be a sacrifice, poured out in the dust, so that the next sister down the line might have a husband, might] *and I began to look ahead of the hills for the candle-shape of Koto come singing through the grass like a carried knife,* [be surrounded by mound of eyeballs like cairns built up to a sightless god, might have daughters under plum trees]

What do you care for plum trees? They do not belong to your origin. What are the trees of Koto, what was the fruit that wet your mouth?

[My trees are the trees of my sisters. They are my persimmons, they are my plums,] *they are my innards* [they are bundles of cherries that sat in my palms day after day. We made the soup of eyes together; we made beds of straw.] *Each huff of smoke-sour want flushed my skin as you came nearer, and the stars were on your collarbone. Hunger spread inky and dark over me, the delicious cascade of color, trickling over my shoulder bones, my ribs, my tail,* [I was born, I was born sixth amid sisters, there have always been women around me, women with dark hair like mine,] *rose erupted in my breast, sliding outwards like a corona, a holy disc of fire. I could not help the groan—you did not seem to mind, after your groaning night—that escaped my throat as it bloomed into the shade of orange-skins—*[and I was born in the laced fingers of my sisters, my trees were my sisters, my fruit the sweet smiles of my sisters,] *and I could be the fruit of your trees, so many colors did I glow in your presence, your snake-fruit, your terror-fruit* [sister-fruit, and what is the snake but a skin for us, a hiding place, like the hollows of the camphor trees, a bark, a crevice, and we, huddled together in the shade] *The Mouth opened between my ribs, its hinges cracking jaw and tongue, the unbolting of this void within me, the glory of its sweet, dark dialect, whispering in my bones, whispering to you, it shudders out of me in a hitching sigh,* [I went into the cool and fog-striated hills after my sisters, to be in them again, in the locked forelimbs of girls dancing under the trees that saw the first breaths of all the rest of them—]*pulling you* [us] *in on the thread of a sibilant breath.*

My back exploded into vermillion and chartreuse.

[But I have no birth story, there is no Koto except Koto-the-sixth-among-eight, I have only them, and their beauty, and their] *light.*

[and their light.]

VII
TAKAMAGAHARA

The stair up to Takamagahara is wrought gold—what else would it be? As I ascended, the heat grew and grew, and the light. The banisters glowed like oven-grilles under my hands, and in the blinding glow of the reed-strewn floor of heaven, Ama-Terasu came striding across to the uppermost steps, and in her footsteps bloomed chrysanthemums red and white. All around her the expanse of Takamagahara had become a garden, and its rice-paddies glittered in her radiance, and cherry trees lost their pink hue entirely in her presence, becoming molten and searing to the eye. Everything was aflame, aflame with my sister, and the sky exploded over and over in adoration of her presence, endless detonations of devotion.

The whole thing gave me a headache.

"Why are you here, mucus-brother?" she said, and her voice was the ground cracking under a broiling sky. "What right have you to come above the cloudline?"

"I came to say farewell, dust-sister. I am to go underground, to join our mother and rule over all that is lightless, all your hem does not touch."

She snorted laughter. "That ought to be a short journey. I hear mother is nothing but a puddle of rot these days. But you can't really be here to say good-bye to me—when have you given me the courtesy of a hello?"

Ama-Terasu is a difficult woman—it all comes of being born first. I cannot explain it, but I did want to speak to her, to touch her light, to feel once as though I had a sister, and that her nature did not stray so far from mine. The instinct of siblings is strange and frequently foolish, but it surged in me, and I wanted her to touch my hair, to call me her little brother, her lamb, her storm-child. I was willing to make the first overtures, of course, and I touched her neck lightly, with a warm palm.

"I do not trust you," she said, but her eyes slid to my hand. "And no one comes here without a demonstration of loyalty—this is the land of the sun, and I am the sun, and my light is law."

"What do you suggest?"

She fingered the sword at my waist, a simple thing, dug from the barrels of the earth by Izanagi for his son. The moon has one like it, I am told. Taking this as invitation, I fingered her necklace, which hung in loops and whorls around her glowing neck, all red beads, carnelian and garnet and ruby. We stood thus for a long while, feeling the heft of each other's belongings, before Ama-Terasu made her bargain—a bargain I should have suspected all along, for she is part of the rutting, multiplying earth, the fulminating green, the doubling and tripling blue. In those days all the world was hemorrhaging offspring. Why should she be different?

"Let us have a contest of childbearing," she said coyly, her golden smile smirking, "and if you should bring forth sons, I will know your intentions are good. But if you should bring forth daughters, I will know you bear me ill—girls are such trouble, you know."

"Oh, yes," I chuckled, "I quite agree. The first troubles of all things troubling. Very well, if this is what you require of me, I will gladly give it."

I moved my palm to her cheek, and tilted her heat-radiating face to mine for a kiss. Was this what I had come for? I could not for certain say no. Her breath smelt of deserts and sweet grasses. I confess it, yes, I confess that for the first time—though hardly first of all things that lusted—my body was moved by a thing which was not grief.

And at the moment that our lips touched, cloud to sun, she broke free of my arms and pulled my sword from its knotted sash. I watched in rain-soaked horror as the bright-belted bitch broke it over her knee in five places—the sound of the shatter was like birds' wings snapping. Her grin was a cracked yellow gourd and her hands moved so fast, so fast, sweeps of light over the metal. Out of the five pieces she fashioned five strong boys, with limbs of quicksilver and eyes like hilts glinting. Their hair was iron; it hung in clanging choruses around their identical faces. Each was sullen as a sword, and each had my eyes, the line of my nose.

I pushed her back from my boys and snatched the red beads from her neck—a burst of scarlet gushed from her, blood-quick—a thousand stones popping from her throat like seeds from a bean pod. I sneered at her; she laughed at me—this is the way of siblings. From her broken necklace I took five beads and stretched them into five children, red of arm and calf—but no matter how I prodded the jewels, they would not make the angles of sons, only curves and breasts like apples, hair unfolding over their ruby skulls like silk. They looked up at me through five identical sets of long, rosy lashes, and snickered behind their hands, mocking and slattern-red as their dam.

"Daughters!" Ama-Terasu crowed, rooster-preening. "I knew you came to harm—you would never come for any other purpose, crow-brother." How she loves to be right!

"Daughters, yes," I said slowly, playing at the craft of an ingenuous smile, "but daughters from your necklace. From my sword, from my body, you see five stalwart boys. They are my issue, these blushing five are yours."

She seemed to waver, unsure of my explanation, but the alchemy between siblings bubbled already away within her as in me, and I could see that she too wanted a brother, that she never saw the moon, and missed the communion of the waste-children, the children out of the Root-Country. She took me by the hand, up the last of the stair and into the corona of the sun.

Behind us walked five daughters and five sons, beautiful as gallows.

I want it understood that I did not intend, at first, to be anything but a sweet and loyal brother to Ama-Terasu. I helped her to comb the water of her paddies for rice; we laughed together when the storm-clouds around my head flashed blue and gold when splashed by the Speckled River-Trout of Heaven. Our ten children followed behind us through the high plains, and we thought them very fine; we broke the Piebald Colt of Heaven into his saddle, and held hands for the first time with real affection while feeding our dun-colored foal apples and sugar.

She blushed in the morning fog as he nuzzled her palm. I stroked her burning hair.

She poured in the evenings a tea all of light, and kept her blazing orange sleeves carefully out of the steam. I roasted octopus for her when she complained of fever. We were happy, brother and sister in one house.

I was bored beyond dreams of leisure.

She thought the rice harvest too meager, the colt not swift enough in its growth. She sniped at me, she taught her sons to reflect the crackling bolts of my storms with their mirror-limbs, taught her daughters to smile behind their hands when I had gone from them. She denied me her gleaming flesh and would not be moved even a step closer to me than she pleased, though we had all these ridiculous babes at our feet. I could not have drunk another cup of tea without gagging on it, and she retched at the thought of octopus.

She was not Mother. Mother would not try me the way she did, would not willfully thwart my devotion. Mother would not exhaust me to the point of the silly tricks I played, would not spend her nights laughing at me behind her hand, when my desire shivered and snapped between us like a lightning-struck tree.

In her hall of pearl and jasper, laid out in flecks from one side of heaven to the other, I pissed out her whistling tea, I squatted and shat out her awful, starchy rice—the pearl stank and the jasper steamed and I was well pleased. She pretended not to notice. She sent our boys to clean it, and the clang of their iron hands on the lacquer scraped my ears spotless.

I walked through the rice paddies we had planted together, hands in the mud, and hers so bright under the sludge that I thought the sludge was itself gold, and what rice would grow from such soil! With my belt of cirrus flashing black, I kicked through her retaining walls and jumped from terrace to terrace, splashing in the sudden water as paddy flooded into paddy, and the rice—not so different than any other farmer's rice—spoiled in the blinding light of Takamagahara. At this she did cry out, and sent our boys to shore up the walls again, but their ore-padded knees rusted in the standing wreckage. Her face was wide and twisted, shining in terrace after ruined terrace. I laughed—the Rice of Heaven was not even good for wine.

But she did nothing to me, she knelt and poured the tea that evening as though nothing had happened, as though she had Mother's patience, and I could not see her stomach flaring through her robes, and her hunger. Yellow-faced fool, she could not touch Mother's patience with the longest of her beams.

Sometimes I feel as though there is something else living within me, a smoke-mouthed and sneer-eyed creature which is me-but-not-me, and I cannot speak to it, but it drives me, drives me after dragons and Mothers and causes me, in its salt-in-wound morbidity, to push further than even I would have if it did not sit like a crow on my spleen, cinching in my guts with its claws. And so I think it was this thing which saw the Piebald Colt of Heaven prancing it its bronze pen, which saw the colt and hopped, horribly, from one black foot to the other.

It must have been this thing in me which opened the pen and put out its hand for the colt to nose, which brought an apple and a lump of sugar and murmured to the beast as it chewed the sweet, wet meat. It could not have been I who stroked its blond mane, called him a good beast, and a kind beast, and put a nose to his. It, and not I, must have felt his hot breath on its cheeks and heard the soft snort as it cut into his flesh, peeling that gold pelt from the muscle, all in one apple-swift strip. I could not have watched the blood of the Piebald Colt of Heaven seep into the celestial plain, the creature I had raised with my sister, had called gentle, and lovely, and ours.

Perhaps it was this thing which had had statues made of it, which stomped snakes with clay soles.

It could not have been I who threw it into the chambers of Ama-Terasu, who laughed at the sodden slap of the carcass on her polished floor, at the high, flute-pale screams of our daughters as they leapt from their sewing, red hair flying, red eyes flashing.

It must have been the storm-seed inside me, for I could never do those things to such a woman as the sun became.

SEVENTH HEAD

I am dragging blood behind me like menses—the grass is full of it, clotted with it, hungry for it, and I pick myself up over the hillocks and dells with a belly bloody and inflamed, a mass of maidenheads burst and gaping *we sit on the floor of the monster like a blister of blood, heavy and black, and we seep through, we seep through, and stamp our wet wombprints on the path from what was once our house to what is now our nest* *I did not mean for this to happen* *did you think you could eat a thing and not become it? We always knew, we who have eaten the soup of eyes every day from birth; what is there we have not seen between the eight of us?* *Kaori, Kaori, it hurts* *yes, it always hurts, we knew that, too, but blood is blood, blood is a portent, and you are beautiful when you bleed, when you bleed for us, and with us, and in us, and around us*

I was so weak when I came to you, Kaori, so weak with the blood bellowing out of me *and your back, your poor back. None of the rest of them saw you as I did, your jeweled skin cracked open, your stomach ruined. No seduction there, only a monster, and terrible* *I could not even cry, the sounds which came out of me were a cacophony, all those voices, all that screeching, I could not hide for the blood and the vomit of voices* *It didn't matter anyway, there were only two of us left, and mother would let neither of us go to the man who was neither well nor sick. His face was moon-blanched when morning found it, his voice gone with my sisters, and he was turned out of our house like a dog, but there was nothing left of him to whip, nothing left but food for other dogs* *There are roots in my vertebrae, twisting and gobbling bone, and I am become the Root-Country, I am Ne no Kuni, all these throats stoppered up with women, women lodged in them like corks and the pain, the pain* *I hung behind my mother's skirts, too young even to look him in the face, and whispered to her that I felt so sorry for him. It was not his fault the snake had taken all his wives, and why should I not have my chance as his wife, when all the others had? I could be a good wife, I told her, I know how to make the soup, I know how to arrange the grass on the floor—why should I not be allowed to wear the rich, thick kimono my sisters had worn?* *Kaori, the blood, where does it come from?* *I was a silly girl, but pity sat in me like a fat baby.* *Something is growing from my shoulder blades, I cannot see it, I cannot see it, but it is there, and its roots seize my eight livers, and its thirst, its thirst—*

It didn't matter, in the end. The man who was neither alive nor dead cut his belly open on our stoop before the day was out. He had seen the snake too many times, I suppose. Mother sighed and sat heavily against the house—I was safe. Kushinada was safe. She had two daughters left to her, and the snake would not come, she thought, now that the offending husband was a cairn of meat on our steps. *It was not him, it was never him, but the blood, the blood sang for you, Kaori, it throbbed hot and thick, and called your name: Ka-o-ri!* *I sat out in front of our little house that night, that warm night, and looked at the stain his suicide had made on the stones. It was such a sad little mark.*

They are sticking out of me like pins, and I can smell them, yes, the trees, all their trees, plum and cherry and dogwood and waist-high reeds persimmon and even the eyes, Kyoko's eyes, they blink on the shell of my back, among the trees, and the trees split me open, they witness my second birth, no longer snake but woman *And my trees, the orange trees of Kaori, white as paroxysms, which saw my birth in the garden, my hardly-marked birth, seventh among daughters, my mother's womb barely felt me leave it, so oiled and hinged by other births was the poor, wrung-dry thing* *yes, yours too, and the fruit is heavy, round as suns, so heavy and I can hardly drag myself among the hills, down to the city, and I know the fruits have no sugar to give, only more blood, more blood, and they will burst and wet the roots again, and they will grow taller and it will go on and on* *but she gave me the meat of the orange to suck, her breasts gone dry with too much milking, and I was calmed by the sweetness of it, the stinging gold of summer, and she sang to me as I nursed the thready fruit, my eyes sliding shut in her arms.*

I slid through the empty streets after a virgin like an opium-eater after a den. *I wondered, I remember, I wondered if you would come anyway* *and I saw you sitting as though you expected me, and the blood was so thick on the alleys and I moaned and all these voices came out of me, you turned as though you knew them* *I knew the voice of Kazuyo, and Kameko, and Kiyomi, and Kyoko, and Kaya, and little Koto, I knew them like my own, and standing on the mark of their dead husband I saw the terrible thing that had eaten them, with their love pouring out of its mouths* *I tried to say 'come to me,' and it came out 'sister, wife, be our sister, be our wife.' * and I knew them for what they were, and I saw the saplings on your poor back, and I knew them for the birth-wardens of my family, and I would not be left out, I would not be left behind, they wanted me, and I ran to you* *you ran to me, and your hair flew like veins behind you* *I ran to you with open arms, and you were so weak* *I could not eat, though the Mouth churned in itself, demanded you, throbbed your name in the midst of all that blood: Ka-o-ri!* *you could not take me; I opened your seventh head myself, and the air from within you smelled of orange blossoms, I patted your head, your blistered, root-ridden, suffering head* *and you stepped inside me with all the trust of a lost child who sees the end of the wood* *and darkness closed around me, but not silence, never silence.*

It took all night to stumble out of the village, my belly so bloodied it might have been a heart, but we were safe, all of us, beyond the blue ridges by the time the sun rose *They married me to him anyway, of course. It was felt that propriety demanded a final marriage for both lost souls—I had said I wanted him, had I not? And he so fond of our family. He should not go down into Ne no Kuni alone.* *We watched, our heads resting thoughtfully on a boulder, as the ghost-wedding proceeded through the village, and a priest said words over empty space, and a feast was eaten while weeping, and an empty bed laid out, clean and white, for the weight of ghosts to rest upon.*

I laughed, and the orange trees on my *our* *back shook, to see my* *our* *sepulchral maidenhead vanish into the cloth*

while we wet the mountains with our red and ruined flesh.

VIII
IZUMO

It was the colt that she could not abide. She would have forgiven the rice and the shit, eventually. But she held its bloodied, skinless skull in her arms like an infant, looked up at me over the whites of its eyes with such betrayal in her stare—for a moment I was shamed, I stood before her like a child caught stealing sweets, but the storm-seed laughed and danced in a puddle of his own making, and I could not conceal, not really, not from her, the joy I took in our daughters chaotic cries, in her own red-streaked gown. She was more beautiful to me in that moment than when she first descended the stair of heaven, cloaked in all the sun's regalia. Her hair was matted with black clots and her sleeves dripped scarlet onto the floor, her fine cheeks were painted with horseblood and I loved her so, I loved her filthy and squalid, swimming in death.

She took me in her arms, finally, and both I and the storm-seed exulted in her heat, her nearness, her light pouring from the spaces between the streaks of horsefat. She took me in her arms and pressed me close, and the gold of her ribs cracked the grey-blue bone of my own, and her face was a boil of grief, and her fire rose up all around me, as it must have risen from Mother, Mother and her boy burning her from the womb out, and my sister burned me from the mouth in, her punishing kiss scouring my flesh of storm, of cloud, of lightning, of sky.

I felt her kiss push me down, down, like a hand on the head of a drowning man, and the sky was caustic, my bones lit up like braziers, and something came spiraling out of me—the strange pearl of Izanami's flesh, the yellowed orb of what she had to give me, the clot of her dust and rot and flesh and Izanagi's fluid—it tore out of me like semen, expelled into the fertile clouds, and who knows what storm it salted there.

It was in Izumo that I landed, face first in the mosquito-mottled grass. Izumo, meaningless village, just over the hills from the stink and sink and sick perfume of Hiroshima.

From far off, I heard my children weeping scarlet, scarlet and black.

KUSHINADA / EIGHTH HEAD

:: Look at you, great enfeebled thing, choking on my sisters, spitting them out of your mouths like chewed meat. ::

Look at you, look at how we sit, like teacher and pupil, you below me with that thoughtful stare, looking up into all these eyes, shaded by the wide camphors like a net of protecting arms. Don't you think it's funny, don't you think it's a classical pose, all the rituals of dragon and maiden observed? I am trying to decide not to eat you, but it is difficult, difficult.

:: I am naked here, and alone, and I am sure that is all as you imagined it, last girl among all the girls, eight, eight—there are always eight, eight of us and eight of you, the eightfold path, and I am at the end, Right Maiden, Right Prey. It is dark here, but my irises have widened, I can see my own mud-streaked limbs, white as poached snails, and I have rocked back and forth on the forest floor clutching them, and I have wondered, wondered when I would join the others, when you would speak to me in their voices, but you will not, you hold them back from me— ::

I hurt. I hurt so much there is no space left in my throats for the hunger. My belly is gape-open, there is so much blood,
{we} never thought (we)
had so much blood in
    me/us,
      |we|
didn't know
    our
flesh went so deep.

It is becoming confused, crowded, and the smell of flowers gags, oh, it
    (chokes)
there was an I before this, I remember it, and all these heads fanned out from it like leaves, and I cannot find it now, it is like looking in a heap of jetsam for the one toy you loved as a child.

:: Look at the monster, holding its stunted hands out to its food, begging surcease. ::

This is your blood, it is all over me,
>   *[we]*

drown in it. Make it stop. I am finished with this now.

:: You wanted all the others—am I not sweet enough to join my sisters? I can hear, at night, the city not far off, the hurrying men with arms full of jars and clothing and cups, but all I see is trees, trees and you, green and terrible among them, and this place is sticky with blood and saliva and urine. It is our nest, and you are like a mother, ripped open to let her babies out, but nothing comes from you, they are stuck, stuck like hooks in a carp's mouth, and I am telling you that I am willing, willing to go where they have gone— ::

Tell me about your trees, Kushinada, tell me what color they will be when they come cracking through

>   *—our—*

spine.

:: Far off from the house my mother :: *Mother!*
>   *[Mother!]*

Always Mother, sloughing her children off of herself like old robes, and then she vanishes, yes, vanishes, and there were no trees where I was born, none at all, but your

>   **our**

mother did it too, she spat you

>   *[us]*

out among the flowers and then filled you

>   */us/*

up with fish eyes until it was time to give you

>   *—us—*

us, yes, us, give us all to the man who was

>   *{neither old nor young,}*
>   *|who was neither handsome nor ugly,|*
>   *(who was neither fat nor thin,)*

neither, neither, neither

:: my mother was fishing, sitting propped against a stone by a little pond, and the air was golden and still, golden and still under the flowering cassia, the yellow blossoms and the red bark, and the smell of cinnamon floating over the rippleless water :: *Mother squeezed* me/us

out into the wriggling silver, the wriggling silver and the salt churn, she pushed
and pushed and I

|we|

dribbled from her like pus, like a tumor, like a

:: she held the pole between her feet; it curved like a lazily drawn bow. ::
leech.

:: There were no tugs at the line; it hung limply as a spare koto-string.
But, as afternoons will, the late sun brought a fish to the morsel of pig-gut
on my mother's crude hook, and in lurching forward to catch the suddenly
taut pole from between her ankles, mother felt something tear inside her ::
Ah, Kushinada!

Kushinada!

I know that tear! Please, I beg—yes, I beg, I am above nothing, lower than
worms, than snails—make the blood stop. Be a good girl, be the good
daughter,

(be a good girl)

{be the good daughter}

put your hands on me and plug up this wet mire

—reach up, baby sister, and we will carry you—

it will ooze between your fingers like menarche but don't fear, don't fear

:: and she caught her belly, gasped, fell forward on her knees and saw
the fish in the water, pig-bowel dribbling from its piscine lip, looking at her
through the filmy green pond. It blinked in the slant-light, and she breathed
quick and fast :: there is a space in me

(there is a space in us)

the space from which all this miasma wells

/the place kept still and soft for you, Kushinada/

and that space was once empty, nothing more than a hollow between muscles

—it is not so bad here—

but now, now there are seven there, and their mouths make a chain, and they

|we|

are waiting for the weld of you, and

[we are the Mouth now,]

and I think if I could turn my heads just so

if we could knot the body just so we might see ourselves

I might see them inside me, holding hands, and out of their heads flower the
branches that shiver my bones

:: quick and fast and low, and the grass was soaked with her water and
her blood; her womb-water joined the green water and flowed in and out of
the rosy fish's gills ::

there were fish at my
                    (our)
birth, too, so many, all silvern and clear, and they smelled, oh, they smelled like
      sorrow
lightning, and they weighed nothing at all, nothing—

:: and she bit down on a cassia branch in agony, and her mouth was
flooded with the murky taste of cinnamon ::

      (we remember how she told this story,)
            |*how she used to give you a flake of cinnamon bark*|
      /*to suck when you teethed*/
I
      {we}
had no teeth, my
      [our]
eyes would not open, I
      |*we*|
could not stand, I
      we
was nothing but a sack sloshing with water, and only the fish would take me,
      —us—
would give me
      (us)
their tentacles to suckle.

:: and the tear in her grinned wide :: *wide, ah, wide!* :: wider than the mouth
of the watchful fish, and she thought her bones would shatter as she squatted
by the green water. I came out of her :: *like a leech-child* :: and her hands on my
soft head were red as paint, and the umbilicus was knotted round my neck
            —yes, she always told it like this: she tore it with her teeth—
/*oh, what a fish mother caught that day, with the pole-and-line of her*
ruined flesh!/
:: And gasping in the flotsam of her body she looked at the rosy fish again ::

the fish carried me
            [it carried us—didn't you feel that we were in you already,
            the promise of us, the taste?]
away from Onogoro; I
    (we floated with you, the seeds of our plums and our weeds)
rested on their backs like the bow of the boat of heaven, island to island, and
the water tasted of mother, and I, I was so alone.
            Oh, beauty, oh self of our selves!
                (You are not alone, we are none of us alone!)
I was alone then, in the dark.
            [Never again, we swear it]
                |we would not let you go into the dark alone|
                    —not without our arms ringed round you—
    :: floating still next to the line. It looked at her silently, without reproach,
and slowly closed the morsel of pig-gut in its mouth ::
                and the tear was so wide and so great in her
—/that mother never gave the trees another daughter/
                |and told us the story of the fish and the cassia|
    {while we stirred the soup}
    We birth each other, over and over, Mouth to Mouth, and it is still dark,
but seven clutch each other,
    (seven clutch you)
and seven clutch me, and I
    [we]
do not remember any longer whether I am eighth or first or last,
                there are eight, always eight
I do not remember any longer what mother looked like, but their
    —our—
cool black braids lie over
    /all of us/
me like first kisses.
    :: My first meal was the mash of that fish's black eyes ::
    My first meal was the slippery skin of those velvet jellyfish, and in those
days we were so like each other, but they did not speak to me like my selves
do now, and
    {we never bled}

|but we ate|

(and we grew)

:: Please, it is cold out here, and I am alone. I taste of cinnamon, and I will lie soft on your tongue. Let me touch your skin—it flames blue and sere!—but let me touch it, let me pry open your lips. It is cold, I want my sisters, I want to be eight-in-one, I have heard them whispering and I know they want me. Lonely little leech, I don't want the soup of eyes. I don't want the bitter tea. I don't want the birth story, the cassia or the persimmon, the plum or the cherry, the weeds or the eyes. I will be your Onogoro, and you will be my Heaven-Spanning Bridge, and I will never leave you. ::

Kushinada, where will I go, when you are all inside me?

/Hush, now, we are infinitely tractable/

(Don't you know how far women stretch?)

There is room, there is room, always room for our sister, our jewel, our little cinnamon-suckling babe

:: Let me in ::

Kushinada!

:: Oh, let me ::

But the blood!

the blood is of us

[and in us]   —and because of us—

/ and from us/ |and it is us|

(and there is always blood)

{when new things are}

born.

IX
MT. HIBA

The white-capped monks shivered—it was night, and the stars gave no heat. Did they weep? I could not tell, their faces hunched together; they all refused to meet my eyes. They ought to have wept—it is that sort of story.

"You see how it was, now," I sighed, "and you will not spread Izanagi's lies any longer, I know."

"No, *musuko*," they murmured, and they turned their faces tighter towards each other.

"Musuko, musuko! What a stupid word. You have no sons at all. But please," and here I leaned close in, hearing my knees creak into the crouch, "I will overlook your wormy vocabulary if you will only tell me why you have those carvings, of the eight-headed snake and I. Did you dream such a scene? Do you know where the snake is to be found?"

The abbot's shining head rose bravely from the throng, which seemed to me in that moment to resemble most ridiculously a bouquet of flowers, bunched together and nodding in the breeze. "Susanoo-no-Mikoto, the serpent carved on our walls has plagued these valleys since my grandfather was a boy. It likes especially to eat maidens and young mothers. We made these icons in the hope that you would vanquish it, cut its heads and tails from its body, and add to your already immeasurable glory. They are our prayers."

So simple, then. They knew nothing they ought not to have known. I was not walking through an already-told tale. I was myself, and no other, not the storm-seed, not the flesh-cased man. I should have known how empty they would prove.

"I have resolved already to kill it, and wed the last girl it seized, if she is still alive. It is only that I cannot find the beast. And I have been distracted by . . . family matters."

"Of course, Storm-Lord! But why would a god marry a poor farm girl?" asked one of the bound novices, his voice thin and chirping as an insect.

"All things must eventually mate," I shrugged, "having been cast into a man's flesh I must do as flesh does. And it hardly matters whether one mates with a woman or a rock or a river—the end result is the same. Once all the world wed stones and trees—but this is a degenerate age, and no one keeps to tradition."

The abbot spoke again among his bright-robed brothers. "The serpent has been quiet of late, but it is easy to spot, for in the last year terrible trees have sprouted from its back, and it drags a train of black, clotted blood behind it like a bridal veil."

"But where?" I cried, and curled my fists, "no one can tell me where it drags its bloody belly, where these trees grow!"

Stroking his beads like a girl brushes her hair, the abbot pursed his lips. "The last time I heard its cries was outside of Hiroshima."

"The city," I said heavily.

"Yes, the city, the city," the monks nodded eagerly, "now let us go!"

"Everyone points me towards that reeking, wasted city. I do not wish to go there, I do not wish it!" I suppressed the urge to stamp my feet and tear my hair. Instead, I simply turned my head to one side and then the other, worrying the serpent in my mind like an old bone.

"Do you make the eight-times-brewed wine in this shrine?" I asked suddenly with a voice like a crow.

"Yes . . . yes," answered the novice, confused, "we have some barrels left, but the brewing season is long past."

"If you will bring eight barrels, and a quantity of sacred camphor wood, I will let you go—but you must come with me into Hiroshima, which stinks of meat and bodies, and do as I say."

The monks wept then, certainly, and shook their knots, and swore they would obey me, whatever I should ask.

"Wait," I whispered, "before we leave—do you know, do you also know where the entrance to the Root-Country is, the path down into Ne no Kuni?"

After a long silence, the abbot folded his hands in his lap.

"No, my lord. No man knows that."

EIGHT

Call us Monster. Call us Leech. Call us Daughter.

We smelled it first. The scents came looping and spinning up through the banyan-roots and into the little clearing where we lay in our cradle of blood, and it smelled, oh, it smelled like warm rice and pickled eyes, it smelled like cassia and persimmon, it smelled like jellyfish thin as breath.

And it smelled like Kazuyo-that-was.

And it smelled like Kameko-who-laughed.

And it smelled like Kiyomi-who-wept.

And it smelled like the Kaya-bird.

And it smelled like Kyoko-who-was-plain.

And it smelled like Koto-who-had-no-story.

And it smelled like Kaori-who-waited-outside-the-door.

And it smelled of Hiruko-who-wailed-for-its-mother.

And it smelled like Kushinada, Kushinada, who tasted of tea.

It smelled like ourselves, and we were drawn to it.

Of course, under that we could smell you, brother—even in your new skin you smell of scorched air and boiling water. But the other smells—the other smells were better smells, and we have wanted better things. It is not that we were fooled, or befuddled. We were fed all our life on eyes: there is nothing we do not see.

We came down after it, down the grassy hillocks and the forest chasms, and our back rolled and creaked like a ship under the weight of flowering trees—but in the reflections of the puddles and paddies we thought ourselves beautiful, and our blood was so red, so red. And we saw the city of Hiroshima, and the river delta, and the sun on the water—and oh! The manifold fence! Out of red and smoke-scented woods a fence had been thrown up, and in it were eight doors, and each door was thrown open as though you were expecting us for festival, brother, as if you welcomed us. Just beyond each door were eight pearl-lined bowls, and each bowl was filled with rice-wine eight-times-brewed. They were laid out so carefully, so sweetly, that we thought—forgive us!—for a moment, that you knew us, and wanted to drink to ghosts among family.

Was it not clever of him, to lay out such well-crafted dishes? I think there has never been anyone so clever as he.

We bend our heads, ducking under the lip of the eight-fold fence, crossing the threshold, threaded as through an ornate needle. Blood pools beneath us—we do not notice. Its warmth has become familiar as a hand. We look hopefully for our brother, to greet us, to toast our health. There is no one; the city below is quiet. Not far from here Kushinada was born in the witness of a fish; not far from here Susanoo-no-Mikoto descended from the rage-blind fire of heaven, the fire which blanches all things to bones. We thought we could still see the afterimage of that fire still laid over the streets, a scald in our vision—but perhaps it is nothing, nothing, perhaps it is a trick of the sunlight, and the wine, which drinks up the gold and throws it up into our eyes like a column of flame.

We look again for our brother-who-is-not-our-brother—the genealogy is muddy, now that we are ourself and no longer a leech and eight girls—we put on our best and most practiced smile like a festival dress. Come see us, come see that we grew up to be beautiful, after all.

There is no one.

The rice-wine smells of fish-eyes, and salt.

It will not hurt, certainly, if we drink a bit before he comes.

He would not begrudge us wet throats.

X
HIROSHIMA

The wretched, stupid thing drank itself into stupor. Its heads lolled on the grass as I approached, looking up at me with great dark eyes, its translucent eyelids opening and closing weakly over sixteen dark irises. It tried to raise each head, one after the other, and let them fall with a heavy slap onto the dirt road beyond the manifold fence. Spittle dribbled from its mouths. It was pitiful; it could hardly moan. Stinking blood ran in arm-thick rivulets from its prone belly, and on its back grew a tangled, stunted forest of trees whose flowers, too, were streaked with bloody muck—in among the ruin there might have been sprigs of cassia, but who could tell? I ran my hands over the massive body, through the thin trunks and the dripping belly. The skin beneath was silver, flushed with blue and gold, rose and green, iridescent as that of a snail.

It was helpless as an infant, unable to stand, and I could smell, still, the skin of Kushinada on its breath.

The monks crowded around, prodding the beast, awe-struck at its size and nearness, this thing they had feared for so long. They tugged at the eight tails, even tasted the oozing blood, and plucked limbs from the forest of its spine. The abbot put a decrepit sword into my hand, the ceremonial blade of their shrine, hardly sharp enough to cut lard. But even below the cellars of heaven, my arms are strong.

I walked to the first head, and in the late afternoon light, the eyes seemed to struggle, the lid seemed to draw aside like pale curtains, and its mouth seemed to protest. With that blunted sword I hewed into the gray-green flesh of its neck—and the blood which flowed from the serpent was red as a woman's, and the jaws sprung open, and its exhale was a shriek:

/Is this how the snot-born earns back his godhead? He slurps us, oh, we are his soup!/

I walked to the second head, and hewed into the silver-blue flesh of its neck—and the blood which flowed from the serpent was red as a woman's, and the jaws sprung open, and its exhale was a rattle:

(Is this how the unloved child punishes the only one less loved than he? He chews us, oh, we are his gristle!)

I walked to the third head, and hewed into the pearl-gold flesh of its neck—and the blood which flowed from the serpent was red as a woman's, and the jaws sprung open, and its exhale was a scream:

—*Is this how the suitor greets his bride? He buys us, oh, we are his prize!*—

I walked to the fourth head, and hewed into the nacreous flesh of its neck—and the blood which flowed from the serpent was red as a woman's, and the jaws sprung open, and its exhale was a hiss:

{*Is this how the dog shows its dam its adulation? He gnaws us, oh, we are his bone!*}

I walked to the fifth head, and hewed into the bruise-violet flesh of its neck—and the blood which flowed from the serpent was red as a woman's, and the jaws sprung open, and its exhale was a sigh:

|*Is this how a cloud shows the sun its strength? He hides us, oh, we are his crime!*|

I walked to the sixth head, and hewed into the tarnished opal flesh of its neck—and the blood which flowed from the serpent was red as a woman's, and the jaws sprung open, and its exhale was a howl:

[*Is this how the hero defeats his dragon? He cuts us, oh, we are his supper!*]

I walked to the seventh head, and hewed into the watery flesh of its neck—and the blood which flowed from the serpent was red as a woman's, and the jaws sprung open, and its exhale was a shudder:

Is this how family honors family? He stains us, oh, he stains us, we are nothing to him! No, please, Susanoo, let me stay, let me live beside you, as Mother meant—

I walked to the eighth head, and hewed into the worm-slick flesh of its neck—and the blood which flowed from the serpent was red as a woman's, and the jaws sprung open, and its exhale was a maddened cry:

"Please, oh, please, I am afraid! The jellyfish, the jellyfish—I can't see! The jellyfish crowd overhead!"

I opened the last neck and lodged there, as though she had just been swallowed, was the body of Kushinada, laid into the green-black flesh like a gem set into a box. She was as beautiful as they promised, her hair wrapping her body, strands sticking in the pooled blood, her pale and perfect face streaked with bile and slime. She lay clutching the length of the serpent's gnarled spine with all her strength, her arms and legs clasped around it, weeping piteously.

"No, no, Kameko, Kazuyo! Kaya, Kiyomi, my sisters! Kyoko, Kaori, Koto! Come back, come back, Hiruko, please, it is cold out here, I am alone, I am alone, we said we would none of us be alone again. Come back!"

I pulled her from her throat-crèche, pulled her out of that wreckage of blood and tissue as a midwife pulls a child from a dead mother, and she trembled beautifully in my arms. I brushed her hair from her face, tenderly and dear.

"You are not alone, Kushinada. I am here, and I have saved you."

But she kept weeping, soft as a mouse, and shaking her head, whimpering:

"No, no."

It became tiresome.

I gave her over to the monks to clean and comfort, for a thing had caught my eye. Kushinada—jewel among maidens!—had clung to the serpent's spine as though it would save her. It gleamed white as a tooth in the slough, the vertebrae knobbled and arched almost in the shape of a sword. I knelt in the sodden grass and pulled the bone from the muscle, ligaments popping and cartilage cracking as it came free. With the blunt and heavy edge of the abbot's sword I hacked at the length of it until it shone with a terrible edge, and a hilt which as so bright and pale as to seem nearly hewn out of diamond.

I sweated in the deepening twilight, but I was proud of my work. I gave the blade a flourish and with one blow halved the trunks of eight tall weeds sprouting from the serpent's corpse. Kushinada gave a sharp yelp like a kicked cat, and fell to her knees, tears steaming on her perfect cheeks.

"That is the flesh of my sisters, flesh of my flesh, bone of our body!"

"No," I answered her, "it is mine, I have made it, it is fine, and I will call it *Kusanagi-no-Tsurugi*, the Grass-Cutting Sword."

I brandished the sword again, and put it into the hands of the abbot.

"Take this to the temple of my sister, Ama-Terasu. Give it to her priests and her cawing roosters, and perhaps the old wretch will make white-haired boys out of it this time. And perhaps she will forgive me the Piebald Colt, who was a good beast, after all."

The abbot nodded and folded up his relic, fading into the city streets, as monks are wont to do.

Kushinada and I were alone in the flotsam of the eight-headed serpent. The sun was almost gone, but still glittered redly behind flax-clouds.

Kushinada sat in the grass, her naked form covered in blood like a dress, holding one of the severed heads in her lap, crooning at it and rocking back and forth.

I watched her for a long while, and smelled with some interest the metallic tang of death hovering over the manifold fence. *Is that,* I wondered, *what Mother's hair will smell like?*

"I have solved it," I called to my bride, "I know now the path to Ne no Kuni, and all because of this brainless drunkard of a snake."

Kushinada wept into the mottled head.

"Would you like to know it? Your husband-to-be is the cleverest of all possible men—will it please you to hear how I have solved this puzzle?"

Kushinada sniffled like a child, and wiped at her bloodied face with bloodied hands. She said nothing.

"You see," I said softly, sitting gingerly next to her as one will sit next to a feral cat one hopes to pet, "I descended not far from here, my first footprints on the earth made their impressions in the dust of Hiroshima and Izumo, and Yasugi and Mt. Hiba. I descended and was made a man, and from that moment I could not find my way into Yomi, the land of shadows."

I turned her face towards me, and the whites of her eyes showed.

"I could not find my way, you understand, because I am a man. No man knows the way. But sitting in all this blood, stepping through the corpse-geography of the serpent of Izumo as my father must have stepped through my mother in the light of his comb, I have solved it: I may go to her as easily as any man, if I am willing to die for her. Who can go into the kingdom of the dead while he is living? Only my father, first of all things that trespassed, and I am not he."

Kushinada's eyes searched mine. "Then . . . then you will let me go?"

I laughed. "Oh, no, you are promised to me—I will die, I will go to the slopes of Mt. Hiba and I will go down into the earth, I will claw the roof of hell until mother lets me in, I will eat earth, I will eat loam and clay until I choke, and she will take me in, and I will become in her primordial womb my old self, crowned in clouds. I will rule beside her in the kingdom of the dead, and when I have shed this flesh I will come back for you."

She crumbled into my lap; her legs tangled in the jaws of the snakehead, and shuddered. "You are neither old nor young, handsome nor ugly; you are neither man nor god, you are neither alive nor dead, and after all this, after all this, I will be the only one of us taken to wife."

I patted her head comfortingly. "It will not be so bad, my love, my love—when I am myself again I will turn you into a beautiful jeweled comb, so that you can come into the land of the dead while you yet live, as my father brought his comb. And I will place you in my headdress, and your teeth will lie close to my scalp, always, so that I know you are there, and that you love me. And every now and then, a jewel will fall from its setting, and those jewels will be our children, and they will grow up to be wonders: your rubies will be samurai and your sapphires will be court poets, your emeralds will be concubines and your diamonds will be magicians, and your silver will be empresses, and your gold will be emperors. They will fall like colored rain onto the radiant flesh of Izanami, and everyone will marvel at the glittering children of Kushinada!"

The mother of all emperors bent double on the wet earth, clutched her belly and opened her mouth to scream, but nothing came, nothing came but spittle and strangled gasps, and then she began that tiresome rocking, rocking and crooning.

I left her there, kissed her forehead like a dutiful husband, and told her I would return. I walked away from the manifold fence with a straight back and a cool brow—I looked back only once to see her with two of the massive, broken heads barely contained within her skinny arms, kissing their gory skin and sobbing.

The guttering sparks of the sun lay over Hiroshima far below, and I thought—only for a moment—that, as if I had already walked there, already eaten and drunk and slept and wakened there, I could see my footprints flaming over the city, burning white and sere, like an afterimage, and a hot wind followed after them.

XI
YOMI

"Mother!" he called to the bloody-flowered acacia.

"Mother!" he called to the top-knots of snow.

"Mother!" he called to the stones from the barrels of earth.

And it was the stones that answered.

"Here," they murmured in their grinding, "here."

Susanoo-no-Mikoto pushed stone aside from stone, slate from shale.

"Here," they sighed, and moved from their loam, "here."

He clawed at the mud, tearing thick furrows in the ground.

"Mother!" he wheezed, falling onto his face, beating his fists against the soil.

And in the long shadows of the night whose shape the sun cannot guess, the black earth closed her arms over her son.

UNDER IN THE MERE

Then quickly rose Sir Bedivere, and ran,
And, leaping down the ridges lightly, plunged
Among the bulrush-beds, and clutched the sword,
And strongly wheeled and threw it. The great brand
Made lightnings in the splendour of the moon,
And flashing round and round, and whirled in an arch,
Shot like a streamer of the northern morn,
Seen where the moving isles of winter shock
By night, with noises of the northern sea.
So flashed and fell the brand Excalibur:
But ere he dipped the surface, rose an arm
Clothed in white samite, mystic, wonderful,
And caught him by the hilt, and brandished him
Three times, and drew him under in the mere.

—Alfred, Lord Tennyson
Idylls of the King

XVII THE STAR

The Lady of the Lake

*So they rode till they came to a lake, which was a fair water and
broad, and in the midst of the lake Arthur was aware of an arm
clothed in white samite, that held a fair sword in that hand. With that
they saw a damosel floating upon the lake. What damosel is that? said
Arthur. That is the Lady of the Lake, said Merlin; and within that
lake is a rock, and therein is as fair a place as any on earth, and richly
beseen; and this damosel will come to you anon, and then speak ye
fair to her that she will give you a sword.*

—Sir Thomas Malory
Le Morte d'Arthur

What damosel is this? What damosel is this? Perhaps I am nothing but a
white arm. Perhaps the body which is me diffuses at the water's surface
into nothing but light, light and wetness and blue. Maybe I am nothing but
samite, pregnant with silver, and out of those sleeves come endless swords,
dropping like lakelight from my hems. Will you come down to me and
discover if my body continues below the rippling?

I thought not.

Look out: the lake's edges blur into the sky, blue to blue. All water flows
into itself—this is the lake; this is the sea. River and shore and flux, we are
all water together, and the moon shows in one just as in the other, a wide
white face and a long white arm.

In the quiet of the dark I have lapped milk from the dish of the moon,
and thought nothing of swords. In the dark of the quiet I have opened my
mouth to let the lake through, and the run-off has been afloat with stars.
And I thought nothing of hilts or pommels or earnest young men with
unconventional grocery lists. Take your basket through the fields—what
does the boy need for his magic kingdom? A magic birth, a magic man, a
magic crown, a magic sheath, a magic sword. I am last of all—you stand
on my white-sand shore and all you need is the sword to set it all going,
like a huge dial in some terrible wind-up clock made of women's limbs and

men's bones and so much gold, so much gold—lift the samite drop-cloth with a flourish and it all begins, it all goes along as the best of the angels of predestination would have it. All you need is the sword. How fortunate for you that we have one in stock.

The little waves wash over your feet, but they do not anoint them. The foam is sweet, but there is salt in the depths. Salt and me. It was good of you to come so far out of the world, so far across green squares of turnip farms and thorny apple orchards and a bridge whose suspensors are strung with the heads of all the kings who have tried to take the sword before you—covered in a sheen of melted pearl and lit up with fire. Check your map: if there are dragons here, I am a dragon, deep in the creases of my lake. Look at your map, Merlin-blessed, and see how far you have come, where the bridge leads and what it spans—it spans the distance between here and there, the rooted compass and the wheeling north, between Camelot and Faery, between the places you would drape with light until there is nothing but radiance and those places whose darkness you cannot begin to touch. Between yourself and your opposite. Between you and I. It arches through the ether; it goes to Annwn, to Avalon. To the otherworld, the otherplace, the othered place.

It goes to the New World. The place where maps shrivel and sodden, where the earth drops into water and water drops into earth. It goes to the sharp margin of everything that is, and there the knight finds the New World, the farthest west, and learns to whisper a word he has never heard: *Cal-i-forni-a*. Whisper it, breathe it, drink it from the droplets of the lake. This is the name of Annwn, of Avalon, this is the name of the underworld. It is written over the gates in chalcedony and drywall. On the other side of the bridge there was no *fiat lux*, only this one word. Say it and it will keep you safe.

I, too, am always at the other side, I and all my brothers and sisters, I and everything which has no place within civilized mortar-and-brick. You must come out to us, again and again, for we are the source of your magic births, your magic men, your magic crowns, your magic sheaths, and your magic swords. It is the chief industry of your reign, the commerce between your world and mine.

But perhaps not. Perhaps I am an old woman living under the water because clams and trout have better manners than kings, and I tell very beautiful lies because I just want the company, and if I lie prettily enough, you will stay and talk to me.

Perhaps I was once nothing but a very young girl, toddling down a stone wall and chasing moths with her pink fingers—and perhaps somewhere along the wet green meadow the wall became a path and the path became a road and the road became a bridge and the moths with the eyes on their wings were always just a little further off, flitting just out of reach, and perhaps the bridge became a lake and I splashed in after them. And perhaps the lake was full of swords and moths and apple trees waving in the current, and perhaps the swords said I was pretty, and the moths said it was all right to touch them, and the apple trees said wouldn't I like to stay, wouldn't I like to learn how to breathe water like a long, slender fish.

And perhaps I grew old down here, while my arm stayed young.

Perhaps I *am* nothing but a white arm, severed, stuck in the lake like a birthday candle.

Yet you see how far you had to come to find me. You cannot deny how warm it is here, how golden, how the gulls keen.

Come closer. Look in: anything could hide beneath the surface of the lake. A serpent, a woman, an arm, a sword. Anything could break the waters and call its own name. This still pool contains everything possible, every woman with necromancy inked on her tongue, every knight tilting, every castle, every grail. A lake has so many voices, you know. The flashes of light slip by on the water, in and out of each other, and each cries out in extremis, each cries out in its gleaming, and is gone. Can you hear them? I have sat at the bottom of the currents, cross-legged as a deva, and watched the green and the pale whicker by, howling, glowing, beaming. The water is so warm, when the choir sings. Lean in, lean in.

I know that I don't matter to you; I am no more than a bucket of water from this lake, something you can take without bargaining or payment. I am the beginning—you only need me to nod my alabaster head, Madonna-gentle, and grant your life permission to commence.

Oh, I am an arm, your arm, mine, theirs, all your boys. I extend, implore, I lavish upon and commit to the deeps. I bless, I strangle. I pull up the lakefloor in the shape of a sword and say: *go, boy, this story has already been told*. And perhaps, when this boy reaches out to take my blue blade, shining like nothing so much as water, my fingers will brush against his—they are warm, and shaking, and he is so young.

. . . and brandish'd him three times

I.

A wide green field, and grass like water waving. There is light here, and thick soil, and hiding hills. Clouds skitter across the hedgerows like rocks skipping on a lake. There are stones: here, there, great gray things, knuckle-knobbled. They lie where the walls will be, corners and lengths and thresholds. You can almost see the glimmer of what will stand, hovering shadow-still over the slabs.

The people come swarming, hammering, boiling pitch, boiling limestone, cutting wood. The most obvious images are best: a beehive. An anthill. Gold-backed, dust-legged, wings folded against the spine, the people stir, pour, smear, nail, pile, hammer, slide. None of them know the name of the man who will live here.

The walls go up first, so that no other bee or ant might suckle at the sweetness of a roof or a palisade. There are slender gaps for arrows, and paths so that helmeted soldiers may stalk their territory like dogs, and slope-shouldered lovers may watch the sun set over the blessing hills. It is good work, and plain: solid and thick and smelling of earth. Peat and mortar, sod and lime.

Second is the cathedral, whose altar was brought up from Cornwall, whose gargoyles were brought over the sea from France—years pass here, under the curling eaves, apples and capons eaten while the scaffolding weathers, a hoary skeleton. Even after the court and market are full of voices, after the stairs have been fashioned sturdy and steep, after secret rooms and passages are dug with due diligence, the cathedral will still be unfolding and spiraling up to the floor of God's house. A father paints the pews; his son finishes the rafters; his grandson strikes the first bell, whose wide bronze bonging tones echo through the valley, now planted with wheat and potatoes and pear trees, hutches of chickens and geese, pens of cattle, now teeming with tenant farmers and broad-bellied knights and harvests of good rain and mild sunshine, harvests that see baskets full of green and gold, brown eggs and thick milk.

The bell-note rolls over all these folk, all these baskets, and some brown-browed folk look up, shading their eyes, when the bell rings its virgin music, but most are unperturbed, pulling carrots and parsnips from the earth, rubbing at sore knees.

X THE WHEEL OF FORTUNE

Kay

Nine nights and nine days his breath lasted under water, nine nights and nine days would he be without sleep. A wound from Kay's sword no physician might heal. When it pleased him, he would be as tall as the tallest tree in the forest. When the rain was heaviest, whatever he held in his hand would be dry for a handsbreadth before and behind, because of the greatness of his heat, and, when his companions were coldest, he would be as fuel for them to light a fire.

—Culhwch and Olwen
The Mabinogion

Morning, First Day

I carry my air with me like crystal capsules—each day I slit one with the edge of my ribs and it is enough, just barely enough, to keep me walking. It is all I was meant for: walking, breathing, cutting. I am an automaton. My brother sets me walking and I keep going, clockworks grinding, bone gearshifts and blood-hydraulics, until I hit something. Sink Kay in the water—it is no matter, he is submersible, he will breathe like a salmon.

Not that I ever thought I would be more. How could I ever have thought myself special, what boy ever thinks he is more than the sum of his meat, when he is knobble-kneed and too tall with a nose that dwarfs his face? What boy thinks so when he is so often fevered that his skin is permanently flushed, and the other boys mock him for his maiden blush, and sweat clings to him like raindrops? What boy thinks so when he likes his horse and his boots and his best deer-hunting bow so much that even his father assumes he is stupid and burl-headed? I dreamed not of kingship, but that I might look up at a forest of men taller than I, a grove of straight-backed birches in which I would be but a stunted sapling.

My brother set it all going; he was a key and he slid into a great machine with jeweled parts. I wonder as I trod jerkily along, obeying his programming, if he ever wanted something more than to be a key, something more than to have opened a closed circuit by pulling a sword out of a stone. I want to say to him: *do you remember when we were brothers? When were not what we are now, toy-men, Hephaestus-cast, rolling along on a track we cannot see?*

But you do not say this to the bronze-footed king on his throne, even if you fear that he has become frozen there, bolted into his regalia, terrified to leave. Instead he sends us out, our quests screwed onto our backs with gold rivets, his words peeling from our tongues as though we had no voice of our own. We are his hands, we are his legs, we go out into the world and we go out of the world and we go where he tells us to go and we are lucky if we remember our names when we return.

I do not complain. It is not a brother's place to complain.

Once he did not cling to his chair—when he was a boy, when he was human and not king. When he was an orphan and chased after me even though we were brothers only by contract, and I actually thought it made a difference whether I called him brother or foster-brother. Then, his feet were always filthy and his clothes were full of bees and frogs and dragonflies and no one paid him much attention. After all, I was the elder. He had no track, he had no rivets. It was I, instead, who sat so often astride a horse that I thought myself half-centaur, who was scrubbed and tutored and dressed up in epaulets and rapped across the knuckles until my country accent faded into rounded vowels and crisp consonants.

Plate by plate I strapped metal onto my body. (And if I was fevered before, this was worse, the sheen of sweat inside the armor, the flushed face beneath the helmet, and after years, even the metal began to blush, until I was a red knight for true, boiling the rain away from me like soup spilled on a blazing anvil.) Then I thought I was making myself a man, but I see now that they were the plates of my manufacture as a king's worker, as the automaton I became. Year by year I bolted on a new body, plate armor like a beetle's shell, with enough holes for that eventual demiurge to slip his orders, to feed in his unalterable programs. A space had to be made for him. A space was made.

I remember that morning, when I slipped out of the world and he slipped into it. A slab of metal in rock—how could such a thing come to mean so much? It was no more or less part of the city than a grocer's storefront or a chipped curb, yet no one proposed that we prognosticate by those. Steel and stone and all of us agreed without speaking, made this covenant with the city streets and skies, that that knife in a rock meant more than melons in a pyramid or old yellow paint in an alley. Even when we had forgotten about it and let it grow over with dandelions and blackberry whips, it did not lose what we had so long ago given it: for my brother pulled it up and the light passed from me to him, the light and the horse and the tutor and the epaulets, which he was welcome to.

His name became like the sword in the stone: write *Arthur* on the skin of your hand and it means more than a boy so named, it means him, always him, forever.

My name became irrelevant.

There is water over my head already, clear and green. I can see the sun, still, shining in shafts through the little waves. What a place this is, how bright, how sere. The water is warm.

Afternoon, Third Day

In my brother's great hall there is a painting. An angel in red so bright it is nearly orange speaks to a scribe, and out of the seraphic mouth comes a long ribbon, winding and whirling and corkscrewing until it enters the scribe's ear. On this ribbon are written divine words, undeniable words, words that originated on the sea of glass and, shard-bright, fell until they tore open the ribbon in shapes of themselves.

This is what my brother's commands are like.

He speaks and I can almost see it, the ribbon snaking out of his mouth, yellow and black, coiling through the air to enter me at the place in my back which was made for him, made for the receipt of quests, made to ingest his desires and make them manifest. There is no sound but the ticking of this ribbon into me, the slow click of a king's calligraphy, holes in the shapes of divine letters slotting into my sinews, whispering angelic and severe, locking my joints in place. His ribbon susurrates in me, insists that an object is required, a child stolen away to the bottom of the sea, to Annwn, the other country, which is west, and there are kabbalistic coordinates which burn themselves into my corneas—but it doesn't matter what the object is. There is always an object. He always requires it. His hunger for them is never quiet. Nor does it matter where they are: they are always west, they are always out, they are always beyond, they are always in the otherworld, which is only to say the other world, anything that is not circumscribed by these walls, these floors, these steels and stones. The ribbon wraps my lungs, sets my constraint: nine days without breath, as near to the limit of my capsules as makes no difference—and this does not matter, either. Everything the ribbons demand extends our limits, no matter what those limits are. If I could hold my breath for ten days, the ribbon would demand ten.

Retrieve object. Return. Simple as stone. Execute.

The ribbon disappears under the plates of my armor, under the beetle-carapace of my second skin. I turn on golden heels. I walk in a straight line, unaltered and unerring until the air is so full of salt my joints cry out.

This is all I am.

West. West is the direction of blue water and gold land—we are aimed this way and thus we go, and we do not stop, we cannot stop, until the Pacific tells us that to go further is to find east and wind and light and silence. We pool in this place, in Annwn, in the otherworld which on maps purchased from salmon and seraphim is called California. Pass through fog and marsh and come out in the desert, pass through the desert and come out by the sea. I walked over the mountains and saw a valley opening up below me like a green lap, and there was a low mist of gold hanging over it, and I cannot but descend into it—I am comically made and even before the plates were fixed to me I walked straight through a river without noticing I was wet.

Yea, I have walked through the valley, and it was the valley of ribbons, swarming everywhere like Eden-exiled serpents, whispering so loud I could hardly hold on to my own, nosing at my feet, at my mouth, at my back. The green valley was choked with them, a paper sea writhing undulate and crisp, slicing characters from each other as easily as scales. I shuddered. Is this where the ribbons are born, this valley of glass grinding against glass, this valley of murmuring directives, of worker-commands without eyes navigating invisible corridors? Is this where they begin, the rustling things, where he found them in the days before he meted them out to us like tickets to a fair? Did he find this place before us all and pass through? What is a king but the source of commands? Am I wrong to remember a brother who let caterpillars sit on his shoulders, as though there was any life before the buzz and hum of Camelot?

There is a sea beyond the ribbons, and they sigh in protest as I walk through the grassy crackle—they cannot find any point of entry. I am my brother's servant, and I have room for no more in me than him.

The light is dimmer now, the water deep and blue. I have seen octopi sloughing by, bulbous heads nodding like proper gentlemen. There is kelp like meadow grass above me, and what sun might be seen is filtered by dark green leaves, the color of the queen's sleeves, descending and descending.

Evening, Fifth Day

I do not know why I expected this place to be full, full of people and things—I suppose I imagined it to be the source of all objects, all quests. Surely the things my brother asks for must be piled up under the streetlamps here like old leaves: girdles, women, swords, grails, wrapped around the light-post, wet and clinging.

But there is only warm air, and empty shops and empty tables and empty streets, and I should have known that the underworld would be a ghost town. Stray ribbons snake through the blazing white buildings like tumbleweed, and there is no sound but the distant sea pounding the distant sand.

Why does he want this boy? This boy who sits cross-legged in the blue, his fine hair blown turquoise, his eyes the dead white of deepwater fish? *Mabon ap Modron*, my ribbon says. But this is nonsense, it means nothing, only words: *Son of a Mother*. He wants a nameless orphan boy who was born with the sun behind his head, stolen to the sea three days after his birth on the back of a green-foam boar.

We all know the story; it is an easy story to know. What country in the world does not have its virgin birth, its martyred babe, its innocent dragged down to the dark depths? They stamp them out like a sheet of cookies these days, little gingerbread boys, all in a row. Why should I hold my breath for one?

But he is my brother, that hemmed-in king. Still trying not to look into the corners of his rooms where a black-haired woman who is not bolted to any dais touches the cheek of another clean-shaven knight. He is my brother and perhaps after all this time I know him, a little. I forgive him for stepping in front of me, and though I was so much taller, obscuring me forever. He sees the stolen child, the sun in his hair. He sees himself, before the ribbons, before the chair and the plates he fastened to his friends. His mother lost him, or gave him to us, I was never sure, being only a breath older than he when they dumped him like a pile of gold on our stoop.

Once my brother might have come himself, breath or no breath, whickering through the ribbons to make this boy a fabled knight with an epithet and a fellow besides—but that time is over. Once the kingdom is won it descends to us, the dumb, mute limbs of a king to push at its edges like soldiers against an iron gate. So I go after the boy, the doppelganger covered in brine, and my ribbon flutters in the sage-edged wind, in the whiskey-and-orange-tongued air, and I will gather him into my arms as my brother might have, and I will carry him on my shoulders the way Ector, our father, once did, and I will try to be happy at the weight of this sun-shot avatar, this twin of the brother-that-was. Perhaps the thing which carries him will have something of the Kay-that-was ricocheting between ether-capsules and parchment-ribbons.

Perhaps that awful sword smoothly excised the boys we were, placed them up on a shelf somewhere, locked into a cupboard. These shoulder-plates and greaves hold only out of habit the shapes of men long dead.

The character of the ocean is variable as a child's—it is violet now, deeper than dye, and the salt is crusting in the corners of my mouth. All around me the heat of my plating causes the sea to recede, boil off. Trickles seethe in—exploratory, hesitant—and hiss into steam when they touch me. It is not quite enough to breathe, but I walk in a warm haze, and bubbles, not of breath but of heat, unbearable heat, waft up to the dark surface.

Midnight, Sixth Day

He sits in the center of the ocean, a silver boy-pin stuck in the floor—the currents move around him like Saturn's rings. Cuttlefish weave through his hair. He opens his mouth and roe wriggle out, floating up like red bubbles.

I open my sixth capsule and stale air fills me up like a sickly bellows.

What is that? His voice ripples the water, even my coat of steam.

It is how I can come to you, boy, down here in the dark. I would lend one, but you do not seem troubled by the water.

He shrugs. *A child learns to love its first milk, mother or ocean. I drink, I breathe. I have been down here a long time. No one came for me.*

I have come for you. Because you look like my brother, not for yourself alone. Because in the concave mirror of his skull he looks and sees you, and wishes that you were not alone as he was alone as he is alone now.

Do you like it here? It is very blue, and the salmon are talkative.

He is a strange boy—but all boys are strange. His feet are covered in infant coral, soft and pocked. It breaks and wafts up as I pull him free, little pink fingers clutching at the thin strands of silver starlight that penetrate—how I cannot imagine—this far. He does not protest; boys this age are used to being carried to and fro and never asked.

Walk quickly, metal man, the boar is only out looking for dolphins to eat. He does not need capsules, either.

Metal man. How a knight must look to a child, plated over with silver and iron and horned helmets, leviathan-sharp. We must look like walking knives. My strides turn the ocean to steam around us, slushing through the sea-sand of the floor, the anemone and kelp-roots. He clings to the nub-antlers on my helmet, the one my brother had made in the shape of a faun's head, as if to acknowledge our common source in bucolic forests. His little legs dangle over my shoulders.

Soon I can feel him sleeping heavily, and I trudge like St. Christopher through the sweet water, bearing the sweat-scalped innocent on my back. His weight is not so much, and he smells like a son, he smells like a brother, he smells like a tired child who has had too much excitement on Christmas night and needs an early bed.

The ribbon in my back is almost shredded. It chews itself as the quest goes on, obliterating unnecessary commands, leaving the core of what I must do. All that is left:

Retrieve. Return.

I am a worker. The factory of chivalry and quests extends ever west, and we go into it in a long, wending line, heads bent, lunches at our sides, lurching forward, lifting stones to find whatever precious object comprises the day's labor. It is no different than the manufacture of linen or gears.

My shift is almost done.

The water is lightening already. Far, far above, I can see the paddling feet of seabirds fishing, and the bottoms of empty boats gliding by.

Dawn, Seventh Day

Arthur came to me with the sword, and he had not even cleaned the moss from it. He did not know what to do. I can say that I was not even tempted to take it for myself, but I cannot tell if that is true, if it did not flash through me like revelation that I was much bigger and stronger than my brother. That I was much bigger and stronger than anyone we knew, in those days before bigger and stronger became colorful balls that so many men fought over. I could have taken it. I choose to believe that I did not even consider it.

Put it back, I said. *Put it back and no one will know and the world will go on as it always has.*

Put it back and you can stay a man, with blood and skin and a stride, you will not have to turn your eyes from your wife and feed ribbons into the backs of your workers like some hellish foreman. You can go home and fish and learn to ride a horse—God knows you need the practice—and no one has to know that you pulled a sword out of a stone. No one ever has to know your name. You're not special: you can't hold your breath for nine days, no one has called you the greatest knight born and no one ever will. You can live in high grass and mote-riddled sunlight until you are an old man—put it back. Just put it back.

You know what happened. You know his name.

He brushed the blackberry brambles away and the swordlight was pale on his face.

Everything is turquoise now, shot through with green light and streams of bubbles. The boy I carry laughs and grabs at them, patting my helmet so that my ears ring.

.   *You are like riding the sun. Faster, sun! Higher!*

Noon, Ninth Day

Sandpipers skitter and stamp on the beach—we rise up out of the surf—whales spouting spray and my body fills with real air, so much and so golden that I feel as though I must burst.

The boy coughs and wheezes—he has never known air. For a moment I want to put him back, too. I do not want to take him to the factory, I do not want to make him into a little copy of us. I take him from my shoulders and pat his back, too hard, at first, but after a long while he begins to vomit up the ocean that has lived so long in him, growing in him and coloring his skin like a pearl. The water comes and comes, the boy holding his small stomach like the Chinese brother in the fairy tale, who drinks the sea, drinks it all down so that his friend can find the tiny jewel at the bottom. Little fish come with his retching, bits of flotsam. His hands sink in the sand.

When he finally draws up, shakily, graceful as a new duckling, the sun seems to settle in him, somewhere at the base of his spine, spreading out around him like a mandorla. I have rescued the sun from the deeps. He smiles, and the beach is flooding with his gold. In the dune grasses, a few errant ribbons snake back and forth—he chases after them, untroubled, but when he touches their tales they burn up, black and ash.

Mabon ap Modron, we must return.

Return? I have always lived here.

No, boy. Home is England. This is hell.

It is beautiful in hell, then.

Yes.

He shrugs, clambers up onto my back again, and we begin the long road over the mountains. A tiny thread of ribbon streams behind us:

Return.

I am bringing the sun home to you, brother. I wonder if it will make you smile. If it will light the shadows. If it will keep us all warm when the snow comes.

Behind us, the water is an unbroken hyphen, blue as heartbreak. There are whitecaps. There is wind. Soon we will not even be able to smell the salt.

XIII DEATH

The Green Knight

And I will stand strongly on this floor
to abide his stroke if thou wilt doom him
to receive another stroke in return from me;
yet will I grant him delay.
I'll give to him the blow,
In a twelvemonth and a day.
Now think and let me know
Dare any herein aught say.

—Sir Gawain and the Green Knight

Black Queen to King's Rook Four.

The sun comes through windows dusted like vellum pages, soft and slant-wise, unable to dream of vertical space, pooling gold paint onto my fingernails. I am yellow as Midas' best loved child, and it is winter in the world.

Outside these walls I can hear the angle of the grass under the wind, grandfather-bent, pointing east, east, east, where all things begin.

I play chess, to pass the time between Christmases. My opponent is a stable boy whose eyes glitter black and silver, the colors of saddles and bits. When the clouds shift, his skin shines horse-pale, and the light plays tricks with the board, flickering like a movie reel—the queens mock each other with sardonic lips. I cannot tell if he is real, if he is ghost or fey, if he has a soul. These things are hard to divine in Hautdesert. But it is pleasant here, in the green mires, all the colors of emeralds crushed between ivory teeth. The hill-mounds curve, humming dusky hymns of earth and root, and I sit in the center, striking a monkish pose with my hands on my mossknobbled knees, dreaming of games within games within games.

It is left to me to wait. Once the challenge has been made, the glove thrown down with all the force ritual can manage, the wager accepted, nothing can be done at all but to wait for the onrush of conclusion like the cold salt tide. So I wait. I am the reed-flute that plays itself, I am the branches waving wild, red stars of holly swelling up under shadow-green leaves, I am the secret places under the hills, where the dark swallows the light with a tender mouth, sweet as well water.

I cannot tell, some days, if I am a man at all.

I am only my shape, grotesque and beautiful, a mask with horns and a grimace. I am bounded on all sides by a light which is not light. A net of spider's legs and gloam, held together by the sputum of diamonds. Here on the low mountains, here on the lips of a turquoise bay, I learn to have no face, to wait and be Quested For, to feel the hands of the sun on my belly.

It is as though I rest within an alchemist's oven—liquids boil and bubble witchwise all around, in silver pots and copper pipes, steam cackles up towards a stucco ceiling and spices hang heavy in the Byzantine air—my head is haloed with these earthen fugues. This is my thatched hut, my kitchen flagstones, my grasshoppered corners and spidered rafters. This little café which burrows under the California light, the unchanging saffron-scented 4 pm sun, liquid and slow, honeycombed wind touching a multitude of skins.

Students cluster as they always have, clutches of infant cats suckling at their books, escaping the great black gates and storming towers of San Francisco in the perfumed loam, in the musk-heavy air. My little bone-china cup opens its lissome mouth to me, breathing into my throat all the satchel-herbs of East and West I long ago forgot—cardamom, cinnamon, cloves crushed like specks of coal, ginger, cocoa.

I have time for a few cups, I think, before he comes.

But each cup is a hundred other cups, journeys on horseback from Persia and India and New Orleans, far off places I relinquish so that I may have this little green hut, round as a heart. Each cup echoes forward and back, beginning and ending at the one cup which is to come—ah, but I get ahead of myself. In the midst of all this human/inhuman hush I drink, and slowly, so that none is spilt.

I can see the Chapel, far off on an island in the snow-gray sea. It has been a year since I have knelt at its altars of manzanita and rough amber, lit the tallow candles which rest in sticks of crushed spectacles, straightened the fern-tapestries and left my offerings of buckwheat flowers and white sage. All those seasons, hissing by like copper kettles, untouchable. Winter comes again on cedar paws, Christmas lights appear out of the sky as suddenly as newborn stars, glimmering red and silver and green. The year stoops and begins his long funeral, laying out a nicely tailored coffin of steel and nettles, gathering his grave goods at local thrift shops. Combing his raw-flax beard into thread, the old year sits in a great blank hall and spins the hair beautifully into silver on his tiny birch-wood wheel. Another will come— years self-regenerate like mites in a haystack. But when the rains come and my elbows ache under those storms which fall graceful and sad, my bones cannot help but whisper their age to one another, and I am weary of it all.

The knight is beginning his pilgrimage now, in his palace, his flame-rimmed cathedrals. He should be bare-foot and rag-clothed, as all pilgrims ought to begin, even if they do not end so. But I can hear the leaf-rustle of his armor and the billow of his starred shield. He knows no better. He guards himself against me—we are all so eager to guard and defend!—I defend my Chapel and he defends his flesh. For him I shall be a monster—because it is expected. If there were no great *monstrum* at the final castle, there would be no quest. And if no quest, what need would there be for knights at all? I am required; without me there is no kingdom.

I lie beneath their courtly cosmos of lighted halls and long-braided ladies to whom souls must be pledged. I lie under their games of adoration and betrayal—I am the wolf-belly and the dreaming trees that crowd in on all sides, the shadows and the sighing fog. I lure them out, I give them my own body to loathe so that they can fill themselves up with light like clay pitchers. I must be the darkness for them, since they fear it so. They must come to my world, and dwell in the dreamlight of my great bronze axe, so that the stars will know them ever after.

White Queen to Queen's Bishop Four.

Smoke converts the Chapel to a bath-house, the smell of rich chocolates and drying apple peels leeches impurities from the skin. The flesh percolates, brimming with itself. Smoke and mist, these are the winter coats I wear, the best mystery-wools and strange-cheeked monk-cowls.

My beard shows best in this light, the bramble of my practiced symbology, holly and yarrow and horehound, the green tinge of next year's wheat, blackberry and hyssop, heather culled with little white knives, shoots of bamboo and snow peas, crocuses sleeping soundly near my chin, wild rose sideburns and mustache of Italian grape and wormwood—I am all the wines ever brewed. It tumbles down to my basil-leaf navel, a tangle of root and branch, huckleberries peeking through and white sage smudging the skin, strawberry leaves sorrowful and low, blue crabgrass and dandelions brushing my elbows. I hide a harvest of gleaming pomegranates in my knees.

I am the Object, I am the Self-Defined. I need do nothing but exist, I draw all men to me as surely as if I were the birth-place of their salmon-hearts. The knight comes and I can hear his progression from square to square, the silky clop of his horse on black and white cobblestones I laid myself in some summer beyond this place, when I was not yet married. I can hear the snow catch in the nutmeg-colored mane, collecting on the reins and hooves when he rests, smell the slush of it in his helmet. There is no step he takes that I do not feel in my ribs and liver and the shaking thorns of my beard.

Boughs of pine hang from high-arched windows, the architecture of cathedrals repeating in this sanctuary like a story told from mother to suckling child. I dwell here, in the skipped frame, the caught film, the grandiose expanse of smelted clocks. I have chosen this place to wait until the new year gnashes its stone teeth and swallows up the old.

This is Limbo—between the first blow and the last, a head for a head for a head. I told the students when I returned last winter how my skull rolled onto the palace floor like a child's ball or a golden apple. The callow youth stood up, his limbs betraying his shuddering heart, whose storm-ridden blood could be heard through the glassy hall. He looked so small with my axe in his hand, the shaft wound with ivy and raspberry bramble—he searched for a place to grip the bronze where thorns would not pierce his tender hands. I waited, as I wait now, patiently as a lion teaching his cub to hunt, for the quick tongue of the blade in my neck.

The spaces between stretch like light, bending their calculated arcs over bodies—the time between the lifting of the axe and the falling, the departure of the boy and the arrival. The nature of the universe is a held breath, a filled lung which never empties into the ether.

When his blow came, inevitable as autumn, I thought he would fall over with the weight of my weapon. The tidal edge came and my blood flowed green as sea-rot onto the vast mosaic floor. Ladies excused themselves in horror, knights vomited into their helmets, children scrambled to pick berries from my hair. The black-eyed Queen looked curiously at the flow of blood nosing her slippers like an affectionate hound. Her eyes strayed softly to a knight, a fearful falcon seeking the hunter's arm. The king laughed too loudly and drank his mead through pale knuckles as though it would save his life.

I lay on that floor cut in two, my own conjoined twin, enwombed and devoured, flooding into my internal seas. I felt the room become the board, the fates of the pieces shifting as the check and escape rippled into clarity. I felt the boy's heart connect to mine.

The separation, the ripping of my heart from my head, was so peculiar—calm spread in me like the tide through salted sand, and as though I called to it through tin cans connected by string, I whispered to my body. The colossus turned, breastplate bristling with mistletoe and strangled oak, groping the silence for purchase. I called quietly to its sinews, familiar as old harp-strings, and I blindly gripped myself by the hair.

Nestled in my arm, I looked at that boy, gone white as whalebone, and said: *Next year in the Chapel, Gawain, next year in Jerusalem, next year in the Christmastide when the stars flash red and green, next year in my castle where the apple-maid has been.*

A bet is a bet—I shall be here when he comes.

White Queen to Queen's Bishop Five.

My wife has no name. She does not come to the Chapel, but lies naked as a lion and turns the sun to dust settling on her gold haunches. Is she the monster I keep in my house? Her lips part and show an endless forest. Did I bring her here, once? Or did she spring from Hautdesert like a water-choked cactus, putting forth her necromancer-flowers?

I think I am inside her all the time.

Even now, even then, in the court with the thousand candles, all around me I saw the walls of her body, slick and butter-warm. In the Chapel, where the altarcloth chants the vespers prayers in a voice dredged from the silt of the sea, I taste her flesh on my tongue like a communion wafer, and this is her body, unbroken for my worship, and this is her blood, poured out for my exaltation. I am a body of her body, and in her deafening heart I am transubstantiated, I become verdant, I become the deepened earth.

When my axe split my cordwood throat, I felt only her tightening around me, her breath wavering in my vision as though I watched the boy through a shroud of heat. I felt her hands on my stomach even when my head's wet veins grasped uselessly at the glassy floor. I wonder if I have ever walked outside the tower of her skin, if I ever really let myself go down beneath the knight's blue scythe. Perhaps I only curl within her and dream, a fetus suckling at her sugar-womb.

Sometimes she looks both north and south. Her northern face is a clutch of stones, slate rasping against granite. This face wears a cowl of nettles, and gnashes black flax with its teeth. From its cracked lips a sallow thread issues like a tongue; where it touches my flesh, I flush green and holly cracks open my pores. Her saliva turns my skin to soil—calendulas sprout in my knee-bones, chrysanthemums fulminate in my mouth until all I can taste is their obscene red. Ivy pierces my septum, stalks filling my body with chlorophyll, shooting through capillaries, thorns sprout from my chest, roots from my thighs—I gag, I spit, I retch in the midst of all this green.

Her southern face is a white river. This face wears a cowl of hair like light, smelling of sage and thistle, the first gold an arthritic miner wrestled from a Californian hill. From its polished lips a thick rope spirals out—silk that was once a worm—and when it grazes my eyes like the pelt of a deer, the pupils flush with blood and smoke. She touches the leaves of my beard and calls it good, she tells me I frighten her, and her skin warms under my blooming hands. My fingers go through her as through a tidepool, and when I draw back, anemones suckle at my palms, blue as kisses. With my hands in her watery hair I am exalted, I am greened and imparadised, I am the Edenic monster.

But I fear her other face, the hag who haunts the dust of a hundred corners.

White Queen to King's Bishop Eight.

The road through the Wirral to the San Joaquin Valley is paved with pulverized magpie bones, and plated in Nevada silver. It is an endless suspension bridge, anchored with horsehair and ambergris. The root system of the bridge connects the water tables, the lightless tide of continents. Neither place is real, but the quest spans all points on all maps, and if the

Gawain-child begins in Camelot, he must eventually pass through San Francisco, swallowing the foghorns as he rides.

And in the thigh of Saint Francis I will meet him and place the sacraments between his teeth, mark his hands with my stigmata, and draw him under the hill—for the Chapel is but the opening to a body, a crevice in the dream-soil, and I am waiting within it, for him to enter her body and mine, the green lord and his two-souled wife.

In Chinatown, the crone spat three times and shook her yarrow sticks at the sky, red and black. Her tar-clouded lungs rumbled, hissing: *Lu. Ch'ien. Sun. The Seeker Descends from Heaven, and Submits to the Gentle Wind.* With her hands pulling at my cheekbones like fish-hooks, she whispered the name of Gawain into my tear ducts, and I wept a tincture of salt and oleander. Am I no other than this, his object, his end? Am I this spectral mask, the giant and the beanstalk in one still-voiced body? There is nothing in it, to sit on the bridge with my holly-beard grazing the water and wait, a fire growing in his mind. I have no tongue, I have no blood. I am only the monster, the false knight, the price of his Christmas feast.

I went across the bridge in my leaf-body because she wished it. After all, we are the witch and the monster that dwell in the glen, it is our duty to set the trials, and draw the boys from their warrens to lie with us.

The winter dark came, and called us across the bridge, and I pulled my hag-wife over me like a coat of folded wings. I stepped into her skin and sealed up the edges with a paste of rosemary, for remembrance. Inside her, I was the Green Knight, and not Lord Bertilak, not myself. I exulted in the grotesqueries of the branch and bramble she lent me, in my seven-mile stride, in the voice that cracked steel. From inside her, I looked on the placid Queen and saw the ocean of that perfect torso twist and roil. I saw her, the king's wife, catch her perfumed breath in fear that the Devil had come to punish her for opening her mist-midden legs.

But it was Gawain and not that faithless who came to us with his green calves quaking, and when his pentangle shield reflected its red on the red of our eyes, we forgot the Queen and her whimpering tryst. We slid into his equation, the quest and the endpoint, we recognized our most beloved Rook, and knew peace when he separated us into heart and head.

But I am not content bridging Christmas to Christmas, holding his purity like a plastic lotus and forcing my fingers into a sullen mudra. I am a bronze Buddha, green with age, motionless, meaningless. My eyes shed blank enlightenment, and he cannot see me as a man. My wife is the storm and the wheatfield, I am only a signpost. Without the mask of her skin I am but Bertilak, and that is less than the weight of the moon on a moth's wing. And Gawain is a milk-brained child staring mutely at the wonders of the world. He will not even mark the passing of the bridge beneath his feet.

Look at the three of us, our little dance. Are we not heroes, are we not terrors?

White Knight to King's Bishop 5th.

The Chapel is filled with sweet smoke, the vanilla and oranges of Christmastide, peppermint candy sticky on my hands. The nave secretes opalescent sweat, flooding the floor with holy vapors. The Lady Bertilak is not here, though I look to the torturously painted tiles of the ceiling and see the arch of her summer-breast.

To you, I would seem only a fat old man bent over a chessboard at Golden Gate Park, slapping the timer with a meaty fist. My belly would hang over patched khaki trousers, bending a leather belt in half. My blue work-shirt would be stained with sour-mash sweat, curling sleeve and collar. My shoes would be bound with duct tape, and you could see the corner of a jaundiced toenail through the ragged blue-striped canvas. You would suspect lice in my beard. But you would keep coming to my table, because I beat you at every game.

On this side of the bridge, I have a flask half-filled with schnapps in my pocket, and a clutch of food stamps in my threadbare wallet. My breath recks of week-old spinach and mothballs, my skin of rotten pages. My biceps bulge under tattoos of anchors and ziggurats, the holly-axe in black ink in the hollow of my elbow. I have a friendly rivalry with a Jewish photographer who leads with his knight, and a regular seat at the soup kitchen.

Only Gawain would know me through that grease-glamour. Only he would see the jade-thighed giant with a Bishop in each hand. Only he would see the two Queens for what they were, would perceive beneath their eyeless crowns the twin ladies of Hautdesert. You would see a blonde waitress and her elderly aunt, but he would know her for the gargantua, the ecstatic beauty that looks both ways, the star of the sea and the apple in the garden.

He is bound to me by this sight, the eyes that scour this gnarled wood of visions and golems like a water diviner. Between us, we construct a map of the world. In the forest of doubles, all geographies are present. The self refracts, into husband and wife, and we wait for our boy.

Red Queen to King's Square.

The Chapel gapes open like a womb. The grasses tangle around it, and the walls slope into the hill. All the altars are hidden, the chalices of baleen and myrrh, the blessed water, the icebound matins of winter. But these are invisible. The Chapel leads into my body-in-hers, a hole in the earth, and it breathes in anticipation.

I spend my nights sharpening the holly-axe, finding the nirvana of the grinding blade, back and forth, the scythe slick and wet. I am the hoarfrost, I am the elk's matted fur, the moon vanishing behind carbon-clouds. I am ready, though I seethe at my position, within her and before him, the Object, without dimension. The smoke of my id spirals against my bones, the friction scalding my beryl-blood. Death sits in my stomach like boot-crushed cigarettes.

He will hear the grind of my axe, all tangled with wild mint and willow, and his belly will clench. He will glimpse the womb-mouth and be struck dumb—neither of us can come too near it. It is her place, though she can never be inside it. She is not built that way. We must act out our morality play beyond its weeping borders. She can only surround us, make our bodies into fantastic cathedrals of flesh, but she does not touch the fall of this axe, or the fall of his. He must betray me, and adore her. But it is the betrayal which is more intimate, the sour congress of our bent throats, the symmetry of a head for a head.

We are nothing but bodies of potential. The Gawain self and the Bertilak-self, moving through seasons, easing into casements shaped to us, glass blown from each step through the witchwood, the wild-limbed Wirral. To speak of us is to enter the unknown—the embryonic. We are fraternal, we are father and son, we are lovers, we are twin salmon swimming in the wife-womb, enclosed. We never cease to be her embryos, our razor-gills brushing in the fluid sky. But within these Chapel-walls we will play our game, the Rook and the Knight. It is my axe, after all, at the end of the tale.

If I glower at the soundless church, if I wish that I were more to him than the emerald-toothed giant, it is only that, at the end of all tales, I am discontent to know my role so well. The Object should not guess its base nature until the end, its lines should not be known too well, or the questing knight will guess that it was all planned from the beginning, to secure three kisses, to secure the green swath around his hips, to secure the wound on his neck which marks him as our own.

But perhaps there is no me at all, no Bertilak, Lady or Lord, only him, gold as a coin, his purity burning the bridge as he comes. I can no longer tell.

He is coming; I am here. I think nothing more is required of me, except that I raise my axe. But in this Chapel of mud and root, in its sodden pews, I pray for his seraphic eyes to see me as I am—though I can no longer tell if that is the green-heart or the freckled flesh—and welcome the parting of his skin.

Queen's Castle.

I am always outside the board as it was meant to be drawn. I care nothing for the mewling white-capped King. But I will not lose the Rook to my own cunning hand. I am doubled, myself and myself, who looks so like a man in his mottled red beard and skin like the white of winter fruit, the other self who knows no secret green spreading in the night like star-fed lichen. He is the singular, the Bertilak, who can move in the upper world, and hunt the fat-haunched boar, and sip tea spiced with cardamom in a chair of oak.

Sometimes I look west and east, and the eastern face is moss-laden, full of blackberry thorns. The nose is straight and fine, laced with dandelion leaves, and the hair falls in hyssop-braids to shoulders heaped in pine boughs. Its laugh is the press of forge-bellows, and it cannot doubt its magnitude. My wife made this face, as if out of clay, and lovingly. If I could dwell always in its net of bones, Gawain could pass through me like air and I would never note him.

But the western face is trimmed by smooth-legged ghost-boys from the wharf, with oiled braids and salt-flecked eyes. That face wears linen and light, its teeth are diamonds set in a cedar skull. It has never dreamt of the color green, it has never watched its arms grow thick with grass. It plays its board with aplomb, while the eastern limbs muddle their game with arcane rites. This is the face that longs, and weeps, and asks for release from duty.

The quest bridges them, and for the breathless moment when the axe falls, before it touches his skin, I am both, I am whole.

Between the four of us—my wife and I with our twin selves, heads bent in conspiracy under the shadows of willows and cypress—we have devised a game for our fifth. Gawain, Gawain, who has no other self, who is pale and brotherless as the moon.

We will split him, so that he need not be alone—he will look forward and back. There will be the Gawain who was whole, whose hair was yellow as a lion encased in ice, whose troth blazed against the turquoise hood of heaven—and the wounded Gawain we will make, our girdled golem, all wrapped in gold and green, the endless green of her belly, which turns knights to feys. The haunted Gawain will return to his court, vomiting shadows into the light until he empties himself. And we will keep the gold-drenched avatar, the limpid hound, our changeling son, our lover incandescent as a scarlet star.

I will hunt the fat-haunched boar.

I will hunt the slack-eared rabbit.

I will hunt the red-toothed fox.

She will hunt him.

And I will trade the animal hearts for his lips on mine, for the lips of the Janus-wife burning through his into me. Hands full of meat and pelts, I will take him in my arms and feed him of my body as she fed me of hers, and like a trunk of apple-wood, he will split under me. I will make a cut in his throat, small and red as a mouth, and kiss the virtue from his blood. Between our bodies, the masters of Hautdesert will alter him, as surely as bread to flesh.

We will deliver the broken brother home in swaddling clothes, a newborn doppelganger, never again able to see without our eyes.

0 THE FOOL

Dagonet

Quoth Sir Dagonet: "I am King Arthur's Fool. And whilst there are haply many in the world with no more wits than I possess, yet there are few so honest as I to confess that they are fools."

—The Madness of Sir Tristram
Howard Pyle

I.

Under the lime trees
I lay my love down
Under the lime trees I lay her

And when she rose up
Her mouth was so red
Sweeter than figs,
Her mouth, so red.
Tan-dara-dara-dei
Tan-dara-dei.

I am the Knave of Dreams. They smote the floor with a stalk of spiderwort and up I sprang, purple and green and all over sweet-smelling, and they tangled me up with bells and bade me dance.

I am happy to dance. The floor of my birth is spangled in stars, painted gold, painted carnelian, painted azure and orange and black, and my feet upon it are light as wort-roots. I am a heart full of foliage—nothing in me is not flower, stamen, thorn, pistil, blossom, blossom, rose. I am a fool, and I am a knight, and my horse is hawthorne and hyssop. I gallop; I canter. They laugh at my silken shoes and sword of campion and rue.

But I see the queen with her girdle of roses—the roses whisper scarlet and white, of where her hips last thrust and blushed, of how her hair whipped linen. I see the best of the knights with his plume of crocus—the crocus murmurs yellow and violet, of how he keeps his eyes open when he kisses her.

I see, I see, and I sing, and snowdrops fall out of my mouth. But I sing of *my love* and *my sweetheart* and *my kisses full tender*—always mine, never theirs—and they think I do not see how their cups flame from the touch of two such burning mouths. But after all, it was a court, it was a starry floor where silk-haired apes danced and wrestled—and such things will happen among apes. Their dance was never a secret, never as high-flown a trespass as lesser poets than I would claim, just so that their verses could scan.

I looked on the queen, too. I marked her honeycomb-hair and her thimble-bright eyes. Like all men my velvets tightened—a fool still owns his blood!—but I sang and sang, and came not near.

Tan-dara-dei.

II.

She came a-walking through the violets
And how did she call to me?
With honeysuckle and meadowsweet and bryony.

Tan-dara-dara-dei

.

She made a place in the wheat for me
and what did she show me there?
Willow whips and strawberry leaves
and fingers clasped in prayer.

Tan-dara-dei.

There was a girl made of flowers, too—the floor was fertile that year. She came up with her black hair all strung with foxglove, and her toes were ringed in coltsfoot. I loved her, I did, but flower calls to flower. She did not sing; I sang for us both. On each of her berry-brown toes was an ivory bell, and I shook them like lilies-of-the-valley, and with buttercups in her eyelashes she laughed like a thrush. The others played at cards which turned up a king, a queen, with lances leaning in, but we played our fools' dice, and were troubled by no dour high-born faces.

Come, Dagonet! Give us a song! Come, Dagonet, show us how you fought a dragon with both hands tied and hopping on one foot!

Ah, gentlemen, I am full tired tonight, and the wine is in my head like a copper tub sloshing over.

Come, Dagonet! Show us how the king looks when he wakes too early!

Ah, gentlemen, methinks the king has drunk enough to wake late for a fortnight.

Come, Dagonet! Tell us a tale, anything, anything! The night is dark, the wine is done.

One tale, then. A fool must earn his penny.

Once, gentle lords, and you ladies with your hair in one thousand knots! Once, there was a poor tile-maker, and his hands were red from the dust of terra cotta, from the dust of all those roof-tiles you see along the road, glittering on wattle houses like a fine scarlet cap! This tile-maker wandered across patches of land like the patches on my own cloak, scouring the earth for bits of bone and feather, stone and glass and seeds like hard little jewels, leaves and hide and fine, sifted soil, husks and bark and jewels like hard little seeds. With these motley things he made mosaics that caught the breath of any who saw them and spun that breath into a shower of golden stars. He laid out the crystalline zodiac on floors and ceilings, with planets of bone and gem-scattered orbital tracks creeping across the rafters.

But it was not often that he could truly ply his art, for such things are expensive, as well you know, my lords. More often the noonday sun found him hammering one red tile to another on the roof of a tavern, swatting at bees that thrummed anxiously around his head. And so the man went in *his* way until a certain palace spat out its foundations on a certain stretch of green sward, and certain men inhabited it as surely as a honeycomb, thrumming anxiously in *their* way. These men called upon the tile-maker and begged him to create for them such a floor that any who stepped upon it would be possessed totally by its vision, and compelled by its beauty to love and serve those who owned it.

The tile-maker considered this for a long while. His little hut was certainly filled with enough bones and stones and skins and powders, paints and feathers and dyes to make such a floor. But he felt that he needed some last thing that he could not quite name, and so this tile-maker whose hair was no less dusty than it had been, went out into the countryside to find the center-tile of his magnificent floor, a floor while had already begun to lay itself out on the bare boards of his heart.

Are you tired already of my tale, gentlemen? You would rather I skip ahead? You do not want to hear of the bridge which spans our fair land and the golden land of the west, where all strange-liveried knights find their origin? You are bored by the nature of floor-making, and desire to hear no more of how the poor tile-maker crossed even into those golden lands to find the sweet, pale bone of a woman drowned for her love, with which to bind the center-tile? Very well—all things for my audience.

The man was ragged as a hare wolf-chased for a month when he returned over that bridge I shall tell you not of, and in his hands he clutched a long white bone, and with brown-beaten hands, boiled this bone with quicksilver in a copper pot until it was passing strange: a lacquer which shone like the very veil of death. He poured this into the core of a milk-stone star he had set in the deep blue floor, and began his work.

And well do you know, my lords, the shape of this floor: how it shows the stars in their spheres and the vines and scarlet flowers of welltilled earth, how it shows Virgo and Taurus and Pisces—glittering virgins astride bulls and fish snapping at the edges of the known world! Well do you know how many fruits and crops twine its borders in green, how many oranges and pomegranates and grapes jewel its corners, how many showers of sweet rain speckled in pebbles and feather-cartilage water how many fields of silver wheat. How many flowers, how many endless flowers, tangle through the stars and the virgins and the wheat, how many peonies and lilies and snowdrops, and yes, roses, and yes, crocuses.

Well do you know, my lords, for you walk upon it.

The tile-maker finished the great work of his life, which was no more than what the men who thrummed like bees would track mud and grass and blood over for a decade or two, and was paid as well as he hoped, retiring to his hut and living happily, if we should wish to imagine him happy, and miserably, should we choose to imagine him miserable—this is only a story, my lords and my ever-dewdrop't ladies, and we may end it as we please.

But one more moment, I beg you, and your Dagonet will be silent as a floor in shadow.

For one evening the floor did lie in shadow—shadow pure as our queen!—and all who looked upon it, and loved, and served, had gone to their slumber or sport. It so happened on this night of all nights that the roof allowed the smallest creep of rainwater through its most noble thatch, and that drop of rain—sweet rain, sweet as golden land beneath a bridge, sweet as a maid long drowned, sweet as the sea that drowned her—fell, perfect and clear, onto that bone-lacquered star-core which the poor tile-maker had traveled so far and through such trials to find.

And what do you think happened? My lords, you will never guess it. It was I sprang from this tile, whole and entire, for there never was a fool who had any land or title, birth or name or worth beyond the grand floor on which he performs, the floor which bears him up while he makes himself ridiculous, makes himself wretched, while he loves, while he serves. The floor is all he is.

Tan-dara-dara-dei.

III.

There my love made a place to lie
and was it strewn with flowers?
Yes, with violets
and bluebells
and lilies pale as hours.

Tan-dara-dara-dei.

There I made my love to lie
and did I love her well?
Yes, with roses
and tulip leaves
and a bird's song like a bell.

Tan-dara-dei.

My lady sprang, too, from that floor—for what can a fool's lady have but the estate of her dearest? And her skirt was all a-snarl with daffodils, and roses red as mouths. We cared nothing, between us, but strode our floor back and forth like lord and lady, measuring and chronicling its every tile. I clutched her roses; she clutched my cap.

Come, Dagonet, you must hunt with us to-day! Put on Lancelot's livery, he will not mind!

Ah, gentlemen, I am full tired this morn. No fox is in danger of me, I am sure.

Come, Dagonet! We will not hear nay! Put on Lancelot's helmet and hoist up his shield—it is no fox we hunt this day!

Ah, gentlemen, and I am no Lancelot. Surely you would rather have a jig? A pratfall?

Come, come! Nothing would amuse us more than to see our own Dagonet dressed up as a knight like a little girl in her mother's gown!

One hunt, then. A fool must earn his penny.

She mounted up beside me on the young knight's horse—a back broad enough to bear Atlas in his blue chair!—and I a-clang in the young knight's armor, a poor Patroclus, all elbows, in Achilles' bronze breastplate. A fool's lady shares in his acts, his pantomimes, his jokes and jibes. She is his straight-man, she is his stage-hand.

Who is to say where Lancelot was that he did not hunt with his men? Not I; not the crocuses; not the roses. Not the queen.

No fox. Not a fox. A breath of white in the linden trees, a breath of ivory and silver against the tall white birches, a breath of hair like spun glass behind a weave of glossy green leaves. Never a fox. And it was my lady who tempted the beast, whose cheeks bloomed with clover and hyacinth, though she laughed like irises opening—*I am no maid*, said she, and it was no jest. From the day the floor pushed her up like a stalk she thirsted for me and I thirsted for her and we were sunlight and water and dirt and air.

But you are a maid, for a fool is not a man, and thus.

Not a fox, not a maid, not a man.

The wood smelled of old campfires and stripped bark. Some flowers were there: mean and nameless things, little more than a smear of red or purple in the brush. Who was I to notice when the birches faded to redwoods and mist covered all things from nose to branch? I thought myself to smell the sea.

It was a unicorn they came to hunt. I tell this tale not to please.

The poor beast blundered into the sward when the apples were firm on the boughs, and was spotted—such a guileless thing cannot help but be spotted, caught, rendered into fat and bone and meat. These boys, these fine boys, a pack of young, bored lions, took themselves up after it, never expecting to find a maiden in any crook of that palace to lure a four-legged pearl from the fog. My lady was the best they could find, and I, as always, amuse them, pass the tedious stretches of a hunt which do not involve gouts of hot blood, but rather cramped muscles and waiting. How marvelous to dress me in a lion's skin. I am a bow-kneed Hercules, and how my Nemean suit clatters and clangs.

My lady lifted her skirt of roses and stepped between the grotesque red trees, calling, calling her thrush-cry voice (*tan-dara-dara-dei*) calling for the unicorn which surely would not come to her, how could it come to her, whose legs clap strong as weeds around my waist, whose lips crushed against mine, whose kisses were so terrible and thick and sweet that our teeth clashed like tiles—what pure beast would come to her? Yet the birches seemed to bleed their white from bark to bark until it emerged, stepping lightly towards her, copper hooves dancing lightly here, there, like an impossibly delicate crab, unsure, hesitant, but drawn to her as though she held him on a string of pale, braided hair.

My lady always had open arms for any lost creature—how else could she have loved me? Her black hair blew back from her face like a nun's veil as she held out her hands to it, smiling, laughing, coaxing, sitting as maidens will do, as they do in all the tapestries I have ever seen, cross-legged on a mossy patch of forest, with red leaves all around her, sticking in her dress and wind-plastered to her skin. In my memory, in my songs, I can never decide if the dress was red, too, or white.

It was a stallion. A fine white down covered his snowy testicles—I noticed that, of all things, thin pale fur like fishbones lying against his pink skin as he sank down into her lap, as if he were tired, an old man who cannot even bend far enough to take off his shoes when the day is done. His huge head nuzzled her laced breast, great black eyes shuddering closed. He quivered, his diamond hide twitched and his teeth ground together—he groaned in my lady's lap, the usurper. And the horn—that horn!—long and twisted like an ice-casked branch, knotted and thick and not at all graceful. It a living limb, no ornament, no pretty bauble stuck to a horse's head. Blood pale as champagne seemed to pulse faintly under the pocked and pitted pearl.

His legs folded onto the moss and my pride was stung—of course it was. They were right, she was a maiden still, and our nights together were as vapor, the seed I left in her no more than a blown dandelion. The head in her lap proved me nothing but a floor-tile, walking like a man, but no less terra-cotta. The silver of the unicorn's cheek rippled against her skin, and she chuckled, my lady chuckled, her laugh like marigolds opening, and stroked his glassy mane. They laughed, too, the men, uproarious, slapping each other's backs and pointing at me, at my lumpish shape which could not even take a maidenhead, swimming in armor too big for me.

It was when she touched him—he must have smelled me on her, must have smelled whatever nameless thing takes the place of virginity, buried deeper in her than other women, for my lady was a floor-flower, and who asks a lily if it has lain with another lily? He snorted; his breath was lilac and ice fogging her knees.

I do not want to sing of this. I do not want to tell you how her cheek flushed as though she had been slapped. I do not want to knit rhyme to rhyme just to tell you how the unicorn drew back, his crystalline nostrils flaring, betrayed and betraying, the scent of her a red smear in his perfect nose, how he drew back—I have no meter for it—how he drew back like an arrow and thrust the limb of his horn into her belly, through the skirt of roses and her belt of thyme, through her leaf-skin, her hyacinth-skin, and my lady opened her mouth as if to protest, and blood dribbled from it, black and ugly, falling onto the flaxen beast in long streams and wasn't it funny to dress up a fool in a lion's skin? Wasn't it funny to call his whore a virgin? Wasn't it funny, wasn't it funny?

The blood seemed to burn him like a brand; he drove deeper into her, the twisted horn working and grinding against her spine, and he was

screaming—a unicorn's scream! A glass-scrape against gold against bone—
screaming and hooves slipping in the moss and bucking against her broken
hips as her belly fell into her hands, and she was not a flower, she was not a
lily, she was wet and red and she was my wife and she is dead, dead, and I
will never sing of anything anymore.

IV.

Stand ye yet, O lime trees
Where we two made our bed?
In the open field
in the open land
where I lay my lover's head?

Tan-dara-dara-dei.

Stand we yet, we lime trees
who watched you lay her head
Here too are grasses
broken grasses
where she made her bed.

Tan-dara-dei
Tan-dara-dara-dei.

But in the end, the floor cannot be unwalked upon. It is not asked if it
would prefer a surcease of shoes. It is trodden; it is worn. It is owned, and
paid for, and it will lie beneath all those feet, it will lie beneath a severed
white head preserved above the mantle, a white head and a gnarled horn, it
will lie beneath those black-glass eyes and never complain. It is not paid to
complain. It will sing, because it was made for singing, and because the feet
would have their song.
Tan-dara-dara-dei.

XII THE HANGED MAN

Lancelot

And when Sir Launcelot awoke of his swoon, he leapt out at a bay window into a garden, and there with thorns he was all to-scratched in his visage and his body; and so he ran forth he wist not whither, and was wild wood as ever was man; and so he ran two years, and never man might have grace to know him.

—Sir Thomas Malory
Le Morte d'Arthur

Vespers—The Psalm of Forgetting

Perhaps I never saw her at all. Perhaps I never caught the curve of her hip in my eyelashes, through the rain-speckled window. Did I never stand below the queen, like Gyges, and dream myself a ring slipped onto her finger? Did I never die on her cross, crucified on the gold-dusted frame of her body? Did no spear pierce my side, the wound irising closed like a cataract?

The faces confuse in my memory—was it one woman or two? I remember the waters closing over me, and a black-tipped breast brushing my lips, and milk flowing into my throat like myrrh and sapphire—but no, that was when I was a boy, when the Lake swallowed me and I saw the paintings on the walls of her belly. When the Lady of the Lake peered up out of the water and thought how well she would like to have a son. But a Lake has no womb—so she took me from my nurse whose cheeks were so fat, and taught me to breathe her blue.

I fell so far, so far. She whispered to me in the language of salmon and bullfrogs, taught my uvula to twist itself into the semblance of herons and leeches. I drank the milk of her body for twelve years, and it tasted of belladonna and lemon rinds, it tasted of verdigris, it tasted of the smoke and mist from an unnamable sea. My heart swelled with it, it replaced my blood, the secret currents of snow-bright mercury pooling in my thirsty ventricles.

She opened her mouth and the Lake rushed out of it, and I had no voice but to adore her and call her my mother, my lover, and my terror, to fall into the tide of her beckoning and kiss the brine from her wavering lips. Her cool skin was my bed and her glassy bones were my meadhall—I drank and drank and there was always more of her to fill my mouth. In the night I slept curled into the blue-black shadows of her hair, and I dreamed that once I had been a human boy, and lived in a house with a red roof, and rode a gray horse.

I live with a skein of waves over my eyes even now, and in my fracturing vision I see their faces merge and separate, the reflections of fish just below the surface, skittering out of reach. Was I, then, the Sword in the Lake? I rose from it by her hand, which dripped with the scales of newborn trout, fluttering from her arm like dandelion seeds. I rose from the water and the reeds sang their canticles. And the king took me in his hand and I have been nothing else since but a stupid sharp thing hacking at bags of blood. If I am the Sword I am innocent; steel cannot sin. If I can be nothing but a dumb blade, I can be forgiven. If I am metal, I have been always in the hand of my friend, and never smelled of his wife.

The last moment in the Lake-mother's arms I wept, and that was the first time I felt the madness coming on, the separating of my skin, the light coughing out from my teeth. I choked, then, who had breathed the Lake for air, and the moon rolled out of my mouth. I stood on the shore, my lungs blazing like saints, and watched her black-flecked eyes disappear, sinking away from me.

Did I suckle at that woman for all my youth? Did I trade my flesh for hers? Or was it all that other she, the one for whom I am punished, the one who will not now hear my name? It is always a black-eyed woman, and I am always prone at her feet, I am always raving at the waters for the false mother—but how sweet the taste of her salt milk, for all her lies—to take me back and wash me clean, take me away from the woman I should not want, from what I have done, from the laughing throat which made me forget that I am only a tool, heavy as a hilt, and all my limbs fold together to make the sleek white edge—I am the musculature of the Lake-knife, and I am not allowed eyes, or blood, or a cock. Yet I strain towards her, always her. Even if I cannot, sometimes, tell the primal her from the secret her.

But I feel it again, I feel the light breaking from my skull like seraphic needles. She will not forgive me, she will not believe me. Her navel spoke to me while her eyes shut my face from the room. It hissed that I was poisoned, poisoned by the Lake, and that I would never be pure enough for the cup to pass to me, I would never be clean of that witch. It hissed like a white serpent and called me damned, and my eyes bled for her, the stigmata of the ruined man.

With my hands in her black hair I screamed the heron-hymns of my youth into her mouth, and she was afraid of me then. She wept and her tears burned constellations into my cheeks, and I'm sorry, I never knew, I didn't know, my love, my love, I thought it was you. But the queen wouldn't listen, she wouldn't forget. And now I am losing her, my Guenevere, I am losing her face in the multitude of faces, and her black eyes bleed into my mother's, and the other one, the one who was not Guenevere, but wore her skin like a dress.

I fell so far, so far. She spat on my hands, and my bones broke like a gate in the wind, and the moon rolled out of my mouth.

Terce—The Psalm of Metamorphosis

It was not only that a hole opened in the world or that in the hole was a garden in which I was the eaten fruit, it was not only that I reached out for a woman and drew back a burned hand. Perhaps I could never have done anything else, and it was all meant to happen as it did, and I was meant to circumnavigate this desert and no other, and pray only to the skulls of buffalo and hare.

I was never innocent, I confess it, as freely as my asthmatic brain will allow. I was a verb, white as opium smoke. I acted, I never stood still. I was the thrust and cry. Somewhere along the way a thing snapped or bent in me and now I can feel my organs expanding like novae, galaxies of liver and spleen, nebulae of bile, of cilia, of obliterated marrow, pounding pulse-rate signals into the blackness of my vast interior—vast enough, anyway, to contain the tumescent moons that spin through me like plates.

But if the geometry of my lover changed underneath me, it did not stop the motion of my hips grinding into her, it did not lessen the red marks of my teeth on her shoulder. The Euclidean planes of her face shifted like glaciers, and her eyes snapped from black to blue. I am guilty, it matters not if I thought that it was the body of Guenevere I loved—it was my fault. I did not die to escape that bed.

But I was not innocent, though I came to that thorn-bed hoarse with faith. I saw it, I saw her lips swell and crack the skein of Guenevere, I saw the Elaine-fruit break its pod, I saw her shiver and her hair flay itself, black slitting to reveal red. I saw it and I did not stop, but I screamed, how I screamed as I felt myself caught inside her, caught as if on a nail in her womb, screaming as I shattered over her body, the glass of my bones pricking her nipples, and her mouth was a trumpet-blare, and the color of its triumph was red, red, red.

The light sluiced from my skin, and her sternum sang my dirge, it gaped between her breasts and I called out her name, her true name which was Elaine, not the white but the clay. I called out her name and her name was the word and the word was the grail and the grail was her womb and my heart cracked like a rotted apple and I was dead in her, I was dead but my son was alive and I could see his face in her belly like the Shroud of Turin and I was lost in the maze of her breath, her wet mouth, her lily-sweat. I was not Theseus, not the hero with the thread of silver, but the mute and rabid Minotaur, raging against flesh-walls and tossing my horns at her phosphorescent ovaries.

Her body seemed to be a cup, and I crushed the goblet to me, and wept into its bowl, and Elaine seemed to smile and promise that she was the only grail I would ever touch, and her mouth was the only life I could ever drink. It was over, over, over and I had betrayed my queen and I clung to the chalice of her, soaked in tears and blood and semen, and her fingers were laced over her liquid belly where the embryonic diamond had begun to swallow its mother in long draughts, the gilled Galahad-thing which I could not now escape.

What a poor beginning for my son, all dressed up in the methane-blue betrayal of morning and grimacing in the light of my skin which was not the light of revelation. But whosoever drinketh from his mother shall have madness until the end of his days and the desert gaping like a jaw at his left hand. I stumbled from the bed and retched a pool of jaundiced stars into the corner, and Elaine was still as stone, listening to the grail-child unfold inside her like origami.

Compline—The Psalm of the Desert Father

I passed out of the world. I ran out of it. I sought out the driest of lands, those red and ochre, burned white and thirsty. I sought out the sermons of the saguaro and the yucca bell. I went deep into the waterless earth, the Lakeless air—in the yellow silt I broke open my skull, and four black opals spilled onto the rock.

Each held a clemency I could not touch, each whispered of purification and hands cleansed of the imprint of Elaine's body. Each reflected my face a hundred times, the hundred Lancelot-selves which I came to bury, the watery proliferation of mirrors I could no longer believe would bear my weight. I gathered up the stones in my arms and cradled them like daughters, daughters I never had, daughters with her hair like cats' pelts, thick with wild scent.

The sun told me a lie, and the lie told me a hymn, and the hymn told me that I belonged to the earth alone. The moon told me a riddle, and the riddle told me a rhyme, and the rhyme told me that only the white sage could heal me, the eating of smoke and darkness. The Mojave opened up to my limbs like a box of secrets, and I went to ground believing in absolution.

The rocks know our story, I do not even have to say our names and they know my sin, they know that there has never been a creature I loved that I did not betray. Oh, but even these red and riotous stones I see through the sick-silvern veil of my mother's skin. They ripple under her water and I am trying, trying, to empty myself of this liquid horror, to exorcise myself in the heat and bleach-dry bones.

Can I never escape these endless bodies, bodies I have entered like a mendicant, asking only for a shower of coins from their eyes, the lustral basins of their throats in which my poor forehead pressed—can I never escape the bodies I have possessed, the plague of hers which were the objects of my aiming?

I went to the waterless lands and still I saw the shore.

I stood on a pole in the desert, and the afterimage of it flashed forwards and backwards, a pin holding a chain of like-footed martyr-lunatics trying to fit the sun into their mouths. If I stand very, very still, and never come down until the coming of the sea, I will be pure again, the wind will move through me like a hand, it will curl up in the cathedral of my skeleton and sing choruses to itself, it will rest in me and breathe, and breathe, and breathe.

If I let my flesh wither to air, I will not be the sword or the lover-destroyer, I will be the saint of the ways, I will be forgotten and the world will close behind me like a drawn curtain. He will smile at her again, and she will laugh. I am the gray-blue stain between them, and if I go, if I go, if I stand and stand and do not move, it will be as if I never came to that castle between the blessing hills.

It is so clear, the glare of light in the desert, the holy emanations of adobe huts and turquoise ring-traders, the desperate clenching of skin against the sand, the divinatory mesas with their pyre-colors. The red crumble of it, studded with those night-blue stones like a spray of seraphic blood—the jewels which have rolled from the skulls of all the mad saints who lost their names in this place, this desert which is all deserts, and if I am good enough, if I am empty enough, it will take my name, too.

This is the end of the world.

I tasted the dust and it was an undoing, and all the wine of the earth became water. I have come as far as I can, there is nothing for me beyond this. The grail was her waist in my hands, and now the cup will never pass to me, except that I touched its rim when I spilled a son into a needled womb, except that I lit with the tongue of that red-haired girl the twelfth star in the crown of heaven.

The open rock begs for rain, and I am a ghost of cloud and salt—I wanted nothing, I swear, I meant only to embrace the mindless loyal *sol invictus* blaze of man and gold, I meant to be stupid and mute like all the other men adoring his light. But the moon is the ruin of me, it always grins, its landscape terrible and sere, knowing it holds me by the screaming scalp, and her apocalyptic touch woke me into shadow, gave me refuge from the topaz sheen of his nodding head, and I was in the Lake again, cool against the belly of a black-eyed mother.

But help me now, help me, wheel of fire, burn me white and chaste and empty of all things but the red rock and the turquoise, make my bones translucent, fill me with light and I will be the spear instead of the cup, I will be tipped in oil and pointed ever skyward, I will stand still as a temple, only take this away, take her away, take all the hers from my tongue, I will never utter the word again, take it, take me, let me become the skull of a buffalo and the jaw of a flat-footed hare.

Yea, though I walk through the valley in the shadow of death I will fear, I will fear and fall, I tremble in the shadowless weeds, I will know nothing but the emptying of my body, the liquefaction of my cyanic organs, the flagellation of my scalded back, for whosoever drinketh from me will inherit a throat of clay and dust, and whosoever eateth from my body will not die, but burn forever in the desert of the lost, and the sun will not forgive.

Sext—The Psalm of the Sun

The mad go to the desert to become holy. Or the holy go to the desert to become mad. It is hard to tell the difference. In the desert, madness is nothing of note, among all those bands of gold dirt. The long bones of the sky metamorphosize the psoriatic brain to sainthood. They become wise men, holed up in caves clotted with beatific filth. Others seek them out, wearing white burns on their thighs, and demand that they create bread from dust, to demand that they be fed, at last, from a hand without shadows.

These are easy words—shadow, sun, dust, mad. They do not touch the salt-scrim of the painted earth, the roads that wend over it like hungry fingers. They do not touch the foot of my spindled pole, the saint's phallus, with its thin shade falling binary and severe onto a pebbled stone tablet. The shadow is not a law, to be scribbled and footnoted—it is an equation, the simple line AB, bisecting crust and mantle, web-gray and endless. Where it falls commandments shiver.

And I above it, with one crooked leg, ridiculous bird that I am, wait to be hollowed, wait to have the muck and grime of her ground away, wait to be dried utterly, to be a magnificent husk, a cicada fossilized into amber on the basin floor.

It is difficult to balance. Like St. Sebastian I can feel holes opening in my skin, pores elongating like throats, rods of light slamming into place, through liver and pancreatic labyrinths, marrow and sweetmeat. Yet I am still wet, water still trickles from my kneecaps, and where it falls the mathematical line wavers—yucca bells spring up, bloody and scowling, from the sand which admits no other life. I am trying so, I have made all the correct calculations, all the alchemical designs inked on my shoulders and scalp, I put myself into the jaw of the sun, and still the yucca bells bloom.

It is the sun, always, which shows truth. When I woke and the sylph beside me was caught in the morning light, I should have killed her. I should have opened her breast before the milk could crack her veins and swell her into a mother. I could have sewn Galahad into my leg and left her a ruin, craggy towers and a vivisected torso. I would have walked with a limp, my thigh slowly becoming round and fat, an egg-thigh, and I this great deformed eagle, lumbering through clouds and the wind-reek of winter. With my moldering beak I could have smoothed the hairs on my leg and whispered to the blue-gilled Galahad, suckling at my sugar-white femur, his little hands opening and closing in the tides of my blood.

And somewhere, somewhere secret, I could have cut open the muscle and spilled out a grail-son onto a nest of sand and pine needles, and hushed his squalls and brought him to the cactus-kings to swear fealty, as I once did, sweating underneath my helmet. And he would have been pure, then, motherless—I could have given him up to the coiled whips of the sun, cauterized his mouth to a thin line, a shadow, an equation.

But I failed him, I let him be born in water and woman, like me, surrounded in that sickening blue, breathing her poison, adoring the sound of her breath. I let him float in the Elaine-lake, where nothing but the detritus of bloated carp can thrive, their coral scales peeling off like pages. I left him to be born in the mud and reeds, a sallow egg, roe, a tadpole—a swamp creature, whatever he becomes. Her fecundity is the rich stink of a dead marsh, and I abandoned him to that false grail, brimming with algae and wet grass.

I am punished, oh, I am punished for it. The sun will not forgive me, it sits on my spine and gnashes its skies. I am not hollow, I cannot be, no matter how I affect this perfect pose, no matter the agave-eyed boys who come to sit at the foot of my pole and stare, playing blackjack on the bedrock, taking bets on when I will fall. I am filled with all this clay, dead loam from a dead river. My heart's chambers press frantically on a glut of schist and volcanic dust. I am the ash-soldier, blasted against the adobe wall by Vesuvius, who could not forgive, either.

But the desert is full of madmen who have found the grail. It is not impossible to find succor in the clattering embrace of ox-skulls and snake-hides. It is not impossible that I may be able to escape the last of them, the water-wraiths that rise from every well and draw me down into dark and silence, into the death of their lips. They pull a son from me, they pull betrayal, they pull what was pure and pale as a tooth from me—all these things spilling from my mouth like a magic trick, scarves shooting endlessly from a painted gut—cobalt, olive, silver, turquoise, orchid, smoke, ink.

It is not impossible that I may find that cup of sage and sweetgrass, and vanish into grace.

Prime—The Psalm of the Roadside Stand

Apples and cherries, grapes and oranges, peaches, apricots, plums and ears of corn like arrows. The desert has no right to these things, this sugar water bursting at variegated skins. I have no right to them. I dimly recall, when I first came, being disappointed that the Mojave was not empty, was not the wasteland I craved. Black-eyed witches and nicotine-toothed magi chewed tobacco and held out hands full of fruits and jewels—I reeled from them, my skull full of tangerines and white jade, groping for hermitage amid all these unmovable faces.

It was the apples I feared most. Everyone knows that red means poison, means a swollen tongue turning black, means years in a glass coffin. And when I was a boy, my mother's breasts tasted of apples, her hair like apple-leaves, and under the surface of the Lake, my mouth was always full of the papery sweetness. I put my mouth to her throat and it was like pulling fruit from a branch, huge and red as a heart.

And there they lay, exuding that same earthy smell, in row after row of identical red—I covered my eyes and behind the lids were only ghosts, with their slim arms full of apple-roots. I went into the salt-flats, where the cool flesh of those fruits could not survive, and I ate mice, cracking open their delicate bones for the marrow.

And still, I could not escape these peddler-crones, holding out their beans and dried peppers like relics to be kissed, mouthed—these idols in orange and scarlet—habanero, poblano, ahi, guadillo, mesilla, shiny with wax and the tender hands of the faithful. Even in the emptiest of flatlands, one will appear as if she had grown out of the rock, slate-gray hair braided under a green bandana and a wide-brimmed hat, and wordlessly hold out the husk of a pepper, desiccated into gold, insisting.

The stars last night huddled for warmth in the shadow of the cliffs, and I shared my fire, my mouse-feast, and the rattling pepper-net I could not refuse, which they quarreled over like wild dogs, tearing into the red and yellow skins, snarling and lapping at the spiced rope.

Afterwards, the stars sat around the flames and I confessed that I was mad, that I was fleeing the water and the threat of apples. They hunched together, coronae bristling like tangled branches, and told me that the curvature of the moon meant rain was coming, they told me that the lizards and sparrowhawks were dancing for rain, that the poppies were singing in opiate harmonies to call down the rain. They told me that the Grail comes up from the bleeding soil, that the rain tells it secret things, and it spins up like wild onion. The bowl of its cup is blue, the leaves are dusty white, sage-white, willow-white, and I will know it by its water, for it will hold the rain perfectly still and not spill a drop.

They accused me of heresy, of turning from the water that gave them the perfume of saguaro flowers, washed their haunches, and fattened the snakes under their feet. I was no madman if I could not weep, they snapped, and weeping is nothing but water. They stroked my stomach with fingers that smoked and sizzled, promising that I would never dry myself to the ruby shell of a roadside pepper, that I would never bind my flesh with those rough ropes or taste the sun's meat.

I wept, under their hands like midwives, and they mocked my tears for water. They pointed at the moon, overturned like a broken bowl, and pulled at my jaw, trying to fashion it into a lunar basket, lips and rushes woven water-tight. They told me that no one with hands so dry could touch the cup of the desert, which was an avatar of liquid things: blood, sweat, milk, tears. They laughed like ravens over carrion at my legs which had not borne a child. They prodded at my old wounds. They sidled into my ears and whispered the names, the terrible names I could not let into me, those acetylene syllables searing through my inner ear, the secret ear which hears only shame:

Arthur. Guenevere.

It was a poor madness, they said, which remembers all its sins.

But I do not have to remember—the desert knows those names, they are written on every hut and dry riverbed, they are in the cave-wall glyphs and scrawled like graffiti on the Anasazi cliff-houses, they are stamped on every fruit in every stall, on the tongue of every turquoise trader, emblazoned on the door of every red-tiled mission with their great lonely bells. It is deafening, it is blinding, and in the night the names couple wildly and reproduce themselves in new crevices, on the backs of whipsnakes and iguana, burros and turkey vultures. Even the stars mouth those names, mash them with toothless gums, roll them over their cold tongues and push them into the earth again, where they will germinate, and under the moon's first rain will detonate into lilies and poppies and knowing anemones.

Arthur. Guenevere.

Nones—The Psalm of Remembering

I walked these last days with my head skyward, until I was blinded by the bleach-boned sun and the expectation of rain. I feared it, I feared its worm-droplets burrowing under my hair, I feared the taste of it mixed with my sweat and blood-dust. I feared that it would know me, and burn at a touch, for all that I have done.

I was not allowed eyes, or blood, or a cock. These things were not given to me the day of my oath. A sword, yes, and a title. But flesh, a tongue, desire? None of these—but when she leaned over me—she, not him, Guenevere, not Arthur—and touched me with the Lake-blade, the diamond at her throat swung forward and brushed my forehead, and I smelled her skin, which smelled of no other thing but apples, and I felt the water floating again over my face like hands, obscuring the vision of king and ceremony, until only she filled me up, the brush of her rainwater-jewel and her lion-braids hanging low like the tongues of church bells.

And later, when I knew what her mouth tasted like, and the milk of her body, when she had miscarried twin daughters, and when her dresses smelled of us, a miasma of apple and horsehide, I could not stop, I could not breathe unless I was inside her, unless I could wend her hair in my fingers and shriek, hoarse and dry, into her neck.

It has always been so. I am always the little boy climbing into the laps of women too big for me. And I am always surprised when they close over me, and I cannot see the sun for the ripples of their tides.

I climbed into the lap of the desert, too, clambering over loose stones, caked in dust that should have been Aramaic, crusader's dust, Byzantine at the least. I scrabbled under scrub-brush and hubcaps for the disc of sainthood, the nova to surround my head, the balm for my drowning, and there was nothing. There is nothing in the desert, there is nothing in women, there is no revelation to be gained by swallowing the sun or by pulling on the body of another like a shirt.

Am I cured, then, by the birth of this homunculus, this black little cherub somewhere in my lower intestine? Should there not be a heroic burst of music, fiddles and drums and low, hooting pipes, as befits the geography? Should not the railroad keep the time, the chuffing trains play metronome to the coyote-sopranos?

The moon is almost upside-down. I lay beneath it and it boils my skin white, white as the tail of a starving deer, white as that mange-ridden stag which bumbled into the wedding feast, gobbling the cakes and shitting noisily on the draped dais.

The signs were there, for anyone to see who cared.

When I left Elaine, Galahad-heavy, she saw—*she* saw, the most perfect of the pronouns that bury me—and Guenevere's glance was the same as it had been on that long ago day, the day she married, when she watched a poor white deer, its mouth smeared with sugar and honey, stumbled into the feast-hall, start and cry out feebly as it was gashed by a dozen arrows. It crashed through the goblet and plate as it fell, legs spasming, spattering the altar with filth. And she watched, calmly, as they carried out the ruin of that sick beast.

Here, too many years hence to admit, my hands still trained to the shape of her waist, I wait for it to rain. I pray, I keep the liturgy of the wolf spider, I ring out the hours on the bare rocks—I pray for the only promise I have left to show itself—that the Grail will bloom out of the desert like a blood-colored marigold, and that I will be pure enough, just enough, to fall into it and cover my body, this mewling body, the splayed thing, hung head-earthwards on a six-spoked wheel made from the twined legs of three women, this horror, cover its shame with light.

I am not cured. I have learned to speak the dialect of the mad saint, which consists mainly of fire and bone, and printed the lexicon on my ribcage, stamped in perfectly even letters, the typewriter-hammer slamming home each time, expressing the virtue of exactitude. But when the bread and water were carried from Rome, they passed me by, deeper into the desert, towards the pepper-stand woman and the star-pack, and I, in my grubby sandals and mantis-hung beard, could not catch them. Canonization is for those who find God in the desert. I found only the smell of the earth before rain, and the memory of wetness exploding in my chest, the ecstatic drops on my blistered lips, my cracked chin.

The moon rolled over and presented her throat to the stars; the stars closed their mouths over her white fur.

Matins—*The Psalm of the Rain*

The fruit stands packed up more quickly than I would have thought possible, collapsing into neat heaps like decks of cards. The pole-children scatter like sullen crows. And now it is truly empty here, as I imagined it, the cross-hatch of railroad tracks binding the expanse of land like a corset, the mesas that clothe the world and meet the sky, and through the heat I seem to see the air shape itself into many-towered Camelot.

But I cannot touch it, the mirage of a well-appointed castle, a castle swollen with happiness and nobility—why would anyone claim such a thing, when we lie around its walls like corpses, genuflecting maniacally, mired in the wreck of it all?

This is my confessional flesh, wet and kneeling even when I stand. Wet and kneeling when the moon empties herself onto my desert, my red rock and whittled canyon. Thin tracks appear over the flats, a race of rivulets, mercurial, sparse as strands of hair. Thatches of green are opening in the cliff walls like eyes, and the rush of water fills my ears, my mouth, closing over me, familiar and silent.

There are arms now, arms in the desert, spinning like the thousand arms of copper-bellied Buddhas, spinning in cattle-horns and barbed wire and agate and gold flecks, serrano peppers burning like sacred hearts, train engines and thirst and burro-haunch, spinning until they are nothing but water, water, and she is here, she is all around me, I am inside her again, beneath the Lake, and her arms around me are as blue as those idols, Lakshmi and Kwan-Yin and the Lady, always the Lady, whose cheek presses against mine.

Her cool skin pools in my hands, and those old black eyes croon over me as if I was a baby again, her own changeling child, down in the deep and the dark, with her and in her and over her. My mother has never said a word to me, but sung in her own liquid language, her burble and splash, her deep thrum which vibrated then in my jaw, but now quivers in my belly. I put my arms up to her, pleading, humble, begging for some surcease, some end, opening my body in supplication to her nebulous form, begging for the Grail from her hands. She gathered me to her breast, and showed me again the place to drink, tipped with black water—and I shut my eyes when she flowed into my mouth, the taste of apples and apple-petals, apple-bark and apple-sugar. I shudder, I shudder, and pull harder against her, sucking her into me, the apple-fire snaking through my veins like honeyed lightning, and the names disappear from the wind, evaporating into nothing, just meaningless letters, wafting up to the sky like ashes.

Arthur. Guenevere. Elaine. Galahad.

There is only the Lake, and the Lady stroking my hair with an azure hand, and my hand twisted in her lightless hair.

When I let her fall from my mouth, and reel upwards at her moon-dark face, I am calm. She holds something in her hand, something I cannot quite see. The small of her back glints in the shadow-and-light of the water, and at the base of her spine I can see a strange root whose tendrils wrap her inky waist. It winds up, around her ribs and cupping the bottom of her heavy breast, curling at last over her shoulder and into her open palm.

She turned to me, and the grail was nestled in her fingers—a flower which was not a cup, and a cup which was not a flower. Its squat stem opened over her hand in white stone, in bundles of white sage, in gnarled lily-roots. The chalice was not a blue blossom, and it was not a black jewel, hollowed like a gourd. Its glass-petals wavered in the current, and it held the rain perfectly still, it did not spill a drop. I looked into her mirroring body, and its light was unmistakable—the light of blood and dark caves, the light of rotted wood and iron, mother-light, the light of the womb filled with stones grinding aside. It cast no shadow, but shone simply as a star.

I reached out for it, extending my fingers in innocence, and she drew away from me, drawing the cup back into her body, under the waters of the Lake, and the light was gone from me. Her eyes (black, still black, black as dreams!) did not blink, or look away, but I knew that I was lost. I fell so far, so far. It was not for me, not her body, not the Grail. It was for the webbed hands growing in a far-off belly, and I could only see, could only watch her open herself into a Grail, and close again. I had drunk and drunk of her, but her Grail-self was forbidden to me, who had killed a deer on the day of a wedding, and clutched a hip which was a lie.

Her hands unlocked from mine, and as fast as water disappears, as fast as the yucca bells close in the desert, her bright body receded from me, flowing back, black and blue, the wave rolling back to the sea.

The stars became waterfalls, and the wasteland was alive with grasses blowing silver and green, brittlebrush and chicory, asters, datura, and bee-plants, verbena, milkweed, and toadflax, globemallow and Spanish needles, creosote and saltbush—and cereus, their white bowls opening with a rush of perfume. Hares snuffed at the suddenly thick air, and sleek mice pattered through the brush.

I looked back towards the road, the great black line bisecting the desert, linear, simple, an equation.

I opened my jaw, and the moon rolled into my mouth.

VI THE LOVERS

Balin and Balan

*Then afore him he saw come riding out of a castle a knight, and his
horse trapped all red, and himself in the same colour. When this
knight in the red beheld Balin, him thought it should be his brother
Balin by cause of his two swords, but by cause he knew not his
shield he deemed it was not he. And so they adventured their spears
and came marvelously fast together, and they smote each other in
the shields, but their spears and their course were so big that it bare
down horse and man, that they lay both in a swoon.*

—Sir Thomas Malory
Le Morte d'Arthur

Balin

Thou shalt strike, he said, *thou shalt strike. Thou shalt strike a stroke
most dolorous that man ever struck.* And he put his hand, speckled like
an owl's with veins and liver spots, on my shoulder as if to absolve me,
or pity me. What entrails or petrified bones did he consult? What cards,
what runes, what bird-flight told him that my hand would find its way to so
many throats? And why was the stroke so dolorous, of all the strokes I have
made? The spear in the king's thigh? Or you, my brother, my brother, on this
crane-nested island, alone and armored all in red? My brother, my twin, my
other face, how could you not have shown me the eyes I loved? How could
you not have made some sign?

But I suspect the old fortune-teller meant the spear and the wasteland.
Fratricide is nothing to them, easily pardoned with the old bleach-gold
words: *ave maria, gratia plena, dominus tecum, benedicta tu in mulieribus*—
what is it to them, who never shared a womb, who never locked translucent
fingers with the child whose skin was white as a mirror, who never rested
within the symphony of three hearts beating?

They all want to talk about the spear, that horrid spear, the great ash-wood
thing dripping with blood, all hung with ripped altarcloths stained with
sacramental wine, a paste of host wafers rubbed into the wood. *Wasn't it*

obvious, they say, *that it was sacred?* Not to be touched? It didn't belong to you, it was plainly meant for someone purer and more pious, *how could you, how could you, how could you?*

How could I? It was easy. My sword had shattered in the battle like a looking-glass, pretty and useless. Room by room I ran with the clamor of men grunting and cutting themselves into corpses rattling in my ears, until I ducked into the chapel and saw the spear.

It was dreadful to see, slick with warm blood—but it was light, it had good balance, a solid heft. I thought nothing at all of it, I took it from its frame and sunk it into the king's thigh—it would have been his heart, save that at the last moment my hand slipped in the blood seeping from the ash and the stroke fell awry. It went into him smoothly, as though his leg was its sheath, and I spat on his beard.

But what is that, what is that compared to you, my brother, spitting blood into my lap? What is that king's coarse nettle-beard next to your downy face? Oh, you were never able to grow a proper beard, it sprang up soft and sparse, moss on a classical statue, and how we used to laugh. What is his gaping thigh next to your chest sucking at the cold island wind, to the birds waiting for us to lie down and change from men to feast?

Why should I weep for the wasteland when we are dying here, together, and the cattails are playing our dirge?

I was there only a moment ago, it seems, in that castle, with my spear in the old man's thigh. And then the pillars began to bleed, too, and the rafters cracked, loosing a clutch of dove-corpses—poor beasts cooked up there by the summer heat—and the thud of their bodies on the tiled floor (in the Moorish style, of course, Pellam was nothing if not stylish) was flat and wet. Then the windows gave, the glass bending horribly before shattering, a spray of pink St. Catherine's nipples and the jaundiced yellow of a dozen angels reciting the Dialogue of the Seraphic Virgin. The shards slashed cheeks and earlobes, and the walls came down like Jericho, like the earthquake of '06, like a blast of steel trumpets.

And I was caught, under one of Pellam's precious black agate busts of Mary, the back of her veil inscribed with the precise genealogy connecting his family to those barn-huddlers, out to seventh cousins and step-uncles.

But the old man came and put his owl-hand on my shoulder, and (*thou shalt strike*) led me out of the wrecked manse onto the clean grass, the

strawberry fields around the house, still peppered with migrants tending the
irrigation and the nascent fruit. I thought he was saving me, a great hairy
angel with scotch-and-water breath, taking me from the endless identical
fields of the San Joaquin to the redwood-chapels, where I could heal. But
he brought me to this murky delta, this chain of islands leading to your
tower—how could he not tell me it was yours? And the mouse-faced little
novice told me to fight the Red Knight—well, what am I for, if not bashing
against things, if not doing what mousy-faced novices tell me to, what am I
for, if not for the kill and the reward and the next kill down the line?

What was the Dolorous Stroke? They will tell me it was the spear, that
I should have known it for a holy relic—but I know, I know as your body
weighs on mine, that the spear was meaningless.

Balan

Red. I was Red, wasn't I? For the tower, for the girl with basilisk-eyes,
who told me how to slip in under the weak left arm of the last knight, and
get my knife up under his ribs? He was red, too, I think—it was so long ago,
now. Red for her lips and her cheeks (though I had always assumed girls like
her didn't blush) red for her sweet little cunt and her masses of hair that I
could wind around my arm like a sleeve. Red for her blood every quarter
moon, and red for the moons when it didn't come, and red for the little
screw-faced dwarves that took our daughters away after dark.

Did she tell you that I lead with my right side, brother? Was she tired
of me? Or tired of all of us, this möbius strip, knight to knight to knight,
and all red, all wearing the emblem of having gotten those hundred babies
on her, all winding her hair around their elbows until her scalp was raw?
Perhaps she saw a way to cut the strip—or perhaps you were simply better
than I—after all, you have spent these years killing kings, and I have spent
them sowing beans and lettuce.

But your shield—it should have been the crossed swords on a field *rempli*,
why was it the cormorant *recursant volant*?

I suppose it doesn't matter, not now.

Do you remember when I brought the dwarf to Cornwall? Bowlegged and
red-nosed—the red of vodka straights, not of the tower-girl—and his many-
colored hat, his deerskin vests still stinking of the animal, his fingernails
caked with dirt, always picking fleas from his pony and crushing them

between those sharp claws. He was one of the dwarves who performed the trick of disappearing my daughters—I followed him to the sea, and watched him, under stars like averted eyes, put my child onto a birchwood barge, with a black sail, into the arms of a woman with hair that absorbed the moon. She took the child in her arms, and smiled—her smile was a sudden snow on my bones, brother—and the barge vanished over the breakers.

I caught the curdled arm of the dwarf and demanded he call back the wild-masted raft, but he would not. Instead, he told me that you had killed a boy, that it could not be kept secret. And I stood by while he accused you in that rancid cream-voice, putting no more than a hand on your shoulder and urging you to be more careful (oh, brother, we do tilt at every living thing, don't we? Is there a tree, a sapling in all the world that is safe from us?) and eating a little bread at your side. I wanted to be back at my tower, at my red woman, at my beans and my lettuce—already I had forgotten the lost daughter.

I wish then I had told you to stay in the valley where the pumpkins grow like little suns, where the orange trees groan with their measure of sugared gold. It was better for you there—you should never have come to the isles, to the mist and the cedars that hide countless towers, that hide countless cursed women, that hide legions of barge-fostered daughters.

You could always take me, brother, twin, my double. I believed in the Red, I believed she loved me. I believed she loved the way her hair could wend around my arm. I believed her hair covered me when I went out to meet any other man, that it arced over my head like a wedding canopy, and that I was safe. I carried my shield with her limbs emblazoned on it, woman rampant, and I believed in the tower, and the dwarves, and the beans and the lettuce.

It is not so incredible, I suppose, that our blood should mix in the dry grass, that we should be clasped, hand to hand as if in prayer, one body again, as we began. Your wound is not so great as mine. (Is it strange to think a wound is like a mouth, to wish it would speak, explain itself, ask forgiveness for its redness?) But your wound is lower, and the seep is darker. Our little pieta, so full of stigmata that there is nothing left but holes, and we fall out of ourselves. Who holds who? Who is the winner? After all this, I still want to beat you once, little brother—yes, little. Do you forget I was born first? Seven minutes, seven minutes before you. I had seven minutes alone with our mother before you came ripping your way free of her.

If I die first, will that even the score?

Balin

It isn't supposed to be like this. Women are supposed to hold us, and give succor, and dry our tears with their veils. How can I give succor to you? How can a pieta stand, when both figures are shivering with blood loss and shock? This isn't the tableau I was meant for, trying to help you into death as if it were as simple as opening a door or throwing a coat over a puddle, trying not to embarrass myself by dying first. Pellam would turn up his nose at this wreck of a death scene—the old man always had a fetish for protocol, for the *mos maiorum*, for good manners in all things—and we are dying in a terribly rude fashion, are we not?

His palace was the height of fashion, Cinderella-spired and Alhambra-fountained, chandeliers from Waterford and spiral banisters carved from solid California oak. It bordered the land where the mist and hulking trees change a man to a beast, the Otherland where quests always seem to lead—the rear walls of the place dropped off with a sickening shear, falling into fog and forest. I was brought in—if you could have tasted the feast, Balan! Of course he had the best—the workers in his fields live on rinds and dimes, but he supped on roasted dove and deer, corn and plum-wine and peaches, carrot soup, strawberries, oranges, potatoes like russet fists, new cream and mint leaves and wild thyme, brandy and port and chocolate dark as the devil's throat. There is nothing that does not grow or breed in that perfect valley, the San Joaquin, heaven's heart. Pellam's table shuddered under the weight of it. And the apples! How can I have forgotten the apples? Pyramids of red and yellow, crowned, each, with a bright green fruit, simmering at the summit like the lamp of a lighthouse.

He began as ritual would have it—as though he would let a chance for ritual slip by! The impeccably dressed (powder blue accented with cobalt) monarch rose at the head of the cherrywood table and recited the litany of begats which charted the genetic drift between himself and the Christ child, tectonic plates buoying continents of paternity, a tree so complex and oft-grafted that Pellam himself seemed surprised had not come out half-dove.

Once the fighting broke out (I suppose you will say that was my fault, brother, that I need not take every challenge thrown up at me by flea-infested second and third sons, but I am what I am) Pellam cracked my sword against one of the perfectly appointed marble steps, and I ran to find another—I only meant to find another sword, you understand. How was I to know he had that ghastly spear hidden away? If it was very important, he would have displayed it in the hall and lectured about it for at least an hour before we were allowed to touch his precious brandy.

There was no crack of thunder when I took it from the altar, no blinding flash of folly or revelation—not even when I buried it in Pellam's femoral artery—I use the precise term in his honor—was there any clap of *cielo furioso*.

Until the house came down.

But by then I had left the spear in Pellam, jutting up awkwardly like an inopportune erection; I didn't connect the wobbling red lance with the sudden seizure of the architecture. Only after I was spirited out from under the Virgin Mary did I understand—the fields outside his house were a gray ruin, the migrants picking at shriveled berries that crumbled to ash at a touch. The orange trees had petrified, the corn-rows calcified, the apple orchards had dropped all their fruit in one gasp, and the wind was snatching up the stench of rot. The irrigation canals had iced over, though there was no cold. They sat sullen and blue-banked, glowering at the hapless workers with their bushels of clay and dust.

Was it his protocols and monotonous ritual that kept the land pushing plenty up through its *crown*? Or the spear in its proper place? You know I have never gotten a handle on propriety. If I had, I would have at least asked your name before charging—but I was tired, I wanted it over and done, I hoped there was a pretty maid in the tower to smile shyly and put a cool cloth on my head.

This island does not have the decency to blight at the touch of our blood. It keeps its swampy councils, and the cranes suck eels from the streams without taking notice of the tragedy nearby. You would think, would you not, my brother, that the noise of such irony as this would be deafening?

Balan

Perhaps it is the fault of our names. Balin, Balan, it hardly makes a difference, does it? Did no one ask where I had gone all those years, while you were assisting suicides and claiming more swords than you deserved? Did no one wonder what had happened to the older twin, the one who didn't run at the other children like a rabid mountain goat, cracking horn against horn? While you were sidling up to Arthur and making battlefield eyes at his knights, did no lady with wild violets in her hair ask if you hadn't once had a brother, and what had become of him?

What was the Dolorous Stroke? When have you made a stroke which was not?

Is she watching us, can you see? My girl? Are there eyes in that tower, feline and yellow—yellow I once thought of as gold, as lion's pelt, as burnished bedposts. Does her red sleeve fall over the parapet—dare I hope that she is crying? I had my quest, finally, and it ended in her, her yellow eyes moving over me, appraising, as the blood of her last knight still steamed on my chest—and I can still smell the metallic tang of that blood as she pulled me down onto her, as it smeared onto her breasts, her lips, as it pooled in her navel—Balin, the smell of it, when I loved her that first day!

Can red have a smell? It must, it must—it must smell of her breath and her hungry mouth when she licked the blood from my fingers.

I cannot turn to look, you must do it for me—my legs have gone numb. If she is there, if her hair is falling over the tower stones, then she loved me and it was not that I was simply next. If she is there then she liked the taste of the beans I planted in the black soil—generations of duels will fertilize the land—she liked the sound of my children's hearts beating against hers, she liked my heavy shape sleeping against her. If she is not—I do not know. Perhaps she betrayed me, perhaps she is at her bath, perhaps she did not hear the sounds of us cracking horn against horn.

I begin to think there is a plexus of these fairy women, a chain, a net, knotted by hundreds of hands in hundreds of towers. They must spread out like veins, collecting each other's daughters, waiting for a chance to escape the pattern of knights and clamber onto that barge themselves.

I want her to have quit that sisterhood, to have hung up its wimple and stamped their prayer beads into glass dust. I want her to have kissed the blood from me and forgotten all her oaths to those witches, those siren-crones, those moon-addled alchemists. I want her to have never known what apples taste like, or stroked another fey-girl's hair with those delicate hands, smooth as candles. I want her to have looked at me and loved me, and turned away from the light of their pale sylph-bodies, away from the forest where masts are cut from strong trunks, and flax crushed between plump fingers, woven into sailcloth.

But I think, even now, she is stepping onto the birchwood and taking deep breaths of the sea wind.

Balin

It was the lady of the house who gave me the shield. It was larger, she said, and more splendid. They would not send me to face the Red Knight with my own, which, she insisted, was little more than a buckler. I admit that it was fine, though the cormorant was unsettling, rising up as if to flee its station.

The old man had brought me all that way from Pellam's castle, and the blasted heath that I had made of the two-rivered valley—I could hardly speak for hunger and tremors of exhausted muscle. The lady put morsels of duck and goose into my mouth, wiped the juice form my chin. She held a cup of hot wine to my lips, and ushered old owl-hands from the castle. Then she told me of a terrible beast who held a maiden captive on an island just a little distant from there. The rushes grew high on that isle, and no road cut through the marshes.

I am what I am, Balan.

I was not even afraid when I saw you, no bigger than I, though your armor flashed scarlet and black in the dim sun, filtered through low fog. You were like a blood-golem, bearing down on me without even a horse, bellowing some name I could not understand. If you had seen my shield, my own, with the two swords—you remember, don't you, the girl with hair like a deer's flank who said no man but her champion could pull the sword? And I took it from her—even Arthur could not! I took it—I alone won two swords. If you had seen the crossed blades, crossed like spears, would you have stopped and clapped me on the shoulder, called me brother, and would we have gone in to feast with your woman? It could not have happened that way, I know that.

Thou shalt strike a stroke most dolorous that man ever struck.

Oh, my brother, my other self, I did not think he meant this. Put your fingers through mine, lock them knuckle to knuckle as we used to, and do not cough so. I will not die before you, I will not go down into the earth without you. I will be your mother, I will be your *pieta*, I will hold your prone body beloved as it goes blue and stiff. I will wait for you to start down the stair, and I will follow after. I am so sorry, I wish your ribs did not show through your skin, I wish I were not so cold, that I could not feel myself emptying from myself. I wish we were whole again, safe in the womb, warm heads pressed together, waiting for a rush of phosphor, for that burst of sound and air scalding its way through new lungs, waiting for seven minutes to separate us.

Balan

I have put my beans and my lettuce to sleep in the earth, my wife to sleep in the tower, and my daughters to sleep on the barge. The cranes have put their heads beneath their wings. Everyone sleeps but us, this huddle of twins in the damp, skin flushed back to the blue of pre-breath infants, whose breath no longer even hangs in the air.

Quiet, now, little brother. I will go first, as I have always done, so that if you fall on the night-stair, I will catch you.

II.

There is not a stone here which has not borne up under a foot. The castle is warm with touching, with hands against walls and spines against floors. Behind the blessing hills, it nearly glows. Knees have worn cups into the floor of the cathedral, and the faithful find their favorite places, nestling into the warm indents that hold them up like palms.

Wells have been sunk. The water is sweet and clear, and tastes a little of new moss, a little of burnt wood. The river is swift and cold and neatly diverted into a hundred fields. There is talk of a new monastery—in thirty years it will be famous for barrels of thick black beer.

The market in the great courtyard passes old money around—each coin has been endlessly fondled, turned into cakes, cloth, shoe-soles, honeycombs, thick red meat strung with thyme and turning slowly on a spit. There are children who have grown up in the shade of the portcullis, and stalls which have been in the family. Seven successive queens have looked down from the topmost tower, each with black braids. Each grew old, each watched their braids turn silver, then white.

There is one up there now—look, you can see the sun on her scalp. Is she smiling? Is she crying? It is always hard to tell with queens.

The lands outside the walls bristle with vegetable, with animal. There are new breeds—someone has even grown a low trellis of grapes. In the winter, they freeze, and children suck on the hard purple fruits. Goats wander shaggy and fat, sheep bleat and roll in the long grass. The clatter of wool-carding is pleasant, and makes little girls sleepy. Taxes are high, but not too high.

Late in autumn, the taxes are not taken—some few guess why. That castle leaks men like a sieve, and they are always out searching for one thing or another. This time it's a cup. They hear. They shrug. Well, everyone needs cups. But the tax-man is busy questing, and the king's tithe is well-put to use in babies' mouths, in old aunts' jugs, in new cows and spinning wheels and a big plow-horse with a white patch on his forehead.

The valley is small and quiet, and the castle sits in its center: safe, familiar, eternal. When was there not a castle here? Curse me if I can remember.

V THE HEIROPHANT

Pellinore

Pellinore, at that time a king, followed the Questing
Beast, and after his death Sir Palomides followed it.

—Sir Thomas Malory
Le Morte d'Arthur

*Of the approximately three thousand species of lizards in existence, only
a few are very large. The legs of some lizards are greatly shortened, or
vestigial, making animals such as the glass lizard or slowworm snakelike
in appearance; they are distinguished from true snakes by their movable
eyelids and by differences in the structure of the skull bones, especially
those of the lower jaw. The bones of the two halves of a lizard's lower jaw are
firmly united; those of a snake are separable. Scales are evenly arrayed in
lines down and around the body. Dorsal scales are keeled while the ventral
scales are smooth; there is little overlapping. Colors are various shades of
brown, green, yellow, even black—some species have lighter longitudinal
stripes or variegated colors.*

*A fold of skin is generally noted running laterally along the length of the
body—some scholars believe that this is evidence of vestigial wings, while
others scoff at the idea that creatures of such size ever flew.*

I will admit, I will whisper into the dust-plated corners, behind bookshelves
and umbrella-racks, sheaves of woolen coats and heavy boots: it is possible
that there is no such thing as a dragon.

It is not the Beast itself that matters, you understand. Leopard or lamia,
there are many hides I could have taken home to Camelot by now, if it were
only the Beast I wanted. I would not travel this way, if that were all, belts
and sashes clanging with sextants and telescopes, magnifying glasses and
monocles, nautical charts, compasses in brass and gold, graphometers,
refractometers, hydrometers, cliometers, and galvanometers, azimuths and
globes studded with malachite and onyx, zinc-carbon batteries, micro-
manipulators and a genuine *camera obscura*—all of my own invention.

There is a gramophone in the saddlebags. But all this *apparati* is not for finding—it is for *looking*.

That is what they do not understand, the boys who rush out wearing braggart swords on bonny hips, astride horses flashing flanks at the sun—only to hurry home as soon as the moon shows her calf. There is sanctity in simply placing one foot in front of the other, again and again, until the foot seems to remember no time when it sat still on a polished floor, and cannot recall what country birthed it—toe, heel, or arch. Devotion to the wood and the wild is a thing of beauty, devotion to the walking staff and the manzanita-bramble, devotion to the beast which may or may not breathe fire, which may or may not possess the ability to fly, which may or may not dream of its eggs, of the shell's slippery hues, ultramarine to indigo, splintering with the pressure of a tiny speckled beak.

In the Sierras, there are places men have never trampled a leaf underfoot. This is, after all, the othered space of fairyland, and if I am to take my chances anywhere, if I am to hope for a green leg, a variegated tail, a clutch of painted eggs, it can be nowhere else but here. I make my little fire in the shade of granite, on the moraine where a glacier once ground its ponderous, imperturbable way through, dropping boulders like shameful tears behind it. Kitchen smells urge their oily gleam through the oaky air—the tea sour and thin, bacon popping and slapping in its grease, leaving a tiny constellation of fat-burns on my forearm, a Pleiades of lard and scorched hair—the sound of it like a spill of salt onto a slick white floor. Coffee speaks its bean-tongue, and the mountains grumble a loamy rhythm of longevity.

The sextant gleams hopefully.

In the center of the head of many lizards is a small semi-transparent spot, which connects to an area of the brain, called the pineal body. A pineal body is a small, cone-shaped projection from the top of the midbrain of most vertebrate species. The pineal body does not appear in crocodiles or in mammals of the order Xenarthra, consisting of only a few cells even in whales and elephants. In lizards, this is a kind of "third eye," thought to detect day length via the angles of sunlight, triggering the breeding instinct in midsummer, and hibernation in winter. It may also allow certain species of green and red lizards to detect the presence of others of their kind, suitable mates or rivals. It has been suggested that the pineal body would account for

the reports of dragons able to eerily pinpoint the weakest part of siege-towers
and other man-made defenses.

Pellinore is a new name. Once, it was *Beli Mawr*, once Bile and Bel. When
the Beast had not yet taught our family to disregard the year's hemlines
we came when we were called, and on boulder-strewn fields we thrust our
fists against the mud. We kept death in the grasses, and when we opened
our mouths, our daughter roared into birth from our jaws. We were moss-
bearded giants, beasts ourselves, and our knees were large as shields. Over
time, we shrunk into the usual span of height, and began to hunt others,
instead of fleeing from earnest young men with nets and tridents.

We became domesticated—it can happen to anyone.

The muscles in our hawthorne-thighs ached with the strain of holding the
down the dark. Stone huts and beds of barley-hulls began to seem sweet as
mountains to us, and we lay down into the sleepiness of country lordships.

But we still resemble boulders enfleshed—occasionally I will find a bit
of lichen or milkweed growing in my beard—our skin is famously tough,
elephant-coarse and the deep brown of men accustomed to carrying the sun
on their shoulders. Roofs do not become us. But I took a roof onto my back,
didn't I? Didn't I agree to put my shoulders to the beams of Camelot, didn't
I let them settle the rafters onto my neck like the fasteners of a guillotine?

I suppose I did, and yet now it seems as though another man asked to be
seated at that table, where no Beast would ever rest its beryl hindquarters.
Someone young and blonde with knuckles like fat golden rings—yet I know
my beard is red. What color could it be but red? My face sprouts fire as the
Beast's does. We are brothers, sinewy and smoldering old goats trundling
about on a mountain neither of us can name. Who was it that clapped
Arthur on the back and ate roasted rooster's combs? I suppose it was me. I
am a Pellinore, the only one living. So, logically, it must have been me.

Perhaps I only wish it were another man, so that I would not now be
this old walnut-husk, so that I would not have walled myself away from the
Beast and the storm-sky's clamor for all those years. Perhaps I once had
yellow hair, and I have forgotten it.

I never told Arthur whether I am older or younger than he—at times I
played the lad, at times I stood for the Merlin-that-was, the Merlin-before-
Nimue, and put my hand on his shoulder—though it is not the owl-clutch

he remembers, my hand is much too heavy for that. But it held the old man's place for awhile.

Do you remember, Arthur, the night you, too, dreamed of the Beast? How you said it had a pelt like a leopard—patently ridiculous, of course—and the feet of a deer—absurd!—the haunches of a lion to top it off—of all the preposterous theories! And you clutched me, sweating, clammy, and whispered that a brother had got a child on his sister, and that child was the Beast, and the brother was punished, punished, in your dream he was punished and the Beast ate him whole.

Oh, my boy. You come to your Pellinore and tell him to wear the band of a dream-interpreter, and I know you are sorry, I know you wish it had not happened, but you needn't tell stories about Beast to torture yourself. He is beyond such silliness. And I told you not to fear—I had hunted him for years and would take it up again for you, and I would ask him myself if all children of a brother and a sister were wicked. As if the Beast knows a thing about it, but it seemed to calm you, and that one night, you feel asleep in my arms, like a son.

I cannot go back now—too many graves, fanning out like sunflowers around its grounds, too many wraiths in the halls, spaces whose edges still burn like cigarette-scars, spaces where people we loved used to walk, and gossip, and trade their cinnamon for lumps of brown sugar. All the men of that place are professional pallbearers now. That great, gabled hall is a death-barrow. It is a mausoleum, tightly shut, scented with bergamot and myrrh. Nothing can live closed inside.

The Beast, oh, my Beast is life. The dragon, its skin hot as a baking stone, its tender snout nosing the air, the space where its skull-plates meet pulsing in an almost intimate rhythm, so that you almost feel ashamed to witness so private a flutter. Nothing about the creature admits the existence of cold—the pouched flaps which might be wings chuff a sirocco off of its aerie, a rush of brown and ochre nest-shreddings. And I, in my lowland hutch, speculating to an audience of three dim stars and a titmouse as to whether the Beast might have some kind of fur over its spine, as smaller lizards are reported to have, fat tufts of hoary tangles—and how would this affect any latent or actual flight abilities?

But the castle beyond the foothills spattered with blackthorn and honey-hearted oak, the castle where the lights have gone out in the tall windows?

That is a dead place, and I would never have found the Beast if I had stayed to die with it.

... most lizards and many other species of reptile have the ability to rejuvenate their tails. The bright coloration of the tail, ranging from vermillion to emerald and into various shades of gold, in some species diverts the attention of predators to the expendable appendage, aiding in escape. (Image Ψ)

Fracture points on the tail bone allow the tail to easily break away. In some lizard varieties, (Image Y), the tail can regenerate itself many times over after detachment, often in entirely different patterns of color than the original tail.

Beast, Beast, when you leave me, I am alone.

When I forget its color—I am almost certain it is green—when I forget that the lining of its nasal passage is coated in opaque mucus which protects the tender tissues from any stray spires of baroque flame, I wake up in the night, shivering, sweating, groping for my notes.

I think, when I was at Arthur's candled hearth, I did not sleep at all. The mornings were all pale as the thronging winter and twice as polluted, scarred like a map, and beyond that line there were monsters, *terra incognita*, alien shores of bleached dinosaur bones, lizards like gods, and I sitting lotus-full in their center, thick as meat. And I was not off the map, I was choked with parchment, when I should have been where I belonged—with the monsters and the deep, outside the grip of longitude.

But Arthur was a beast himself in those days—the tawny bear-king slapping lazily at bees with a massive paw. I contented myself with measuring his stride and analyzing the musculature of his broad back—I told myself that was enough, to watch the lion lying on his stone slab, and his mate languid in the shadows. I told myself that there were no dragons, or if there had once been, they were long extinct, long extinguished, dead as diamonds.

But at night, I would wake and my lungs would seize, I would scramble for my cliometer and hold it to my heaving chest. I would calculate the Beast's probable heart rate, its respiration, its molting-day three years hence, until I was calm again. As time went by, more and more recitations were necessary to calm the panic burbling up in me like cauldron-brew. I was not Merlin, I could not be the old man of the law-bench and banquet-hall—I could only be the old man of the mountain, and that only by the grace of the Beast.

I longed for the mountains, the mountains which hunch and huddle like my own body, clutches of wild ponderosa and star thistle grinning in the knee-joints and elbow-sockets. I longed to sniff the baroque, three-pointed footprint of the Beast, to measure it precisely and note the length of the talons in my notebook. I longed to smell a fire gobbling up the green branches, I longed to sleep on hard ground and wake to the sound of a tail whisking by, just a little further on, always a little further on.

I didn't even have to creep, or muffle my footsteps. By the time I heard the great gate swing closed behind me, there was no one left to care that I had gone.

The scales of certain lizards are shaped like small beads. Only the beaded varieties are venomous; therefore, if one can get close enough to a specimen or obtain a corpse for study, this can be useful in taxonomy. Of course, dragons have no need of venom, being capable of generating streams of multicolored fire from glands corresponding approximately to lymph nodes in humans. My opponents maintain that there is a relationship between reports of fire and reports of venom—that the two have somehow become confused in folklore, and that the image of the great-winged, fire-breathing dragon so popular in the peasant psyche is, in fact, a small, bead-scaled creature no more than three feet in length capable of producing a venom which may or may not paralyze small vermin such as mice and voles.

It is always dangerous to leave the mountains.

If one leaves them for Camelot, one may at least be sure that one travels form linear space to linear space, that molecules and sky-motes will behave approximately as they do elsewhere.

Any other destination is suspect.

When I first went down from the granite cliffs, when I despaired of my Beast, when I had lost the trail of its scent (bayberry and sulfur with an underwaft of jimson weed) in the Butterfly Forest, I had meant to go to Camelot. After all, where could I find better maps, better records of past hunts, better genealogical archives which might have recorded sightings

long since forgotten by the peasants—in short, I meant to go for the purposes
of research. I say I meant, for Camelot did not rise to meet me, as the tales
assure one that it does, cresting the hills with its golden turrets to the sound
of trumpets and of flutes—I found darker places before I found Camelot,
places of red smoke and hushed voices. The path which was supposed to lead
up the fabled hill until Camelot itself took hold and laid itself out before the
weary traveler—me—like a new bride lost itself, curled on itself like the tail
of the Beast, and swallowed me up. I hardly knew the pebbles underfoot had
changed before I could no longer guess at the geography of England, could
no longer spin my compass to the capitol.

Around me, before I could draw breath, was a town of oak-shacks and
dark seal-heads floating grim in the morning, a town full of trickling
wells and streets that blew dust at themselves. I could see no one, only the
murk of dun and gray creeping along empty, plantless ways. I rode into the
Underworld on the singing angle of my golden sextant, eyes open, charts
asplay, and yet, and yet. I suppose I ought to have known. The place wore
all the vestments of hell: smoke closed around me, red as eyes—floats of
yellow-gold flared and sputtered in the waft, and my feet crushed the moss,
and my fingers groped for a gate. But there was no gate, no lock like a gape-
mouth slavering for its key. There was no dog—I was quite hoping there
would be a dog. I would have liked to scruff it behind the ear and call it a
nice pup, a good chap. I would have liked to take dictation, to note down its
long tale of service and meals of damned marrow thrice daily. But there was
no asphodel, and no moon-eyed wolf. I lay down on a couch of flesh, and
there was a discord of music, a silvern jangle that slid over scales as though
cut by them. Smoke vomited itself from glass pipes, from ivory lips, from
pools of paint like open veins. I fell, I fell so far, and the green fields of Dover
frayed into emerald string, into the spines of serpents corkscrewing in the
airless sky, slips of tongues like letters snapping through their phonemes. I
seemed to see a woman's face above mine, her black hair drawing its curtains
around my jaw, and she put a flute of whalebone into my throat. When she
blew, I filled with her white exhalation, fat as bellows, and my navel burst in
a spray of star-sputum.

I fell. I fell so far. And the Beast was there at the bottom, a belly as big as
the world, banded in nacre, rolling on his back, a beached turtle on black
sands.

He did not look at me—of course not. I was a mote in his perfect eye, flashing in the dim, yes, but no more than a flash. His forelegs clutched at the downbreath of Stygian air, mottled green and yellow as cholera—his bunched hindlegs flexed lazily, muscles bulbous-blue. As if in water, his jaws opened and shut, clacking together desultorily, without hunger or malice. At last I saw the pink of his cheeks, his gullet, his marvelous tail slapping heavily on some unguessable floor. A leathery plume sprouted braggart-red from his head, and oh, it was so like the plumes of those poor, ruined dolls winding down their clockwork way, fused to horses, prancing in a jerky sort of grace towards their fossil-frieze.

It was so like the plumes I wore.

Beast! Oh, Beast, when you leave me, I am so lost. I cannot paste the pages of my manuscripts together to make anything like your shape. If you were to look at me—I do not ask for more than a glance!—I would be young again for you, a boy hunting his favorite lizard across the hot stones, pricked over with bright burrs. I would be gray of eye and gold of hair for you, the height of scientific fashion. I would be hotheaded and rash, I would forget the cubic measure, I would forget, even, to note the circumference of your jeweled skull. I would be just your own lagging lord—but what is a Beast without his Huntsman?

Surely we are connected, the Beast and I, surely within that geologic musculature he knows he is mine, my Quarry. Surely his bones know that he is captive, that we are locked together in step and follow—it cannot be that he has ambled on his way and never heard a desperate pant not far—not far at all—behind.

I fell. I fell and he never glanced up, never heard the whistle of my descent, of the air through all my ticking instruments. I only fell, and fell into him, into the globe of his stomach, and the skin, the spotted, spackled, glowing skin, only gave a little before breaking under the needles of graphometers, refractometers, hydrometers, cliometers, galvanometers, and azimuths, all bristling from me like natural defenses, and they tore into him, they opened him up like an egg, and I went down into the swim of his viscous self, I went down through the banded gate, and my face was erased in the acid of him. He saw me then I am sure, I know it. His eye rolled downward to me, expressionless, yes, but he witnessed my rapture, I am certain, I am certain. In his entrails primordial I was helpless, and his black blood pooled around me like a sea lapping against a ship whose loss is forgone. But he saw the wisps of my hair and the earnest gleam of my study, even proud—he must have been proud!—to allow me to finish my work, intimate, close.

He extended that elegant snout to me and his nostrils flared sulfurous-sere. I touched it—I touched it with awe, and the warmth of his tympani-heart barreled up beneath me, slamming a sun back and forth between its sixteen ventricles, and I was a part of that violent sway.

And then my face was wet, and the woman with curtaining hair was emptying a copper flask over me, and thin-lipped she dragged me to a veiled door. The Beast was gone, the vision detonated in a splash of algae-ridden water. His belly was sewn up without me, and I could not even find his scent in the murky air. There was no gateless void, there was no endless fall, and on my instruments there remained not one drop of precious blood to tell me its secrets. I stumbled, no better than a drunk bereft of tavern, and the black-haired creature flung me from the door, into the wood and the wold again, with nothing but mewling magpies flitting stupidly ahead of me.

Beast, when you leave me, I am so lost.

Lizards utilize a combination of high heat, fermentation and stomach microbes to break down their food. Dentition is a secondary mechanism, as the fiery interior of their bodies is fully capable of both killing and in some sense cooking their prey. Teeth are used only to crop large pieces of meat for ingestion and subsequent incineration.

The structure of their gastrointestinal system is similar to that of herbivorous mammals including a greatly enlarged, elaborate colon, almost baroque in its labyrinthine design. Seared flesh passes through the small intestine into the large, cup-like anterior colon. The lizard colon contains many folds and partitions which act to slow the passage of flesh, giving increased time to fermentation and cremation while allowing time to work on the ingested foodstuff by the microbial inhabitants of the colon (protozoa, bacteria and nematodes).

The interior of a dragon is a cathedral constantly engulfed in holy flame, and the flesh of the devoured lies within, consumed in that incorruptible holocaust.

The wood is cool and pale; ashes from my night-fire still comb through the air, delicate as sheets of vellum escaped from some celestial library. There is gooseflesh. There are cracked lips. I crouch in the crevice between granite and juniper, and my knees creak—of course they creak. That is the office of an old man's bones.

It has been weeks since I found even a snapped branch that might tell of the Beast's passing. I sold all my instruments in that strange and dreaming town, to the perplexed palms of a blacksmith who will surely melt them into slag, and then into horseshoes. Somewhere a horse will clop its way from stable to hall on hooves of golden calipers and brass clockworks. I am all that is left—but I am pure, I am ready for him, I have nothing more to learn—I only ask to be in the presence of that skin-heat, that baleful eye, to in truth be in his orbit, just a small, unassuming moon, content to radiate his verdant light.

In the black-cake soil I illuminate, monk-intent, the text of my Beast, his lymph-canticle, the scripture of his taxonomy. The loam is my bestiary, and he is the only inhabitant of my dust-opus. The curve of his spine is there, the web of his toes. In the mire, his plume is enshrined, his terrible belly is recorded for the rain and the fog to witness. Tales of his ferocity, of his mercy, of his depthless hunger, insatiable, incomprehensible. The folklore of his birth is etched in pinecone and birchbark, the fire-birth of the cosmos, and he a crystalline sphere of ineffable green. I am his lonely scribe, who was once—but who can remember now?—the scribe of that other plumed beast, that other strutting sire at play in his menagerie, galloping among the tigers and serpents and great, graceful deer, the dancing bears and the hoopoe, the salamanders and the crows snapping at the tendons of winter.

I could not bear the noise. The contests of mating, the territorial screech. And in the end, I could not bear the meathouse slaughter, the shanks of wildcat piled red and dripping, the pearlescent feet pickled in so many glass jars.

The Beast is blessedly silent, he has no hooting language, no raucous claim. And if I have any fealty left in me, it is owed to the gilt-lined innards of the untouchable leviathan.

I will wait, and I will walk in the ash-strung wood.

And in the distance, there will be, before the end, a green flash in the mere.

IV THE HERMIT

Galahad

Then took he himself the Holy Vessel and came to Galahad; and he kneeled down, and there he received his Saviour.

—Sir Thomas Malory
Le Morte d'Arthur

Last night I was a lily, and very purple. I sat on the water with my toes in the silt, and my petals curled darkly up at the juniper forest. Thick violet lips reflecting the light of flickering fish deep in the lake, surfacing to nibble at my lily-flesh. But I do not taste like a dragonfly, and they never eat me entire.

A flower is very still, still in a way I can't imitate in the suntime. I grow legs and fingers and breasts, and lost my purpleness. I begin to notice imperfections—my coffee cup is chipped, I haven't made my bed in days, I stumble under the almost-raining sky like a doomed gazelle. And oh, the ocean here is not so wide or deep as I had hoped. It does not swallow me, or demand, or promise like the ocean I remember. When I am a lily I am not disappointed, the lake moves through me and I can let it.

You understand, of course. You know the nature of lakes. Water passes over you in sunlight and moonlight and grasslight and fishlight and you love it for its passage. I envy you your capacity for silence, and waiting. Do you know the Question already? Or does it wait in your mind like a hibernating bear, ready at the precise aural combination to stretch its furry legs and roar out its relief? Funny how "question" contains the word "quest" inside it, as though any small question asked is a journey through briars. You want me to push towards you, to believe in you, to want you and strive to achieve you. To be bent upon your purpose and wear white robes, passing though trees like a fiery-eyed wraith, filled with your flame. To encircle the globe with desire for you.

But a lake is a deep-within place, within a forest, or mountains. And I am by the Sea, an edge-place, the end of the world. And somehow, because it is beautiful, and sparkling, and very expensive to stand on the seashelless sand, I feel I should not be so disappointed, that I am not allowed to be.

But still, I will not come to you, will not succumb to the destiny you have written for me. This is not a quest, but a battle, and my will is as strong as yours.

Let me tell you a little story. You know it already, of course, but here in Southern California, it floats between the boardwalk shops like half a memory. You see, on the voyage home from windy Troy there was a place called the Island of the Lotus Eaters. It was on the coast of Africa (which in the Western Mind is somehow all Sahara, all sand and desert with an occasional cheetah or jackal). But the flower-eaters island wasn't like that. It was full of green, and lakes and rivers, and beautiful, bulbous blue flowers that grew everywhere like dandelions. They covered the rocks like foam, and rippled like laughter at the base of the swaying trees. Pale, child's eye blue floated over the island, and the petals tasted sweet, like spun sugar, their fuzzy texture melting on the tongue. And the men ate the flowers, and they were always happy, and serene, and they could let the water pass through them. Through the flowers shining and dancing, through the skein of cerulean and silver-white, they thought their land was the best and the most wonderful, and no one wanted to leave. Their tall ships against the bleeding sunset seemed ugly, monstrous skeletons, which had once seemed so graceful and sleek. Happiness forever seemed to hang like a jeweled necklace in the air, the promise of an eternity without intellectualized discontented winters.

And you know, the people here remind me of that a little. There is a thought that inhabits many of us, not quite generated of our own brains, that this is the best of all possible worlds. Sand and water alone somehow constitute paradise, and to be unhappy here is sacrilegious. To think this ocean different from the others and too warm. Everyone eats the flowers and never wants to leave. And I am a soldier-sailor, I want to go home, if my ship would steer that way, home from the Crusades through the musky domes of Los Angeles, the myrrh-scented incense of San Diego. The rain beads on cafe tabletops like tears, and gold-plated hooves stamp on sanctified alleyways, the smell of palm-wind and cinnamon weaving the air. I would walk these roads, if I could, where everything is gold, threads of light leading away from you, towards release and illumination. Beyond them lies destiny as I would craft it, in the mountains and rivers I have never seen. A hermitage of the crags and meadows, devouring time.

Here, in these strange lands that lie on the homeward route from broken

Constantinople, through the Red Sea and Santa Monica, gold dust covers my toes in a fine mist, it is spun out clear and pure, translucent in the windowpanes, beaten into coronas around the heads of dark-eyed women— alive? Dead?—with their bundles of rushes and blue-flowered rosemary, cobbled onto the rooftops that spread out in an infinite line, like the sea. The sun turns cities into novae.

In a thick stream, gold is drunk in coffee-shops and eaten in musky theatres. I would pull this curtain of light over my body and hide from you forever. I can see its sheen billowing behind me like a sail, making me invisible, bearing me home in a wash of sun. This, that is Holy Land, drowns in its beauty and golden lights, until there is nothing but the light, covering everything, swallowing the body and smoothing the universe into a long, gold altar cloth.

But I don't want to eat the lily; I remember what happened to Eve. Never eat the fruit another offers you. Because then I will forget what fire and darkness are. I will forget my wounds, my blood, and without my scars and sacrifice, what am I? What am I without my pain? What if I did not storm and weep and rail at the sky, if I did not leap with madness or rapture, did not pound my fists against anything? What if I did not resist? Would I know myself? Would anyone? What if I were a simple man, kind and true, full of unadulterated light, walking the earth only outside my own door, not wandering like a nomad on a bedraggled camel? What if I were not driven to do these things? What if I were not filled with desire and expansiveness? Would I be anything? Am I anything without my drive to see, to experience, to devour?

What if I never despaired, never doubted, never considered the ravening advance of time, never thought of death? What if I merely yielded to you? I would not know myself, would not recognize my own sinews. The flame that keeps my flesh crackling with light, if for a moment it were calmed and turned civilized, I would cease to be. I, the thing that is I, would vanish. If I did not resist you, did not clamor against you, did not open my throat to swallow everything, as though to ingest some power to allow me to keep out the tympani of your call.

Can you see this? Or is the bear pacing within you, the creature that yearns only for the right question to be asked to release you? Is he deaf to all other questions save that One? But last night I was the lily, and I was content, and forgot.

Last night I was a silver trumpet, and I roared out the beauty of caves for you to hear. The goblet of my metal rim gleamed in dim, smoky light. My voice was crimson and it sparked like a blacksmith's forge. I thought of you, because of your silence, because of our oppositeness. It was good to be loud and colorful at last. I have felt so much gray and amorphous lately. But to dispel that ashen self, someone had to find me, and polish me, flick my keys with their fingers to test me out, and force air and sound out of my throat. Someone's lips wrapped around me, forcing me to sing, pushing a wash of color out of me. It leaves me pale and shaking, but scoured clean. I have made something beautiful, and it is enough. I wonder if I will always need someone else to make me useful? How used to lying in a cedar box in an attic have I become, someone's once-beloved instrument, a glimmer of metal with a corona, like a Byzantine Madonna? Someone once ran their fingers along me, almost faint with desire, the music in him rushing to bloom into the world. I once carried a universe of possibility. Before potentiality sharpened to a fine edge.

Attics are soft and warm, they do not require my loudness or my weeping notes, they require only my inactivity, so that they can settle dust over me like a lover's hand. How comforting that once was. But it is only like a lover's hand, it is not. Softness and gold half-light sing the mind to darkness. And this place, the woven gold of the California desert, is an attic that wraps you in warmth like a chain. It is good to be quiet and think, but it does not quite satisfy the belly. And to be this brazen thing, to make something red, something else must supply the air, or I am silent. You understand, of course. You, too, require another to complete you. Your purpose is unfulfilled by solitude. Alone you are an old man sitting on the pier, drinking bourbon and feeding seagulls. Alone, passing teenagers toss a thoughtless coin into your gray felt hat, half-smile in pity and leave you in the dust of their red leather high heels. But this is not you at all, you are a King and it is the quest that makes you the King-Who-Waits. It is at your feet the salamander sits, showing his glinting emerald loyalty. But sometimes I smell your cigarettes from far away.

I thought of that last night, as my trumpet-voice drank the smoke of cigarettes from quietly disintegrating club-goers, and moved through a woman's hair with such softness, such an ache, taking a black strand of it tenderly from her mouth. I wanted to show you this thing, this thing that you sacrificed. You desire only the one who finds without seeking, how can I tell you what her hair felt like? How can I give you the serpentlyric I cried out over her dark head?

You stand at the center of all human paths, but you know nothing of us, of me, who you call to yourself like a child, of the woman I touched, how beautiful she was. You don't know what it is to want, except the one who can find your temple in the forest that is not of trees.

I wish I were that one, that I were innocent enough, and patient enough, and that my hands did not bleed so.

I am not your one.

You play the harp, and your notes are silver and slinkingly soft, all glissando. You call me with this wind harp, call me to the dust of the pilgrimage path through California desert instead of Byzantium. You call me to the rim of crusader's footprints. But last night, at least, I was the trumpet, and not the kind that is mournful and low. The kind that deafens the harp.

I can't help that I am too loud. My voice would break the glass of your trees. I am all fortissimo, and I can't change the need for that thumping clamor beating at the ears. I can't always be the water and the silence that you inhabit in tortoiselight forever. I'm so sorry, because I want to know, I want to walk where you have passed, and I want to see the chalice shining through the tree-shadows. But you can't make me into a crusader. This is not my quest, not my question, not my life, not my desire. Not my fault.

Last night I was a hummingbird, and it was a thoughtless jewel of green and pink, existing in between dewmeals. I tasted the thick orange-red lips of bougainvillea like dusky honey, and the jacaranda flowers like pale cold wine. There is so much desert in California, I seize like one starved upon the beauty of a few bright things alive in the dark. It occurs to me that when I write to you of my night metamorphoses, I always tell you about drinking. Perhaps because I associate you with water, and rivers, and seas and rain. My father was afraid of the water, he ran from it, all the way to the desert. But to me, you are the king of waterpaths, and I think of that all the stories I tell you, you most like to hear about the liquids I encounter. It is why you found me in California, where the sea walks in my skin. It is how

I commune with you, when I drink the lakewater, and feel the damp sky on my skin. When I am immersed in the water of your mind, I feel as though I have not disappointed you, and I am with you in the night.

Because I have disappointed you, haven't I? You wait and wait, silently watching the lake ripple in blackbirdlight, and you expect that any moment I will appear out of the shadows, cloaked in white light as you always knew I would be, and rest my head on your silver knee.

I prefer my little lives to your uninterrupted living. Last night I flittered down the street that leads west to the Pacific, I reveled in the syntheticness of the streetlights which in the movies always glimmer like tiny moons, pure and perfect. But in the world outside Casablanca, they are orange-yellow, and insects thrum around them in a corona. I could have eaten a few, when they are in the light like that, they act like opium-eaters, swaying on a wind sweet only to them. But I was not (could not be) wholly hummingbird, and mosquitoes taste like bad vodka. You live in a mythical Morocco, you wrap yourself in the sea and white streetlamps. I feel their radiant falseness on my wings.

Sometimes I hate you. Your silence claws my throat, your own private knife under my ribs. You know I will come to you, even when I run and fly with shutterblink wings to escape you. You know, and I hate that smugness, even though you are incapable of such a selfish thing as smugness.

Or is it only that I want to see you without human faults? Perhaps if you are not human it will be easier for me to submit to you in the end. Then I will have had no choice, it will not be from failure of will that I yielded.

They call you a King. The Fisher King. And if you are a King, a monarch with absolute power, not a gentle sort of steward, then it won't be my fault that I couldn't refuse to come, bearing the sun to you in my arms. It is who I am, what I was made for, for pain and the quest. If I deny it I will be driven below the waves by the weight of that denial of purpose. Is this how others will see me when all this struggle is over? Do I need you to be beautiful and sage, the father when he is still worshipped by his cherubic child? Will they need me to be perfect for them? Will they need my purity like I need yours? My inhumanity? Galahad the White, the Pure? Will a river of light be emblazoned on my shield, will that be my symbol?

But I know I am not capable of your silence, I don't want any part of this wide-gaping fate. I want to be a hummingbird, to be thoughtlessly dazzling, an aviary seraphim without the burden of paradise.

I want to be wordless.

Instead I overflow with words, offering them to you like sacrificial bulls, and if the blood runs red enough over the garlands of jacaranda, will you, Jupiter-like, release me from this?

Last night I was a salmon. Salmon go home. They have such a powerful drive towards the little stream of algaelight that threw them forth. It calls and calls them, a siren cry that promises life and death and sex all in one. You understand, of course.

You call like that, too.

Salmon are silver-rose scaled, and their eyes are pupilless and strange. This is what I was, but it was winter, and the spawning season waited on the turn of equinoxes. The sea slid through me like mercury. I swam thoughtless with thick ranks of silver-rose fish, and I was not separate from them, but they were my brothers and sisters and we were one liquid arrow of movement.

Let me tell you a longer story. You know it already, of course. A woman told me this story in a tarot-reader's shop in San Francisco, as she shuffled her cards with hands like a hawthorne tree. And I think that she knew from the lines on my palm that I would meet you when I grew up, because now I know this story is about you.

Once there was a boy, and he was very bright, the most promising child in his village. His hair and his eyes and his skin were all gold, so that he looked like a young lion. His father was very proud of him, and smiled when he saw how strong and clever his son had grown. But he worried that since everything came so easily to this boy, that he would never be the kind of man to lead the clan. So one day when the boy was fourteen years old, lean and strong and skilled with his fishing-spear, his father took him away from the village, to the edge of the forest, and told him:

"My son, I am very proud of you. You have become the strongest and cleverest of your brothers. The women in our village look at you with willing eyes. But though you are as tall as I am, you are not yet a man, and I fear that you will always be clever, but never wise. So you will go into the forest for seven days, and you will not take your fishing-spear. You will not take your hunting-knife. You will not take your water-skin. You will go away from the clan and seek the manhood you have not discovered in your father's house."

The boy was afraid, for he had never been away from the village without his father or one of his red-haired brothers. But he knew that he should not show his father his fear, and turned silently to go into the forest. But his father called after him:

"Wait, my child. Like all warriors who go into the wild, you must have a geas put upon you, a thing forbidden. Listen carefully, for if you break your geas, you will never lead the clan. Whatever you catch to eat, whether it be rabbit-flesh, or mouse-haunch, or fish from the river, you must roast it over a fire, and not touch it, or eat of it, until it has been scorched black. This is the way of your geas. Come back to me with your belly full of this scorched flesh, and you will be a man, and not merely a clever boy."

So the boy went into the forest, and he found it full of voices, the voices of trees, and streams, and the earth covered in dry leaves. For three days he could not catch a rabbit, or a mouse, or any fish, since he had not taken knife or spear. On the fourth day his belly ate at his spine, and he walked into the cold and racing river to catch fish the way he had seen the old men of his clan do to impress the boys, with their own hands and no spear. He walked into the river until it licked at his waist, and he shivered, peering into the swift water for a glimpse of silver fish.

Three times he saw a fat salmon, and three times he plunged his thin hands into the water and felt the slick animal escape. He began to cry in frustration, even though he knew it was not strong or clever to cry, and his father would be ashamed. Night was coming, and he was certain that he would never have to worry about eating foul-tasting scorched meat, because he would never be a man, because he could not catch anything.

As the shadows grew long over the water, he saw another fish, but this one was thin and small, hardly the length of his hand. Once again he pushed his hands into the icy river, and this time he felt the fish firm in his grip, and he drew it out with a whoop of triumph which the oak trees heard with satisfaction. The boy made a fire to roast his victory, and soon the salmon was blistering away in the red-gold flames. The boy thought how proud his father would be, and how his broad-chested brothers would clap him on the shoulder and tease him over the size of his catch. The smell of the fish was rich and sweet, and it was beginning to blacken.

But the boy was a boy, and very hungry. He looked at the fish, which was not at all scorched yet, and with the eyes of hunger thought it to be quite black enough for him to have a little bite. He put his fingers into the fire to tear off a piece of fish, but the flames burned his thumb and forefinger, and he put them to his mouth to ease the pain.

And then the boy saw why he had been forbidden to do this. For some of the oil of the fish was on him, and when he tasted it he knew in a torrent all the things in the universe, and he understood the voices of the trees, and the river, and the earth covered with dry leaves. He knew the thoughts of his father and his mother and his red-haired brothers. He knew all the things that were and would be, and he knew that he could not now lead the clan.

So the boy went deeper into the forest, further than any of his clan had been. And he was mad for a long time, with these things scorching his mind. But one day the madness passed over him, and he was a pool of standing water with the moon on his back, and he stayed in the forest, finding his fate in the deep-within places.

And your father wept, for you never came again to the village.

Perhaps that salmon was like me, not a salmon, not at home in the fish-skin, a wanderer whose journey to the sea ended in your campfire. I journey to the sea now, that's where all these forms take me, slowly, against my will which is not strong enough, to you who wait in the forest, on the long pier in seagullight, at the end of the gray and foggy streets of Southern California. Because all these places are the same place, and I know with the certainty of an earnest seeker that the locus of the Grailcastle is nowhere/ cannot be sought, unless one eats the salmon and his insides are lit up by it like a silver-rose lantern.

Last night I was a pen, and it was a sigh of movement. Motion, motion, linear and serene. My consciousness focused in the brass tip, fierce and sharp, devouring the parchment in swoops and whorls of black ink, diving like a seabird, in and out of the golden sea of paper, catching fat fish of verbs and participles in my metallic beak. And swept back, the rest of me flowed like a wave of light, into a long, creamy feather tipped in scarlet, I quivered and vibrated with the shivering motion of writing, illumination, conjugation, culmination of thought, spilled in a rush onto the expanse of page.

I danced with myself: tip, quill, ink, in waltzing time, Viennese in the extreme, the vanilla of silken feather as it crossed highways of finely wrought paper, crescendo, denouement, a box-step of being, tip yielding to the forward motion of statement. I yielded, yielded, to the waxy cold of the scholar's hand that deftly drove my length, his skin made phosphorescent by moonlight singing in through the iron-crossed window, shifted into cobalt by the stained glass. We swam in blue, were washed in it, purified as though floating in the hand of a river-nymph. The scholar's lashes fractured the light, casting long, sweeping shadows on the page, blue within black within blue, bars of darkness breaking the expanse of watery light, as though waves blowing forwards and back, whitecaps of my own quick steps through the lines.

It was relief. I did not have to create. The salve of his icy hands on my feather-spine, flowing over me in a blanket of snowy flesh, silencing my voice grown so hoarse with speaking, with screaming over the sea to be heard. He slid me through words, through the alpha and the theta, through the wide forest paths of chi, the violet shadows of omega. He made his letters carefully, small and delicate, dipping me into his little clay pot of ink which swirled around and into me in a rush of glistening darkness, like the Nile through the throat of a crocodile, glutted my mouth with black, with thick, with the absence of light.

It flowed in and out of me with equal ease, in inklight and moonlight, and I could let it because I did not initiate motion, because I was an instrument and not the voice, the ever-sounding voice that could not afford silence for a second, else the world would fail. I could release something nameless and accept the passage of liquid through me, and its pouring of self onto a valley of dry and rasping manuscript. The glyphs formed so beautifully, shimmering slightly before drying. The cuneiform magic of their arch and fall sang through me.

And yet how strange to be vertical, held upright like a heron poised on one leg, maintained in a tall line, the mast of a ship catching wind and expelling storm. How strange to feel inkblood draining out of me, all sensation focused downward as the vellum received my raven-throated exhalations. Horizontal is the direction of dreams, of the otherworld, of sharp-hoofed Time and the eventuality of death. Thus we lie on slabs and mounds of furs, on cots and grasses. We lie and gaze upwards into a sky-mirror, there to see ourselves become fantastic, become legend. Verticality denied me this, I could not cast upward to the sun. I was timeless in the hand of icicle-skin, without present, in motion so slidingly that pause by death or dream was inconceivable.

Is this what you feel, out beyond the breakers, beyond the desert and the stream? You do not move, but are in motion, shaking with it, sylphlike in the water-shadows and reeds? Your tentacles and umbilici snake out over the miles of earth and sand, coils of bodylight snatching at the air to find a remnant of me still gasping in the wind.

I want to shake you, as I have been shaken by you, to see the lake ripple behind your eyes and demand, demand, demand:

"Why are you drawing me?"

My voice is pathetic to my own ears, a whimpering, sheeting tears, child's wet-nose:

"Why me?"

Why is my figure so circumnavigated in your mind, so realized and defined, drawn as surely as a an angel out of Raphael, shaded and colored by your palette alone? Why am I bound to you?

It isn't worth anything, protestation. In these metamorphoses how rarely do I have pockets for a few dismal coins, but no lump of copper or silver would make a single cry of negation a thing of substance or meaning. I know it, I know it, I know why this road was built, why it goes forward and not back, what lies at its end.

I am peeled like a raw almond, bright green, down to the pure whiteness of fruit, so that you can take my skinless and shivering form into yourself and make me like you. Purity flows from your hand like a curling vine, and you will have me white or not at all. Purification, purification, scouring the sands of rivers dark and hushed from my arms, pulling the mosaic teeth of ritual crocodiles from my feet streaked with the black mud of the Delta. My body is restful and leaping and rippling like the lake that bore the sword, but it cannot yet birth such a thing.

I hate what you want to make me. You encourage my limbs, seduce them into rigidity, into dissolution, into the silver aurora of a blade, beguile the line of my lips into the twisted gold of a hilt. Or is it the stem of a Cup into which you would have my body form itself? My mouth open to the heavy sky in its silent howl to mold the agate and ivory bowl of the chalice? Are the very fingernails of my hands to comprise the milky jewels of its rim?

Yes, I am angry. I have floated like a barge of lashed birchwood on the fantasy of my Will, and you steal it from me. Every time you smile beneath the curtain of your briar-beard, every time your face goes benevolent and sorrowful my hatred rumbles like a sheet of tin. If I shrink into the corner of a cinnamon-scented café, if I bury my face in a chipped green cup so that the steam will encircle and hide me from you, you appear before me to ask in infinite gentleness if I want another.

If I recede behind a bookcase in the Library, examining the bindings, you materialize to tell me that silence is mandatory in such places. I cannot escape you and I will never forgive you that. Only in the nights, as I flee into shapes and lines not my own do I find respite from your compulsion and sympathy. You see in me some core of purity beneath all that which does not exist. You will allow me no humanity.

Last night I was a a glass of beer. I was foamy and golden, and slender and bitter-earthy. I think I was a microbrew of some kind. I sat on a coaster with a picture of a mallard flying low over a marsh on it. The marsh was wet with spilled bourbon. I sat for a while the woman who bought me talked to her suitor, laughing synthetically and stroking her swan-cheek with grape-colored fingernails.

I wondered if I could taste myself while she regaled him with tales of her corporate dragon-slaying. If I could taste my own liquidlight, then I would know myself, whether the foreigners I feel was by the brewer's design. But while I mused on the taste of myself, the woman stopped trying to be seduced and sipped me in silence. I felt the warmth of her throat, the slickness. I sighed into the heat of her body, letting desire pass over me in sunlight and moonlight and grasslight and fishlight, and I did not try to hold it with both hands. Soon I had passed of necessity from the beerself to the glasself,

and I rested in my own emptiness, foam clinging to my cupbody. I was transparent, the clarity of my bones was sweet, and I reflected a myriad of eyes, like a crystalline Argus. And for a moment, in this glass in an antediluvian bar, in the hands of a sad and lovely woman whose belly cried inside her I was the grail, open and clear. For a moment which slid away as quickly as a strand of beerfoam, I was no longer my own ever-striving self, but a chalice of blown glass, yawning to encompass the sky and the sea, floating in dolphinlight, I was not a questing knight with tobacco-stained hands, I was you, the king in the forest, and I wept into my own lake, watching the ripples expand into fractal infinity.

And then I was not a glass, or beer, or a lily, or a fish, and the grailight was gone. I was alone in the dark, and even the alcoholic fishermen who dread their children had dragged themselves home. I crumpled in the shade of a brick building, my belly betrayed my grief and I vomited the Pacific into the street, my throat flaming—I was the Chinese boy who drank the sea, and I gave it back and back until no more would come and still my body convulsed in anguish for the moment I could not keep. In fear for my sanity, in fear that I was a hallucinatory Fool with the black dog at my back, who dances in beerlight alone on the cliff edge to the tune of a man who may not/I want not to exist.

And I was ashamed of this so-human act.

Last night I was my father. I looked at my mother from above her body, and I saw, not her face, but the face of another woman, with hair like the spaces between stairs. I did not understand, and when her mouth shifted, red to pink, it became my mother's mouth, the mouth I knew, and in my father's skin I cowered, I crawled away from the slick of her belly, and the moon rolled out of my mouth.

Last night I was my father, and I went into the desert. I yearned for the cup, the cup, always the cup, the thing you offer me so easily, that he could never hope to touch. His hands were hung with women—my hands are empty.

You cannot bear any hands which remember other grails. They must be pure, they must have been waiting for you since they first turned brown in the sun. My father died in the desert like a man who stuffed his mouth with peyote, and when he returned, his eyes were full of dead lakes. He patted my head and draped himself over a cross until the chapel stank of his sour sweat and shit. He never spoke to me, not a scrap of scripture or drunken curse for my mother—in both his hands he gave me silence like a black ball of opium.

But last night I squatted in his skin as though it were a sacred hut, I breathed the sage-smoke rolling off of his bones, I drew patterns in the sand which had settled on the roof of his stomach. I put my toes into the water that filled him, and writhed with him under the rain-bringing moon. I was sick with the thickness of him, I asked for nothing but escape, I longed for my salmon-skin—yet I had swum to the stream of my birth, as a salmon must, and the water choked me. I spluttered and flailed in the wake of it, trying to touch the rim of my mother, somewhere in his desert geography—but she was not there. I was not there. We did not exist for him; we were not the saguaro and the yucca. This is what I understood in his marrow—I was encased in a vial of water, and he wanted only sand.

And now I seek the waters of you, because no black-eyed queen ever looked at me with fire cutting her fingers.

In the cell of him, floating over my mother and the painted desert, I tasted the apple-bile of his sorrow, and forgave that cairn of murdered words. Perhaps I would not have survived that gaze.

He should have known better than to seek you in the wild—a cup is a thing of the city, it is civilized, it sits at a hundred thousand tables and travels from wood to mouth. A cup is only needed when joined hands at the river have failed, when an adobe hut is raised up, and a stone oven shaped into the wall, and dried flowers thrown into a pot. He sought the Lady, I seek the King.

Perhaps there is no difference, perhaps the King wears a gown of river-white, and the Lady binds her breasts under an ermine robe.

Last night I was Lancelot, and I fathered myself on a woman I hated, and I begged forgiveness from a lake of night.

So this is the end.

I walked with heavy feet to the end of the pier last night, and looked into the sea which is the rim of the western world, and wondered when I accepted that this was inescapable. I still hate that you did not think me strong or clever enough to turn from this road. (And of course I was not.) But there on the pier was a little fisherman's hut, white paint curled back by sea wind, and it glowed softly in porcelainlight.

I stood outside for a long time, and the door seemed to grow to enormity, to much for me to dare. I felt and still feel that this is all too big for me, that I am a salamander before the throne of the King of Spears. The threshold mocked me, and whispered that I was a very clever child, the strongest and cleverest of my brothers, but I would never, never be wise, there is no forest deep enough to purify me, my madness will last and last. So in the end it was pride that drove me through the door, that I would show myself to be pure enough, just barely, to finally see you.

And there you were,

not so powerful-looking, an aging man, but not infirm, the gold of your hair not quite conquered by snow. You sat in a deep leather chair, your left hand held an ancient fishing-spear, your right held a cup of living glass. Yet in the lines of your body there was a darker shape, a liquid self moving behind the lines of your skin, holding black-tipped breasts out to me with both hands, like a sacrifice.

You looked at me with laughing eyes, and I saw that sleek shape moving behind them. I wondered then if I saw you with a beard because I could only give myself over to a father, to a King, and the rest was beyond my touch—pure enough for you, but not for her. I suppose it doesn't matter, in the end—if you are doubled, if you are twinned, I will know in a moment, when the chair is mine, and I vanish into the glass.

You could not speak, that was not the ritual, it was mine to ask the question you have desired. But you laughed because you understood, of course. You know the nature of quests. You know that this has been the question, all these words to you on the road to this temple/hut. You know that my fighting has burned this body hollow, and made it ready for this. You know that the end of the quest is silence, only the quest is the sound and dancing and galloping toward.

And so I reached out, able to do nothing else but dare this thing, and touched the rim of the cup/lake.

And the burning filled my vision.

And the sea swallowed my voice.

XVI THE TOWER

Mordred

The art of war, then, is governed by five constant factors, to be taken into account in one's deliberations, when seeking to determine the conditions in the field:

I. Moral Law

*Moral Law causes the people to be in complete accord with their ruler,
so that they will follow him regardless of their lives,
undismayed by any danger.*

The morning before the war begins, there is not much to do but sit on a sand-choked embankment and tell yourself lies about how you got here.

I am a good liar. I have always shown a talent for it. When other children were discovering that they could paint or sing as though their little throats were coated in gold, I reached within my own skin and drew out a body of falsehood, a chalice-eyed homunculus with beautiful fingers, clasped together in saintly gesture. This other boy was more pleasing than I, he stood straighter and rode with thighs more steady. When he spoke, glittering ladies patted his scarlet cheek and called him clever; when I spoke, they yawned and asked if perhaps the room had not become uncomfortably cool. It was not long before I had given myself over entirely to him, his baroque, mincing speeches, his fantastic tales of his own marvels, his great strategies—oh, the strategies, the ambitions! Laid out like a litter of manticore at his bedside, how they grew and grew, and how their tails bulged with venom. The lies lay over my tongue like a melt of stained glass, and I was praised, I was praised for them.

I came to the desert and lied a war into the golden air. The other boy rode very high on a brown horse and hoisted a banner into the sun-hung sky. He made it look beautiful; he made it look like a war—everything glittered as it ought, everything spangled and shone the way it will before blood and lymph come slithering out onto the thirsty dust. I walked the walls—ah, those light-swallowing walls!—I walked the ditches and the drainage pits, I watched the city chuff out its jeweled effluvia and starve for more than it could eat. I came to the fat city of skinny angels and tasted the salt of its sweat, and my tongue was as crystalline with lies as ever it was. The city shivered in delight; lies are her peculiar fetish.

Besides, men would hardly know how to fight a war if it did not look like a war, if the lies did not line up in formation, if lies did not sit about with rifles and knives leaning against trees, chewing black bread, cracking jokes and knuckles and hiding the shaking of their hands. If there were no lies floating through the morning fog—that strangling, choleric fog, even in the desert, even so, when the sea is not so far off, when behind the bolt of mountains sailboats in turquoise marinas dip their prows like women's needles through the surf, that filthy, shit-sludge fog, nicotine-wet, sops up all imaginable sound—if lies did not prick through it they would not even know to blow their trumpets twice, three times. Lies stick to everything, even the sun, forcing that warm, balding brow below the horizon like the victim of a drowning.

My little fire is a recalcitrant smear of red in the brown and the gray, the unfathomable gray, and the scrub crackles on the coals, manzanita and pine, sending up a fragrant, clutching smoke which is, in the end, indistinguishable from the fog.

The other boy, with his crow-tongue a-grin, says that we are here, in the mountains where the river Cam flashes green and gold and the aqueducts glare straight and narrow through the land like cutting knives, because our father is wicked, and it is the duty of all those who carry light in their bellies to thrust something very sharp into the wicked. He says that it is the natural way, for the wild and toothed to tear apart the house of order before it freezes the world into statuary, before it spasms in a glut of compulsion, and all men walk gray and dull, in lockstep, abased before the altar of chivalry. He says our father is a goat dressed up in a tin tuxedo, and the sun ought shine on a finer beast than that, a jungle-beast, a desert-beast, a thing with red teeth and hindquarters rampant. We are here, he says, because we are the apostles of a savage virtue, and we must teach it to the old debauch.

That is what he says.

I crouch here with the small of my back against the stone wall, the concrete stinking and steaming, peering into the ripples of gold, the otherworld-veils hanging from the sky. I am afraid to walk in the fog—it gnaws at my vision, and I cannot see. I am afraid to go down to the sea, into the other city, which shows against the daub and wattle of Camelot like a metallic negative: many-knived and spiraling.

It is not long before we are all—soldiers, cooks, squires, smiths—weeping like pieta in the brume, salting the earth with secret tears, pissing ourselves fearful. It comes blooming up from the city and fills our gullets like old beer, brown and sickening. The sere of it, the cough and lag and blear of it, blinds and burns, bubbling over our knuckles like bile from some wasting creature.

The roof-tiles of the city are musky and mired in the brown, as we are musky and mired on the desert rims of those ghost-streets, as the streets are musky and mired in their wheeling and spoking, out from some center I cannot guess at. The mute, silent squalor pricks at my eyes, and the horizon wavers like a lie, and there is no father in this, the throat-saw and the sour-eyed bleed. There is no order or pride, no frieze of dead lords marching, nothing but spittle and the scrub, the unending sun—I can see nothing, nothing at all.

Hinc illae lacrimae, hinc illae lacrimae.

There has never been any father, only a burning plain skirted in stone, and a boy vomiting his breakfast into the weeds.

I do not know why I am here at all.

II. Heaven

Heaven signifies night and day, cold and heat, times and seasons.

My mother has no name. Or she has dozens—but when you have so many, like jewel-boxes lined up around a great, high bed, it is just as well to say you have none. Her nameless womb crushed my body into something like a boy's shape, something like limbs and skull and digits, something like primogeniture, something like alive. Did she have dark hair? Did she keep her milk? Did she watch the umbilicus that once connected us shrivel and blacken like a spent candlewick? Each of these things she kept in a box by her bed, boxes of silver and chalcedony and iron slugs. Each of these she kept locked away from me like a name, and I never knew them scattered clear on my hands like drops of water.

But isn't that always the way? How we rotten, errant sons do love to drape our worm-eaten souls around our mother's shoulders. My mother didn't love me: the chanson of the tyrant.

My mother loved me. I believe it; that must make it so. Out of all those names I pull a woman-aggregate: she had dark hair. She played with my toes. When I took my first step, she was there to tell me I had pleased her. When I crawled under light-diffuse linens next to her, and her black hair branched all around like an old tree, there was always milk, secret and sweet, and her voice was a consonant-less hum, like bees or gray wings.

I do not remember these things, but I would like to. The other boy remembers them—he says that we looked so like her that it was whispered we had no father at all. But then, lies involving parentage are the most common of all, and he mastered that species early on. I watched them with each other: dark mother sopping at the skirts with lakewater and my double, my twin, whose tongue was all bound up in deceitful sapphires. There was always milk for him, yes, but I was always thirsty.

What was the first lie?

Do you love your mother?

Yes.

No, no, that came later, later, when there was no more milk for either of us, only empty, hardened breasts, and linens rough and unbeaten, and hair like snakes snapping. The first lie, which seeded me with my brother as though I were a woman, and she a father:

Isn't he lovely? I am his aunt.

And the other boy formed inside me, like water freezing to the shape of its bottle. This other boy who was her nephew, who was charming, precocious, and doesn't he look marvelous in his uniform, marching along just like a little soldier! But I was her son, inside the golden clockwork boy, pawing at her under the bedclothes, with only her sorrow-bent stare to feed me: they cannot know. *If they knew they would take you from me.*

But still, I was born a lie, I was made a secret, and that sort of thing can't help but leave a mark, like a slap. How could I be anything other than this, hunkered down in the dunes with the scorpions lashing their tails at the moon? A man told his sister he loved her—what of that? Tawdry tragedy, except that a child was all hung with shadows, a child that no one could ever know about, lest it get its fool head knocked out on some unfortunate granite stairs.

I am no one.

I was not supposed to be.

I have no name, either. No one would give me one, for to name a thing means it is real, it exists, it displaces air.

Please, father, look at how I move the air around me. I am right here. Look at me.

III. Earth

Earth comprises distances, great and small;
danger and security; open ground and narrow passes;
the chances of life and death.

This is La Cienega. This is Camlann. There is a river; there is a sea; there is sand and the wend of snakes rattling through the throat-scoured soil. There is stone and a road and light like albumen floating yellow and white. I walk down to the city because I have to, because the light is also a lie, but it lies only about itself, and is holy. I have always been told that light is holy. Even I cannot quite imagine a world where the dark is sacrosanct—I am a mushroom fulminating in shit and decay, but still I acknowledge the sun, though it too lies. It lies and says it is the center of everything, the source of all possible light.

I go into the city because my mother lives there still, and my father will smell her like a deer, and go after her, hoping to find her gracefully bent in the snow, her nose snuffling out acorns under the ice. I know she would never do such a thing; I look for her as she is. This is her place, all full of glamors and illusions and images spinning.

A son told his mother he loved her. What of that? I have heard of a man in Thebes who fucked his mother—he made four children in her, two kings, two beauties, and one of those beauties was an anti-establishment revolution in a twelve-year-old's body. Certainly this bested the previous score of one shriveled, club-footed boy, marked on that tired womb with a Greek fingernail. I confess I had hoped, too, to best my father, to people the vineyards and humble little rivers with laughing, dark-eyed revolutions. But somewhere in the city's dark crease she found a lesson learned: no more children hung with shadow, no more lies hung upside down from a weeping woman, umbilicus black and blaming on their little throats.

No more nephews, she said to an apothecary with eyes like spinning wheels, whose counter was greasy with *aqua vitae* and typical tonics—what otherworld physic does not vend hemlock, belladonna, mandrake? The wheels clicked round—thirty times left, twenty times right, ten times left again, and out of a dry drawer popped her panacea, and though her legs were open to me her body was shut, and she put her hand on my face when I came to her and whispered that a ruin called to a ruin, and what were we both but stones already crumbling, and what did it matter after all, what was any of it but solace, and solace she had, solace thick as clouds.

The other boy breathed heavy and gold. The other boy told her to lie to him.

I love you, she said.

We never spoke of my father when I was young. The universal pronoun. The only possible him. He hung in our house like Cicero's head, but we never looked, we never spoke of it, how its blood dripped on the tablecloth, spattering the spoons. Instead of a father I had two crows, pets caught out on the moor by young girls with leather cages and horsewhips at their hips. I did not call them Thought and Memory. I called them Gaheris and Agravaine for the brothers who were not brothers, and therefore would not look at me, would not speak to me, but chased the girls with the leather cages and caught them round the throat like thrushes. I called my birds brothers and they cawed in my ears, perched on my bed while I slept, shook their feathers and clacked talons against wood when my mother lay beside me.

Gaheris and Agravaine pick through the trash which blows along the central thoroughfare of Camlann, which is Los Angeles, which is not a road but a river, which is not a river but a road—Gaheris picks up the refrain, disappearing down alleys glutted with old paper, crying: *a river is a road, a river is a road*—gray and flat, ripple-less, proceeding on and empty, and if she is there, if my mother is there and my father, I can catch no sight of them from here, where lights flicker behind monoliths—light of the moon? Of stars? Of sickness and electric haze? Agravaine tosses a beetle into the air and severs it with a snap of his black beak.

The sun is coming up, banging over the black hills like an old, dirty shop-sign.

IV. The Commander

*The Commander stands for the virtues of wisdom,
sincerely, benevolence, courage and strictness.*

There is a crown lying on an iron grating. It is studded with opals and cat's eyes. A crown always watches you, you know. Watches for the smallest weakness, the smallest excuse to roll off, grinding over the ground to another bone-battered skull. It sees me, but it won't move towards me, not the smallest inch.

The other boy would grab for it. Gaheris and Agravaine, my crows, my true brothers, snap at the blinking jewels. I hunch under a little bridge and stare at the circle of metal. The troll under the bridge—when have I been anything else? I am crypt-hidden; I am secreted, and the secreted thing wants nothing more than to come into the light—no, to be beckoned into it, to be called, to be invited. The other boy put on a coat of red and black; the other boy stood at attention and drilled the mission into me.

We are here because the old man has bound himself up in virtue, and would bind the rest of us so, would tell us how to be, how to think, would tell us what was right, what creature virtue, and no inch of space would be left for us to see behind him, beyond him, to see anything but him. He would take up our vision like a sun, a lying sun who screeches that he is the source of all possible light, and would burn our eyes under we saw nothing but holes in the sky, purple and green. Of course, those he loves, those he cannot live without will be pardoned, with a kneel and a dry kiss, for any breach.

Except us. We are unforgivable. His whoring wife has grace and we have a broken staircase and an old beehive, exile that tastes like desert weeds.

The old man worships order, and those who worship order cannot abide anything which is not-order. We are not-order. We are a cut in the immaculate flesh. We are not allowed to be; he will not let us be. He is not Hammurabi, not Moses—what right has he to hand us laws in stone?

I put my head on my knees. I want to be called into the light. I am here to be asked into the gold, to be beckoned, I am here to stand on the stone and wait for my father to tell me it was all a mistake—had he only known, had he only known.

A river is a road, caws Gaheris, down a gutter, past a courtyard which still seems to hold the refuse of pilgrims, old relics sucked dry of divinity, shoes more hole than leather, crosses dented and softened at their joint by rust and rain, swords and sackcloth and old paper, blowing in whip-wound dervishes, tentpoles and helmets and bibles empty of pages. They were here, in Camlann, on La Cienega, in Holy-Land. I am here—I should not have come down into the city. Cities connect to each other, some dark, glittering network, they know each others' secrets, they pass each other's fluids down sluices of concrete and thatch and creaking, swinging iron.

Once, I saw my mother as he must have seen her. She was down at the riverside, fishing with her hands. We lived alone by then, the other sons gone, the young girls she collected like butterflies alighting on her lips grown and wandering, wild as she. We were alone, she and I and that old crumbling manor with its stairs breaking off into nothing, an arm dashed at the wrist. We ate honey from her bees and wore cloth spun from her spiders and chewed the bones of her frogs and my mother was always the queen of small and creeping things—which is why she drew me from the deck for a son, I suppose.

I saw her waist-sunk in the river, her long black hair floating around her like water-snakes, her strong brown face searching the sun-flattened ripples—and now and again she would pull a squirming, gasping fish up to look it in the eye before smashing its bony head against a flat stone. She always did that, looked her fish, and her bees and her spiders and her frogs, in the eye before spilling their brains out on a stone. The light was so bright on her hair that it shone blue, and I saw, for a moment, how a brother could not care, could see nothing but the blue in her, nothing but that dancing cyan, and move staircases and rivers and worlds to touch it with one finger of his hand.

We crouched by the stump of a rotten elm, the other boy and I, unified for once in our admiration for the long lines of blue that shot back from her clear brow. We felt like our father, primeval and golden and never secret, as though we could stride towards her just then, just then, and she would welcome us as she had welcomed him. We felt as though she was constant, her blue was constant, and we had a right to the blue, inherited, just like this blasted land, from that tattered old lion we would spend every day after chasing.

That was the first night we spent in her.

In the mere, in the mire and the rubble and the slow blinking light of a street in the other-city, the fairy city I touch only now, after they have both passed before me into it, along the slow, creeping aqueducts which steal water from richer lands, I see—yes?—a flash of blue dancing forward, a long line like fishing-silk, and I will not, I will not call her name, not any of them, as I run after it, as my feet catch on old bottles and broken windows, as my breath comes hoarse with the poisoned air. I will not. The other boy makes me a fool.

He calls joyously into the shadows.

Morgan. Morgause. Morgana. Mother.

V. Method and Discipline

By method and discipline are to be understood the marshaling of the army in its proper subdivisions, the graduations of rank among the officers, the maintenance of roads by which supplies may reach the army, and the control of military expenditure.

A father hangs in the dark like a noose, his feet already reliquaried, his brainpan already opened to silver needles, dissection-angelic, searching for the kernel of light that must make a king a king.

But he is not dead yet and all I can see is the shape of him against the night. The smell of the desert is coming over the hills: not sweet sage and agave, but dead mice, old bones, and the droppings of buzzards. The shape of his back. Of his lie. But I am the shape of his lie and I cannot be expected to do anything in this place but stand my ground and tell him that order is inherently oppressive, as though that means anything at all when our eyes are the same shade of green, and our forefingers crook identically to the left.

The other boy's forefinger is straight as an accusation.

There are men back there, beyond the hills, who are playing ridiculous games with rattlesnakes, baiting the poor green creatures, laughing when they snap. They came because I told them to, and I am very beautiful when I command, and they didn't want to pay a pair of oxen to the old king when a little sweat-work might save the cow and make the new king look kindly on them.

I will not be king. I know that. Secrets aren't kings. Genealogies are meant to be worn on one's chest, not held under the tongue like a communion wafer. I wait for it to melt and it stays hard and sharp against my mouth. The other boy still thinks there is a destiny here. I have heard his wife never had a child; I would have given her one, if I had survived this place. If she had had blue in her hair. And that boy would have been king and no one's nephew—but you cannot be king when you cannot, even for a moment, stand in the light. I knew it when I came here, I knew it when I walked off of the desert like sea-fog pooling in a valley, I knew it when I followed my mother to him like a hyena following the water to a wounded gazelle. The crown wouldn't look at me. He wouldn't look at me.

She is standing in the Pacific, waist-sunk. The sun is on her hair. Her dress billows like a sail. She is the ship of dreams.

Did you grow up strong?

Yes, the other boy lies.

I'm glad.

She reaches into the salt foam and pulls me in beside her, her cold, wet hand on the nape of my neck. She looks me in the eye.

It's surprising how much a body weighs. I can't remember which corpse I dragged along the beach, though it seemed like my own black insides pouring out on the sand, over the little holes the sand-mites make with their leaping. It seemed like his gut opening clam-thick. We are both so black inside, and maybe he was a secret, too. Secrets beget.

The other boy leaps and slaps his thigh in triumph, struts like a yellow-headed parrot, teaches lessons so that our father will know how wise we have become in his absence.

When seeking to determine the military conditions, let them be made the basis of a comparison, in this way: Which of the two sovereigns is imbued with the Moral Law?

This is what happens: the son replaces the father. It's the heart of every story. But I am not in a story. I never existed, he was my uncle, wasn't he? Silly boy, thinking you had a father, that you started in someone's body. I stuck in my father as he stuck in my mother and there was so much black, so much red, and his eyes were so tired. I walked from his ruin, ruin from ruin, and the flags went up in the distance, the flags, and the trumpets' long, clear calls.

Which of the two generals has most ability?

This is what happens: the king is sacrificed; the new king ascends. I didn't want to hang him on the oak tree, I didn't want my crows to peck at his intestines. I didn't want to watch him remember that he had a son once before the moon ate his skull in one swallow. The other boy was so sure, so sure he was right, that this one thing was no lie: the old king was rotten, corrupt, cuckolded, senile. It was our duty. This is how histories of the kings of frozen islands are written. I stepped up, behind his body, and there was only the same oak tree, wide as the world, and waiting.

With whom lie the advantages derived from Heaven and Earth?

This is what happens: a boy sees his father in the dark, and calls out to him. The father turns, not, in the end, particularly surprised. He sees blue in his son's hair, and almost manages a smile. The other boy leaps first, and he can taste the metal of the cat's-eye crown, and the family cuts into itself like meat. They lay together on the beach, and there are sandpipers all around, and the sun is over the horizon, whitened to a tumor by fog.

It was an accident. I meant only to show him I was strong. He was always too old for this; his bones like an string-necked chicken's. A lung shot through with blue like a woman's hair spat blood into his mouth. I cradled his head as if he were my son. When he died, the grief was like a child in me, though my stomach lay open and bleeding, a gift of his antler-hilted knife. I gave birth and the strangled child was death, our death, and I whispered songs to him while the gulls snapped mussels from the gray-spackled rocks.

I never touched her, you know. Did you really believe all that Oedipal nonsense? The other boy told you that—he is convincing, an orator wrapped in white. He was always the best of us. I was no Sphinx-solver, I could not fill her up with kings. I slept against her; she was so cool and soft, as if her strands of blue retreated in the night and ran all through her body. I slept against her as a son will. And once, oh, once, my breath so thick in my throat, like throttling wool, I cupped her breast in my hand and she turned that great black stare on me—father, you know that stare—it rippled with such pity. She took my chin in her hand. She looked me in the eye.

You look like your father.
Who is my father?
The man you look like.

I came to the city. I looked into a mirror of flesh and it broke, a long silver crack.

This is what happened: I killed my father. He got his knife into me when I leapt—stupid, not to keep my guard up.

The streets shine with flotsam.

XXI THE WORLD

Bedivere

*Then Sir Bedivere departed, and went to the sword, and lightly took it up, and
went to the water side; and there he bound the girdle about the hilts, and then
he threw the sword as far into the water as he might; and there came an arm
and an hand above the water and met it, and caught it, and so shook it thrice
and brandished, and then vanished away the hand with the sword in the water.*

So Sir Bedivere came again to the king, and told him what he saw.

—Sir Thomas Malory
Le Morte d'Arthur

*Therefore, said Arthur unto Sir Bedivere, take thou Excalibur, my good sword,
and go with it to the waterside, and when thou comest there I charge thee throw
my sword in that water, and come again and tell me what thou there seest.*

It's amazing how heavy a sword really is. You never think about it—spend
your life heaving them into wood and silk and leather, into earth and mire
and stone, into bone and meat. It becomes part of you—you do not have a
hand of flesh, but an arm which ends in metal, a long, curving finger which
accuses, always accuses. You stop thinking about how thick and still it sits
in your fist, the heft of it, the swing and the slog of it. It's a hammer, and a
club, it's your own bone and gristle, and if the light is beautiful on the blade,
if it is even like water, like a lake-edge, that does not mean that it was built
for less than cutting, less than bludgeoning, less than pulling flesh from
flesh.

You told me to come here, and the sea is on the shore like a tablecloth,
more blue than I have seen together in all my days. I am tired, tired in my
perfect sinews—recall how they used to call me that, how the women used
to cheer for Bedevere, the Knight of the Perfect Sinews, and I never knew if
it was mockery or not, if they snickered at my stump-wrist while praising
the one hand left to me. But we were young, we were so young, and names
of that sort seemed so important.

I am tired—there is no water here which is not full of salt, no wind that is not a hot clutch at the throat, a flaming sash, a flaming favor. I cannot see what color I might have been before the blood, before your son's blood—how heavy was he, too, when I pulled him from you like a skin from an apple!—my blood, your own clotted last. The books always say that a dying man's face is gray—I always thought that a poet's silk-calved dream of what death might be, but your face, your face with its evening stubble stippling the skin like grass, it is gray after all, gray as the moon, and I am still so warm and red.

It is not a one-handed sword, your old blade, and I had to drag it from your body to the sea, two limping footsteps and a deep, worrying furrow in the sand. Bees buzz around my gore-stuck hair and lizards snap at fleas in my shoes. Kelp collects at the sword-tip; wet sand pulls and sucks at it, as though the earth would have it before the brine. My good arm aches as though I spent the day heaving a silver axe into cedar—you used to tease me when I filled my own wood-grate, told me you had men to do that for us.

Of course you do, Arthur, I said, you have me.

There are islands out there, beyond the sunline, but I cannot see them except as lashes of whipped light against a too-bright horizon. Dawn slants down like a glass window dropped into the whitecaps, and the whole world is waterside, how am I to know where to throw it? How am I to know where it ought to fall? How can I choose the place, who was never one of you, one of the boys who heads beamed with so much light that to look in on your suppers was to look into a painting, choked with coronae. I never wore anything on my head but my hair, and you were all too beautiful for me to feel like much more than an altarboy at some terrible, radiant Mass. I was thick at the ankle, at the waist, at the shoulder, no part of me was slender or elegant. They called me perfect and I winced at the lie, at the joke, the hulking man who could hardly cut his own meat for the mottled stump at his wrist where his hand used to be.

But I know you did not mean to be cruel. Such a thing was not in you.

Of all the places I went at your side, I never imagined this would be the last, this long strand, like a thick rope laid below the dark city, the strange half-place where the Cam whorled and looped into the not-Cam, into a road I could hardly fathom as a road—yet who could think that the dead air could empty itself in a sea so clear, so bright, that I cannot look at it, cannot look out on that perfect shore, that perfect sea.

The breeze smells of clean grass—the dunes prickle with it, curving back over the headlands. The blue batters at my skull, and out of the surf comes the strange, foreign cry of dolphins, their chirping litany, their barking lament. Their blue heads stud the water like sapphires set in steel—like the stones on the hilt of this cleaver, this hack-saw you loved so well.

I know a secret: it is your own arm I carry to the waterside, severed from you—you are like me, now, at the end, limb-hewn—embarrassed by its own jewelry, but no less your own, hung at your wrist all those years as though by joint and sinew. I have dragged it through the barnacled sand, this arm, this pommel, this elbow, this cross-guard, this shoulder with its sparse golden hair. I know it for your arm and no blade, and I cannot fling it away as though it were a scrap of palimpsest blowing through the streets of that city by the sea.

I cannot cast off this thing which has been your body, cast it into the water like a fishing line. I cannot do it. I will keep it for myself, and fold it beneath my floorboards, wrapped in rags and furs and covered in pine which does not quite match the surrounding ash, so that in the smallest of all night-hours, I may pull up the planks like exhuming a grave, prying up the coffin-splinters, so that I may uncover it like an old bone, and look into it as a mirror, lay beside it as beside dust, and know my friend is near.

I will not do it.

What saw thou there? said the king. Sir, he said, I saw nothing but waves and winds. That is untruly said of thee, said the king, therefore go thou lightly again, and do my commandment; as thou art to me as life and dear, spare not, but throw it in.

The sun is so high and hot that it will allow nothing green beneath it—everything here is hard and gold, hard and blue, hard and white. The hilt is warm in my hand; the blade is incandescent, star-shot. I am almost used to it, stranger to my palm before you turned gray and coagulate.

Lumps of city scatter off to the west, houses like red ant-cairns, roof-tiles shining back the endless light, light that must have weight, weight like shoulder-plates, like liquid, pooling silver. The sand has dried in the noon so that the furrow I leave this time is neat and sighing. Its sides trickle in behind me.

There has been a beach like this before, though never a sea like this, never a sun like this. But there was a strand—oh, does he remember it, in the long line of things he has killed which must string together in his breast like old ornaments? St. Michael, St. Michael, the castle and the tide, and the fires burning like infidels stuck on the ramparts. We went into that place, and I never came out, that place so like this one, as though all places which are not Camelot must run together into one country, long and strange and serrated, along the coast of another sea.

Arthur did not want to go. I understood immediately, because I did not want to go either. I saw in the ogre-keeper of that place my own hulking, muscle-bound form, horrible in its meat-pounding arms, its swollen legs. I did not want to go down across the green fields when the strawberries had just come through, still small and hard and pale on the stalk, I did not want to go trampling over their little beads in order to kill something so like myself. I have always pitied ungainly things, things born too big for the world. I never forgot my own inelegance, my own boar-belly.

There were a line of girls at the gate in those days, crying dirt-tears, eyes spinning in their heads like weathervanes. They held their fists between their legs and the blood had dried to black there. Mouths hung open, missing teeth, and they just stood still, all in a row, so quiet, like nuns, their breasts beaten flat. Arthur did not want to look at them: he knew their faces. He remembered that his mother looked like that every time his father came home from campaign, sweat-stung and hard, that it had never gotten better or easier for her, not the littlest bit, and he knew from the time he was hay-haired and jam-stained that she probably looked like that the morning after he was made.

Every morning there was another woman in the line, beads on an abacus, and someone, somewhere, tallying, tallying. Finally I went out to them, and found the first in that blood-wan sisterhood.

Who did this to you, Lady? You must know that this is the house of justice—we manufacture it here, like wooden toys.

Her eyes rolled back and I could see the tiny scarlet veins in the white, like the strokes of a brush.

The Beast of St. Michael pushed us open until we could not but crack. I cannot feel my spine, but I can feel him, still, inside me.

Still, he did not want to know. He did not want to remember that he could not sit on his mother's lap for days after his father had left again, door a-slam and finally soft. He did not want to think that his own blood was full of numb spines and cracked hips. But I could not watch them add to their number, day by day, like a faucet dripping.

She is dead, and beyond him now.

He, too, is dead, sighed Arthur, *and gone after her. What if still he breaks her beneath him on a rack of clouds?*

I pulled on his shirt and strapped this very sword to his waist, though his limbs were frozen and heavy. I dressed him like a baby. He could not raise his head to them as we rode out, though they beat their bellies until the blood began to run red and wet again, and we were heralded in crimson all the way to the sea.

The castle stood on a strand like this one, though the sea was gray, not blue, and the sun was a white disc, not flaming as if to purify a sinning sphere. Far out into the slate waves it frowned, piled on itself like a fallen cake, sullen, gouged windows and doors bolted like torsos. Here and there, it was burning, tall, thin flames hissing as they met the damp sky, steaming in rain that slanted into the brine-pitted walls, and surely to him it must have looked like home, must have looked like his mother's bed, must have looked like his father's grinning face.

Of course, he would not remember the girl. Only I saw her, only I touched her. If I were a better man I would confess my sins to my king before he dies, but I cannot unstring my lips after all this time, and see his pupils widen, then shrink. I was once a good man. I was once his man.

We slayed a giant together, my friend and I, a giant with no beanstalk or harp of gold, only a wretched castle hollowed out for him by whale-speckled tides, only rough, mucus-yellow eyes and an expression like a lamp that once shone and has long gone out. The usual business of slaying occurred—we have done this before. There were bellows like shades blowing open in a storm, and once the skin of a thing is broken,

I am always reminded of heifers calving on my own father's land—my father, who never knew, as I do, how much blood you could let out of a woman and yet keep her living—arms deep in hot, swampy flesh, pulling at bone, at kicking hoof. We reached into him as into a breach-birth and pulled at his kicking spleen, pulled at his huge heart until the chambers tore one from the other in our hands.

The blood coated us, made of us red knights. We laughed, pulled greasy strips of giant-flesh from each others' hair like apes picking lice, and set out searching for harps or geese or whatever a giant holds dear enough to build a castle to keep. My eyes were still blurred with exertion and triumph, gore still thickening and drying on each of my perfect sinews—my whole skin thrilled and pricked like a plucked guitar, as it will when you have killed a thing much bigger than yourself, and much stronger. Even my eyelashes seemed to vibrate, to sing some dark and untaught tune.

It was in this state that I found her. If I had been un-frenzied, if the giant's blood in my mouth had not been so like boiling wine—

She was not young. Her skin was deeply lined and sunburned; her hair was matted and gray and hung like long iron bars all around her, hung in her face so that her dark eyes peered through them. She was naked, and her arms clasped above her head with chains of bone bolted in bronze, her ankles nailed through, like a crucifixion, the skin long healed and grown around the nail-shaft. She sat on a low wall, perched as well as she could with her arms pinioned so—and all through the grass-stuck mud wall march a line of small graves.

She shrieked when she saw me, so like the giant, and painted in his corpse. She shrieked, tired of shrieking, but knowing that the giant would always expect her cry. Her howl was dry and breaking, like pine needles crushed underfoot. The fires of the castle still burned in its higher terraces—the rain scissored down through dark clouds and the sound of the giant dying, of the sear of it, was still in me, battering back and forth between my bones, so loudly I could hardly hear her weep with sweat-sour relief, knowing her salvation had ridden to her bearing a silver cross.

The giant pulled up my daughter and I from our country like crickets from a hay roof.

Ah, the chains of bone! My blood sang high and taut.

He tried to have her, but she was always so pretty, and so frail, and his love broke her hips open like two halves of an apple.

Ah, how black her eyes! My blood hummed low and loose.

He fell on me then, and it has been years. I was always stronger than my girl. That is her, buried there, buried first.

The blood in me and the blood on my back seemed to stretch towards each other, and the rain and flames were so hard and bright, and I could not see anything but her splayed legs, without the smallest modesty—what blush should she have left for me?—though the stain of the giant's last visit still streaked her skin like a tiger's hide, black against brown. After the giant, I thought, she will hardly feel me. I have done so much for her today.

I thought that. I.

With the titan's ruined heart still in my hand I pushed her knees open, and I did not even notice the caked blood, but I saw her clamp shut her mouth, and her eyes roll up to heaven, and you know, she never even made a sound, though I heard her old bones creak—I was so full of slanting flame, so full of blade-swings and axe-wield, so full of fur and bone and bile, all thumping and throbbing within me, and I was the giant, his innards draped me like sacramental robes. I was the giant, and my boulder-knees scraped the stone wall. I was the giant, and I wanted her to cry out beneath me.

Another knight would have knelt and hoisted her to his horse, given her over to convent, washed her wounded womb in a clear river. It is what we were trained to do. How many of us failed to do it? Or was it only I who fell so far?

I rolled off of her and there were no stars behind a skirt of clouds. She stared at me, expressionless, and the blood ran from me then, and I was not the giant, I was a gristle-clung ape and I had done what apes will do. I turned and vomited into the gravestones, spattering their rough granite with sickness.

Those headstones—how bitter and terrible her growl!—are for the children I bore the giant, all the babes he threw from the ramparts to watch their skulls crack on the surf-sharpened rocks. Don't you worry, chevalier, *I'll make sure your little one is not parted from his brothers and sisters. I am not so old yet that I can yet leave the funeral trade.*

I ran from her, I ran and I screamed horse-horrid, I rode and rode and Arthur could not keep with me, and I would not answer when he asked what had bitten my heels—how could I? How could I tell him I was his father, I was the giant, I was a hundred kings before him and after? The blood was never so hot in him that he could even dream that one day he might imagine that he could grind an old woman's back against a stone wall.

I left her there. I left her in the rain and the fire.

The winter passed and no one questioned me. Feasts were held for the giant's death. Games and hunts. I did not hunt, or play.

I went into the forest to cut wood, I told him. It is my way, never-mind how you chide me. My silver axe and my Hephaestus-gait, dragging the ash-handle behind me, leaving a furrow in the loam. I cut oak and pine and green birch, and held each log in place with my huge gnarled hand. I watched it every time the blade fell. I watched the hand that had held her down, the hand that had bruised her mangled breast, the hand that had whipped my horse away from her, leaving her in her clutch of bone. I watched that wicked, shaming hand, I watched it curl around a log like a throat, and it seemed better to sever it like a side of beef than to let it go on dangling from me after it had played a giant's paw.

An accident, I said. *It might have happened to anyone.*

Yet here I stand on a shore pebbled with clams, the holiest of things clutched in the other hand—as if that hand, too, did not clamp down on her mouth, as if that hand did not hold her hip to mine. I cannot cast off this thing: if there is something in that sea which wants it, which longs for it, it would not accept tribute from me, I am a monster, a giant, a thing to be slain, a thing to stand before a real knight and be cut down in his turn. I am no bright-souled saint, to deliver the divine to the divine. I have no right even to look at my king, even to look at his blade.

I cannot do it.

What saw thou there? said the king. Sir, he said, I saw nothing but the waters wax and waves wan. Ah, traitor untrue, said King Arthur, now hast thou betrayed me twice. Who would have weened that, when thou that hast been to me as life and dear? And thou art named a noble knight, and would betray me for the richness of the sword. But now go again lightly, for thy long tarrying putteth me in great jeopardy of my life, for I have taken cold. And if thou do not now as I bid thee, if ever I may see thee, I shall slay thee with mine own hands; for thou wouldst for my rich sword see me dead.

There is so much light here.

I cannot bear it. I have not earned the gold of this place.

The king was shivering, this time, when I left him, dragging that old cleaver after me, that metal which must still possess the giant's perfect sinews, some shred of his vein-stitched heart, too small to see. He does not understand. He thinks I am a magpie, over-fond of things which glitter and shine.

I think that while I stare out to sea like a child who cannot remember the simple task his father has set him, he will shudder his way out of this air, this salt, this sun. Bits of shell crackle in the furrow I leave—the sky sighs and blushes blue, blue as grace, blue as a hem. The moon is up, but not yet lit; it floats in the sky like a broken skull. Like a manacle of bone.

I am the giant, in the end. I hulk on a beach-head and keen my sorrows to the surf—I am penitent, penitent, but the wind in my mouth always and forever tastes of her, the crone I left bolted to a wall, buried in her own dead infants, and my child too—was there a child? Was there not?—squirming from her with my eyes, starving into a skeleton on the wall, another bone to link her chain. I became nothing after her joints bent under me, I only walked to her prison and exchanged seats with the colossus. If the book had but opened in another place, if I had but turned another corner in that moldering castle, come upon an empty crèche, or a sack of gold, or a giant's broken bathtub, I might have been Lancelot, a knight of blue and silver and love perfect as pearls. The queen might have looked on me with cool black eyes and thought me the best of them all, might have loved me, too. But my pages opened onto gray hair and twelve little lumps in the earth, and I am but a hulking, bent-backed shadow of Lancelot, crouched and sneaking behind him like a starving bear.

All I have to do is throw it. Easy, yes? For any other of his boys, easy. For Lancelot, easy. I should not be the last. Some other man should remain to witness us. What loyalty can I give him who could never confess how far I fell from the gold-shot grace of his hall? The loyalty of carrying his jetsam to the sea. Am I a pall-bearer, hoisting his last living limb, or a garbage-carrier, shifting scrap-metal from one sand-dune to another?

Could I but erase myself in this, erase my name and all my deeds in this light, scrub my sinews clean. Could I but be remembered for this only, and not that other shore, that other sea, that other self. Once, I was a good man. We were young together, Arthur and I, and the catalogue of our deeds unspooled from an angel's mouth.

So much light: the moon ignites itself, sparking into silver like an altar candle. In its shadow, I see—do I? Yes? No?—something break the sheen of sea. A hand, it must be a hand, whole, perfect, scaled in trout-mail, a hand from every story he told when he was drunk and sloshing over with sorrow, a hand open, waiting, a hand open and lying on a birch-trunk, axe-shadows playing on the lines of its palm, a hand, withered and wiry, clenching and twisting, caught in a cuff of bone.

It strains towards me. Open, beckoning. Calling me to drown, calling me to kneel and serve her as I ought to have done. Palm-lines curve away from my sight, and I want to believe that the hand does not open only for the sword, that the fish-scale nails and looping threads of silver-pregnant silk do not only rise from the foam for him. I want to believe there is forgiveness in that hand. I want to believe there is grace. I want to believe that it will take my stump in its grip, which will be soaked with brine and draped with seaweed, and that in the press of its fingers will be understanding.

Leave your giant-skin behind, that press will say, *and become Bedevere again.*

The moon glints on the sword-edge as it turns, hilt over point, in the air. The hand catches it, as I could not. The ivory chain-links jangle. The blade whirls once, twice, three times. An ocean beyond any blue I have known closes over hand and blade and all, and I am alone, on a long, low shore, in a dusk so deep and bright.

There is so much light here, unbearable light. Water which conceals a forest of crones' hands seems to open before me, seems to promise, seems to cajole. I can almost see them in the waves, when the moon shines through them. Fingers like kelp, kelp like fingers.

The taste of the sea is so like skin, you know.

A wide green field, and grass like water waving. There is dusk here, and thin, over-tilled soil, and hiding hills, still those blessing hills. Clouds skitter across the hedgerows like rocks skipping on a lake. There are stones: here, there, great gray things, knuckle-knobbled. They lie where the walls once were, corners and lengths and thresholds. You can almost see the glimmer of what stood then, hovering shadow-still over the slabs.

There is no one here. Old, dry-clawed crows hop from stone to stone, pecking at the first blocks of the cathedral, which are also the last. A wild, shag-pelted pony wanders, chewing at the tough grass. The market has gone, so too the farms and the monks and the cows. The ground refused to give up any further beans or turnips—it was hoarse and tired and coughed up its last cucumber long ago. The wells are brackish and thick with slime; a slow drip wears away the cisterns. A withered grapevine crawls along a low line of stones, hung with yellow leaves that are almost, but not yet, dust.

The base of the old tower lasts longest—rain and wind pit and streak it until it forgets all the queens it ever knew, and dreams under the new hills, which cover the ruin like grave-mounds, snaking around the valley, eating what is left of this place, modestly drawing themselves up over the bones like shrouds.

In a century, no one will remember what this place was called. In five, someone will say that it was seventy miles south and in another country besides. Someone else will say they have dug it up and wouldn't you like to buy a bit of soil, a bit of rock, a bit of bone? Someone else will say there was never a castle here—the land is too poor to support a population.

Occasionally a shepherd will try to feed his sheep on the yellow, fibrous grass that is left. The animals bleat pitifully and will not touch it: it is so bitter. The flock moves on.

Under the blessing hills, a thousand dreaming bones shiver in their sleep.

XX JUDGEMENT

Morgan le Fay

And when they were at the water side, even fast by the bank was a little barge with many fair ladies in it, and among them all was a queen, and all they had black hoods, and all they wept and shrieked when they saw King Arthur. Now put me into the barge, said the king. And so he did softly; and there received him three queens with great mourning; and so they set them down, and in one of their laps King Arthur laid his head. And then that queen said: Ah, dear brother, why have ye tarried so long from me?

—Sir Thomas Malory
Le Morte d'Arthur

Away in the apple-groves I dreamed of you, and you seemed so still and grave—once, you and I ran laughing from our mother's house, and hid in the forest, and told each other tales of terrible boars who would snatch us away to prisons made of pomegranate and whalebone. Even then you tried to kiss me, when the afternoons were thick and yellow, and the dust-motes swam in the air.

I blushed—I was not brave enough.

They took you from me—remember how you cried? You grabbed at my dress, my hair, clung to me, trying to stay. For your safety, they said.

I cut my hair the day they took you. I burned it in our forest. The ash smelled like us.

Why have ye tarried so long from me? Away in the mint-fields I clapped a hand against my shorn hair and learned things I will never tell you about. I did not see you again until after the crown clamped on you like a lamprey. You had married her already—and do not think I did not note her deep black eyes, so like mine.

They will say we didn't know; they will say it was an accident. How could I not know? How could I not see how tired you had become? How could I not see your too-thick hair that still would not obey and the three little lines in your forehead—how could I not know my brother?

Do you remember how we walked together, in the forest which was not our old forest but was green enough for walking, for talking of grain and crops and how green sashes were in fashion at court that year, and I could hear the weariness in you, how it pulled at me like a hook in my throat? I stroked your head against my breast like I used to, innocent as a sister, innocent as a nun, and you kissed me again, and I was brave that time, wasn't I? I was brave and the dust-motes floated in my hair which was not as long as it had been, and you moved against me in the shade of a old hollow oak, and your kisses became cries, and your cries became a son—

Oh, my brother, I should not speak of our son. He will say he had nothing like a mother, and I do not call him a liar, but we all try, we all try so hard. Sometimes I think it is all our trying that has brought us here, all our struggling and trying that sets up all these tragic scenes.

We grew old—did you notice? I did not. One day I had white hair instead of black and spots in my skin like a leopard. I was suddenly slow, and bowed under a woolen hood. I could not stay with you—I went over the bridge to the other world, the other Camelot that is called Avalon and hell and California. I learned to make orange-cakes, learned to make the rain come.

I learned to look both north and south.

And I tried, once every decade or so, to pull you over the bridge with me, I tried every colorful thing I knew to draw you: I sent my girls out into towers with red armor in their arms, I sent you a dream of a beast with a dragon's head and a leopard's skin, I took a boy down into the water not once but twice, just so that you would come after him. But you did not come. I sent my champion all wrapped in leaves and green, in a mask, with an axe. I sent unicorns; I sent giants.

But you would not come. You would not come to me no matter how I lined that bridge with sweets. You loved your wife, more fool you. You loved that place. You thought, I know, that I would always be here when you reached out in the dark to find me.

I suppose you were right.

I have missed you so. Why could you not come into the golden country with me? We would have been happy. There would be now no cold seashore and a widow's barge. Do not laugh—the blood is too bright in the fog. Yes, I am your widow. I have mourned you all your life.

My brother, why have ye tarried so long from me? Away in the orange groves I once made a rind-golem of you. I piled up the wet, sour peels into something like the shape of you. I was lonely, and it was an easy trick.

I gave it eyes and breath and life and it was golden like you, and sweet like you, and it looked at me with eyes of dusty green leaves and said:

I forgive you.

I forgave the orange, too, and they fell into a pile of lifeless husks, already turning brown at the edges.

Do you see the light in the distance? That is Avalon, which is the underworld, an island in the Pacific where where I have spent my days in apple orchards and mint-fields and orange groves and rose-thickets and glistening lakes. I am your Hades, and you are my spring. I will steal you away to sit on a yew-throne and tell me stories of your knights and how you were so young, once. I will feed you pomegranates and make you a shield of whalebone, and we will chase each other through the forest on knees that do not crack or buckle, and I will be brave, always brave.

It will be wonderful, Arthur, you'll see, and if I was nothing but a white arm before, I am your sister now, and I love you, and I will wrap you warm in my best samite, and my white arms will carry you home.

It is so bright, the sun on the water, on the lake, on the sea, and the dust-motes are so thick I can hardly see the shore.

THIS IS NOT A BOOK

In an odd turn of synchronicity, I sit down, by a tall window looking out on a Maine bay, to write about my first novel nearly exactly nine years after I began writing it, by another tall window, looking out on another bay, in Rhode Island. It's pure coincidence that I started writing fiction in New England—a place haunted and possessed by its writers—and now, years down the way, I live and love and write there in a more or less permanent fashion. New England has been good to me. All those wide grey seascapes and sudden snows and endless tiny graveyards, like monuments to tribes of hobgoblins. All those winding, narrow streets and mists and cobblestones. How much like another world. How much like Europe, as seen through Poe's eye.

How much like a maze.

It sounds so silly now: I wrote *The Labyrinth* to see if I could. To see if a piece of long fiction was something I had any facility with or ability to accomplish. I had no idea if it was. Until then I had been a poet, and not a very successful one. I had written exactly one short story, which appears, fittingly enough, as a chapter in another novel in this volume. I had no idea if I could write something longer, something more complex. I had no idea, to be honest, whether I was really a writer at all. I was planning to teach Greek at some university at some point. Like many folks right after college, I loved to write, wanted to write, but had no notion of how it was actually done. Writers seemed like superheroes to me, and the thing about superheroes is that you're either born a mutant or you're not. (I know that's not really true now, but it I believed it then, and writing a novel was a kind of personal laboratory test: Did I have the mutation?) So in my little apartment, on my little computer a friend had bought me (after its predecessor had been mutilated and finally killed dead by a stray cup of coffee and a drunk freshman) because he couldn't bear the thought of me not writing, I wrote a few words, and then a few more.

I was twenty-two, my poems were too full of fairy tales and adjectives, and I was terribly lonely. I'd just graduated from college and moved back to the

States from Scotland. My boyfriend was in the Navy, we were supposed to be getting married but I don't think either of us really knew why, other than that the Navy offered certain concrete encouragements to do so, and I was working in Newport, RI as a fortune-teller. I was good at it—after all, it's not much more than sizing a person up and telling them a story, guided by a few symbol-dense images, designed to evoke a feeling of surprise, recognition, and finally, revelation. And I found myself typing away between readings, in this little room in a gothic tower that used to be an armory, on a velvet covered table. The room did double duty as storage for a local theater company, and I spent my afternoons surrounded by Macbeth's throne, Ibsenesque dressing tables, Yorick's skull—I'm sure Chekov's gun was in there somewhere. There, and at a local Starbucks, in case this is getting too atmospheric for you, and at a particle-board desk in an apartment with no air-conditioning, I wrote *The Labyrinth*.

I wrote it quickly—I have always been fast. And when I look back I feel as though I was waiting to write it for a long time. Saving up for it, mulching. And when I actually sat down at the keyboard, I wrote what I knew to write. What formal training I'd had was as a poet, and little enough of that. I had three freshly-baccalaureated languages banging around my head and a lifetime of voracious reading, but I didn't know the rules. I didn't know what I was or was not supposed to do. I didn't know how to reign myself in in any real way. I smushed words together and I made up new ones because I liked to and it seemed to me to have meaning. I don't think this is a bad thing—just doing it, before you know how it's meant to be done. It was terrifying and exhilarating and I had no idea whether I could ever get it published. Later, when told it was not really a book at all, and accused of passing off some kind of neo-Beat poetry as a novel I was righteously indignant, but the truth is that's about the size of it. I didn't know how to write a novel. I knew how to write a two hundred page poem with no columns and my whole heart. It was, if not perfect, at least pure.

I wrote it merely to write it, and I poured into it everything I thought I knew, all of the hurt and uncertainty and depression and mania and wildness and misery of my twenty-two years. At the time, I thought it was probably the only book I'd ever write.

Of course, I made myself a liar almost immediately. A few days further into October, I opened up a blank file and wrote the first words of what became *The Orphan's Tales*.

It was a strange, long, inchoate summer. But out of it came everything else.

Three Days in the Archetype Mines

Fast forward a year and I had just gotten married, just moved to Japan, just gotten a fluffy yellow dog and a house in the suburbs of Yokosuka. I was installed in it like any housewife of 1957, meant to wait for my Naval officer husband to come home at infrequent intervals and entertain myself.

I wrote *Yume no Hon* as an entry for the Blue Lake Books 3-day Novel contest. The thing I remember most about those three days was that Blue Lake required someone else to sign a form certifying that you had written your manuscript in three days as per the rules—and I didn't have anybody. My husband was at sea and I had no friends. I called the only other person in town I knew, who happened to have been my high school sweetheart, years ago. He'd joined the Navy, too. He signed the form and we had nothing to say to each other.

Yume is a novel of loneliness first and foremost. A hymn or paean to being alone—though it does not praise it. It seeks for the light and the hollows in solitude, solitude being what I possessed in abundance. I had discovered the strange, gorgeous names of the Heian calendar, and as I watched those times of year come in Japan, an utterly other calendar than the one I, California girl, was used to, I began to think of Ayako, and how she might dwell within those seasons, in and among and beside them.

I have occasionally referred to *Yume* as the suicide note I never delivered on. How's that for an introduction to a poetic little novella? Well, so it goes. It is the work of a person profoundly not alright, a person living a Betty Friedan life in a post-Paglia universe, a white woman living in Japan, a twenty-three year old who saw no end to the isolation and sameness of the life she had chosen for herself. It is all of those things, and it is also a novel of feminine archetypes, of Pele and Tiamat and Isis and the Sphinx, all of whom live in a broken old hermit named Ayako, as they live in all of us or they wouldn't be archetypes. How those archetypes want us to survive, and to survive in us, how they evolve and force us to evolve. It deals in physics, the physics of infinite paths and worlds and states of being, infinite ways of being here and yet not-here.

In my life I have often been accused of being deliberately obscure in my writing, of meaning nothing, of being pretty for pretty's sake. Perhaps you can see that all the things I write about, and am still writing about, have always seemed vitally immediate to me. They are not even truly metaphors. Ayako is her dream. There is no difference. And everything she dreamed was everything I could not process outside of fiction. What it meant to be alone. What it meant to be a woman. What it meant to make choices I imagined a better woman would not make. I have always been a confessional writer, and if anything can be said of the period of my work covered by this collection it is that this was my most confessional time. I had not yet learned how to tell anyone else's story, only to drape silk and history over my own. Of course, perhaps we never really do anything else.

This is, at its purest essence, a book of choices, and the punchline, if such a thing applies, is that they are all taken eventually. That literally, not metaphorically, we life every life, and some of those are lava-goddesses and some of those are husks that used to be human, clinging to a mountainside. It is a book that helped me live.

I lost the contest.

When, ultimately, *Yume no Hon* was published, we decided to print two editions, one red and one blue. Given that the novel deals with light and physics as much as dreams and myth, I chose to separate the book along the light spectrum. It seemed to me to say that this one book could be any book, any path taken, any choice, any author, any reader. We have chosen to print the blue version here.

Some 170 words are different between the two editions, and to make it easier on readers who are not collectors, I print the differing texts here:

Blue:
On the other hand, the wavelength of each potential self is determined by its distance from the fulcrum-crone. But if we

understand any of an infinite series of women and ur-women to be fulcra, the wavelength of each self is also infinite, both infinitely short and infinitely long, infinitely red and infinitely blue. Instinctively, these selves seek each other out and merge, unable to comprehend the depravity of their conviction that a single woman can serve as a hinge around which they all turn. The resulting sea of constantly merging and disengaging selves resembles the primordial mitosis-swamp—the infinite female, treading water in a mass of pure, white light.

Red:

On the other hand, the wavelength of each potential self is determined by its distance from the fulcrum-crone. But if we understand any of an infinite series of women and ur-women to be fulcra, the wavelength of each self is impossible to determine, being both identical with and impossibly far from its point of origin. In the yolk-riddled void, these photon-bodies float, flashing red and blue, containing within them all possible redness and blueness, joining together like spinning gears, and at each notch exploding into a third (or fifth, or eleventh,) mirror-self, gashing the darkness in its birth pangs —a wash of pure, white light.

An Eight-Headed Problem

If every novel has a seed, this one lay in a confluence of myth and history and my traveling in Japan—that Susano-no-Mikoto, the Shinto god of storm and wind, completed his major myth cycle, destroying an eight-headed dragon, in the city of Hiroshima.

These things seemed to go together to me in some fundamental way. Huge ribbons of history pinned in this one place. And yet, at the same time, I had such terrible sympathy for Yamato-no-Orochi, the dragon in question. He or she or it spent most of their time roving the countryside and eating maidens, a common hobby for dragons in all cultures. Yet it is summarily executed, by Susano, who is no one's idea of a hero and is not meant to be seen as one. Instead, he is a trickster, and I found it hard to exult in his victory.

This is probably the most textually experimental and angriest of my work.

Its feminism is not only one of giving the maidens names and hopes and dreams, of speaking for the monster, but of rage at the constant helplessness of simply being female in a world of hyper-idolized masculinity, of being traded, a trophy for one god or a meal for another. There is a small comfort in community, of women similarly devoured, similarly in the dark, turning the identity of the monster into their own identity. You are what you eat, you become what you destroy. Having often been treated as a problem to be solved rather than a person in my familial and romantic life, well, I felt I had something to say about all that.

I have always been fascinated by the monster and the maiden—they are my yin and yang, constants in mythology and folklore, constants in life, though in life the innocence, if there is any to be had, is not always all on one side or the other. Japanese art is full of examinations of young girls and monsters, and though in American geek circles this is often played as a joke, I felt there was something deeper there. I wanted to write the book of the monster and the maiden, and in connecting that to Hiroshima and the monstrous acts there, it came to encompass the entirety of the Shinto creation myth, which begins with an act of terrible, brutal denial of feminine agency, even existence, and bounces through another and another—not terribly different from Western creation myths, really.

I should mention that in the original myth cycle, Yamato-no-Orochi is not the leech-child born of Izanami and Izanagi's first meeting. No further mention is made of the child in any text I could find. I struggled for a long time over this change in the original story—it seemed to me to fit, like a puzzle piece, but I am not a Japanese woman and I did not want to appropriate or disrespect a culture I had come to call, at least in some uneasy part, home. In the end, however, I realized that I would change a piece of Greek or Roman or Celtic myth, if it opened up a new window into the story. I felt that in the absence of an ending for the leech-child's story, I could fill in the corners, shade and shape. I hope I have done well by that poor creature.

This novel bridges my last days in Japan and my coming back to America. My world was changing, the snakeskin of my old marriage falling away, the mutant maiden-monster of my new self emerging into a new world. I was working on the second book of *The Orphan's Tales*, what would become *The Book of the Sea*. In the end the two books came out within weeks of each other. This was a difficult book to write, because of its anger, perhaps, because of the trapped women in it, who so nearly resembled my own situation. In the end, however, it is one of my favorite of my own books, I am proud of it and its anger, and it is a gift to the country I lived in for so long, struggled with, and finally came to love.

My Dinner with King Arthur

The inclusion of this last novella might seem anachronistic, as it came out in the fall of 2009, three years after *The Grass-Cutting Sword* and four years after *The Labyrinth*. In fact, it came out on the day of my second wedding, on a bright day in November when the world was much better than it had been for some years. However, it was written much earlier. Novellas are notoriously difficult to find publishers for, and it stayed in my "trunk" the word we still use to describe the no-man's-land of our crowded hard-drives where unpublished work lives until it does or does not find a home.

In fact, the Galahad chapter of *Under in the Mere* is the first piece of fiction I ever wrote when I was twenty, for a class in experimental writing in which I wholly failed to impress upon my professor that I had any ability whatever. She thought there was something to this chapter though, written as though Galahad were wandering through San Diego, where I then lived, looking for his Grail.

All of these books have strong ties to the places I lived when I wrote them. *Under in the Mere* is no exception—but I wrote pieces of it in San Diego, San Luis Obispo, Japan, Virginia, and finally I finished it in Ohio. It is part of that confessional style, that other period of my writing, before I ran out of my own angst and had to start figuring out how to tell someone, anyone else's story.

And this was the beginning of that.

I have been obsessed with Arthuriana since I was a child and my father, who had some peculiar ideas about baby's first King Arthur, gave me Steinbeck's Acts of King Arthur and his Noble Knights. I loved Morgan le Fay—she was described in Malory as a "clerk of necromancy" which I took to mean she worked at some kind of magical grocery store, packing bags of spells and potions. Later, I found out clerk meant cleric, and my image of her changed to a magical secretary. Morgan was the hero of my childhood.

When I grew to be a teenager, my circle of friends and I not only obsessed together, but wrote an Arthurian play and, when it was performed, we played the parts we had always assigned to ourselves in our fey afternoons in the California woods It's not hard to guess who I was. It is to that circle that the book was eventually dedicated.

And yet when I came to write about King Arthur, it was in the 2000s, when Morgan and her sisters had been done to death in the fantasy of Arthuriana market. And really, no one writes about Arthur himself—it's always his friends that steal the show. I felt I could say little more about her, other than my grocery-girl or my secretary. I was moved instead to the minor knights, and the idea of the Otherworld all Arthurian knights must eventually travel into as California. California, where I moved when I was thirteen, has always seemed to me a kind of Fairyland, a desert of illusion, full of the fey and the cruel as well as the kind. I couldn't let go of that connection, and this book, which took as long to write as books of mine three times the size, came out of that. Each chapter is a connection between the modern and the ancient, and the knight is the path between them, with its Kay as a Turing machine or drunken Galahad. It is a work full of both my youthful not even knowing what rules to break, just rushing pell-mell at literature like Chung Li in the old Streetfighter game, her legs on fire, and my graduate study in medievalism. If you are a medievalist, well, you're welcome—this is a book full of the tiny and irrelevant and beautiful and mad things we know. If not, I hope it will lead you to our little fortress.

It was also my first work to deal primarily with masculinity and masculine POVs, something that excited and worried me—would I get it right, so many do not, when dealing with the opposite gender. I hope I have done well by that, and most especially by the stories that have possessed me since I was a girl.

I sit by my long window in Maine and a storm slowly clears outside. Blue sky peeks through the deep forest just outside my house, the old hoary New England forest that might be full of anything, maidens or monsters or knights. Spatters of rain start to dry on the glass, and my chickens crow for the sunshine.

There is a kind of map that connects these four novels, a ley line connecting Rhode Island to Japan to Ohio to California and finally to Maine. A map with strange place names and stranger roads, perhaps the kind of map a kid draws when they don't know how to stay in the lines, perhaps the kind men drew a thousand years ago, when the difference between the real and the unreal seemed less important. It is a map of my heart, a heart in four chambers.

ABOUT THE AUTHOR

Catherynne M. Valente is the *New York Times* bestselling author of over a dozen works of fiction and poetry, including *Palimpsest*, the Orphan's Tales series, *Deathless*, and the crowdfunded phenomenon *The Girl Who Circumnavigated Fairyland in a Ship of Own Making*. She is the winner of the Andre Norton Award, the Tiptree Award, the Mythopoeic Award, the Rhysling Award, and the Million Writers Award She has been nominated for the Hugo, Locus, and Spectrum Awards, the Pushcart Prize, and was a finalist for the World Fantasy Award in 2007 and 2009. She lives on an island off the coast of Maine with her partner, two dogs, and enormous cat.